"It doesn't get an
—The Ror

New York Times and *US*

CANDACE CAMP

HER REGENCY ROMPS ARE . . .

"DELIGHTFUL." —*Publishers Weekly*

"DELECTABLE." —*Booklist*

"SPIRITED." —*Publishers Weekly*

"CAPTIVATING." —*Romantic Times*

"ENGAGING." —All About Romance

"ENTERTAINING." —The Best Reviews

This "talented craftswoman" (All About Romance), who
is "renowned as a storyteller who touches the hearts of
her readers time and again" (*Romantic Times*), presents
Willowmere, a sparkling new Regency series featuring
three noble English bachelors, raised as brothers, who are
suddenly saddled with four American cousins, all girls of
marriageable age! Scrapes, romantic complications, and
misunderstandings cannot fail to ensue. . . .

Look for more of the Willowmere series from
Pocket Books in the months to come!

A Lady Never Tells is also available as an eBook

CANDACE CAMP

A *Lady* NEVER TELLS

POCKET **STAR** BOOKS

New York London Toronto Sydney

Pocket Star Books
A Division of Simon & Schuster, Inc.
1230 Avenue of the Americas
New York, NY 10020

This book is a work of fiction. Names, characters, places, and incidents either are products of the author's imagination or are used fictitiously. Any resemblance to actual events or locales or persons, living or dead, is entirely coincidental.

First Pocket Star Books paperback edition May 2010

POCKET STAR BOOKS and colophon are registered trademarks of Simon & Schuster, Inc.

For information about special discounts for bulk purchases, please contact Simon & Schuster Special Sales at 1-866-506-1949 or business@simonandschuster.com.

The Simon & Schuster Speakers Bureau can bring authors to your live event. For more information or to book an event, contact the Simon & Schuster Speakers Bureau at 1-866-248-3049 or visit our website at www.simonspeakers.com.

Designed by Jill Putorti

Cover illustration by Alan Ayers
Hand lettering by Ron Zinn

Manufactured in the United States of America

10 9 8 7 6 5 4 3 2

ISBN 978-1-4391-1797-2
ISBN 978-1-4391-5770-1 (eBook)

For my grandmother, Lula Lee Bibby Irons,
who was never too busy to join in a game of make-believe

Acknowledgments

This book would never have come into being without the help of my agent, Maria Carvainis, who often supplies me with a handy backbone.

Thanks, too, goes to my editor, Abby Zidle, for her invaluable insight and suggestions.

And most of all, I would like to thank my husband, Pete Hopcus, and my daughter, Anastasia Hopcus, who provide great sounding boards for all of my (often-tangled) ideas.

Chapter 1

LONDON, 1824

Mary Bascombe was scared. She had been frightened before—one could not have grown up in a new and dangerous land and not have faced something that set one's heart to beating double-time. But this wasn't like the time they had seen the bear nosing around their mother's clothesline. Or even like the way her heart had leapt into her throat the day her stepfather had grabbed her arm and pulled her against him, his breath reeking of alcohol. Then she had known what to do—how to back slowly and quietly into the house and load the pistol, or how to stomp down hard on Cosmo's instep so that he released her with a howl of pain.

No, this was an entirely new sensation. She was in a strange city filled with strange people, and she had absolutely no idea what to do next. She felt . . . lost.

Mary took another glance around her at the bustling docks. She had never seen so much noise and activity or so many people in one place in her life. She had thought the docks in Philadelphia were busy, but that was nothing compared to London. All around them were piles of goods, with stevedores loading and unloading them, and people hurrying about, all seemingly with someplace to be and little time to get there.

There were no women. The few whom she had seen disembark from ships had been whisked away in carriages with their male companions. Indeed, all the passengers from their own ship were long gone, only she and her sisters still standing here in a forlorn group beside their small pile of luggage. The shadows were beginning to lengthen; it would not be long until night began to fall. And though Mary might be a naïve American cast adrift in London, she was smart enough to know that the London docks at night were no place for four young women alone.

The problem was that Mary didn't know what to do next. She had expected there to be an inn not far from where they left their ship. But as soon as they disembarked, she had realized that the area around these docks would not house an inn where a respectable group of young women could stay. Indeed, she was reluctant for them even to walk through the narrow streets she could see stretching out in front of her. A few hacks had come by and Mary had tried to stop one or two, but the drivers had simply rolled past, ignoring her. No doubt they presumed from the rather ragtag pile of luggage that Mary and her sisters would not be a good fare.

They could not stay here. Unless a carriage happened by soon, they would be forced to pick up their bags and walk into the narrow, dingy streets beyond the docks. Mary glanced uncertainly around her. Several of the men loading the ships had been casting their eyes toward Mary and her sisters for some time. Now, as her gaze fell on one of them, he gave her a bold grin. Mary stiffened, returning her most freezing look, and pivoted away slowly and deliberately.

She studied her three sisters—Rose, the next oldest to Mary and the acknowledged beauty of the family, with her limpid blue eyes and thick black hair; Camellia, whose gray eyes were, as always, no-nonsense and alert, her dark gold hair efficiently braided and wrapped into a knot at the crown of her head; and Lily, the youngest and most like their father, with her light brown, sun-streaked hair and gray-green eyes.

All three girls gazed back at Mary with a steadfast trust that only made the icy knot in her stomach clench tighter. Her sisters were counting on her to take care of them, just as Mama had counted on her to get the girls away from their stepfather's house after their mother's death and across the ocean to London, to the safety and security of their grandfather's home. Mary had managed the first part of it. But all of that, she knew, would be for naught if she failed now. She had to get her sisters someplace safe and proper for the night, and then she had to face a grandfather none of them had ever met—the man who had tossed out his own daughter for defying his wishes—and convince him to take in that same daughter's children. Instinctively, Mary clutched her slender stitched-leather satchel closer to her chest.

At that moment, a figure came hurtling toward them and careened into Mary, sending her sprawling to the ground. For an instant, she was too startled to move or even to think. Then she realized that her hands were empty. *Her satchel!* Frantically, she glanced around her. It wasn't there.

"My case! He stole our papers!" Mary bounded to her feet and swung around, spying the running figure. "Stop! Thief!"

Pausing only long enough to cast a look at Rose and point to the luggage, Mary lifted her skirts and took off running after the man. Rose, interpreting her sister's look with the ease of years of familiarity, went to stand next to their bags, but Lily and Camellia were hot on Mary's heels. Mary ran faster than she had ever run, her heart pounding with terror. Everything important to them was in that case—everything that could prove their honesty to a disbelieving relative. Without those papers, they had no hope; they would be stranded here in a huge, horrid, completely strange town with nowhere to go and no one to ask for help. She had to get the satchel back!

Her sisters were right behind her; indeed, Camellia, the swiftest of them all, had almost caught up with her. But the wiry thief who had taken her case was faster than any of them. As they rounded a corner, she spied him half a block ahead, and realized, with a wrenching despair, that they could not catch him.

A few yards beyond the thief, two men stood outside a door, chatting. In a last, desperate effort, Mary screamed, "Stop him! Thief!"

The two men turned and looked at her, but they made no move toward the man, and Mary knew with a sinking heart that her sisters' future was disappearing before her eyes.

Sir Royce Winslow strolled out of the gambling hell, giving his gold-headed cane a casual twirl before he set its tip on the ground. A handsome man in his early thirties, with blond hair and green eyes, he was not the sort one expected to see emerging from a dockside gaming establishment. His broad shoulders were encased in a coat of blue superfine so elegantly cut that it could only have been made by Weston, just as the polished Hessians on his feet were clearly the work of Hoby. The fitted fawn trousers and white shirt, the starched and intricately tied cravat, the plain gold watch chain and fobs all bespoke a man of refinement and wealth—and one far too knowing to have been caught in the kind of place frequented, as his brother Fitz would say, by "sharps and flats."

"Well, Gordon, you've led me on another merry chase,"

Sir Royce said, turning to the man who had followed him out the door.

His companion, a man barely out of his teens, looked a trifle abashed at the comment. Unlike Sir Royce's, Gordon's clothes evinced the unmistakable extremes of style and color that branded him a fop. His coat was a yellow reminiscent of an egg yolk, and the patterned satin waistcoat beneath it was lavender, his pantaloons striped with the same shade. The shoulders of the coat were impossibly wide and stuffed with padding, and the waist nipped in tightly. A huge boutonnière was thrust through his lapel, and his watch chain jangled with its load of fobs.

Gordon drew himself up in an exaggeratedly dignified manner, though the picture he hoped to create was somewhat marred by the fact that he could not keep from swaying as he stood there. "I know. I beg your pardon, Cousin Royce. Jeremy should never have told you."

"Don't blame your brother," the other man replied mildly. "He was worried about you—and rightly so. You were being fleeced quite royally back there."

Gordon flushed and started to argue, but the other man stopped him with an adroitly cocked eyebrow and went on, "You'd best be grateful to Jeremy for coming to me instead of going to the earl."

"I should think so!" Gordon admitted in shocked tones. "Cousin Oliver would have prosed on forever about the family dignity and what I owed to my parents."

"With good cause."

"Here, now, don't tell me you and Cousin Fitz never kicked up a lark!" the younger man protested.

A faint smile curved Sir Royce's well-formed lips. "We might have done so, yes—but I would never have gotten myself kicked out of Oxford and then gone to town to throw myself into yet more scrapes." He narrowed his gaze.

"And I would never have taken it into my head to wear that yellow coat."

"But it's all the crack!" Gordon exclaimed.

However, his companion was no longer listening to him. Sir Royce's attention had been caught by the sight of a man tearing down the street toward them, clutching a small leather satchel. What was even more arresting was that running after him was a young woman in a blue frock, her dark brown hair loose and streaming out behind her and her gown hiked up almost to her knees, exposing slender stocking-clad legs. Behind her were two more young women, running with equal fervor, bonnets dangling by their ribbons or tumbling off altogether, their faces flushed.

"Stop him!" the woman in the lead shouted. "Thief!"

Royce gazed at the scene in some amazement. Then, as the thief drew almost abreast of him, he casually thrust his cane out, neatly catching the runner's feet and sending him tumbling to the ground. The man landed with a thud and the case went flying from his hands, skidding across the street and coming to a stop against a lamppost.

Cursing, the runner tried to scramble to his feet, but Royce planted a foot on his back and firmly pressed him down.

"Gordon, fetch that leather satchel, will you? There's a good lad."

Gordon was gaping at the thief, twisting and flailing around under Sir Royce's booted foot, but at the older man's words, he picked up the case, weaving only slightly.

"Thank you!" The woman at the head of the pack trotted up to them and stopped, panting. The other two pulled up beside her, and for a moment the two men and three women gazed at each other with considerable interest.

They were, Sir Royce thought, a veritable bevy of beauties, even flushed and disheveled as they were, but it was the one in front who intrigued him most. Her hair was a deep chocolate brown and her eyes an entrancing mingling of blue and green that made him long to draw closer to determine the precise color. There was a firm set to her chin that, along with her generous mouth and prominent cheekbones, gave her face an unmistakable strength. Moreover, that mouth had a delectably plump bottom lip with a most alluring little crease down the center of it. It was, he thought, impossible to see those lips and not think of kissing them.

"You are most welcome," Sir Royce replied, pulling his booted foot off the miscreant's back in order to execute a bow.

The thief took advantage of this gesture to spring to his feet and run, but Royce's hand lashed out and caught him by his collar. He glanced inquiringly at the women.

"Do you want to press charges? Should we take him to a magistrate?"

"No." The first woman shook her head. "As long as I have my case back, that is all that matters."

"Very well." Sir Royce looked at the man he held in his grip. "Fortunately, the lady has a kind heart. You may not be so lucky next time."

He released the thief, who scrambled away and vanished around a corner, and turned back to the group of young women. "Pray, allow me to introduce myself—Sir Royce Winslow, at your service. And this young chap is my cousin, Mr. Harrington."

"I am Mary Bascombe," the young woman replied without hesitation. "And these are my sisters Camellia and Lily."

"Appropriately so, for you make a lovely bouquet."

Mary Bascombe responded to this flattery with a roll of

her eyes. "My mother had an exceeding fondness for flowers, I fear."

"Then tell me, Miss Bascombe, how did it happen that you are not named for a flower?"

"Oh, but I am," she responded, smiling, and a charming dimple popped into her cheek. "My name is actually Marigold." She watched him struggle to come up with a polite response, and chuckled. "Don't worry. You need not pretend it isn't horrid. That is why I go by Mary. But . . ." She shrugged. "I suppose it could have been worse. Mother could have named me Mugwort or Delphinium."

Royce chuckled, growing more intrigued by the instant. The girls were all lovely, and Mary, at least, spoke as perfect English as any lady—even though there was a certain odd accent he could not quite place. Looking at their fresh, appealing faces or hearing her speech, he would have presumed that she and her sisters were young gentlewomen. But their clothes were not anything that a young lady would wear, even one just up from the country. The dresses and hairstyles were plain and several years out of date, as though the sisters had never seen a fashion book. But, more than that, the girls behaved with the most astonishing lack of decorum.

There was no sign of an older female chaperoning them. And they had just gone running through the streets with no regard for their appearance or the fact that their bonnets had come off. Then they had stood here, regarding him straightforwardly with never a blush or averted gaze or a giggle, as if it were perfectly ordinary to converse with strange men. Of course, they could hardly be expected to follow the dictum of not speaking to a man without having been properly introduced, given the way they had met. But no well-bred young lady would have casually offered up her name to a stranger even if he had helped her. And she certainly would not have volunteered the girls' first names as Mary Bascombe had just cheerfully done. Nor would she have commented in that unrestrained way regarding her mother's naming them. Most of all—what in the world were they doing down here by the docks?

"Are you—Americans?" he asked abruptly.

Mary laughed. "Yes. How did you know?"

"A lucky guess," he replied with a faint smile.

Mary smiled back, and her face flooded with light. Royce's hand tightened involuntarily on the handle of his cane, and he forgot what he had been about to say.

Mary, too, seemed suddenly at a loss for words, and she glanced away, color rising in her cheeks. Her hands went to her hair, as though she had suddenly realized its tumbled-down state, and she fumbled to repin it.

"I—oh, dear, I seem to have lost my hat." She glanced around.

"If I may be so bold, Miss Bascombe. You and your sisters are—well, this is not a very savory area, I fear. Are you by chance lost?"

"No." Mary straightened her shoulders and returned his gaze. "We aren't lost."

Behind her, one of her sisters let out an inelegant snort. "No, just stranded."

"Stranded?"

"We got off the ship this afternoon," explained the youngest-looking of the Bascombe sisters, turning large gray-green eyes on him. Her voice lowered dramatically. "We are all alone here, and we haven't any idea where to go. You see—"

"Lily!" Mary cut in sharply. "I am sure that Mr. Winslow isn't interested in hearing our tale." She turned to Sir Royce. "Now, if you will be so kind as to hand back our case, we will be on our way."

"Sir Royce," he corrected her gently.

"What?"

"My name. 'Tis Sir Royce, not Mr. Winslow. And I will be happy to return your case." He plucked it from Gordon's clasp and handed it to Mary but kept hold of it, saying, "However, I cannot simply walk away and leave three young ladies alone in this disreputable part of the city."

"It is all right, really," Mary argued.

"I insist. I will escort you to . . ." He paused significantly.

"An inn," Mary said firmly, and tugged the case from his hand. Her chin went up a little. "Indeed, we are most grateful for your help, sir. If you will but direct us toward an appropriate inn, we shall not bother you anymore."

Sir Royce bowed to her, schooling his face to hide his amusement. Her words were a dismissal as much as a thanks, he knew. Well, he thought, Miss Mary Bascombe might find dismissing him was easier said than done.

Mary watched as Sir Royce stepped into the street and casually lifted his cane. To her amazement, a carriage a block down started toward them. She turned back to him with a newfound respect.

She had not been sure what to think when she first saw this elegantly dressed gentleman standing in the thief's path. He had hardly seemed the sort to engage in any sort of rough-and-tumble with the fellow who had just stolen her precious satchel. Yet, with seemingly no effort, he had tripped up the thief and given her back her case. And now he had managed to conjure up a hack for them in this uncongenial place.

Mary studied Sir Royce. She had never seen anyone with quite his air of sophistication and elegance. His clothes and boots were impeccable, and he moved with a sort of languid grace that bespoke a man of leisure. Yet it was plain to anyone with eyes that the shoulders beneath his jacket were broad and the thighs encased by his tight-fitting pantaloons were firmly muscled. This was not the effete, weak aristocrat she had heard more than one American describe as a typical British man.

She must have been staring, for Sir Royce offered her a smile. Mary's stomach fluttered in a most disconcerting way. It was absurd, she told herself, that Sir Royce's smile should have such an effect on her. Indeed, if she was honest, everything about the man, from his thick blond hair to his leaf green eyes, seemed to affect her in an unfamiliar way. It simply was not like her to be so strongly aware of a man's looks—much less to feel her pulse speed up when he smiled at her. What was this peculiar warmth that curled deep within her as she gazed at him? And why did that dimple in his strong chin seem so appealing?

Sternly, she pushed such thoughts from her head. This was no time to turn foolishly girlish. She had heard tales of the sorts of people who lurked in cities, just waiting to swindle the unwary—or worse.

"How is it that you are able to summon a hack so easily?"

He raised an aristocratic eyebrow at her tone. "Suspicious, Miss Bascombe? You are probably right to be so. But I am not a white slaver patrolling the docks for lovely young American girls to abduct. And it is no hack, but my own carriage. I came in it because I was searching for young Gordon here, and I was unsure in what state I might find him. I had no desire to escort him home afoot if he was, um, a bit worse for the wear."

"Oh."

Mary studied him. There was no way to know if Sir Royce was trustworthy. But he had, after all, tripped up the thief and returned her case to her, which indicated that he was a law-abiding sort. And while this Gordon fellow with him was most oddly dressed, Sir Royce appeared eminently respectable. Even to an unpracticed eye such as hers, his glossy boots and elegant coat bespoke a man of wealth, and his bearing was certainly that of a gentleman. He could be all pretense, she supposed, but she and her sisters outnumbered him; surely he could not overpower them all. Besides, they had nothing that anyone would wish to steal—that thief would have been severely disappointed when he opened her case and found it contained nothing but documents. She had heard tales of white slavers, of course, but Mary could not believe that a white slaver looked and acted as this man did.

"Please, allow me to escort you to a respectable inn," he urged.

Mary hesitated for a moment, glancing at her sisters. Lily looked decidedly wilted, and even Camellia nodded, pulling her hand out from her skirts to show Mary the knife she held. "I can take care of him, Mare."

Sir Royce's eyebrows vaulted upward, and Gordon, following Royce's gaze, goggled and exclaimed, "Bloody hell, is that a knife?"

"I believe so," Royce replied calmly, adding, "Language, Coz—there are ladies present."

Gordon appeared as if he might dispute this statement, but at a look from the older man, he subsided, saying only, "Beg pardon."

"Gordon—can you manage on your own?" Royce continued. "I fear there isn't enough room in my carriage for all of us."

The other man, still eyeing Camellia's knife, nodded. "Of course. I mean, if you're sure it's safe . . ."

"I think I can hold my own," Sir Royce assured him. "Will you promise me that you will go straight home?"

"Home! Not there!" Gordon protested. "Mother's in residence here."

"Very well. Then straight to your father. He's at the estate, is he not?"

Gordon looked pained, but nodded grudgingly. "Yes. I'll go to Father and tell him everything."

"Good. If I find out differently, I shall lay this all in Oliver's hands."

Gordon groaned, but nodded again and trudged off down the street.

"Will he be all right?" Lily asked, watching him walk away. "He seemed a trifle, well . . ."

"Drunk," Camellia helpfully added.

Sir Royce looked somewhat nonplussed, but said only, "Yes. You are correct. I am afraid he has overindulged somewhat. But I think he will manage well enough."

"Is that why he is dressed that way?" Lily asked. "Because he has been drinking?"

Royce let out a short laugh and shook his head. "No, I fear he was probably quite sober when he bought those clothes." He glanced around. "Now, um, I assume you had some baggage?"

"Oh! Our bags! Rose will be worried sick about us," Mary exclaimed. The girls all whirled around and started at a run back in the direction from which they had come.

With a sigh, Royce stepped up onto the tiger's footplate of his carriage and grabbed the handle, gesturing the coachman forward. "I fear we must follow them, Billings."

"Aye, sir," the coachman replied, his colorless voice indicating that he had long ago accepted the fits and starts of his employer.

The girls ran to the docks, the carriage lumbering behind them. Royce's jaw dropped open when he saw, perched atop two battered trunks, a raven-haired, blue-eyed beauty . . . with a long rifle resting across her lap.

"Good Gad!" Royce hopped lightly to the ground and strode toward the cluster of girls. "There is another one of you."

"Yes, this is my other sister, Rose."

"Of course it is." He made an elegant leg to the lovely young woman, who shyly nodded back. "And I see that you brought a rifle with you."

"Of course. We couldn't just leave Father's gun behind."

"Naturally . . ." Royce replied faintly. "And who knows when one might have use of it? Any other weapons about your persons? Pistols, perhaps?"

"They're in our bags," Lily told him. "We didn't think we would need them, really."

"Mm. I would venture that a rifle—and your sister's knife—should be enough for everyday occurrences." He turned toward his driver, who had followed him from the carriage. "Well, Billings, load up the luggage, and we shall be on our way."

Royce opened the door of the carriage and stretched out his hand toward Mary. "Miss Bascombe . . ."

Mary herded her sisters over to the vehicle, and Royce handed them up into the carriage, Mary hanging back until last. She would have liked to grab the handle beside the door and swing herself up into the carriage, but she could not, without rudeness, ignore Sir Royce's outstretched hand. She couldn't explain even to herself quite why she was reluctant to take Sir Royce's hand. She only knew that she dreaded the contact—and at the same time was somehow eager for it.

Royce turned from handing the last of her sisters into the carriage. Mary hesitated, then reached out and slipped her hand into his. His fingers closed around hers lightly. She could feel the heat of his skin; he seemed unusually warm to her—or was it just that her own hands had grown suddenly icy?

She looked up into his face. She was closer to him now than at any time before, and she could see clearly, even in the growing dusk, how sinfully long and thick his lashes were. They were the same rusty brown as his eyebrows, darker than his thick blond hair, and they accentuated the bright green of his eyes. He was looking straight into her eyes, and there was in his gaze an intensity, a heat, that made her feel suddenly shy. She cast her eyes down; she could feel color rising in her cheeks. Almost imperceptibly, his fingers tightened on hers.

Mary stepped quickly up into the carriage, and for an instant it seemed as though he might hold on to her hand, but then he released her. Her three sisters had squeezed onto one seat, so she sat down on the seat across from them, realizing that she would have to ride next to Sir Royce, who, after a moment's consultation with his driver, entered the carriage and sank onto the soft leather seat beside Mary.

Mary, avoiding his gaze, looked around her at the luxurious vehicle. She had never been in a carriage of such elegance and comfort. It was roomy, with wide benches cushioned in dark red leather, and behind their backs were squabs of the same butter-soft leather. Short, heavy curtains framed the windows, drawn back to admit the dwindling evening light.

The carriage started forward over the uneven cobblestones. Mary was very aware of Royce's presence beside her. His broad shoulders seemed to take up a great deal of space, and his muscular thighs were only inches from her. She held herself tight against the other wall of the carriage, afraid the vehicle might lurch and send her knocking against him.

For a long time, there was only silence in the carriage, the four girls and their rescuer regarding each other carefully.

Finally, Sir Royce said, "May I ask whence you young ladies have traveled to London?"

"Three Corners," Lily answered promptly. "That's a little town not far from Philadelphia. In Pennsylvania. The United States."

He nodded. "I see. And what brings you to England?"

"Lily . . ." Mary sent her sister a warning glance.

Lily looked at her, surprised. "But what's wrong with—"

"No, no doubt your sister is quite right," Sir Royce said easily. "One can never be too cautious in the city. It can be a dangerous place. Though," he added with a glance toward Camellia, "I am not entirely certain that holding a knife at the ready is necessary. It could lead people to leap to the wrong conclusion."

"We don't usually go about bearing arms, Mr.—I mean, Sir Royce," Mary put in. "But, as you said, the city can be a dangerous place. So Camellia decided to wear her knife today."

"Wear?" He looked blankly at Camellia, as if he would see it hanging about her neck.

Camellia smiled faintly and reached down to lift the hem of her skirt, exposing a bit of her shapely calf, to which was strapped a small leather scabbard. She bent and slipped the blade she had been carrying back into the scabbard, then shook out her skirts and regarded Sir Royce evenly.

"I see." It gave Mary a small spurt of satisfaction to see the man, who was far too cool by half, look faintly disconcerted. "Handy. Well, clearly, I need not worry about your safety."

"No," Mary agreed firmly. "You need not."

Mary was not sure why she was so reluctant to reveal anything about herself or her sisters to this man. He had, after all, done nothing harmful to them—or even suspicious. On the contrary, he had done them more than one good turn. Perhaps it was simply that this Englishman affected her in ways she was unused to or that she felt somehow unsure of herself around him. Or maybe she was just irritated by the relief that had swept her when Sir Royce had taken charge of their problem and set out to escort them to an inn. It was so nice, so easy, to put all her worries into someone else's hands for once, to not be the one in charge, entrusted with protecting her sisters and leading them to a better life.

But that was something she absolutely could not do. She had learned from her mother's bitter experience that putting one's entire welfare in a man's hands was foolish. Better by far to rely only on oneself.

Sir Royce held her challenging gaze for a long moment. There was something in his eyes—interest? amusement? a challenge of his own?—that both intrigued and confused her. Finally it was Mary who turned her face away, no longer able to hold his gaze.

After that, there was silence—even Lily, usually curious to a fault, was too exhausted to ask any questions—until the carriage rolled at last to a stop in the courtyard of an inn. Sir Royce got out, telling the girls to remain inside. Mary and her sisters exchanged a glance and promptly scrambled out of the vehicle after him, following him into the inn.

When they walked inside, they saw Royce speaking to a small man who was nodding and smiling obsequiously. Royce turned at the sound of the sisters' entrance and cast them a wry look, but made no protest at their ignoring his instructions. He turned back, said a few more words, then withdrew something from his pocket and handed it to the man.

The man scurried off, and Sir Royce came over to Mary and the others. "Holcombe is the innkeeper of the Boar and Bear, and he has suggested that you wait in the private room while he makes sure that the bedchambers are turned out in the quality you deserve. My driver will bring in your things."

A maid appeared to show them into one of the private areas set aside for the drinking or dining convenience of their guests who did not care to rub elbows with the other occupants of the tavern and inn. After a few minutes, she appeared again, carrying a pot of tea and mugs for the girls, as well as assurances that she would soon bring them steaming bowls of stew if they liked.

All the girls agreed that they would very much like it. Sir Royce cast a comprehensive glance around the room and said, "Well, ladies, it appears that you are well settled here, so I will bid you adieu."

Mary's sisters clustered around him, showering him with thanks. Even shy Rose offered him a blushing smile with a soft assurance of her gratitude. Only Mary kept her distance, watching Royce with a cool and thoughtful air. When he had bid each of the others good-bye, Royce turned to Mary and swept her an elegant bow.

"Miss Bascombe. It has been a pleasure."

"Indeed." Mary nodded, realizing that her gesture came out too primly. She was, she thought, appearing ungrateful, but she could not seem to relax around him.

He hesitated, then reached inside his coat, saying, "Allow me to give you my card, in case—"

Mary held up her hand. "No. Please. That is very kind of you, but I assure you, we will be fine. I will contact our grandfather tomorrow."

"Ah, then you do have family here?"

"Yes." Mary could see further questions forming in his eyes, and stepped forward quickly, opening the door into the hallway and turning to him in a clear gesture of dismissal. "Thank you, Sir Royce. I appreciate all you have done for us."

With a wry look at her, he laid his card upon the table, then tipped his hat to Mary and stepped past her into the hallway. Mary, with a quick glance back at her sisters, followed him into the hall, closing the door behind her .

"Sir Royce . . ."

He turned inquiringly.

"As I said, I appreciate what you have done for us, but—I saw you give that man money."

"Man? What man?"

"The innkeeper. I cannot allow you to pay for our accommodations. We do not even know you. And I am quite capable of paying our way. We are not penniless, I assure you." That, she thought, was not entirely a lie; there were still a few coins left in her purse.

"Of course not," he replied smoothly. "I would never presume in such a manner. What I gave him was not payment for the rooms. 'Twas merely a trifle, a small . . . incentive, shall we say, to ensure the innkeeper's immediate attention to rooms for you."

"Then I shall pay you back for that."

Sir Royce waved such an idea away, and Mary set her jaw mulishly. "I insist, sir. I have no desire to be beholden. I cannot, of course, compensate for the kindnesses you have done us, but I can and will repay you for any money you have spent on us."

"My dear girl, it was nothing. I haven't even any idea what I handed him."

He regarded her blandly, and irritation rose in Mary. She knew that he was purposely thwarting her, and she could not help but be suspicious that Sir Royce was lying to her. It was most kind of him, of course, but still . . .

"I cannot allow you to leave without repaying you," she told him stubbornly, planting her hands on her hips.

He regarded her for a moment, and his eyes began to twinkle. "Well, then, allow me to take this in exchange."

And with that, Royce took a step forward and wrapped an arm around her waist, then bent his head and kissed her.

Chapter 2

Mary froze in surprise. It wasn't as if no man had ever tried to kiss her before. She had had a few suitors, even if they did not number as Rose's did. And there had been men in the tavern who, laboring under the mistaken notion that any woman in or around a tavern was fair game, had grabbed her and tried to steal a kiss—or more. She had taken care of all of them in ways ranging from subtle to painful.

But she was unprepared for this man's kiss—not only the smooth way he swept her in, but also the intoxicating effect of the kiss itself. His lips were firm and warm, pressing into hers with soft insistency, opening her mouth to his. The dark, subtle scent of his cologne teased at her senses, combining with the heat of his body, the taste of his lips, the feel of his chest pressing against hers, into a swirl of sensation that left her breathless, even dizzy. Mary felt herself warming, melting, and she realized that she was no longer standing stiffly in astonishment but sinking into Royce. It was, she knew on some level, reprehensible. But right here and now, she didn't care about anything but what she was feeling.

Then, as suddenly as he had whisked her into his arms,

Royce released her and took a step back. Mary saw mirrored in his eyes some of the same amazement she was sure was in her own gaze, but he recovered more quickly than she.

Giving her a quick, impudent grin, he tipped his hat a fraction. "There. I think that's adequate recompense, don't you?"

Before she could dredge up a single thought, much less come up with a rejoinder, he turned on his heel and strode out of the inn. Mary watched him go, sagging against the door in sudden weakness. Even after he was out of sight, she remained where she was, her brain a whirl. Whatever was the matter with her?

It occurred to her that she was standing in the hall of an inn, where anyone could have seen them kiss, and she straightened, quickly glancing up and down the corridor. A blush rushed into her cheeks as embarrassment seized her. She had acted like a common hussy!

She raised shaky hands to her cheeks to cool the flames that burned there, and tried to pull herself together. She could not let her sisters see her so agitated. Sir Royce had not behaved like a gentleman, and she had responded in a way not at all like herself. No doubt she should have slapped him—or, at the very least, pushed him away. But it had been a very trying day; it was no wonder she had been slow to react. In another moment or two she would have shaken off her strange stupor and pulled out of his arms. Wouldn't she?

As for the strange sensations that had flooded her while he kissed her—the heat, the eagerness, the wild fizzing of her nerves—well, she would not think about that now.

Mary drew a deep breath and smoothed down her skirts; then, lifting her chin, she turned and opened the door, marching back into the room. Her sisters turned to her.

"What happened?"

"Where did you go?"

"What did you say to Mr. Winslow?"

"Sir Royce," Rose corrected Camellia. "Now that we are here, we should learn to use their terms."

"Sir. Mr. What difference does it make?" Camellia retorted. "He's the same man whatever title you give him, isn't he?"

"Yes, of course," Mary said. "But I suppose it's impolite for us to address him as 'Mr.'"

Camellia shrugged. "If someone told you to call him Emperor, would you do it?"

Lily rolled her eyes. "Oh, Cam, honestly, it's not a crime to have a title. I think it's romantic."

Camellia made a face. "You think everything's romantic."

"All right, girls," Mary said automatically. "There is no need to fuss at each other."

"Why did you go out into the hall with him?" Lily asked.

"I just . . . thanked him again for what he did for us." Mary felt her cheeks grow heated, and she prayed that her sisters did not notice.

"Don't you think we should have told him who we are and what we're doing here?" Rose asked, frowning. "He probably could have helped us find our grandfather, couldn't he? Why, he might even know the earl; he seemed a very fine gentleman."

"Dressing like a popinjay doesn't make you a gentleman," Camellia pointed out.

"He didn't dress like a popinjay," Lily protested. "It was that other silly man who looked like a bird."

"A bird in lavender-striped trousers," Camellia agreed, grinning.

"What?" Rose looked from one to the other. "What are you talking about?"

"Oh, you should have seen him, Rose!" Lily jumped up, her heart-shaped face alight with laughter. She posed, her hand on one hip, her chin tilted up, looking at Rose down the length of her nose. "He stood like this, and he looked so silly, and you could see his coat was padded out to here." She held her hands out on either side of her shoulders.

Rose giggled at her antics, and Mary smiled. It seemed as if Rose had hardly smiled since they left America. More than one night Mary had heard her sister crying softly in her bunk on the ship, after she thought all the others had gone to sleep. It was a relief to see her laugh again.

"He had a flower in his lapel the size of my fist," Mary added, wanting to keep the smile on Rose's face.

"No! Really?"

"Yes, and his coat was canary yellow," Mary continued.

"That's unkind to canaries," Lily protested. "It was a perfectly vile color."

"You should have seen his face when he saw my knife," Camellia put in. "I thought his eyes were going to pop out of his head."

"Sir Royce called him his cousin, but he wasn't like Sir Royce at all." Lily shot a pointed glance at Camellia. "Sir Royce is a gentleman."

"Perhaps Sir Royce is exactly as he seems," Mary agreed, bringing the conversation back to its original topic. "But we can't know that for certain. It's better not to take strangers into our confidence. If you remember, even Sir Royce agreed with that. That's why we can't tell him all about us."

"But he was kind to us," Rose reminded her. "He brought us here, and you told me he stopped that thief and got back your case. I don't know what we would have done if that man had gotten away with all our papers. How would we have proved who we are?"

"Yes, he did help us. But it's one thing to go to the aid

of four young women who are clearly of no great wealth or consequence. Even a thief or cardsharp or bamboozler might do so, particularly if it is no great trouble to him. But what if such a person then found out that these four young women were actually the granddaughters of the Earl of Stewkesbury? It isn't just ourselves we have to consider now. We must think of our grandfather as well. We can't waltz into his life bringing cheats and scoundrels along."

"I suppose so," agreed Rose with her usual amiability.

"I don't know why we should care about the earl so much," Camellia retorted. "He threw his own daughter out!"

"Yes, the way Mama described him, he sounds like a disagreeable old man," Lily agreed.

"I'm sure he's stubborn and autocratic," Mary admitted. "And it was terrible of him to cut her out of his life. But Mama was certain that he would have come to regret his decision over the years. And he *is* our grandfather."

"Besides," Rose pointed out with the practicality that often surprised people, given her soft, almost angelic demeanor, "we are here to throw ourselves on the earl's mercy. We have nowhere else to go, no one else to turn to. We cannot afford to offend him."

"I hate that." Camellia grimaced.

"I hate it, too." Mary looked at her sympathetically. "But we cannot escape the truth. It would be different if we could have stayed and run the tavern. But with Mama dead and our stepfather inheriting everything, you know we couldn't. What else could we do? Where were we to go? You wouldn't have wanted to stay with Cosmo, would you?"

"No! Working for that old lecher?" Camellia's face turned fierce. "He wouldn't even have paid us. He'd have said we ought to be grateful for the roof over our heads and the food we ate."

"And no way to escape except marrying," Lily put in. "I

refuse to marry just to have a house of my own. I want to marry for love, like Mama and Papa. Remember how happy they were?"

"We all were," Rose agreed, her voice tinged with sadness.

Mary nodded. Until their father had died six years ago, their lives had been good. They had never had much money. Miles Bascombe, a charming man full of dreams and plans, had tried his hand at dozens of different things in an attempt to make a living—farming, teaching, even being an itinerant artist—but none of his careers had been successful. They had moved from one place to another, living first in Maryland, then in two or three different areas of Pennsylvania. Their mother, Flora, having been raised an aristocrat, had had little idea how to cook or keep house, much less manage a budget. As a result, their lives were often chaotic, to say the least.

But Miles and Flora had been fun-loving, kind, and terribly in love with each other. They had given their children warmth and love. If the Bascombes had not had much, at least they had not starved, and they had enjoyed life.

Their father's last venture had been a tavern in a small town on the road to Philadelphia. In his usual careless way, he would doubtless have run this business into the ground, but for Mary. Fourteen at the time, she had become adept at keeping the household going, and she had taken over much of the operation of the business as well, not only keeping the books but also overseeing the day-to-day running of the tavern. She could not entirely save the tavern from Miles's mercurial and usually ill-fated business decisions, but she did manage to keep the place running in the black.

But then her amiable father had died, and his partner in the business, Cosmo Glass, had arrived, intending to sell out. Instead, smitten by the lovely widow, he had remained, operating the tavern and wooing Flora. Their mother, grief-stricken over her beloved husband's death and recognizing her own lack of competence in regard to business, had been persuaded to marry him. It had been the only way she could see to provide for her daughters.

In the ensuing years, Flora had come to bitterly regret marrying Cosmo. He had proved to be an unsavory sort, always involved in some moneymaking scheme or the other. Bad-tempered and given to drinking, he blamed everyone around him for whatever went wrong. Neither a good husband nor a good provider, he had been a dark presence in their lives. Once again, the actual running of the tavern had fallen to Mary, although Cosmo had time and again asserted his authority, insisting on changing a supplier or canceling an order, always with a detrimental result. Often he took money from the till and set off to pursue one or another of his schemes; and while all the girls—and Flora—were glad to be rid of his presence, this habit left the business perennially strapped for cash.

There had been other aspects to him that Mary despised even more, though she had been careful not to express such views to her mother. However mistaken Flora had been, she had sacrificed her own happiness for the future of her daughters, and Mary could not bear to increase her mother's feelings of guilt. She had kept quiet about the drunken advances Cosmo made toward her and Rose, taking care of the matter herself with a sharp knee to Cosmo's groin and a warning of what would happen should he ever try such a thing again. She had also made sure that all the girls slept in the same room and that their door was securely barred at night.

A few months ago, Flora had fallen ill, and as the weeks went by, it had become more and more apparent that she was not long for this world. She did not mind dying, she told them, for she would be reunited with her beloved Miles. But she could not bear to think of what would happen to her daughters upon her death. They would be at the mercy of Cosmo Glass, for in marrying her, he had acquired the entire tavern. She had nothing to leave her daughters except a few small pieces of jewelry. Finally, one morning she had called her daughters to her and told them about their grandfather.

Flora had never spoken much about her father or, indeed, about her life before she married Miles Bascombe. But now she explained that their grandfather was a powerful and influential man, the Earl of Stewkesbury. When Flora had fallen in love with Miles Bascombe, the penniless younger son of a minor nobleman, the earl had become enraged and had forbidden the marriage, telling her that if she disobeyed, he would cut her out of the family forever. Flora had defied her father and run away with Miles to America.

"But you must go to Father now," she had told Mary, her worried face as white as the pillow beneath her head. "Surely he has forgiven me after all this time, and you are, after all, his granddaughters. He would not turn you away."

"No, Mama, no." Mary and the others had assured her that she was not going to die, but Flora had only smiled wearily, knowing as well as they that they lied out of love.

"Yes." Her voice was firmer than Mary had ever heard her. "You cannot stay here with *him*." Her emphasis on the word carried all the venom she felt for the man she had married. "Promise me, Mary. Promise you'll take your sisters to my father."

Mary had promised.

She had hated to leave the home they had known for the last twelve years as much as her sisters did—Rose was not the only one who had shed a few tears in the middle of the night. But she had given her word to her dying mother—and she knew her mother was right. They could not remain with Cosmo.

He had never been a good man, but after his wife's death, he had grown worse. He took to drinking more heavily and at all hours of the day. He had turned his leering gaze on all the Bascombe girls and seized every opportunity to brush up against them, so that the sisters made sure never to be in his presence alone. He was apt to fly into a rage about the slightest thing—and sometimes about nothing at all. Once he had even swung at Camellia in a fit of temper, and it was only her quickness and his drunkenness that had kept her from being injured. She had picked up the closest thing to hand, a cast-iron skillet, and chased him from the kitchen, but it was clear that Cosmo was becoming a danger to them all.

Worst, when he returned from one of his weeks-long trips, he had brought with him a man named Egerton Suttersby. Suttersby was pale and quiet, with the dark flat gaze of a snake. He wanted to marry Rose, an idea Cosmo thoroughly endorsed. Suttersby had courted Rose assiduously despite her clear attempts to avoid him, and Cosmo had harangued her about it at every opportunity, alternating between threats and descriptions of the wonderful world that would await Rose if she accepted his suit. The two had been so insistent that Mary had begun to fear that they might try to spirit Rose away and force her to marry the man.

So Mary had scraped together all the money she could and sold her mother's bits of jewelry, and as soon as Cosmo left on another of his trips, the girls had run away from Three Corners, taking their mother and father's marriage certificate, the girls' birth certificates, and a sealed letter from Flora to her father. Mary did not know what was in it, but she suspected that her mother had tearfully thrown herself on her strict father's mercy, begging him to take in her children.

It galled Mary that her mother had had to beg for anything. She wished she herself did not have to face the man and ask him to take them in. But her mother had put her in charge of the girls, and Mary was determined to carry out her mother's wishes.

"Approaching the earl is the only thing to do," Mary reiterated now, casting a look around at her sisters. "You know as well as I do that we can't stay together any other way. What could we do to earn money? None of us would qualify to be a governess; we haven't enough education. We could sew, perhaps, or be servants somewhere, but we'd never all be hired in the same house."

"Besides," Rose put in quietly, "we promised Mama."

There was a moment of silence after her words, all of them feeling again the pain of Flora's passing.

Mary nodded. "Mama was certain that he would have come to regret his words. And he could not be so heartless as to throw out his own granddaughters."

"I don't know." Lily shook her head. "How could anyone be so heartless as to cut someone like Mama out of his life just for going against his wishes?"

"He's an old autocrat, obviously. But living with him would have to be an improvement over starving to death. Or being dependent on Cosmo Glass."

"Or having to marry that odious Egerton Suttersby," Rose added with a shudder. She glanced over at Mary a little worriedly. "We are well away from him, don't you think? He wouldn't follow us, would he?"

"No, don't be silly. I don't think even Mr. Suttersby would

be so ardent as to cross the Atlantic in pursuit of a woman who doesn't want him."

"I would have thought any man would have taken the hint that she didn't want him weeks ago," Camellia put in, rolling her eyes. "He must have seen her slip out whenever he entered the tavern. Sometimes I thought I must be struck down for the absolute whoppers I told him about why she was not there."

Lily snorted. "As if those were the worst lies you've told." She turned to her oldest sister. "So what are we going to do now? How are we going to find our grandfather?"

"I don't know," Mary admitted. She sighed and flopped down in a chair. "I had not expected London to be so *big*. I mean, I knew it was a large city, but I thought it must be something like Philadelphia. But this . . . ."

"That is why Sir Royce could have helped us," Rose pointed out. "He might know where the earl lives."

"Perhaps." Mary grimaced. "But I have no desire for that—that rake to know our business."

"Rake!" Rose looked at her sister with raised brows. "But I thought he acted the perfect gentleman."

Mary felt a flush rising in her cheeks. She wasn't about to tell her sisters about the incident in the hall. "Well, perhaps not a rake. But he certainly isn't anyone we know. I have no desire to go about telling everyone our life story. I am sure that I will be able to find the earl's address somehow or other." She paused, then went on, "I think that I should go by myself tomorrow morning to find him. It will be easier than having all of us present ourselves on his doorstep."

"But I want to meet the earl, too!" Lily protested.

"You *will* meet him. Don't be silly. As soon as I explain everything to him, I am sure he will welcome us all into his home," Mary told her with more conviction than she felt.

One reason she wished to see the man by herself first was that she feared his reaction to the news that he had four granddaughters he had never known existed. She did not want her sisters to hear what he might say when she told him.

"Mary is right," Rose put in, backing up Mary, as she could be counted on to do. Several years older than Camellia and Lily, with only a year between them in age, Mary and Rose had always had a special bond. "It might overwhelm the poor man for all of us to show up at once."

"But what are we to do while Mary's gone?" Lily argued.

"It will be deadly dull," Camellia agreed. "But no doubt it will be even duller to visit some old earl. At least here we can go down to the stables and see the horses."

"Oh, who cares about the horses?" Lily replied somewhat sulkily.

"There might be shops close by," Camellia pointed out, and Lily brightened.

"No!" Mary's eyes widened in alarm. "You mustn't go out walking. What if you get lost? What if something happens?" She turned an appealing eye to Rose. "Rose, you must see that they stay here while I'm gone."

"You are such a mother hen." Lily rolled her eyes. "Camellia and I can take care of ourselves."

"At home, you can. Even out in the wilds, I wouldn't worry. But it's different here. The people are different. Promise you will not."

The girls argued for a bit more, but the serving girl's arrival with a tray of food put an end to their protests. It had been some hours since they had eaten, and the prospect of a fresh meal after the days of shipboard fare was mouthwatering. They sat down and fell to eating with relish. When at last they were sated, all arguments had long since flown from their heads, and they were more than ready to follow the innkeeper to their rooms.

Lily and Camellia shared one room, and their two older sisters were next door to them. Mary was pleased to see that the door locked from the inside. She turned the key, and beside her Rose let out a sigh of relief.

"I was afraid we wouldn't be able to lock the door." Rose sank down onto the straight chair that stood beside the door. "This place frightens me."

"The inn?" Mary asked, a trifle surprised. "It seems quite respectable, I thought."

"No. The whole place. The docks. London. It's so big. So dirty and . . . squalid."

"It's been a difficult day." Mary hopped up onto the bed. "It is very different from home. But I am sure the docks are worse than the rest of it. Things will be different tomorrow. You'll see."

Rose gave her sister a faint smile. "You are always so full of confidence."

Mary shrugged. "I never like the alternative."

"You must wonder sometimes how we could be sisters. I feel as though I am frightened by everything."

"Don't be silly. You sat there on the docks all alone, guarding our bags. That's hardly the act of a coward."

"Well, yes. I mean, I had to. But I was scared the whole time."

"But that's the whole thing about being brave, isn't it? Standing your ground even though you're afraid." Mary leaned toward her sister, frowning a little. "Rose, what is all this talk about? What's bothering you?"

Rose shook her head. "It's just all so strange. What if our grandfather turns us away? What if we can't find him?"

"Don't think that way." Mary slid off the bed and went

to her sister, slipping a comforting arm around her shoulders. Rose had always been the most tenderhearted of them, ever willing to offer sympathy, but just as easily hurt and far more likely to worry than any of the others. "You're just tired, so it all seems worse. But things will get better now. You'll see."

She watched as Rose got up and began to get ready for bed. Mary was not about to admit to her sister how much the events of the day had shaken her as well. It chilled her to think what an awful situation they would be in if Sir Royce had not stopped that thief. She should have been more careful, Mary told herself. More watchful. She would have to learn how to deal with the dangers of a new city and country.

And that included men like Sir Royce Winslow.

How silly it was to even think of Sir Royce. The kiss had meant nothing to him—any more than it had to her, of course. She would never see him again. It had been foolish but utterly harmless.

Still, as she unbuttoned her dress, she could not help but remember the way his lips had felt on hers—the soft, insistent pressure . . . the heat . . . the promise of further delights.

Flushing a little, Mary yanked her plain white cotton night rail over her head. Firmly she pulled her mind back from its wayward path. She would not think about him, she promised herself. She would not let her thoughts drift to his thick hair, the color of wheat in the sun, or his grass green eyes, or his strong, competent fingers as they curled around her arm.

No. Definitely. She was done with Royce Winslow.

Mary set off the next morning for her grandfather's house in far better spirits than she had enjoyed the evening before. A good night's sleep and a hearty breakfast had done much to chase away her troubling thoughts, including those relating to the handsome Sir Royce.

She was certain that her fortunes had turned when she asked the innkeeper if he knew the address of the Earl of Stewkesbury and, after a quickly suppressed look of surprise, he had told her that Stewkesbury House lay on Bariston Crescent and any hack in the city would know where it was.

A few minutes later, dressed in her best day dress and bonnet, her hands encased primly in ladylike gloves, and wearing the dainty silver earbobs she had inherited from her mother—for she was determined not to look like the impoverished relative that she was—she set out from the inn. It was easy to hail a vehicle here to take her to the earl's house, and she settled into the seat with some satisfaction. It did not have the elegance of last night's conveyance, of course, but she had at least managed it on her own. She thought that it boded well for the project before her.

It was not until the hack stopped in front of an imposing gray stone building and Mary climbed down from the carriage that she realized with horror that the only coins in her purse were American. The driver had jumped down and stood waiting expectantly as Mary tucked the case containing her papers under her arm and dug in her reticule.

"I-I'm sorry!" Mary stammered, a flush rising in her cheeks. She pulled a few coins from her coin purse and held them out to him. "I haven't any English money. Will these do?"

The driver stared at her as if she had taken leave of her senses. "No money! 'Ere, wot's this? Tryin' to gull me, are ye?"

"No! No, truly—though I'm not sure exactly what that

means. But I am not trying to deceive you. I just arrived here from the United States, you see, and I haven't any money except American coins. I haven't had time to—to exchange it. Indeed, I don't really know how to do that. But if you could just wait, I am sure—"

"Wait? Wait for what?" The driver eyed her suspiciously. "Don't try any of your stories on me, missy. I'm no Johnny Raw."

"No, indeed, I am sure that you are not. But my grandfather is inside, and he will have some British money to—"

"In there?" The man nodded toward the grand house behind them. "Aye, and I'm cousin to the Duke of Clarence."

"You are?" Mary asked, taken aback for a moment. "But why—oh, oh, I see. You are being facetious."

The driver grimaced. "I don't know about that. But I'm telling you, I'm not leaving 'ere 'til I get my blunt!" He narrowed his eyes. "If you ain't got coin, I reckon I'd take them little earbobs."

"No!" Mary's hands rose instinctively to cover the tiny silver loops that hung from her ears. "Those were my mother's!"

The man continued to argue, and Mary noticed that a passing couple had paused to stare, then hurried on, and the boy sweeping the crossing at the intersection had strayed down the street to watch them. Soon, she thought, they would attract a clot of onlookers, and her grandfather would not appreciate that.

"Here!" she said finally, in desperation taking out a silver coin and thrusting it toward him. "It's silver! Even if it is American, it has to be worth far more than a mere ride across town. It wasn't even that far!"

The driver grumbled and examined the coin, even biting it, then finally pocketed it with a bitter remark concerning mutton-headed Americans and climbed back onto his seat. Mary closed her purse and thrust it back into her reticule, letting out a sigh of relief. Her hands were trembling from the confrontation.

She turned and walked up the front steps, then paused to set her case down and smooth her skirts. She reminded herself that she was the earl's granddaughter and he was bound to take her in. Picking up the satchel once more, she raised the large brass ring that ran through the lion's head knocker and brought it down sharply against the plate.

The door opened only seconds later to reveal a man dressed in old-fashioned blue breeches and coat, with a powdered wig on his head. He had a long narrow face centered by a long narrow nose, down which he stared at her coldly.

Mary, somewhat startled by his rudeness as well as his odd attire, stood silent for a long moment, gazing back at him. The person who answered the door must be a servant, she thought, yet why was he dressed in the sort of wig and clothes that were usually seen only on very old gentlemen?

"The service entrance is to the side," he said, and stepped back, starting to close the door.

"No!" Mary cried, recovering her voice, and she reached out to grasp the edge of the door. "No, wait. I am here to see the earl."

"The earl?" The man's brows rose comically, but he pulled his expression back into its former cool blankness. "I fear you are much mistaken. Now take yourself off."

"I must see him!" Mary said quickly. "I have very personal business with him. He will wish to see me, I swear. I am here from the United States. I know I should have written first, but there wasn't time, and a letter would not have arrived before I did anyway, and—"

The man took her wrist firmly and pulled her hand from the door, thrusting her back. "Take your stories elsewhere, you doxy, and stop dirtying the earl's doorstep."

With that, the man closed the door in her face.

Chapter 3

Mary stared, mouth open, at the smooth expanse of the closed door in front of her, too astonished to speak or even move. A saving fury washed through her, and she grabbed the knocker, bringing it down several times. She paused, and when there was no response, she began to hammer again.

At long last, the door opened. The same man stood before her, his face red now with anger. He came out, pulling the door shut behind him, and Mary was forced to move back and down onto the top step, almost dropping her satchel.

"Cease that noise this instant!" the man exclaimed. "I told you to take yourself off. The earl doesn't have time for bird-witted hussies cluttering up his doorstep."

"Hussies!" Mary faced him, eyes flashing and her free hand planted pugnaciously on her hip. "How dare you! I am no hussy!"

The man cast a sardonic glance down her form and let out a snort. "Aye, 'tis certain you don't dress like one. Well, he has no use for dowds harassing him, either. Whatever you're collecting for, try around the side, like I said, or get you gone altogether."

"I am not collecting for anything!" Mary retorted, stung by his comment on her best dress and bonnet. "I told you,

I am here to see the Earl of Stewkesbury. I demand that you tell him I am here."

The man crossed his arms over his chest. "No one sees the earl without Mr. Hooper's say-so."

"Then let me see this Mr. Hooper, whoever he is."

"He's the butler. And I already told you—go around to the side."

Mary regarded the man for a long moment. She had not expected this obstacle to her plans. She had known she would have to convince her grandfather of the truth of her claims. It had never occurred to her that she would have to convince some strangely dressed servant merely to let her see her grandfather. But it was obvious that she could not shove her way past him.

Turning on her heel, she descended the steps and went around to a narrow path along the side of the grand house. At the end of the walkway, a few steps led down to a door of much less grandeur. Mary trotted down the steps and, tucking the case under her arm, rapped sharply upon the door. Her nerves had long since vanished, burned away by her righteous indignation, and she was eager to launch into battle with Mr. Hooper.

A young girl in a mobcap opened the door and gazed blankly at her. Even after Mary demanded to see Mr. Hooper, the girl continued to look equally unknowing.

"We're not 'iring," she said at last, turning to speak to a tall woman with muscular arms who was stirring a pot. "Are we, Cook?"

The woman thus addressed frowned at the girl. "Course not. Wot are ye doin', Millie? Get back to the pots."

The girl nodded, saying, "Yes, ma'am," and started to close the door.

"No!" Mary was faster this time than at the front door, and she jumped inside, bringing up her forearm to stop the closing of the door. "I am not here looking for employment. I am here to see the earl."

Both the cook and the girl regarded her doubtfully.

"The man at the front door said I must speak to Mr. Hooper," Mary went on. "At this door. Now, will you kindly inform Mr. Hooper that I am here and wish to speak to him?"

Something in her voice must have convinced the girl, or at least the cook, for after a nod from the tall woman, Millie turned and headed off into the recesses of the house. Mary waited for an interminable time, during which she found herself the object of all eyes in the kitchen—and that, she realized as she glanced around the cavernous room, was a very large number indeed. The kitchen could easily have held two or three of their tavern's kitchen back home, and the number of people working in it was daunting. Was this not a private home? How could it need such a large kitchen? And what could all these people possibly do? She noticed two or three other men dressed in the same way as the man at the front door.

A very tall, very thin, very elegant man with snowy white hair strode into the room. In his black jacket and trousers and starched white shirt, he looked so imposing that Mary knew at once that this must be the earl himself. Millie must have misunderstood and had fetched Mary's grandfather herself.

Mary's stomach quivered at the thought of meeting her grandfather, but she faced him squarely. He halted in front of her and regarded her with an unwavering gaze.

"Yes?" he intoned at last, drawing the word out and investing it with a decided frostiness.

The apparent contempt on his features raised her hackles, but Mary kept a firm grip on her temper and bobbed a polite curtsey. "How do you do, my lord?" She had quizzed her fellow passengers aboard ship about the correct way to address an earl. "I am Mary Bascombe, and I have come to see you on a very important matter."

The man's eyebrows shot up, disturbing the careful reserve on his face. "I fear you are mistaken. I am Mr. Hooper. The butler of Stewkesbury House."

Mary flushed, aware of the titter that was running around the room. "Oh. I-I see. I beg your pardon." She straightened her shoulders; she was not about to let her mistake intimidate her into forsaking her mission. "I am here to see the earl. It is quite important."

"His lordship is not receiving," the man answered shortly. "And I cannot conceive of any business that you might have that would necessitate speaking to the Earl of Stewkesbury."

"My business with the earl is not your concern."

"I am afraid it is. I do not allow strange young women access to his lordship whenever the whim strikes them. I can take care of whatever 'business' you think you have with his lordship."

"I fear you cannot." Mary set her jaw and regarded him steadily. "My business with the earl is personal. I do not think he would appreciate my sharing it with anyone else, including his servants."

They stood, eyes locked, as the room around them settled into a hush. Mary suspected that few had ever dared stand up to this tyrant. Finally, in a carefully uninflected tone, the butler said, "If you will leave your card, I will make sure that his lordship receives it. If he wishes to make contact with you, I am sure he will."

"My card?"

"Yes. Your calling card."

Mary remembered the small white card Sir Royce had tried to hand her last night. No doubt it was another mark against her that she did not have one to produce.

"I don't have a card. I shall simply wait for the earl."

"I think not. It could be hours before he returns from his club."

"Then I shall go there. Where is this club?"

This announcement sent a ripple of horror across the man's face. "You cannot go to his club!"

"I don't see why not. Just tell me where it is, and I—"

"Young woman!" The butler's voice cracked like a whip. "It is time that you left this house. I suggest you go back to"—he cast a disparaging glance at her dress—"whatever village you came from and cease this nonsense."

"I came from America!"

"Ah. That explains it, I suppose. Still, it gives you no reason to see the earl. Kindly take your leave."

"I will not!" Mary wanted to scream in frustration. "I am the earl's granddaughter."

Her announcement did not have the effect she had hoped for. If anything, the butler's face grew even more remote, and his voice was like ice as he turned from her. "James. Escort this person out immediately."

The footman who had run her off from the front door strode forward now from the rear of the kitchen. There was a purposeful look on his face that left Mary in little doubt that the fellow would pick her up bodily if necessary and put her outside. In order to retain what little dignity she had left, Mary turned and stalked out the door. She heard it close solidly behind her.

Fighting back tears of fury and embarrassment, she marched back up the stairs and along the narrow walkway to the street. It was then that she realized that she had no idea how to get back to the Boar and Bear where her sisters were waiting.

Hiring another hack was not an option since she had no English money to pay for it. Nor did she know how to go about getting her American money exchanged for British. She would have to walk back to the inn. It had not been terribly far, but she had paid little attention to the route.

She set off in what she hoped was the right direction and stopped the first gentleman whose path she crossed to ask for directions. He looked askance at her, then shook his head and pointed vaguely, saying it was no doubt to the east. Next she approached a pair of women who were strolling along, parasols raised to ward off the sun, but they shook their heads and quickly skirted around her. The young boy sweeping the crossing was equally little help, though he was happy to talk. As Mary could understand less than half of what he said in his thick accent, she soon moved on. It was a woman pushing a cart full of fruits and vegetables through the streets who finally steered her in the right direction.

As Mary walked, she noticed that more than one passerby shot her a quick, curious glance. She supposed it was her clothing, for her dress was plain and she could tell from looking at the few other women on the street that it was out of style, as well. But more than that, she realized after a few minutes, she was the only woman who was unaccompanied, except for the vegetable vendor. Most women were on the arms of well-dressed gentlemen or hidden away inside carriages, and the rest had other ladies with them or maids trailing along just behind—or both. It seemed quite peculiar to her. Did women remain in the house if they couldn't find another person to drag along?

The distance was longer than it had seemed in the carriage, and Mary got lost a second time. The trek was made no easier by her gloomy thoughts. How was she to talk to their grandfather if she could not get inside the house? She had known that she might have a hard time convincing the old man that she and her sisters were his granddaughters, and she had not been certain that he would take them in.

But it had never occurred to her that she might not even be able to present her case to him!

At last, bone-weary and dejected, she reached the inn. The first thing she heard as she stepped inside was the merry sound of her sisters' laughter coming from the private parlor, so she turned her steps in that direction. Knocking on the door, she went in and stopped abruptly.

There, sitting with her sisters, looking quite composed and devastatingly handsome, was Sir Royce Winslow.

Sir Royce had not intended to concern himself further with the Bascombe girls. He had seen them to a respectable inn; they had assured him that they were able to take care of themselves. There was no need for him to worry about what became of them.

He was not, after all, the sort of man who took everyone else's problems on his own shoulders. Let his stepbrother Oliver hold himself responsible for every person within his reach, however tangentially. Royce was a different sort. He was not the head of the family, merely the son of a nobleman with a nice inheritance. He looked after his estate, of course; the old man had drummed that into him. Any of his tenants could turn to him in need, just as they could expect fair treatment from him. But Royce had always been careful not to take on added responsibility. He was not one to stick his nose in where it did not belong.

And the four young American women he had encountered last night were no business of his. He could not have left them alone by the docks; he was, after all, a gentleman. But having seen them to safety, he considered that he had done his duty.

However, he found that he could not stop thinking about them. They were so odd—at once quite pretty and yet far out of the mode, they were naïve and innocent, but at the same time bizarrely able to take care of themselves. Whoever heard of a young lady strapping a knife to her leg? Or of four young gentlewomen traveling alone across the ocean, as they seemed to have done? Why, Charlotte and his other female cousins had never ventured as far as the park without a chaperone, at least in the form of a maid.

And what, he wondered, was in that satchel that was so important to them? He supposed it must be their money; yet it had been quite light, as if containing very little. Certainly it was nothing heavy like coins or jewelry or even stacks of paper scrip.

Most of all, though, Royce found himself thinking about Mary Bascombe. But, no, that was too common a name for such an uncommon woman.

"Marigold," he decided, and a smile curved his lips.

Certainly she was no flower—what a blunt, unrefined, direct creature she was—but the exotic quality of the name suited her. He had never met anyone quite like her. She had none of the airs of a lady, no girlish simpering or missish indecision. She had not cast herself at him, playing the help-less innocent as most young women would have, seeking his aid in her desperate situation. Indeed, she had been, if anything, reluctant to receive his help.

But there was nothing of the jaded sophisticate about her, either. She was far too fresh, too unaware of the dangers of their situation. And despite the astonishingly straightforward way she had talked to him, a strange man, it was clear that she had had no experience with men.

A smile touched his mouth again as he remembered their kiss, her lips soft and yielding beneath his. He had not in-tended to kiss her—he had been certain that, despite her odd ways, she was well brought-up—but at the last mo-ment, he had been unable to resist. He had had to taste that luscious full mouth. She had melted so easily against him, her response untutored yet eager. It had been far harder to pull away than he had expected.

And far harder to forget.

It had taken him a long time to go to sleep, and the next morning, as he dressed and shaved, he found that Mary Bascombe was still on his mind. And her sisters, of course. They were, he thought, mere babes in the woods here in London, completely unprepared for the pitfalls of the city. Mary had said that they would contact their grandfather, but what sort of grandfather would fail to come to the docks to greet them, or at least send someone in his stead? He could not help but wonder if she had told him the truth or if they had some other plan entirely.

No matter what the girls had planned, Royce had a strong suspicion that they would find it more difficult than expected. Set down in a strange country, not knowing where anything was, they were bound to need help. And there were many men with far from savory intentions who would jump to help four such attractive females. Besides, even though the Boar and Bear was a perfectly respectable inn, it would not do for the sisters to go exploring—which was, when he considered it, precisely the sort of thing they would do.

With a sigh, Royce acknowledged that he would not be able to spend a peaceful morning until he had visited the Bascombe sisters again and elicited from them a more thorough explanation. And, he admitted to himself, he would not mind having another look at Marigold Bascombe. Therefore, after breakfast he set out for the Boar and Bear. Normally he would have walked or hailed a hack, for it wasn't far, but today he had his carriage brought round, suspecting that before the day was over, he would once again have use for it.

He was somewhat surprised to find the girls tamely whiling away their time in the private parlor—Rose occupying herself with darning while Lily read aloud from a book and Camellia appeared to be repairing the sole of a ladies' boot.

"Ladies." Royce swept them a bow as he entered the room, quickly taking in the fact that Mary Bascombe was not among them. "I hope I am not interrupting you."

"Oh, no!" Lily cried, closing the book with a thump. "I mean, well, yes, you are, of course, but I am very grateful. 'Tis the dullest book imaginable—there's not a single mad monk or rattling skeleton or even a ghost."

"Shocking."

Lily laughed. "You may pull that face with me, but I warrant you would find it dreadfully dull, too. It's horridly uplifting, all about a boy who wants better things, which seems to me perfectly reasonable, but then these dreadful things happen to him because of his pride. And really, that sort of comeuppance so rarely happens, don't you think?"

"Too true."

"Whereas one often meets mad monks," Rose teased.

"Oh, you know what I mean. That's not real either, but at least it's fun!"

"In any case, at least I shan't have to feel guilty for intruding upon you," Royce said.

"Goodness, no."

"Anything would be a relief after hearing about that watery Hubert," Camellia agreed, then blushed a little. "That is—I didn't mean that you were just anything, or anyone— I mean—"

Royce laughed. "Oh, no, don't apologize. Your bluntness, Miss Camellia, is admirable." He glanced around. "I see that your sister is not here."

"No, she has gone to—" Lily stopped short. "I forgot. We are not supposed to tell you."

"I see. Well, I would not wish you to go against your

sister's edict, of course. But I could not keep from worrying that I had abandoned you to your fate. I wanted to offer you my further help."

"That is very kind of you," Rose told him. "But Mary will be able to handle everything. At least . . . well . . ." She trailed off uncertainly.

"I see." Royce studied the girls' faces. "Has she been gone long?"

"Forever," Camellia said, with a look of relief that told him he had found the precise point of their concern.

"It has been a good while," Rose agreed, frowning. "But I am sure that she is all right. It probably takes longer to get places here. We are not used to a large city."

"It's been almost two hours," Camellia pointed out. "How could it possibly take that long? She went in a hack."

"Indeed? Well, then at least she should not get lost." Despite his cheerful tone, Royce could not help but feel a twinge of alarm. "Can you not at least tell me to which area of town she was going?"

"We don't know," Rose confessed. "She asked the inn-keeper, I think, where it was, and he told her, but she didn't say what area that was."

"Perhaps we should ask the innkeeper," Royce suggested. "Surely if it is all right for him to know, it would not be amiss for me to know as well."

"I suppose not." Rose frowned thoughtfully.

"Oh, really, Rose," Lily grumbled, "you cannot believe that Sir Royce is a swindler. Or that he is going to take ad-vantage of our—well, you know who."

"And he's right—Mary must have told the innkeeper," Camellia pointed out.

"Yes, but though she may have told him *who,* she did not tell him *why* she was going to see . . . this person whom she was going to see." Rose began to chuckle even as she finished her sentence, and the others joined her in laughter. "I am sorry. This is awfully secretive, isn't it?"

"Positively furtive," Royce agreed. "In another moment, I shall become convinced that you are involved in a secret society."

"Like in the *The Secret of Castle Ordeyne*!" Lily sat up straighter, her face glowing. "Where the wicked count is part of a group that supports the false prince, and they all dress up in hooded robes and meet in the dungeon of the castle."

"Precisely."

Lily let out a huge sigh. "Well, it's not at all like that."

"No? I am downcast." Royce smiled.

"I think we should tell him," Camellia offered. "Mary has been gone too long. I'd go looking for her myself, but I haven't any idea where to go. If she's lost or in trouble, we need Sir Royce's help. And it isn't as if our grandfather—"

"Your grandfather? Then he lives here in London?"

"Yes. That is where Mary has gone, to see our grandfather."

"Why did he not come to meet you at the docks? Or send someone for you?"

"He didn't know we were coming," Rose replied.

"He didn't know we were alive," Lily added.

As Royce was absorbing this bit of information, a knock sounded on the door, and it swung open. Mary Bascombe stood on the threshold, looking flushed, tired, and thoroughly irritated.

"You!" Mary said in accents of loathing.

She wasn't sure why it was so irritating to see Sir Royce Winslow. But it seemed the final humiliating cap to a dreadful day to arrive, red in the face and perspiring, her hair damp and crushed under her bonnet, fuming from her encounter with her grandfather's servants, and find Sir Royce here, looking handsome and carefree, so utterly relaxed as he joked and chatted with her sisters. Mary was perilously close to the edge of tears, and it would be the absolute worst to bawl like a child in front of this man.

"Yes, I." Sir Royce rose with easy grace and went to the bellpull. "I think something to drink might be in order. Some tea, perhaps?"

"Anything." Mary jerked at the bow tied beneath her chin, eager to pull the hat from her head, but the bow had turned into a knot during her long walk, and her sharp movements only served to make it tighter.

"Allow me." Sir Royce came over to her and gently pushed Mary's fumbling fingers aside.

He smiled down into her face, his green eyes alight with amusement and some other quality Mary could not quite identify. Despite her annoyance, Mary felt herself relaxing. It was difficult to keep her lips from curving up in response to his smile. And there was something so capable, so calm about him; she could not imagine anything ruffling him.

His fingers grazed the underside of her chin as he worked at the knot, and it was all Mary could do not to shiver. It felt so pleasant and yet so different; she found her mind wandering to how it would feel to have his fingers trail all the way down her throat. She remembered the touch of his lips on hers the night before, and her cheeks warmed even more.

Mary looked away, unable to meet his eyes. What if he realized where her thoughts were straying? What if he was thinking the same thing himself?

"There." Royce gave a final pull, and the ribbons fell apart. He reached up and took off her bonnet, turning to set it on a nearby table.

"Thank you." Mary hurried over to the mirror.

What she saw there was not reassuring. How had he looked at her and not burst out laughing? Her face was shiny and her cheeks beet red, and her eyes were still bright with anger. Mary dug in her pocket and brought out her handkerchief, wetting it in the washbowl and wringing it out, then smoothing it across her face. She picked at her hair and repinned a few strategic pins.

"Mary! Do stop primping," Camellia told her. "Tell us what happened."

"We are all dying of curiosity," Rose added.

"We were beginning to think something dreadful had happened to you." Lily's voice was concerned—and just the slightest bit hopeful.

"I am not primping!" Mary whirled around. Her eyes went first to Sir Royce, who was now lounging beside the fireplace, one arm resting on the mantel, watching her. Had he thought she was primping for him?

She lifted her chin challengingly and swung away from him, going over to sit down on the couch beside Rose. "Nothing happened. Well, nothing helpful. I was thoroughly embarrassed, but I am beginning to think that will not be an uncommon occurrence in this country."

"Did you not find our grandfather?" Lily asked.

"I found his house. But they would not let me inside."

"He denied us?" Rose stared at her, shocked.

"No, not *him*. His servants would not let me in. They sent me round to the back door!"

Sir Royce smothered a groan, and Mary turned to glare at him. "You people are insufferably rude. Why would anyone tell their servants to behave like that? To treat people as if, as if they were—well, he called me a hussy!"

Her sisters erupted into gasps and exclamations. Sir Royce just closed his eyes and sighed. "Oh, dear."

"Oh, dear?" Mary repeated. "That's all you have to say?"

"No. Of course not. It was quite dastardly of him." A grin quirked the corners of his mouth. "Shall I call the fellow out?

No, that would not do; he is, after all, a servant. I could demand satisfaction from his employer, of course—but then, he is your grandfather, so that would scarcely work. Perhaps I should just give the scoundrel a good thrashing."

"Oh, stop making jests. No doubt that is exactly the sort of thing you instruct your servants to do as well. The butler told me I should leave a card, but of course I didn't have one, and then he said I should write a note and the earl would see me if he wished to. But he will probably just tear it up if I am not there to explain it all to him."

"The earl?" Sir Royce's eyebrows rose. "Your grandfather is a peer?"

"You needn't look so amazed." Mary crossed her arms and glared at him. "It is quite true. Our grandfather is the Earl of Stewkesbury."

The effect of their relative's name on Sir Royce was astounding. He stiffened, his face going rigid and carefully blank. The casual arm draped along the mantel dropped to his side as he took a swift step forward.

"What?" His voice was as cold and brittle as ice, as stinging in its force. "Is this some sort of jest? Or was all this an elaborate ruse, designed to pull me into your little scheme?"

Chapter 4

Mary and her sisters gaped at Sir Royce in astonishment. He had changed in an instant into the very picture of a haughty aristocrat. Even his calm was different—now the silent intensity of a predator.

"Well?" he snapped when they said nothing. "Answer me! Was that arranged last night—did you plan it to draw me into your swindle? Am I intended to be your means to get to the earl?"

Anger flooded Mary, releasing her from stunned inaction, and she jumped to her feet. "I haven't the slightest idea what you're talking about! But I can assure you that I have no swindle in mind. Do you think I arranged for a thief to steal our papers just so we could meet you? I must say, you have an awfully grand idea of your importance. I didn't know you last night; I still don't, beyond what you yourself have told me. And I have even less notion of what you have to do with the earl!"

"You think we're imposters!" Lily exclaimed, looking less indignant than intrigued at the idea. "That we are like the wicked Cynthia Montrose, taking the place of the Lady Anna while her horrid brother keeps Anna locked up in the dungeon!" She turned to her sisters, explaining, "They wanted the old lord's money, you see, and they thought to trick him out of it by pretending Cynthia was his daughter, only—"

"Yes, I understand what Sir Royce thinks of us." Mary's eyes flashed. "He believes we are scheming adventuresses. He must also think we are rather spectacular in our abilities. Not only did we arrange for someone to steal our case and dash past him with it, we also knew that he would be stepping out of that door at exactly that moment. I'd like to know how he thinks we managed that! Perhaps he'd also like to tell us why we should set up this elaborate farce for him when it is the Earl of Stewkesbury whom we want to reach."

Royce gazed at her for another long, considering moment, but Mary could see him subtly relax. "Do you honestly not know who I am?"

Mary frowned. "You are Sir Royce Winslow. At least, that is what you told us. But perhaps I have been too trusting. It seems to me that someone who is as suspicious as you must engage in a bit of double-dealing himself, else how is he so familiar with swindles and frauds?"

He let out a short laugh that was signally lacking in humor. "I have had quite a bit of experience with those wishing to get closer to the earl. You see, the earl's father married my mother thirty-one years ago. We grew up in the same house."

Once again, Mary stared at him in confusion. "But no, the earl—we cannot be talking about the same man. Is there another Earl of Stewkesbury? He was my mother's father; he must be an old man."

Again he regarded her for a time. "What was his first name? Do you know?"

"Reginald. That is what my mother wrote on the envelope—Reginald, Lord Stewkesbury."

"That is the old earl. The present earl's grandfather. I

am sorry to tell you that Lord Reginald died more than a year ago. Reginald's son, Lawrence, had predeceased him, so Lawrence's son Oliver became the earl."

"Then he would be . . ." Rose stopped to work out the relationship. "Lawrence must have been our mother's brother. And that would make the present earl . . . our cousin?"

"But that is wonderful!" Lily blurted out. "Then you are our cousin, too!"

A flicker of dismay ran through Mary at her sister's words. This man, whose kiss had sent fire sizzling through her, was her cousin?

"No!" Royce's eyes slid to Mary for an instant before going back to Lily. "No, we are not related at all. You see, I am not a Talbot." At their confused looks, he explained, "Talbot is the earl's family name. *My* father was Sir Alan Winslow. He died when I was young, and my mother, Barbara, later married Lawrence, Oliver's father. Oliver's mother had died when he was but three, leaving Lawrence a widower with a child to raise as well. Lawrence and my mother had another child, Fitzhugh. Fitz is my half brother through my mother, and he is also Oliver's half brother through his father. But Oliver and I are merely stepbrothers. Lord Stewkesbury and Fitz would be your cousins if your mother was Reginald's daughter, but I am no relation to you at all."

"Oh. Well." Mary turned away to hide the relief that his words brought. She reminded herself that she was irritated with Sir Royce. "It scarcely matters anyway, does it, since you believe we are common thieves."

"Oh, no. You are most uncommon," he retorted, and a ghost of a smile hovered on his lips. "As to your thievery— well, I must admit, it does seem unlikely that you could have arranged our meeting."

"That isn't the same as saying that you believe we are the earl's cousins."

"You must allow that there is little way I could know that."

"Some people are able to judge one's honesty just from speaking to a person." Mary made a dismissive gesture. "In any case, it matters little whether you believe us or not. We are not asking for your help in presenting our case to the earl."

"But, Mary, why not?" Lily protested.

"It seems to me that Sir Royce would be most helpful," Rose agreed. "He could tell the earl our story, and then he would be more likely to see us."

"I will find a way to address the earl." Mary set her jaw. "I shall locate this club of his and go to see him there."

"Good Gad!" Sir Royce looked shocked. "You cannot go to his club!"

"I don't see why not."

"For one thing, they will not allow you in. It is a gentlemen's club. No woman of any sort is admitted. And if you showed up on their doorstep, it would ruin you socially."

"As if I care for that!"

"You should, if you and your sisters are who you say you are," he shot back.

"Then I shall sit down and write the man a letter and take it round to him." Such a tame course was not what Mary wanted to do, but she was not about to ask this arrogant man for help.

Royce sighed and came over to her. "Miss Bascombe, I apologize profusely for any insult I may have offered you. Pray, sit down and tell me your story. Then we will see what can be done."

Mary would have liked to hold out a little longer, just to show him that she wanted nothing from him, but her pragmatic nature won out. "Very well."

She sat down on the sofa beside Rose, and Royce pulled

over one of the straight-backed chairs and settled into it, as if preparing for a long tale. "Now . . ."

"Our mother was Reginald's daughter Flora," Mary began. She proceeded to tell him the full story of her parents' hasty wedding and the earl's disapproval, though she skipped over her mother's second marriage to the odious Cosmo Glass, as well as her and her sisters' hasty departure from the United States.

"We have papers showing that we are Flora's children," she finished. "It isn't as if we expect the earl to believe us without any proof."

"I see." Royce regarded her, a twinkle growing in his eyes. "Well, well. I wonder what the righteous Oliver will have to say about this."

"I am so glad that our situation provides you with amusement," Mary snapped.

"Oh, no, your situation does not. I am in full sympathy with you, I assure you. It is the thought of Oliver's expression when I present you to him that amuses me."

"You mean you are going to take us to him?" Mary asked, her irritation vanishing in a flood of relief.

"I have little choice in the matter, it would seem."

"When?" Lily asked eagerly. "When can we meet him? Tomorrow?"

He gave the young girl a smile. "I see no reason to wait that long. I suggest we pay the earl a visit this afternoon."

Chapter 5

Mary's second arrival at the home of the Earl of Stewkesbury was a far cry from the first one. This time she and her sisters stepped down from Sir Royce's elegant carriage. And when he knocked and the same haughty footman opened the door, the servant's face immediately was creased with a broad smile.

"Sir Royce! Good afternoon, sir." He stepped back to allow Royce to enter, and his gaze fell upon Mary, standing at Sir Royce's side. His jaw dropped. "You!"

He looked as though he was about to say more, but he saw Sir Royce regarding him with cool inquiry and shut his mouth.

"Yes, James?" Sir Royce asked. "Is there a problem?"

"I—well, no, sir. That is—" He cast another disbelieving glance at Mary.

"Why don't you tell Lord Stewkesbury I am here?" Royce suggested, ending the man's dilemma.

"Yes, sir, of course, sir." James bowed and hurried away.

As the footman headed up the stairs, Mary looked around her. Even the grand kitchen had not prepared her for the splendor of the entry hall of Stewkesbury House. Large squares of black and white marble stretched away from the front door into an enormous room that rose two stories. On the walls hung massive portraits and landscapes and even, Mary noticed in some amazement, a large oil painting of a black horse. There were heavy padded benches and chairs scattered around the walls and long wooden tables holding large urns and candelabra. The centerpiece of the hall, however, was the grand staircase that rose before them, twice the width of an ordinary staircase up to the first landing, then splitting into two as it continued in either direction to the second floor. If this room had been built and decorated to awe its visitors, Mary thought, it certainly succeeded. Glancing at her sisters, she could see that their impressions were the same.

Rose turned to look at her, and Mary saw the almost fearful look in Rose's wide blue eyes, a look that said, *Surely we don't belong here!*

"Well, ladies . . ." Sir Royce turned to them, seemingly undaunted by their surroundings. "Why don't we wait for the earl someplace a trifle less drafty?"

He ushered them across the entryway and into a large room. Two sets of tall windows hung with red velvet drapes looked out onto the wide street outside. Dark teak furniture dominated the chamber, and it took Mary a moment to realize that the arms of the sofa and chairs ended in carved dragon's heads. Red silk cushions padded the seats, and gold-and-white–patterned wallpaper repeated the theme of Chinese dragons.

The girls stared about the room in amazement.

"Forgive the décor," Sir Royce told them. "One of Oliver's aunts became rather obsessed with chinoiserie during the Prince's building of the Pavilion in Brighton. I cannot imagine how she ever persuaded the old earl to let her do it. However, it is the most comfortable drawing room in the place."

Mary glanced around her at the elegant silks and velvets, the smooth rich wood, the thick rug beneath their feet, and wondered how this could be classified as "comfortable." She had never seen anyplace that was at once so elegant and so exotic.

She glanced at Royce suspiciously. Was the man serious? Or had he brought them here purposely to intimidate them? He appeared to be without guile as he directed them toward the sofa and settled in one of the chairs beside it.

Mary perched on the edge of her seat and steeled herself for the moments ahead. Her chest was so tight she felt she might choke. Her mother had said that their grandfather was a wealthy and influential man, but Mary had pictured him rather like Mr. Treadwell who owned the mill in Three Corners. She was discovering that she had not understood the sort of wealth and position her mother meant—and in which her mother had once lived! It was bizarre to think of her mother sitting in this very room when she was a girl, feeling at home in the way that Sir Royce clearly did.

Mary turned to look at him. The laughing light had returned to his eyes, and she wondered why he had been willing—nay, almost eager—to bring them here after his initial protest. Perhaps he was simply being gentlemanly or kind, but there was something about the hint of laughter twitching at the corner of his mouth that made him look like a naughty schoolboy about to play a trick on the teacher.

"Chin up." The corners of Sir Royce's eyes crinkled as he smiled. "The earl's not so fearsome really. Just stand your ground."

Something eased inside Mary. Whatever mischief Royce might be up to, he also wanted to help her.

"Royce!" A man strode briskly into the room, his mouth curving up into a smile. "I scarce believed my ears when

James told me you were here. What brings—" He stopped, taking in the sight of the four girls grouped on the settee, and his expression changed to a look of faint puzzlement. "Oh. Beg pardon. James neglected to mention that you had brought company." He ended his statement with a look of polite inquiry toward Sir Royce.

Mary regarded the man with interest. This must be her cousin, the man who would decide her and her sisters' fate. He did not look fearsome, she thought. He was handsome, more so when warmth had lit his features as he greeted Royce than a moment later, when he realized he was among strangers and his face settled into a cooler, more distant mask. He was tall, though not quite as tall as Sir Royce, and he had the broad shoulders and well-muscled arms of an avid horseman. His hair was dark brown and his eyes were gray, the color of a stormy sea. He was dressed impeccably but sensibly, eschewing the high collar points and patterned waistcoats sported by some of the men Mary had glimpsed that afternoon. Even his snowy cravat was tied in a most unremarkable way.

"Hallo, Stewkesbury." Sir Royce rose to greet him. "Pray, allow me to introduce you to Miss Bascombe and her sisters, Miss Rose, Miss Lily, and Miss Camellia Bascombe."

"Welcome to my home." The earl bowed, then glanced once again toward his stepbrother.

"The Bascombes are from the United States."

"Indeed? Well, you have come a long distance indeed." His expression was much too polite to give away any curiosity. "From which part of the country do you hail?"

"Pennsylvania, most recently," Mary answered. She studied him, looking for any sign of kinship. There was the dark hair, of course, such as she and Rose had, but beyond that . . . Was there any likeness about the eyes? The chin? She had to confess that she could detect nothing.

"Indeed? I know less than I should, no doubt, about America."

Mary knew that he must be wondering what the devil they were doing here, and she cast about for some polite way to ease into the subject.

But Royce was already plunging ahead. "They have come from the United States expressly to meet you," he told Oliver. "They are, it seems, your cousins."

The earl absorbed this knowledge with admirable aplomb, not betraying his surprise with more than a blink. "Ah. I see. I am doubly happy to make your acquaintance. You are, um, related to us through . . . ah . . . ?"

Mary seized her courage and stood up, taking a step toward the man. "My grandfather was Reginald, Lord Stewkesbury."

The other man's face went still, and his eyes flashed toward Royce. "Is this your idea of a jest?"

"You *would* think so of me," Royce replied. His voice was easy and light, but there was a steely quality underlying the tone. He picked an indiscernible speck of lint from the sleeve of his jacket. "However, jests are more in Fitz's line than mine, wouldn't you say? In any case, I had nothing to do with it."

"Other than bringing them to meet me."

Royce shrugged. "I met the young ladies quite by chance. I had the opportunity of offering my aid to them, and when they told me who they were, I knew that you would wish to be the first to meet them."

Oliver swung his gaze over to Mary. Under the full force of his cool gray stare, Mary revised her opinion of him. The earl was, apparently, capable of seeming quite fearsome.

"I am afraid that I have never heard of any American cousins." His words dropped like small hard stones into the silent room.

Mary squared her shoulders. She could not let this man intimidate her. "You don't believe me, of course. I didn't expect you to. Perhaps your grandfather never mentioned his daughter Flora, who ran away to marry the man she loved."

Stewkesbury's eyes widened a fraction, and Mary knew that her last remark had struck home. "She married Miles Bascombe and moved to the United States. We are their children. I realize that you must be suspicious, so I have brought proof."

Picking up the leather case she had set down on the low table in front of the couch, she pulled out several papers and handed them to the earl. Somewhat reluctantly, he took the documents and began to read them.

"There is my parents' marriage certificate. Also, each of our birth certificates, stating our parents' names. Well, all except Camellia's. The courthouse burned where she was born. However, we can attest to the fact that she is our sister."

The earl studied the documents in his hands and turned to his stepbrother.

Royce raised his brows eloquently. "Well?"

Oliver shrugged. "Grandfather had a daughter Flora. He quarreled bitterly with her over the man she wanted to marry, and the girl ran away. He never knew what became of them."

Royce nodded. "He mentioned to me that he was estranged from his daughter, though I don't recall her name."

Oliver turned back to Mary. "Where are your parents now? Why have they not come as well?"

"They are both dead." Mary saw no sense in trying to soften the statement. "Our father died several years back. My mother passed away a few weeks ago."

"Why did your mother not return before now?" he asked.

"The earl told my mother that he was cutting her out of

the family. I think she had little hope of welcome from him. Besides, she had sworn she would never speak to him again as long as she lived." Mary could not hold back a small, wry smile. "My mother could be rather obstinate."

"I see."

"She would not have sent us here if she had felt that she had any other choice. She did not even tell us about what had happened between them until she knew she was dying. It was only that which drove her to tell us to seek her father's help."

The earl's gaze held hers for a moment longer before his eyes dropped to the papers in his hands. He shuffled through them. "What is this?" He plucked one out, extending it to Mary.

She took it and cast an eye over it, coloring a little. "Nothing. I mean, nothing related to this. It is just one of our papers, a deed to the farm in Pennsylvania that my father owned."

"And what of this?" He held up the letter Flora had written her father, still sealed with the wax she had melted onto it.

Mary reached out toward him, then pulled her hand back. She wished that she had thought to take the letter out of the satchel when she learned that Flora's father was no longer alive to read it. "My mother wrote that to her father. I am sure that it was personal and meant for him alone."

She hated to think of the stern-looking earl reading Flora's tearful apologies to her father and her pleas with him to look after her children. It had gone against Flora's grain to beg him for help; only the utmost love and fear for her children could have driven her to swallow her pride and apologize to her father. Somehow it seemed even worse for those painful words, her mother's dying fears and hopes, to be read by this cool, remote stranger.

The earl regarded Mary assessingly. "It is addressed to Lord Stewkesbury," he pointed out. "I think I should read it, don't you?"

"Perhaps you'd like to compare it to my mother's handwriting, just to make sure she wrote it," Mary snapped, washed with the humiliation she knew her mother would have felt at the exposure of her innermost feelings to someone she didn't even know.

The earl said nothing, merely raised a single eyebrow as he looked at her, and Mary immediately felt small and foolish. With an inarticulate noise, she turned away and sat down. The earl broke the seal on the paper and began to read. The room was deathly silent. Mary could not bring herself to look at her sisters. If this man scornfully dismissed their claim, she would have failed her family. She knew that none of the girls would blame her, but she would blame herself fiercely.

After a few moments, the earl folded the letter. He cleared his throat. "Well, ah, it would certainly appear that Lady Flora made her case."

Hope fluttered in Mary, and she looked at the earl, trying to read his impassive face. Was he saying what she thought he was? She glanced at Royce, who smiled at her. "What does that mean?" She turned back to the earl. "Are you saying that you believe me?"

He made a slight bow toward her. "Welcome to the family, cousins."

Chapter 6

"Thank you, sir." Mary's heart leapt, but she struggled to appear calm, as if she had expected his approval all along. "We are honored."

"I have never . . . um . . . been in this position before," Stewkesbury admitted. "I am not quite certain how to proceed. But clearly you must stay here, at least for the time being. I shall send someone for your things."

He walked over and tugged at the tasseled cord beside the door. A moment later, the magisterial butler to whom Mary had spoken this morning glided into the room. His eyes slid over to her, and there was a spasm of astonishment on his face, quickly suppressed. Mary pressed her lips hard together to hide her little smile of satisfaction.

"Yes, my lord?" the butler asked, his tone betraying not even a hint of curiosity.

"These young ladies will be staying with us, Hooper. They are my cousins."

There was the slightest pause before the butler replied, "Indeed, sir. I shall have rooms made up immediately."

"Very good. In the meantime, I think tea might be in order. Oh, and send the coach around to fetch their things."

Sir Royce told him the name and location of the inn, and Hooper bowed out of the room. As soon as he had gone, Mary turned to the earl.

"It is very good of you, sir. Thank you. We do not for the world wish to be a burden on you. . . ." She trailed off. There was something about the earl's polite gaze that she found extremely inhibiting. It was difficult to tell what he was thinking. He hardly seemed welcoming, but she supposed that no one could wish to have four young women dropped in one's lap.

"Nonsense. Think nothing further of it. You are my aunt's children, after all." The earl tucked her mother's letter into an inside pocket of his jacket and sat down.

A long moment of awkward silence ensued. Finally Sir Royce broke it by saying, "I am afraid that I do not remember Flora, Stewkesbury."

"I believe she was my father's youngest sister. She was away at school when you and your mother came to Willowmere," the earl told him. "After that, she was in London, making her debut. Then she disappeared. I never heard her spoken of again. I remember asking Aunt Phyllida once where she was, and she looked horrified and hushed me up. It was only years later that I understood that Aunt Flora and Grandfather had quarreled and she had left the house. Of course, we rarely saw much of the aunts anyway, stuck up there in the nursery as we were."

"I remember Euphronia well enough from those days," Royce commented dryly.

"Good Gad, who could not?" Stewkesbury paused and looked thoughtful. "I suppose we ought to introduce you young ladies to your other relatives. I shall invite the aunts to dinner this evening. Royce, you must come as well."

Royce looked at the earl askance. "I? Why must I come?"

"Family dinner," Oliver replied. Mary did not know the earl well enough to be certain, but she thought she detected a hint of laughter lurking in the man's imperturbable gaze.

"Not my family," Sir Royce pointed out.

"I am sure Fitz will be there."

"I can see Fitz anytime I want."

"But what about your duty to these young women?" Stewkesbury went on. Mary was certain now that there was contained mirth in his voice. "You cannot mean to desert them so soon."

"Oh, yes," Lily piped up, turning a pleading look on Sir Royce. "Please stay."

Mary would not have admitted it as freely as her sister, but she too wished that Sir Royce would stay for the meal. She dreaded the thought of meeting more unfamiliar family members, but it would not seem as bad with him there.

"Of course, if you ask me," Sir Royce told Lily gallantly, though he shot his stepbrother a hard look.

The butler carried in a large tray containing a tea service and cups, followed by another servant with a tray bearing a variety of cakes and biscuits. There ensued the formality of serving the tea and cakes, as well as a smattering of stilted conversation. Mary could think of nothing to say, and though Royce tried, he could not get much of a conversation going. The earl asked a few questions about their trip and their home, but Mary could not decide if he was expressing a polite interest or trying to find out information about them. She had the uneasy feeling that he was not entirely certain that they were really his cousins.

It was a relief when the tea was finished and the earl rang for a servant, remarking that he was sure the young ladies would like to be shown to their rooms to rest before dinner.

He turned and bowed to the girls, said he would see them at supper, then strode off down the hallway.

"I should take my leave," Sir Royce added, rising.

Mary turned to him, saying, "But you will be here for supper, will you not?"

"Oh yes." He reached out and took her hand, bowing over it. When he raised his head, he stood holding her hand for a moment longer as he smiled down into her face. "Nothing could keep me away this evening."

His hand was warm against hers; she was very aware of the texture of his skin, and her own flesh tingled in response. She could not seem to pull her gaze from his. At last he released her hand, and it was as if his movement released her from her own paralysis. She took a quick step backward, turning her face away from his. She knew a flush was rising in her cheeks but did her best to ignore it. When was she going to stop reacting this way to this man? Surely she would grow accustomed to his presence at some point. The memory of his kiss last night would fade. She would begin to view him as she did other men.

Or would she?

Mary watched Royce as he bade good-bye to her sisters, then turned and walked toward the front door. A poke in the side from Camellia's elbow made her jump.

"What did you do that for?" She frowned at the other girl.

Camellia pointed toward the maid who stood waiting just inside the doorway. "She's trying to take us to our rooms, but you are too busy mooning about over Sir Royce."

"I was doing no such thing," Mary whispered fiercely as she fell in beside Camellia, following their other sisters out of the room.

Camellia rolled her eyes. "I'm not blind, you know. Whenever he's around, you look at him."

Mary blushed to think that she had been so obvious. "Of course I look at him. He's—he's different."

"I didn't notice you staring at the earl."

"Don't smirk. It's unbecoming."

Camellia chuckled and leaned in closer, linking her arm through Mary's. In a low voice, she went on, "It's all right. He's terribly handsome. Even I noticed that, and you know I am not the sort to get all dreamy over men."

The maid led them up the stairs, and they emerged into a wide hallway of highly polished dark wood. A tall window facing the street let in a stream of sunlight to brighten the corridor, which was further illuminated by sconces along the walls. To the left a long wall was hung with paintings, its length broken now and then by a bench or a narrow table displaying a vase of flowers. The maid went to the first doorway, opening it to reveal a large bedchamber.

"I'm afraid there's only two chambers made up, miss," she said, curtseying. "There's others, if you want us to make them up too, but they're not as nice as these."

"I am sure these will be fine," Mary responded faintly, looking around the enormous room.

As Lily and Camellia followed the maid to the next room, Mary slowly turned to take in her surroundings. It was almost as large as the drawing room downstairs. The room was papered in a white and blue pattern, and long drapes on the two sets of windows matched the blue of the wallpaper, as did the heavy draperies of the four-poster bed. The bed was massive, its mattress luxuriously thick, and there was a small step placed beside it to help one climb in. At the far end of the room was a fireplace, and in front of it stood a low round table and two wingback chairs. There was also, Mary noted, a wardrobe, a dresser, and a vanity, as well as a long wooden chest at the foot of the bed. What was more amazing than the amount and size of the furniture, however, was that the room was so large that it did not seem crowded.

Mary turned to Rose and saw the same expression mirrored on her face.

"I never dreamed it would be like this!" Rose exclaimed in a hushed voice.

"Nor I." Mary shook her head.

"It's no wonder Sir Royce and the earl were suspicious of our motives. There must be any number of people who would love to live here. Do you really think he is going to let us stay here?" She looked a trifle scared at the idea.

"I don't know. He seemed to have believed us."

At that moment, Lily and Camellia came flying into the room, their faces flushed. "You should see our room!"

"It's almost as big as the strange Chinese room downstairs!"

"I know." Mary waved a hand around at her own room.

"I thanked the maid, and she looked at me most oddly," Lily went on. "I thought, well, she doesn't know who I am, so I introduced myself and tried to shake her hand."

"She was positively shocked," Camellia added, throwing herself onto the bed. "Ahhh." She let out a satisfied sigh. "This is soft."

"It's beautiful here," Lily added, and clambered up onto the bed beside Camellia. "I've never seen so many fine things—did you notice the velvet drapes? And those statues that are scattered around! It's enough to make you feel as if you're in a palace." She paused, then added thoughtfully, "But the people are odd."

"What do you think these aunts are like?" Rose asked. "Is the earl asking them here to get their opinion of us?"

"No doubt they are horrid and stern," Lily ventured. "They'll probably order us out of the family."

"If they're anything like their father, they very well might," Mary agreed. "However, I have the feeling that the only opinion that matters here is the earl's."

"Have you ever seen anyone so . . . so . . ." Camellia began.

"Aristocratic?" Lily offered.

"I would have said *auto*cratic," Mary retorted dryly.

"He *is* rather arrogant," Rose allowed. "But maybe you can't be aristocratic without being arrogant."

"I don't know," Lily argued. "Sir Royce didn't strike me as arrogant, and he is quite aristocratic."

"Watch out, Mary, you have a rival for the gentleman's affections," Camellia warned playfully.

"What?" Rose turned to regard her sister with interest. "Do you like Sir Royce? Truly?"

"Camellia is being silly." Mary shot a dark look at the other girl. "I have no interest in the man."

"Why not?" Lily piped up. "I think he's awfully handsome. And so courtly. Did you see his bow? I have never been bowed to so elegantly."

Mary rolled her eyes. "As if I care for that."

Camellia snorted. "When have you ever been bowed to at all, Lily?"

Lily tossed her head. "Well, perhaps never before. But I have *seen* bows. Mr. Curtis always—"

Their conversation was interrupted by two footmen carrying in their luggage, followed by two maids. When the bags had been sorted out to the right rooms, one maid went to Lily and Camellia's room while the other began to put Rose's and Mary's clothes away in the wardrobe and dresser. Mary felt odd, just sitting there and watching someone else take care of a task she could easily do, but when she offered to help, the girls gazed at her with such astonishment that she quickly subsided.

It was not as if she had no experience with servants. There had been a cook and servants at the tavern, of course. But Mary and her sisters had taken care of their own rooms and clothes and had also pitched in to clean the tavern or work in the kitchen whenever they were needed. It was most peculiar to do nothing concerning her own dresses.

It was even stranger later that evening when the maid returned to help the girls dress and do their hair. When Mary politely declined the offer, she could see from the girl's expression that she had again stepped astray. And though the maid said nothing, Mary also suspected that she had found Mary's and Rose's dresses wanting. Her mother had told her that they had dressed for dinner every evening when she was a girl, so Mary and the others had been careful to choose their very best dresses for tonight, the ones they wore to church on Sunday. However, when Mary saw a shadow flicker across the maid's face, she knew that their best was not fine enough for a British lady.

But it was not until she and her sisters trooped downstairs that Mary realized just how far short their attire fell. The earl and Sir Royce were waiting for them, wearing black silk breeches and jackets, with snowy falls of cravats down the fronts of their white shirts. A flash of rubies glinted at Sir Royce's cuffs and nestled in the folds of his neckcloth. The earl was more subdued, with onyx gleaming in his cuff links and stick pin, but Mary had no doubt that what he wore was the equal of anything that adorned Sir Royce.

There were two women with them—one an imposing female with iron gray hair and hard eyes, the other a younger copy of the first, her hair still dark and her form more slender. The older woman was dressed in black satin with an overskirt of lace. The neckline was low, exposing more of her bosom than Mary was accustomed to seeing, especially on a woman her age, and the sleeves were elaborately slashed and puffed. Diamonds winked at her ears and encircled her throat and wrist. The younger lady wore a burgundy silk dress in the same high-waisted style, with ruffles of lace cascading down the bottom third of her underskirt. Slippers in the same shade of burgundy peeped from beneath her dress. Pearls adorned her throat and ears.

Mary's first thought when she saw the group was how utterly handsome Sir Royce was in evening attire. His lean, masculine build and sharp, aristocratic profile were perfectly complemented by the luxurious materials and elegant lines. Her pulse quickened in response.

Her second thought was an acute consciousness of the inadequacy of the dresses she and her sisters wore. Their frocks were clearly out of style, with waists that were too high. But more than that, they were far too simple, too plain, with no more than a ruffle of the same material around the hem. The people waiting for them looked ready to go to a ball. Mary suspected that neither of these women would have considered Mary's dress acceptable to wear even to the market—not, of course, that they would ever go to the market.

Surprise flitted across the faces of the earl and his companions when they saw the Bascombe sisters, and Mary's cheeks burned with embarrassment. Then Royce strode forward, smiling at her.

"Miss Bascombe. What a pleasure it is to see you again." He swept her a bow, then took her arm to steer her toward the others.

Mary let out a tightly held breath, grateful for his support. "Thank you."

"It is you who do me the favor. A gentleman always appears to advantage with a beautiful woman on his arm."

"I fear we are terribly underdressed," Mary began in a low voice.

"Nonsense. Your face outshines any amount of jewels and silk."

He was speaking foolishness, she knew, but his extravagant compliments warmed her and steadied her nerves.

The earl stepped forward, saying, "Miss Bascombe, pray allow me to introduce my aunt, Lady Euphronia Harrington, and her daughter, Lady Elizabeth."

Mary noticed that he did not explain who she and her sisters were, and she wondered if for some reason he did not want his relatives to know their identities. Was he putting them to some sort of test? Seeing if they would pass muster with the rest of his relatives before he acknowledged the Bascombe girls? If so, Mary had a sinking feeling that she and her sisters were doomed to failure. She could not see even the slightest warmth or interest in these two women's faces as they gave Mary and her sisters the slightest of nods and a murmured greeting.

They stood in an awkward group for a few minutes before two more women arrived along with another man, a rotund, smiling sort who greeted everyone with bluff affability. Both the women had dark hair shot through with silver, but one of them, Lady Phyllida Kent, was almost as tall as Lady Euphronia, and the other, Lady Cynthia Atwater, was softer and shorter than the others and possessed of a certain vague sweetness of expression. The gentleman, Mary learned, was the husband of Lady Phyllida.

There was a faint resemblance among the three older women, and Mary could see something in them that reminded her of her own mother's face—though it was hard to catch it in the stiff arrogance that stamped these women's features.

The earl took a look at the watch that was tucked into his waistcoat pocket and sighed. "Apparently Fitzhugh has chosen not to honor us with his presence. One never knows whether to wait for him, so I suggest that we move forward. Aunts, Cousin Elizabeth, I am sure you are rather curious about the reason for my invitation. . . ."

Lady Euphronia gave him a regal nod. He drew breath to continue, and at that moment, a man came striding into the room.

"Sorry. Am I late again?" He came to a dead stop as he caught sight of the older women. "Aunt Euphronia! Beg pardon." He made a bow that, even to Mary's untutored gaze, surpassed all the other men's efforts. "Aunt Phyllida." He spoke to each of the women, then to Sir Royce and the earl, his expression growing increasingly puzzled as his gaze traveled from one to another, ending with the Bascombes.

His greetings gave Mary and her sisters ample time to observe him. This, Mary thought, must be the man Sir Royce had referred to as Fitzhugh. He was the earl's younger brother—as well as Sir Royce's—if she remembered correctly Sir Royce's explanation of the family tree. Mary could see the resemblance. This man was tall and broad-shouldered like the earl and Royce, though Fitz was the tallest of the three, and his figure was more lithe than powerful. He was also almost dazzlingly handsome. His hair was thick and black and perfectly styled in a carelessly windswept way. His eyes were a brilliant blue, and his face was almost too well-modeled—but a mischievous twinkle in his eyes and the deep dimple that creased his cheek when he smiled saved him from the blandness of perfection.

"I beg your pardon," he went on, casting an engaging grin at Mary and her sisters. "Did I know we had guests this evening?"

"No. I invited our aunts to meet these young ladies. You will be interested in their history as well, Fitz."

Mary and her sisters were now the object of several interested stares. Mary forced herself to remain still under their scrutiny, as if she were unbothered by the situation. She was glad that Royce was still standing by her side.

"The Misses Bascombe are our aunt Flora's daughters—your nieces, ladies, and our cousins, Fitz."

For a moment the room was completely silent. Then Fitz let out a crack of laughter. "Cousins, is it? No, really, I think you are far too lovely to be related to this old fellow and me. But if we are cousins, then I must claim the right to welcome you to the family."

He bent and kissed each of the girls lightly on the cheek, engendering a series of blushes and giggles. Stepping back, he went on, "I cannot simply call each of you Cousin. You must give me your names. I will start by telling you that I am your cousin Fitz."

With more smiles, the sisters went through their given names.

"Flowers," Fitz remarked. "Most appropriate."

Aunt Euphronia snorted. "I must say, it does sound like the sort of silly thing Flora would do."

Aunt Cynthia smiled at them. "Rose rather looks like Flora. Such a pretty girl."

Aunt Phyllida studied them, frowning. "I really could not say for sure."

"No, I would not want to decide too hastily," Aunt Euphronia agreed.

"Dear aunts, I fear you misunderstand." The earl glanced over at the older women. "I did not ask you here to judge my cousins' legitimacy. Their papers seem to be in perfectly good order. They are Flora Talbot's and Miles Bascombe's legitimate children. I merely thought that you would welcome the opportunity to meet your nieces."

Aunt Euphronia favored the earl with a frosty look, but Aunt Cynthia nodded. "Of course." She turned to the girls. "I always wondered what happened to Flora. I wished that she had written me and let me know where she was. Father forbade us to correspond with her, but I would have, anyway, if only I had known where she had gone." She took a step forward. "Is she here as well?"

"No, ma'am," Mary told the woman. "I am afraid my mother died several months ago."

Aunt Cynthia's face softened with sadness. "I am so sorry. Flora was a bit unconventional, of course, but I thought that Father was too harsh with her."

Again Aunt Euphronia snorted. "She was wild as a March hare, and we all know it. Father had every right to cast her off."

"No doubt." The earl cast his aunt a quick, tight smile. "However, that is neither here nor there. I believe it is time for us to dine. Aunt Euphronia, if you will allow me to escort you?"

Everyone sorted themselves out, the men offering the women their arms to escort them the few feet down the hall, in some sort of order that the earl and his British relatives all seemed to understand, though Mary could not see how the matter was decided. Lord Kent did not escort his wife, she noted, and the order did not seem to follow along lines of age, but she was rather glad that Sir Royce offered his arm to her.

She slipped her hand into the crook of his elbow and they followed in Lady Phyllida's wake, her sisters trailing along behind them.

Royce glanced down at Mary, his eyes glinting. "Had your fill of the aristocracy already?"

"Everything seems a bit . . . formal."

"Mmm. Stewkesbury is . . . a traditional sort of man. He does not even have to consider what the rules for an occasion are; he simply knows."

"Then he knows what to do when a gaggle of cousins is dropped on him unexpectedly."

Her companion let out a laugh. "No. There, I think it is safe to say, he is a mere novice. As completely ignorant as I. It's rather refreshing to see, actually."

"And you're enjoying that."

He chuckled. "A bit."

"Why? Do you dislike him?"

Royce glanced at her, startled. "My, you are one for bluntness, aren't you?"

Mary shrugged. "Are you one for answering bluntly?"

"I am not averse to it. However, you have asked a question that is—well, a trifle complicated to answer. And, as we are already here, I fear there is no time."

They had walked down the hall as they spoke and entered the next room. A long table surrounded by heavy chairs stood in the center of the large room, dominated by a huge vase of dried flowers. Two smaller epergnes of fruit were placed halfway between it and both ends of the table. A sideboard along the wall at one end of the room was flanked by servants.

There seemed to be an order to the seating as well, Mary noted, and again, everyone else went unerringly to the correct seats. After seating Mary, Royce took the place next to her. Servants jumped to pull out chairs for the other three girls. Lily sat down beside Mary and Camellia and Rose were seated across from them, spoiling the careful man/woman arrangement about the rest of the table.

Mary looked down at the table before her. There were plates of varying sizes and bowls and glasses, not to mention a plethora of forks, knives, and spoons. She realized that she hadn't any idea what three-fourths of the utensils were for. Down the table, she heard Aunt Phyllida begin to describe the opera she had attended the evening before. Mary sighed inwardly. It was going to be a long and excruciating evening.

Chapter 7

Servants moved around their table, carefully filling glasses or dishing food onto plates. Rose thanked the footman with a smile and received a sharp glance from Aunt Phyllida. Mary suspected that Rose had made some sort of faux pas, but Mary could not worry about that. She was far too involved in determining which utensil to use to eat her fish.

She cast a furtive glance at Sir Royce on her right, and when he picked up a knife and a fork, she chose the same utensils beside her plate. As they ate, she began to notice that Royce reached for his utensils each time with great deliberation, lingering over the right one before slowly picking it up, and she realized that he knew what she was doing and was trying to ease her task. Mary let out a giggle, cutting her eyes over to him.

He shot her a playful wink and returned to his food.

Conversation at the table was slow and erratic. Most of the early conversation consisted of polite general remarks about such things as the weather. Fitz, however, seemed determined to get the group talking. Over the soup course, he smiled down the table at Rose and Camellia and asked where they hailed from in America.

"Pennsylvania," Rose answered softly. Mary knew that Rose did not like talking to strangers, and she was sure that this situation inhibited her even more.

"Ah." Fitz smiled. "Philadelphia, yes? That is in Pennsylvania, isn't it?"

"Yes," Mary put in, coming to Rose's rescue. "But that isn't where we are from. We are from a much smaller town— Three Corners."

"But we've lived in quite a few places," Camellia spoke up.

"Oh, yes," Lily added. "Maryland for a while. Then there was the farm."

"Your father farmed?" Aunt Cynthia asked. "How nice. Did he have many tenants?"

"Tenants?" Lily replied blankly.

"Yes. Perhaps you use a different word. The people who worked the land."

"He didn't have any workers," Mary assured her. "Except us, of course. He did the work himself."

All the rest of the table froze, staring at the girls.

Mary gazed back at them, annoyed. What was the matter with these people? They seemed appalled by the simplest things.

"It was on the frontier," Mary went on. "The farms were small, worked just by a family. We all helped with the planting and the harvesting."

"I see." Aunt Euphronia raised her brows disdainfully.

Some imp in Mary made her add, "Except, of course, that one of us had to carry the rifles and stand guard."

All the heads swiveled back to her.

"To warn everybody if we saw Indians coming," Mary explained.

Aunt Cynthia gasped. Across the table, Rose made a strangled noise and raised her napkin to her mouth, coughing.

"Indians?" Lord Kent asked, his eyes going round. "You mean wild Indians?"

"Very wild. It was the edge of civilization, you see." It was wrong of her to goad them this way, but Mary could not seem to stop herself. Her aristocratic relatives' attitude was simply too annoying.

"And you—you girls carried a gun?" Aunt Phyllida looked even more appalled at this than at the idea of marauding Indians.

"A knife as well," Camellia added.

"We had to be able to fight," Mary explained calmly.

This statement elicited a gasp from one of the aunts, and Mary heard a muffled noise from Royce beside her. She slid her eyes over to him and saw that he was studying his plate with great interest, his lips pressed tightly together.

"It came in very handy later, too, when Papa bought the tavern," Rose piped up.

Mary shot a surprised glance at her sister. Apparently even gentle Rose had become tired of their aunts' quiet condescension.

"The tavern? Your father owned a tavern!" Aunt Euphronia's eyebrows appeared in danger of climbing into her hairline.

"Yes. We lived above it."

"You lived there! Four young girls!"

"We were not terribly young by that time," Mary pointed out. "We were all old enough to help—cooking, serving the food, sweeping up, that sort of thing. I kept the books, as Papa was not fond of that."

"Dear Lord," Aunt Cynthia murmured.

"The pistols were handier there, of course," Camellia said judiciously, "when you had to break up a fight. The rifle simply wasn't practical for close-in situations."

Fitz let out a bark of laughter, and Sir Royce closed his eyes, quickly covering his mouth with his hand. From the end of the table, the earl shot a look at his brother and stepbrother, then regarded Mary and her sisters sternly.

"Heathens!" Aunt Euphronia exclaimed. She swung round to the earl. "Stewkesbury, they are absolute heathens! I hope you are not contemplating trying to bring these girls out in society. It simply would not do. We would be the laughingstocks of the beau monde."

"A Talbot living above a tavern!" Aunt Phyllida chimed in. Across the table, Aunt Euphronia's daughter nodded vigorously.

"Flora must at least have taught them how to speak, for their English is decent, if somewhat spoiled by that accent— but everything else!" Aunt Euphronia fairly quivered in her outrage.

"We are sitting right here," Mary pointed out, anger rising in her like steam. "If you wish to criticize me, you should say it to my face."

The older woman swung to look at Mary, her gaze so haughty that Mary was sure it had withered many another person. What it engendered in Mary was a strong desire to hit her. "I was speaking," Aunt Euphronia said in a slow, measured way, as if she were addressing someone hard of hearing or mentally deficient, "to the earl, as he is the one who has charge of you lot. It is he who must exercise some control over you, God help him."

"He is not in charge of Mary or any of us!" Camellia shot back.

"As long as you are living on his generosity, I should think he has every right to control your behavior! Heaven knows, someone needs to. A more rag-mannered group of girls I have never seen."

All four of the Bascombes jumped into the conversation at that remark, and as Aunt Phyllida, Lord Kent, and Aunt Euphronia also chimed in, the result was pandemonium.

"Silence!" The earl's voice cut like a knife through the din, and the table immediately fell quiet.

"Now." He looked at Mary and her sisters. "You will not speak to your elders in that way. It is most impolite. Aunt Euphronia, Aunt Phyllida, I would remind you that these young women are indeed my charge and not yours. I assumed that you might welcome the opportunity to meet your late sister's children." He swung his head back to the Bascombe girls. "And I thought that you might wish to meet your relatives. Clearly I was wrong on both counts. You do not have to like one another. However, I do insist on everyone behaving with some decorum when you are seated at my dinner table." His gaze moved around the table, taking in each of the combatants.

Mary flushed, abashed. "You are right. I am sorry."

These women were her mother's sisters, and she should have reached out to them, not judged them on the basis of their clothes or their manner. She knew, deep down, that part of her resentment was based on her own embarrassment.

She turned to her aunts. "I apologize for behaving rudely. I should not have spoken as I did. I assure you that my mother taught me to treat my elders with respect, and she would be most upset to see me ignore her lessons."

Her sisters chimed in with subdued apologies. Aunt Cynthia smiled at them, and Lady Euphronia answered with a frosty nod of acceptance. Mary noticed that neither she nor Lady Phyllida was moved to respond with an apology to their nieces.

The rest of the dinner continued in a more subdued manner. As soon as the meal was finished, Mary asked that she and her sisters be excused, pleading tiredness. Beside her, Sir Royce jumped to his feet, pulling back her chair, and offered his arm.

"Pray allow me to escort you."

"I think I would be able to undertake the long trek to our rooms on my own," Mary replied with a twinkle. But she slipped her hand into the crook of his elbow.

Her sisters went ahead of them, obviously eager to escape the dining room. Mary strolled along more slowly at Royce's side.

"I hope you will not allow the aunts to, shall we say, discourage you . . ." Royce began.

Mary cast a sideways glance at him. "I am afraid you do not know me very well if you think that they will discourage me."

"No, I suspected they would not. But let me assure you that they are a trial to everyone in the family—and outside, I suspect. I make it my business to avoid Aunt Euphronia whenever possible. I hesitated about coming tonight, truthfully, but I pulled my courage together. I could not in good conscience allow you to face her on your own."

Mary chuckled. "You are a brave soul."

"I have suffered enough cuts from that razor tongue to be wary." He smiled wryly.

"Thank you for your kindness tonight."

He cocked an eyebrow. "I appreciate your words, but I don't know what you mean."

"I noticed how you indicated which fork and knife to use. I would have been lost without your direction. And do not try to deny it. I appreciate the help—heaven knows we need all the help we can get here, I fear."

Royce shrugged. "'Twas little enough. I know how difficult it is to be an outsider among the Talbot family."

They stopped at the foot of the staircase. The other girls were already running up the stairs, chattering, but Mary paused and turned to face Royce, holding out her hand. He took it in his.

"I am mindful of all you have done for my sisters and me, and I am most grateful. We are *all* most grateful," she amended quickly.

Royce did not let go of her hand. She knew that he should, that she should pull free of his grasp. Instead, she looked up into his face, neither of them saying a word.

It would be easy to get lost in his eyes, she thought. They were dark green now in the candlelight, the large pupils softening the sharpness they had held earlier in the day. She was aware of an urge to reach up and caress his cheek; she wanted to learn how his skin felt against her hand. Indeed, she wanted, God help her, to feel his lips on hers again.

Mary wondered if he was thinking the same things as he looked down at her, if his mind, too, strayed to the kiss they had shared the evening before. When his eyes darkened further and his gaze flickered for a moment to her lips, she knew that his thoughts had indeed mirrored hers. He would not be so brazen as to do it again, she thought, not here, but there was some part of her that boldly wished he would.

His mouth softened, and Royce bowed, his lips brushing the back of her hand. Mary shivered, feeling the velvety touch all through her. He straightened, his eyes glinting, and a slow, knowing smile spread across his lips. He knew her reaction, she thought; indeed, he had intended to produce exactly that response.

"Good night, Miss Briscombe."

"Good night." She could barely get out a whisper. She turned and ran up the stairs, not looking back. But when she reached the top, she could not keep herself from turning and glancing back down the steps. Royce was still watching her.

Mary hurried on to her room, unable to erase the smile from her face.

Rose was in their room undressing. To Mary's surprise, the maid Jenny was there too, efficiently undoing the buttons down Rose's back. Rose shot Mary a pained look as the maid bobbed a curtsey to her.

"You needn't have stayed up to help us," Mary told the girl.

Jenny gazed at her in the puzzled way that Mary was becoming accustomed to. "But, miss, it's me job."

"Yes, well, I'm sure you could do with a bit of extra sleep, and Rose and I have been helping each other with our buttons for years."

The maid hesitated, looking at Mary, and Rose took the opportunity to slide away from the girl, holding her dress up with a hand to her chest.

"But what about your hair?" the girl protested. "Don't you want me to take it down and brush it?"

"We are quite capable of doing that ourselves as well." Jenny stood there indecisively, and Mary remembered how the earl had dismissed the butler that afternoon. "That will be all now."

"Yes, my lady." She bobbed another curtsey and left the room.

"Thank goodness!" Rose exhaled a sigh and let her dress drop. "When she told me she was here to help me undress, I didn't know what to say to her! I didn't want to be unkind, but how can I take off my clothes in front of a complete stranger?" She bent and picked up the frock, carefully folding it and setting it aside before she began to undo her petticoats. "I don't understand these people. They don't even brush their own hair!"

"It is a very different place." Mary turned so that Rose could unfasten the back of Mary's dress. "If we are helped to dress and undress, they certainly will not stand for our sweeping the floors or even dusting. It is nice not to have to work, but . . . what are we to do all day?"

"I don't know. Oh, Mary . . ." Rose's voice caught. "I wish we could go home!"

Mary turned and hugged her sister. "Rose! Dearest, don't cry. Are you so unhappy here?"

Rose swallowed hard and stepped back, giving Mary a small smile. "No, of course not. I'm being foolish. No doubt I am a bit tired. It is all so strange."

She went over to sit down in front of the vanity and take the pins from her hair. Mary shrugged out of her unfastened dress and changed into her nightgown, watching her sister closely.

"It is strange," Mary admitted. "But I am sure we will become used to it after a while."

"No doubt." Rose sighed. "It's just that I miss home."

"I know. I do too."

"Here everything we do is wrong. Our clothes are out of fashion—no, worse than that. We looked like Quakers tonight compared to those other women."

"Mmm. Poor Quakers, at that."

Rose smiled faintly at her sister's wry comment. "Yes. Very poor Quakers. I know it's vain of me, but I don't think I can bear to look dowdy everywhere we go! Even the men dress more elegantly than we do."

"You could never look dowdy," Mary assured her. "Even in rags, you would far outshine the other women there."

"You, of course, are not at all prejudiced." Rose flashed a fond smile at Mary. "You are far prettier than any of them, too, but still . . . weren't you embarrassed? I felt like a fool; I know they thought we were so provincial we didn't know how to dress." She sighed, then added, "Of course, I guess we are. Even after what Mama told us, I never dreamed they went to supper looking like they were going to the Governor's Ball."

"I felt out of place," Mary admitted. "We *are* out of place."

"The servants think we are odd," Rose went on. "Nothing looks familiar. I'm scared to touch anything in this house for fear I might harm it. Our relatives hate us and wish we had not come."

"I am sure they do not *hate* you. Cousin Fitz seems quite nice and friendly. He didn't act proud or offended. Indeed, I am quite certain he was laughing during our . . . performance."

Rose met her sister's eyes in the mirror, grinning. "It was awful of us, wasn't it, to horrify them so?"

"Terrible," Mary agreed, grinning back. "But I could not keep from . . . exaggerating."

"Exaggerating! I am quite certain that you did not carry the rifle into the fields to ward off Indians. Why, you were no more than ten when we left the farm. And I don't recall any Indians."

"That may have been a bit of a lie. Still, we did live above the tavern and work there. And there were fights from time to time."

"I can't be sorry we said those things," Rose admitted. "I could not resist when I saw the shock on their faces."

"I know. Still, one of them was not so awful. Aunt Cynthia actually smiled at us, and she seemed to wish she'd heard from Mama."

"That's true."

"Perhaps the others are not as bad as they appear. We

should try harder—be more civil to them. Once they get to
know you, I am sure that even our aunts will come to love
you. Everyone does, after all."

Rose grimaced. "Don't be silly. Not everyone."

"Well, perhaps there is some person whose soul is so
shriveled that he cannot love you. But I do not know who
he might be."

"Sam Treadwell's father," Rose said with a touch of bitterness.

Mary glanced at her sister, surprised by her tone. "The
mill owner? Pah! He scarcely knows you."

"He knows me well enough to say that a tavernkeeper's
daughter is not good enough for his son."

"What?" Mary went over and knelt beside her sister.
"Did he actually say that? Did Sam Treadwell ask you to
marry him?"

"No, of course not. He knows his father would not allow
it. And Sam would never go against his father." Rose began
to yank her brush through her hair with a good bit more
force than was necessary.

Mary gaped at her sister. Sam Treadwell was one of many
men who always seemed to be hovering about Rose back
home. He was a good-looking, good-natured fellow, but he
had never stood out in any way to Mary. And while she
could remember Rose talking about Sam now and then, relating some bit of news he had told her or some witticism he
had made, she could not recall Rose ever stating a preference
for him.

"Rose! Do you—do you have *feelings* for Sam?"

Color rose in Rose's porcelain cheeks and she glanced
away from Mary. "No. I mean, well . . ."

"You *do* like him! Why didn't you tell me?"

"It wasn't any use. I knew his father would never allow it.
Sam said he was trying to win his father over to his way of

thinking, but I know Mr. Treadwell isn't the sort to change his mind. I didn't want to tell you; I was afraid you might say something to his father."

"Indeed I would—as if you were not good enough for his son! You are good enough for any man."

Rose chuckled. "You see my point, then."

"Yes. But I wish you'd told me anyway." Mary paused, considering. "Rose…did you not wish to leave him? Would you rather we had stayed?"

Rose shook her head firmly. "No, of course not. Sam said a lot of splendid things, but he didn't ask me to marry him. I doubt he would ever have gotten up his courage to do so. His parents are horridly snobbish." She let out a little giggle. "They should see how our cousins live!"

Mary smiled. "No doubt. I'd like to see Mr. Treadwell say you're not good enough for his son now."

Rose shrugged. "Anyway, I'm not about to grow old waiting for Sam. And Mama was right. This was the best thing for us to do. Lily and Camellia will have a better life. And I know that if we had stayed, Cosmo would have somehow forced me to marry Mr. Suttersby, and I could not! You know how in Lily's books, the women are always declaring that they would rather die than endure some man's advances?"

"Yes, and a more muddle-headed lot I cannot imagine. It seems to me far preferable to do away with *him* rather than oneself."

Rose let out a chuckle. "No doubt you would. But that is how I feel about Mr. Suttersby. I think I would rather kill myself than have to marry that awful man. His hair is gray, and his teeth are brown, and when he looks at me . . ." Rose shuddered.

"Well, you shall not have to do either," Mary told her stoutly. "We left him far behind us. Good riddance to Sam

Treadwell, too, if he is that weak-kneed. You will find some-one far better to marry here."

"Oh, Mary!" Rose reached out and hugged her sister. "Do you think we will really find any man like that here? Everyone seems so—so stiff and cold."

Mary's mind went immediately to Royce. She remembered the feel of his arms around her, of his lips upon hers. No, he was not cold, she thought, a secretive little smile hovering on her lips. She would not call Royce Winslow cold at all.

But she said only, "We have met few men here, after all. I am sure that you will be bound to find one to your liking."

"Of course. You are right. And the earl does seem to have accepted us as his family. Everything will be fine. It seems strange to us now, but in time we will become accustomed to it all." Rose straightened her shoulders and smiled at her sister as she rose from the vanity, braiding her hair into a single thick plait, her fingers quick with long practice.

Mary knew Rose well enough to be aware that the smile was forced. But she was also sure that Rose would try her hardest to make her words a reality. Because of her shyness and her sweet, compliant nature, people often mistook Rose as weak, but Mary knew that there was a quiet strength inside her. Their starched and prosy aunts would surely come to accept Rose.

It was Camellia and Mary herself, she knew, who would be the problems. Mary sighed as she took her sister's place at the vanity, unpinning and brushing out her own hair. She would speak to Camellia tomorrow about the need for diplomacy and tact, especially in the beginning. But she would also, for all her sisters' sakes, have to put a curb on her own unruly tongue. However much it might go against the grain, she would try to get along with these people.

It was some time before she finished her evening toilette and, rousing herself from her thoughts, turned to see that Rose was already sound asleep. Mary was tired, but as was often the case, she was too restless to sleep. Slipping on her dressing gown over her night rail to keep the chill at bay, she curled up in one of the chairs before the fireplace. But her thoughts did little to make her drowsy, filled as they were with apprehension about the future.

A book would help keep her mind off such thoughts. They had had to leave all their books behind; they were far too bulky to take to England. However, there must be a library somewhere in this house. Mary hesitated, reluctant to go creeping through a strange house this late, clad in night rail and dressing gown. What if she met someone? But surely the guests had all gone by now, and the earl would have retired to his own bedchamber.

She lit a candle from the lamp on the dresser and slipped out of the room. It was a little surprising to find that the sconces still burned at a low level, casting a dim light through the corridor. She went quickly across the hall and down the stairs, her footsteps in her soft slippers almost noiseless.

She turned down the hallway they had taken when they went to supper, thinking that it was likely the library lay along it. Mary peered in the first doorway and saw another elegant gathering room, even larger than the one they had been in this afternoon. As she walked on, she became aware of the murmur of voices. She stopped, listening. Were there still servants about? Then came the sound of rich masculine laughter, and Mary realized that it issued from the dining room. The door was ajar, and light spilled from it onto the hall floor.

For a moment she wondered if the guests could possibly still be here. But no—it was far too late. There was no other sound or movement of servants, and the lights were out at the back of the house. It was, she thought, only the brothers, probably talking over brandy or port. Mary turned to go back upstairs, ready to abandon her search. But curiosity got the best of her, and after a brief hesitation, she moved quietly down the hall, closer to the slightly open door.

To Royce's relief, the aunts and uncles had not lingered long after the Bascombe sisters retired. After the others left, Stewkesbury had dismissed the servants, and he, Royce, and Fitz had settled down at the table with their port and cigars. For a while, they sat in the companionable silence of long custom, sipping their drinks.

Fitz cut his eyes toward his eldest brother. "Well, Oliver, it appears that you are going to take on the role of father now."

Fitz glanced toward Royce, and they exchanged a grin.

Oliver scowled. "Easy for you two to smile about it. You haven't had a set of marriageable cousins plopped in your lap."

"Especially these girls," Fitz responded, chuckling. "Did you see Aunt Euphronia's face when Miss Bascombe was talking about carrying a rifle to defend them from Indians?"

"I thought Kent's eyes might pop right out of his head," Royce added.

"Yes, well, it's all very amusing to tease the aunts," the earl said somewhat sourly. "But I am going to have to do something with these girls." He turned toward Royce, fixing him with a hard gaze. "How the devil did you come up with them, anyway?"

"I didn't 'come up with them,' " Royce protested. "It was sheer happenstance. They were chasing some fellow down the street, and I stopped him. Seems he'd stolen their satchel. I could see they weren't the sort one would normally find wandering about down by the docks."

"The docks! Good Gad, it just gets worse."

"They had just arrived from America and clearly had no idea where to go or what to do. So I took them to an inn and settled them there. But I still didn't know who they were. This morning when Mary told me she had been here knocking on *your* door, I was sure she was cutting a sham. That they had arranged to run into me. But I couldn't see how that was possible. They couldn't have known I would be at that den of thieves, chasing down Gordon."

"Gordon!" The earl's brows flew up. "Aunt Euphronia's Gordon? What the devil was he doing there? He's supposed to be at Oxford."

"Bloody hell!" Royce grimaced. "I forgot. I told him I wouldn't let on to you if he went to his father and confessed."

"Sent down from university, eh?" The earl sighed and waved his hand dismissively. "It doesn't matter. Let his parents see to him. I have enough problems with my new cousins."

Royce paused, studying his stepbrother. "Are they really your cousins? Are you sure they're legitimate?"

The earl sighed and took another drink. "I'm afraid they are. After our meeting with the girls, I went to the nursery and searched for my aunt's old books."

"So you did check up on their mother's handwriting!" Royce exclaimed, remembering Mary's taunt to the earl this afternoon.

"Of course I did." Stewkesbury raised his brows. "You didn't think I would simply take her word that my aunt wrote that letter? Aunt Flora's name was written in several books, and there were a number of her old composition books as well. The dratted letter matched them all." He stared down broodingly into his brandy snifter. "I also looked at the portrait of Grandfather's children that hangs in the second-floor gallery. Aunt Cynthia was right—Rose Bascombe looks a great deal like Aunt Flora."

Fitz raised his brows. "So they really are our cousins."

Oliver nodded. "I believe so. The only possible question would be whether the marriage and birth certificates are legitimate. They could be forged, I suppose, and I would have no way of knowing."

"If they were forged, the girls could have been born out of wedlock."

"Yes. But it seems unlikely. Aunt Flora disobeyed her father, but that does not mean she would have entirely flouted convention and not married Miles Bascombe. Indeed, the whole point of contention was her marrying the man, so I would presume that she did so once she was out from under her father's hand."

"Isn't one of the birth certificates missing?" Royce asked.

"Yes, but to my way of thinking, that makes it even more likely that they are telling the truth. If one were planning to gull someone into believing that several illegitimate children were legitimate, it only stands to reason that one would forge *all* the birth certificates. Why leave one out? It creates doubt. Why make them each come from a different place? It's a great deal of work to no purpose. No, I fear this tale bears the messy hallmarks of reality."

Oliver reached over to pour them another drink.

"What do you intend to do with them?" Fitz asked, taking a sip.

"Clearly, I have an obligation to them. They are Talbots, after all."

"And, of course, that is what matters," Royce murmured.

The earl frowned at him. "Well, I would think it is when one is talking about providing for four people. I have no interest in taking in every stray orphan off the street."

"Don't get on your high ropes, Ol," Fitz drawled. "You know Royce cannot pass up the chance to point out that he is not a Talbot."

Royce cast a jaundiced eye at his younger brother. "I beg your pardon. Need I remind you that I can still draw your cork?"

Fitz let out a bark of laughter. "You haven't bested me since I was nineteen."

"Yes, yes, no doubt you are both exemplary pugilists," the earl put in. "But we are talking about the Bascombe girls."

"A delightful topic they are, too." Fitz heaved an exaggerated sigh. "So sad that they are relatives."

Both his half brothers rolled their eyes, and Royce went on as if Fitz had not spoken. "What do you plan to do about them?"

"Obviously, I cannot toss them out to starve. Besides, I think Grandfather would have mended the rift with his daughter if he had had the opportunity."

"The old earl spoke to me once of her," Royce said. "I had forgotten all about it until this came up. He did not say her name, as I remember, but he spoke of her with regret."

"Too bad he didn't change his will to reflect that," the earl remarked.

Royce shrugged. "I imagine he didn't consider the possibility of Flora returning. I think he believed she was dead. He wouldn't have known about her daughters."

"I haven't the slightest notion what to do with four young

girls!" Oliver burst out. "Especially ones as unready as these for London society. I feel I ought to do more than feed and clothe them and immure them somewhere in the country. Surely they deserve a marriage portion and a Season—a chance to find husbands and marry."

Fitz grinned. "I can see Camellia at a ball now, describing how best to wield a knife at close quarters."

Stewkesbury groaned. "That is precisely what I mean. Much as I dislike the Season, I could steel myself to that, I think. But the entire *ton* would be appalled by them. They would have no hope of marrying well—or even of being accepted by their peers."

"Too bad you can't marry them off before they face the world," Royce joked. "Find some squire or Cit happy to ally himself with the Earl of Stewkesbury. Then it's his worry."

"Perhaps you would like to marry one of them and take her off my hands," the earl tossed back lightly. "Grandfather would have been pleased to see you tied to the Talbots."

Royce's face tightened. "I should shackle myself to a half-civilized hoyden of questionable origins just for the honor of attaching my name to the Talbots?"

"Bloody hell, Royce." Oliver returned his frown. "Don't be a fool; I was jesting. You know I wouldn't expect you to take on a wife like that to rid me of a problem."

Royce grimaced and started to retort, but at that moment the door swung open with great force. Mary Bascombe strode into the room, clad in dressing gown and slippers, dark hair tumbling in a wild mass over her shoulders and her face lit like an avenging angel's.

"Don't worry your head over marrying us off, either one of you," she announced. "My sisters and I will leave your house tomorrow, and you won't have any 'problem' to deal with."

Chapter 8

For a moment, the three men sat stunned, gaping at her. Oliver recovered first. He rose to his feet, all dignity even in his shirtsleeves and with his cravat loosened, a glass of liquor in his hand.

"Don't be absurd. I told you I accepted you and your sisters as my responsibility. There is no need—"

"We were looking for our *family*," Mary cut in, her words like acid. "Not someone to take on a 'responsibility.'"

Her eyes burned through him. She pivoted, sending that same red-hot gaze searing into Royce. "We certainly were not asking anyone to sacrifice himself in marriage."

Mary whirled and strode out of the room, leaving the men staring after her. Fury drove her, hot and consuming. Clearly, it was true that one never heard good about oneself by eavesdropping. Mary's cheeks burned with humiliation. The way Royce had rejected her! The words he had used to describe her! It was too much to bear.

"Mary!" Sir Royce's voice echoed down the hallway, and there was the sound of running footsteps. "Mary, wait!"

Mary walked faster. She was at the foot of the stairs when he caught up with her.

"Mary! Blast it, stop!" Royce grabbed her arm, pulling her around to face him. "Don't run off like this. Listen to me."

"I have heard enough from you. I don't need to hear any more."

"You mustn't act hastily," he told her, his handsome face so earnest it hurt her to look at him. "Oliver is not a hard man or unkind. I am sure he doesn't think of you as 'problems.' He was simply blindsided. He doesn't know what to do with young girls."

"Don't you mean he doesn't know what to do with 'half-civilized hoydens of questionable origins'?"

Royce flushed, and his jaw tightened. He dropped his hand from her arm. "I'm sorry. I did not mean to speak so harshly. I—it's just Oliver. He's bloody infuriating, the way he tries to control everyone around him. Always playing the big brother. I was irritated at Oliver, and I didn't mean—I wouldn't want you to think—"

Mary crossed her arms over her chest as he fumbled to a halt. She raised a skeptical eyebrow. "What? What would you not want me to think? The truth?"

"No! It wasn't the truth! I don't believe that."

"Don't you? What exactly did you say that you didn't mean? Do you not think I am a hoyden?"

"No, not a hoyden," he demurred, a smile twitching at the corners of his lips. "Perhaps more of a romp."

Mary let out an inelegant snort. "Perhaps it's the 'half-civilized' part you didn't mean. Is that it?"

"Mary . . ." He shifted uncomfortably.

"Then maybe it's the part about not wanting to marry one of us that you didn't mean. You *do* intend to ask for my hand. Is that it?"

"No," he snapped back. "I bloody well don't."

"That's fortunate, since I would not marry you if you were the last man on earth!"

Mary whipped around and ran up the stairs. Sir Royce started after her, but stopped on the second stair. His jaw clenched as he stood there for a long moment, scowling. He stepped back down into the hall and glanced toward the dining room, where Oliver and Fitz stood in the doorway, watching him. With a grimace, Royce turned and stormed out the front door.

"Well." Fitz turned toward his half brother. "That certainly went well."

The earl sighed. "I hope this is not an indication of what my future evenings will be like."

"From what I have seen, I fear that your life of quiet order is finished—unless, of course, you can find someone on whom you can foist our American cousins."

"Would that I could." Oliver walked back to his seat. "But who? None of the aunts would take them, and even if they would, I couldn't be so cruel to those poor girls—or even to Aunt Euphronia—as to throw them together."

"Mmm. I fear there might be murder done."

"Probably mine," the earl retorted dryly.

"Of course, Miss Bascombe could do as she threatened and walk out of here with her sisters. Then all your problems would be solved." Fitz dropped into his seat, stretching his long legs out in front of him.

Oliver grimaced. "I suspect a cooler head will prevail on the morrow. She must know the prospects that await her if they leave my protection. If she does not, I will point them out. I cannot allow our cousins to roam the streets of London, penniless."

"Still, her feelings were wounded, and she seems a most headstrong girl."

"She appears to be a shrewd one as well. She had the wit to come here and present her case to me, after all. She must be aware of the advantages of being acknowledged a Talbot. I am sorry that she overheard our comments—and even sorrier that I invited the aunts to meet them. I was hoping I could induce one of the aunts to take the girls on, but I should have had the foresight to realize what would result."

"I doubt anyone could have envisioned the tale of standing guard against wild Indians along the frontier."

A smile twitched at the corners of the earl's mouth. "Indeed. I'm not sure which appalled Aunt Euphronia more—that or their living above a tavern."

Fitz let out a crack of laughter. "God, yes. I'd have given a yellow boy just for the chance to see that look on Aunt Euphronia's face." He paused, then added meditatively, "I wonder if any of what they said was true."

"Who knows? What I do know is that the majority of the *ton* would react as Aunt Euphronia did. And their clothes— I never dreamed that they did not know to dress for dinner. Or did not have the proper clothes. I would have expected them to be out of fashion, but . . . surely even Marigold Bascombe must see how inadequately prepared they are for society."

"Still, one does not always like to hear the truth."

"No, but I will make sure that she listens to reason." Oliver sighed and swirled his brandy around in his snifter, looking thoughtful. "I wish I were as certain about my ability to deal with Royce."

Fitz waved a negligent hand. "Don't worry about Royce. He will be fine."

"I have no doubt. But I will assuredly have another black mark against my name. Why is it that whatever I say to him strikes him the wrong way? I did not mean to offend him when I said he might marry one of the Bascombes. I was only joking—I would not try to saddle Royce with an unsuitable wife."

"He knows that."

"Although I would like the connection, really. I've always considered Royce a brother, but I know he does not feel the same. If he were married to our cousin, the tie would be stronger, more legal. Of course, I should have realized that Royce has little interest in being tied to me. Still . . . he was fond of Grandfather. I would have thought he might like the idea of being married to one of the old earl's grand-daughters."

"He was very close to Grandfather. But this whole issue of family is, well, something of a sore spot with him. You know he's always felt a bit of an outsider."

"Then why wouldn't he want a closer tie?"

Fitz shrugged. "People don't always act logically. I know that must be a trial for you."

His older brother rolled his eyes in response.

"It isn't that he doesn't want to be connected to you," Fitz went on. "But he chafes at—well, you have always had a tendency to, um, arrange people's lives."

Oliver's brows shot up, and he opened his mouth to speak.

Fitz added quickly, "For their own good, of course." He cut his eyes toward his brother, mischief glinting in them.

Oliver had to chuckle. "Yes, so I have heard. Many times." He sighed. "I do not mean to annoy Royce, you know. Or run his life. Yours either."

"I know. I am sure Royce knows that, too. Deep down."

"Very deep down," Oliver added with a wry smile. "Ah, well. Enough of such gloomy talk." He shrugged. "Let's speak of something else. Tell me the gossip. I heard you shot out the lights at a gambling hell last Tuesday."

"Untrue—untrue!" Fitz protested with a laugh. "It was not a hell, but a perfectly respectable club, and I shot out only one light. Fullingham bet me that I could not take out the central candle without hitting any of the others. I could hardly allow that to pass, could I?"

"Indeed not," Oliver murmured.

And, pouring another drink, the two brothers settled down to convivial conversation.

Seething from her confrontation with Royce, Mary ran into her bedroom and barely kept from slamming the door after her. Casting a glance at her sister's sleeping form on the bed, she pushed the door shut with a quiet snick. She did not want to have to talk to anyone at this moment, not even Rose, to whom she usually told everything. She was too embarrassed.

No, embarrassed wasn't even the word for it—humiliated, that was what she was. To think she had believed Sir Royce liked her! He had not kissed her because he had been attracted to her particularly. No, it had been because he thought her a woman "of questionable origins"—too low in stature for a gentleman to have any concern for her reputation.

She had thought him kind because he had brought them here to meet the earl. Now she saw that it had all been a joke to him. He had wanted to cause his stepbrother consternation. All the times he had smiled or winked or warmth had glinted in his eyes, he had merely been laughing at her. She remembered the way she had responded this evening to the mere brush of his lips upon the back of her hand, the shiver of desire that had shot through her. She had thought that the glint in his eyes meant that he had felt it too—when all it really signified was that he was amused at her naïve reaction.

Mary winced as she recalled the anger and resentment in Royce's voice when he rejected the earl's suggestion that he marry one of the Bascombes. It had been painful hearing the earl say that she and her sisters would not be accepted by London society, but it had not surprised her. The earl's reception had been anything but warm, and she suspected that he had invited the aunts to dinner simply to drive home to her and her sisters how little they belonged here. He had intended to show them up as country bumpkins, without proper clothes, manners, or sophistication.

But she had thought that Sir Royce would defend them. That he would point out that they were clever or self-sufficient or pretty—something besides social pariahs. Instead, he had rejected with great indignation the idea of marrying one of them.

She had been an utter fool. All she could hope for was that Royce had not realized how much she was drawn to him. Mary tried to remember if she had appeared to flirt with him. Had she looked at him like some moonstruck young girl? She knew she had responded to his kiss, but surely any woman would have done that. It had been far too exciting not to respond.

But maybe other women—sophisticated women, those raised to be ladies—would not have kissed him back. Perhaps that was why he had called her half-civilized. Her thoughts went round and round on this track for some time, and the more she thought about it, the worse she felt. She could not bear to think of facing Royce. Perhaps he would not come to the house tomorrow, and she could leave without seeing him.

She ignored the pang that idea caused and tried to focus on leaving. She would have to explain it to her sisters, of course, and she dreaded that. It would hurt them to learn what she had overheard. But she could hardly expect them to go just because she told them to. It made no sense to leave just when they had finally achieved their goal. No, she would have to admit that the earl and his relatives did not find them good enough. Then her sisters would not wish to remain any more than she did.

The problem, of course, was where they would go. They had no money and knew no one. They could not return home; they hadn't enough money even to pay their fare. They would have to find a place to live and some sort of employment to keep themselves fed. It was a daunting prospect, especially in an unfamiliar city and country. Still, she told herself, there was nothing else she could do. They could not stay here, knowing how the earl—and the others—felt about them.

Her eyes filled with tears, but sternly she blinked them away. She would *not* cry. She refused to let Sir Royce make her cry. She wished with all her heart that she had never gone downstairs tonight.

When Mary awoke the next morning, she found herself alone. Rose must have already dressed and gone downstairs. It was quite late, she realized. She had slept poorly, waking from vague, half-remembered dreams that left her unsettled, even afraid. Accustomed as she was to the quiet of their small country town, every unfamiliar city noise—from the sound of a late hackney rolling down the street to the rumble of vendors' carts and their cries early in the morning—had brought her awake.

Mary pulled herself out of bed and dressed sluggishly. She wondered whether there would be any breakfast left or whether she would have to leave the house on an empty stomach. It would make for a more satisfying, dramatic exit if she did not prosaically go downstairs to eat breakfast—the heroines in Lily's books would not even think of food. However, Mary was aware that she was far too dull and pragmatic to be a heroine. She hoped that at least the earl would not be there at such a late hour.

When she slipped into the dining room a few minutes later, she was relieved to see that the earl was, in fact, not at the table. Unfortunately, his brother Fitz was. She hesitated in the doorway, tempted to turn and flee, but Fitz rose gracefully to his feet and the chance was gone.

"Cousin Mary." He smiled, the corners of his blue eyes crinkling in a charming way. "Just the person I was hoping to see."

"Indeed?" Mary walked to the table. Fitz nimbly rounded the corner to pull out her chair, and by the time she had sat down and placed a napkin in her lap, a footman was pouring her tea.

"Thank you, Will," Fitz told the footman. "You may go now. We will serve ourselves this morning."

The footman nodded and left the room.

"Hope you don't mind," Fitz said to Mary. "But I particularly wanted to talk to you, and it's better without servants around. Shall I fill your plate for you?"

He turned toward the sideboard, where an array of chafing dishes stood, and picked up a plate. Mary jumped up and followed him.

"I can get my own, thank you." She jerked the plate from his hands and started down the line, slapping a little something from each dish onto her plate.

Fitz waited to pull out her chair again before returning to his own food, already half-finished. He was silent at first, but when the first sharp edge of Mary's hunger was taken off and she settled back in her chair to sip her tea, he pushed his plate aside and leaned forward.

"I want to apologize for both my brothers. They are, quite simply, fools."

Mary set down her cup and crossed her arms. Fitzhugh Talbot was entirely too easy to like, and she had the suspicion that many people had found themselves agreeing to whatever he said before they even realized what they were doing.

"Yes, they are," she agreed, steeling herself to ignore his charm.

"You, however, are not a fool. We both know that. And it would be foolish in the extreme to depart from this house because of a wayward remark or two."

"It wasn't the remarks. It was the opinions behind them. The earl does not want us here. We are an embarrassment to him, as well as a burden."

"My dear girl, believe me, Oliver does not worry about embarrassment. Talbots, you see, are above that sort of thing. I do not know how much you overheard last night, but I can assure you that my brother was not worried that other people might look down upon him."

"Surely you cannot expect me to believe that."

"I assure you, 'tis true. The thought, quite frankly, would not occur to Stewkesbury. He has never shown the slightest embarrassment over the fact that my mother's father was"— Fitz leaned forward to deliver a mockingly scandalized whisper—"*in trade*. You may be American and not, shall we say, bang up to the mark, but your family lines are quite unobjectionable. Your father was penniless but from a good family. So if *my* origins don't shame him, I cannot imagine why yours would."

"But he said—"

"You walked in on the middle of a conversation. As it happens, we were discussing the difficulties a group of young ladies presented for Oliver, for he is not a particularly social man. He generally dislikes the social whirl and finds most parties boring. Receiving polite calls from friends and relatives is even worse for him."

"I don't understand what that would have to do with us."

Fitz cocked his head and studied her. "But surely you

must see, with four eligible young ladies, he must bring you out?"

Mary frowned. "Out where?"

Her cousin laughed. "Out into society, of course. You must be introduced to the world we live in. The beau monde. The *bon ton*. Young women make their debut."

"Why?" Mary stared at him blankly.

Fitz's return gaze was equally blank. Finally, he said, "Why . . . um . . . because it is what one does. How else is a girl supposed to meet her future husband?"

"In the usual way, I suppose. In the course of life."

He looked at her oddly. "That *is* the course of life. Our life. You see, one comes to London for the Season. One goes to parties and the opera and the theater. One rides or drives in the park."

Mary's gaze was disbelieving. "And that is all you do?"

"Oh, no, I do other things. There is my club—well, for men, of course. And Tattersall's, for the horse sales. Women shop. And receive visitors, make calls, all that sort of thing."

"What about work?"

"I beg your pardon?"

"Doesn't anyone work?"

"Of course people work. Not me, you understand. I am like the lilies of the field. I neither toil nor do I sow." He paused, frowning. "Or is it reap?" He shrugged. "Well, it doesn't matter really—I don't do either." A gurgle of laughter escaped Mary's lips, and Fitz flashed her a grin. "But Oliver is in his study diligently going over his books and such half the day. In any case, work is not the point of this discussion."

"Quite frankly, sir, I am not sure what the point is," Mary responded.

"You and your sisters staying here. I was explaining to

you Oliver's trepidation. It was not about you causing him embarrassment; it was dread at the thought of embarking on the social whirl."

"But there is no need. Why must he introduce us to society?"

"You are our cousins. He has taken on responsibility for you. And Oliver is a man who takes his responsibilities quite seriously."

Mary cast him a skeptical look. "You are a pretty talker, but I don't believe that was exactly the import of his words. He said we would not be accepted by our peers."

"Doubtless he fears that on your account. He would not wish to see you suffer embarrassment."

"Like our clothes last night?" Mary's cheeks flushed at the memory.

"Exactly. You see, he did not realize the problems that would arise. Oliver was most chagrined that he did not foresee the situation."

"Mr. Talbot—Lord—I don't know what to call you—"

"Cousin Fitz would be best." He grinned. "Or just Fitz. I am a great believer in American informality."

"All right, then. Cousin Fitz. It is very good of you to take up the cudgel in your brother's defense. However, I must tell you that it makes no difference. It is clear to me that even though the earl has accepted responsibility for us, it is not something he wishes to do. He will be well pleased that we are gone. And my sisters and I would prefer not to be where we are not welcome."

"My dear cousin, I fear you are wrong on both counts." Fitz's usually lighthearted expression dropped into serious lines. "You will not prefer leaving Stewkesbury House. Where will you go? What will you do? How will you live?"

"I don't know," Mary answered honestly. The same

thoughts had kept her awake half the night. "But we will find a way. There must be employment."

Fitz's eyes widened in shock. "But you are a lady. However you may have been raised, whatever you did in the United States, here it simply would not do. The only acceptable employment would be as a governess or a companion, but—I am sorry, but I must be frank—what Englishman is going to hire an American for a governess? And companions are never lively, attractive young women. There is no place where the four of you could go together, even if someone were willing to hire one or another of you."

"We are quite capable. We can cook and clean and—"

"You are suggesting that you go into service?" Fitz could not have looked more stunned if Mary had suggested that she and her sisters take to walking the streets. "Mary! You cannot." He shook his head in bemusement.

"Why not?"

"You would not enjoy it, I assure you." He gazed at her solemnly for a moment, but then his usual grin lightened his countenance. "Besides, I do not believe you and your sisters have the, ah, temperament to be servants. Anyway, my brother would not allow it."

"What business is it of his?"

"The Earl of Stewkesbury's cousins living hand-to-mouth? You cannot think he would stand for that."

"We wouldn't say anything. No one would know we are his cousins."

"*He* would."

"Oh."

"Oliver is a man of firm beliefs. He has accepted you as his responsibility. He would not toss you out, and he would not allow you to put yourself in that sort of position either."

"There's nothing he can do about it," Mary protested. "We are grown women."

"As far as *you* are concerned, perhaps he cannot do anything—other than prose on at you for hours, which I can assure you is far worse than a thrashing. However, I have seen your birth certificates, and your sister Lily is not of age. Nor, I warrant, is Cousin Camellia. Clearly, Oliver would be their guardian, and he would go to court to establish that if he had to."

Mary stared at him, speechless.

Fitz smiled and reached across the table to take her hand. "Come, Cousin. We are family, and relatives have their little spats. But they don't go haring off because there has been a disagreement. Think of your sisters. You cannot condemn them to a life of poverty and toil simply because of hurt feelings. Because of pride."

Mary jerked her hand away, glaring at him. "That is exactly what my mother said!"

Fitz chuckled. "You see? Family. This is what your mother wanted you to do; she understood what sort of life it could be for you and your sisters. There is just a . . . small period of adjustment." He paused. "What do you say?"

Mary set her jaw mulishly. The thought of staying galled her, no matter how diplomatically Fitz had presented it. Unfortunately, she knew he was right. She had brought her sisters here precisely because the future had been so bleak for them in America. But here, alone in a foreign country, it would be far worse. She thought of all they had done to get here. It would be extremely foolish, just as Fitz said, to throw away that effort because of her hurt pride.

Last night she had promised to make a better effort to get along with her new relatives. She had sworn to herself to hold her tongue. Then, before the evening was out, she had flown into a temper and rashly declared that she would leave their benefactor's house. She had not thought about her sisters or what would happen to them or, indeed, about anything but herself.

Besides, deep down she knew that it was not really the earl who had angered her. Sir Royce's words had cut her to the quick because she had foolishly let herself imagine that he was interested in her, that he liked her, even desired her. Her sisters should not have to suffer simply because she was behaving like an adolescent girl.

Mary sighed. "You are right. I cannot argue. We have no choice but to stay."

He smiled. "You will not regret it."

"I hope not." Mary could not bring herself to return his smile. She had done the right thing for her sisters, but all she could think about was that now she would have to face Royce.

She was not sure whether that idea filled her with dread . . . or anticipation.

Chapter 9

As it happened, Mary did not have to wait long to find out what her reaction would be when she saw Sir Royce again. She and her sisters were sitting down to tea with the earl and Fitz that afternoon in one of the drawing rooms when the butler announced the arrival of Sir Royce Winslow and Lady Charlotte Ludley.

Mary, who had been adding sugar to her tea, felt her heart flip in her chest, and her fingers involuntarily tightened on the little spoon, sending sugar crystals tumbling into the saucer. She occupied herself with replacing the spoon in the sugar bowl and setting down her cup, gathering herself inside, before she looked up at the two visitors standing in the doorway.

Her eyes flickered over the attractive woman dressed in what Mary assumed was the height of fashion and went straight to the man standing beside her. She had hoped that now that she knew what Royce was truly like, he would not look the same to her. Unfortunately, she could not deny that a sizzle still ran through her at the sight of his tall, muscular figure. Royce's green eyes met hers, and Mary braced herself. She would not lower her gaze before his; after all, he was the one who should feel ashamed. If she was going to stay here, she would doubtless encounter the man on a regular basis. She had to establish that she did not give a whit for his opinion of her.

She held his gaze for one long beat without expression, then turned her head to look at his companion. She saw a woman slightly older than herself, with dark brown hair pinned up under a ruched silk bonnet of palest gray decorated across the crown with a cluster of bright red artificial cherries. The woman wore a carriage dress that matched the hat in color, and Mary noted that although its waist was still higher than one's natural waist, it was definitely a good bit lower than those on the gowns Mary and her sisters wore—clearly the new style, like the aunts' dresses last night. Beneath the bonnet the woman's face was pleasant and rosy-cheeked, with bright hazel eyes and a rosebud mouth.

"Cousin Charlotte." Both Fitz and Stewkesbury rose to their feet, smiling.

"I was most sorry you could not come for dinner last night," the earl said, stepping forward to kiss the woman on the cheek.

"Not as sorry as I after Mama visited me this morning and told me whom she had met." Charlotte's eyes went past her cousin to the Bascombe sisters, grouped on two short sofas.

"Allow me to introduce you to your new cousins," Oliver told her, turning toward the Bascombes and running through the list of their names. He added, "Charlotte is your aunt Cynthia's daughter."

"Oh, my! How pretty you all are!" Cousin Charlotte exclaimed, coming forward to shake the girls' hands. "Royce told me you were, but I thought he must be exaggerating. I can see now that he was not." She cast a mischievous glance at the earl. "Oliver, I fear you will have your work cut out for you, fending off these girls' suitors."

"I think that will be sometime down the road," Oliver replied noncommittally.

"Not this Season, of course. Why, 'tis almost over. But next Season they will be sure to make a splash." Charlotte sat down in the chair closest to the girls. "You must tell me all about yourselves. Mama said you gave Aunt Euphronia quite a turn. Do you actually carry guns? Royce swore to me that you had a rifle with you when he met you, but I was certain he must be lying."

It was clear that the girls had found an appreciative audience, and they proceeded to launch into more realistic versions of the tales they had told the evening before. Mary allowed her sisters to take the lead in the conversation, concentrating on ignoring Sir Royce's presence. It was, she found, excessively hard not even to glance at him—especially since she could feel his gaze upon her throughout most of the conversation.

Finally, during a lull, Charlotte turned to the earl and said, "Oliver, Royce tells me that you might be in need of my help."

The earl immediately brightened. "Indeed. Have you come to offer to sponsor our cousins through their Season?"

Charlotte responded with a musical peal of laughter. "Are you mad? With my three rampaging boys? No, thank you. I have more than enough on my hands, believe me. Besides, I am not the sort of sponsor you need to make a path for our cousins." She turned toward the Bascombes, adding, "And, indeed, much as I like all of you, there is a great deal to be done to prepare you for your entrance into society."

"I am aware of that," Oliver told her. "In fact, I have sent round to an agency to find a chaperone who can also teach them the social skills they need. As soon as I hire her, I shall send them all to Willowmere. They will have ample time and quiet there to learn all they need to know."

"What?" Mary glanced at her sisters, on whose faces she saw the same expressions of surprise and alarm. "You are sending us somewhere?"

"Yes, to Willowmere, the Talbot family estate. It is north of here, in the Lake District."

"I see. Someplace far from London. Where we will be less trouble to you," Mary said caustically.

Lily sucked in a breath. "Oooh . . . you're locking us away? Like the wicked duke in *The Shield of Montague*!"

"Who?" Oliver looked at her, startled.

"It's a book." Mary shrugged her sister's remark aside. "Don't you think, sir, that this is a bit high-handed?"

"Don't mind Oliver," Charlotte told her. "He is high-handed with everyone. Isn't that true, Fitz?"

"Absolutely." He gave the Bascombes a wink. "You mustn't hold it against him. He cannot help giving orders."

"But what if we don't want to go?" Camellia protested.

As the earl's brows drew together, Charlotte jumped in. "You will like it there, honestly. Willowmere is a wonderful place—so beautiful, and such a relief after the bustle of London. Actually, it is the perfect plan. I know it's maddening, but that's the way it is with Oliver—he is invariably right. You don't want to be thrown into the Season with no preparation. It could be an absolute disaster. I am sure that it is very different here from what you are used to."

"That's an understatement," Camellia muttered.

"There, then you know what I mean. You have been in America all your lives; you can't be expected to know what's what. But the sad truth is that everyone will expect it anyway. Looks, I fear, will only take you so far. In any case, the Season is almost over, and everyone will leave, and it will be deadly dull. In the meantime, you will be at Willowmere, learning all you need to know, and—"

"But what is that?" Mary asked. "What are we going to learn?"

"Deportment, dances—whatever you'll need." Charlotte gave an airy wave of her hand. "This woman Stewkesbury is hiring will take care of that. Then when you come for the Season next year, you will be ready to take the *ton* by storm. And I know just the woman to introduce you to society, if she will do it. Lady Vivian Carlyle."

"Vivian Carlyle?" Oliver echoed. "You mean that annoying, carrot-haired, skinny chit who used to plague us at Willowmere?"

Cousin Charlotte cocked an eyebrow at him. "Vivian Carlyle is a leader of the *ton,* as you would know if you spent more time in London."

"I do know," he retorted. "But from all I've heard, Lady Vivian is a sad romp. It can't help these girls, who are much too wild already, to have an example set for them by someone with as little regard for propriety as a Carlyle."

The Bascombes all bristled at this description of them, but before they could speak, Charlotte was already saying, "Oh, Oliver, don't be such a prig. I'm not talking about them *living* with her, after all. And they would keep their chaperone, of course. But if Vivian were to sponsor them—"

"I am sure that one of our aunts is fully capable of sponsoring them."

Charlotte rolled her eyes. "Please. I will be the first to agree that the Talbot name is old and well respected. But it hardly carries the weight of the Carlyles'. Besides, you could not be so cruel as to saddle these poor girls with Aunt Euphronia. It might be too much to ask Vivian to sponsor all four of them. But if she were to invite them to a few of her parties or single them out at a ball or let them share her box at the opera, that sort of thing—well, it would mean their instant acceptance into the *ton*. Lady Vivian is all the crack."

"But a Carlyle!"

Charlotte pulled a face at him. "There has never been even a whiff of scandal associated with Vivian. And she can scarcely be blamed for the scandals that past generations of Carlyles got into. Those are all long forgotten, anyway."

"*I* remember them."

"I mean, by people besides you. Vivian does exactly as she pleases, but she cannot be accused of immorality. And she is the daughter of a duke."

"Just a moment," Mary interrupted. "Don't we have anything to say about this?"

Charlotte turned toward Mary. "You will love Vivian. No need to worry over that. And I suspect that she will like you just as much as I do. Viv and I have been friends for years. Perhaps when the Season is over, I can persuade her to come to Willowmere to see you. She could visit her uncle."

Charlotte stopped as soon as she uttered these words and cast a quick, almost guilty look toward Sir Royce. Mary's eyes went to him, but she could see no change in his expression; indeed, his face was blank. However, she could feel a rise of tension around the room. Oliver and Fitz glanced at Royce, then at each other.

Charlotte rattled on, a little breathlessly, to Mary and her sisters, "Vivian's uncle, the duke's younger brother, lives near Willowmere, you see, and, uh . . ." She looked almost beseechingly at the earl.

Quickly, he put in, "Certainly. Consult Lady Vivian, if you wish."

Mary could not help but wonder what had just happened beneath the surface of the conversation, but Charlotte was already plowing ahead.

"Good," she said, beaming. "That's all settled. Then all that's left is the matter of clothing."

The earl let out a small groan. "Of course. I knew it would come down to that."

"Well, of course you did," Charlotte agreed. "It's quite obvious. They cannot be seen in public in these garments."

Mary looked down at her dress. Their clothes were a trifle dated and had been worn for some time, but she had never guessed that their frocks were so unpresentable as everyone here seemed to think.

Charlotte turned to the girls in great good cheer. "Your come-outs will require whole new wardrobes, of course, but for now, we must come up with a few new things for everyday wear. I know! I'll see if Vivian would like to accompany us on a little shopping expedition. We can go to Grafton House and purchase some fabrics. I know a seamstress who can whip up some dresses for you. The finished frocks can be shipped to you at Willowmere. And, of course, we must visit the milliner's. I am sure you must need new bonnets—and gloves. Oh, and slippers!" She smiled broadly. "This is going to be such fun."

Somewhat stunned by this flow of words, Mary said nothing, visions of rolls of fabric—dainty dimities and elegant silks and sprigged muslins—filling her head. She cast a sideways glance at her sisters. Rose looked happier than she had in days, and Lily was positively aglow. Even Camellia was smiling.

"We can go tomorrow afternoon—no, wait, I must call on Ludley's deaf old grandmother tomorrow afternoon. It's a great trial, for she cannot hear a word one says, so that one has to shout. And she takes snuff—can you imagine! She's an utter throwback, of course—she still wears panniers and face paint and a moth-eaten old wig. But she's the power in his family, and poor Ludley lives in absolute fear of her."

"You might mention that Ludley is your husband," Royce put in in an amused tone. "I believe you have quite befuddled your audience." He nodded toward the Bascombes, who were gazing at her in confusion.

Mary glanced at him, almost smiling; but one look at his handsome face reminded her all over again of how painful it had been last night to hear him discount her. Her features froze before they could reach a smile, and she turned back to Charlotte. She could feel Royce's eyes upon her, but she steadfastly ignored him.

"I'm sorry! Sometimes I am such a rattle. Well, the dowager baroness is neither here nor there. The fact of the matter is that we cannot go shopping until the day after tomorrow. But that will give me time to invite Vivian along, so it turns out just as well, doesn't it?"

As Charlotte continued to discuss the arrangements for the shopping expedition, Mary's thoughts turned inexorably to the depleted state of her purse upstairs. The thought of new and fashionable frocks was a powerful lure, but she felt sure that Charlotte was unaware that her cousins' resources were far more limited than her own. Much as Mary hated to put a damper on Charlotte's enthusiasm, it would be even worse to have to admit their inability to buy a new wardrobe later.

Steeling herself, Mary said, "It sounds lovely, Cousin Charlotte. But, well, I'm afraid that we—I don't think we could—" A blush rose in her cheeks, and she lifted her chin a little. "The truth is, we haven't enough money to buy anything."

Charlotte stared at her blankly. Lily let out a long-suffering sigh and sagged back in her seat. Besides that, there was only silence. Mary felt sure that she had made another faux pas; no doubt these people did not discuss anything so crass as money. But Mary could not let Charlotte proceed merrily with her plans when there was no hope that Mary and her sisters could buy anything.

Finally, the earl spoke up. "I fear you have misunderstood, cousin. The bills will be sent to me."

Mary turned to him, astonished. "But, no—I mean, I—you should not have to buy us clothes."

The earl lifted one brow. "You are my charges now. Did you think I would not provide you with the necessities?"

"Well, yes, of course." Mary had to force herself not to squirm under the man's cool gray gaze. "But I didn't think— I mean, it seems too much. You shouldn't have to pay for our clothes as well."

"I can hardly expect you to wear the same frocks for the remainder of your lives, now, can I?"

"No, of course not," Mary agreed, feeling more foolish than ever.

The earl inclined his head. "Then it is agreed." Amusement lit his eyes as he said, "Perhaps you shall provide a valuable restraint to our cousin's spending habits."

"Ludley never complains," Charlotte told him haughtily.

Mary had to marvel at the other woman's ease with the formidable earl. Mary felt she had to square her shoulders and screw up her courage whenever she faced him. But that ease, she supposed, was what came from belonging . . . as Mary and her sisters did not. As they never would.

It was not long before Charlotte took her leave, promising to see the girls in two days for their shopping expedition. Warmly Mary bade her good-bye, and since Sir Royce had risen and walked with them to the hall, Mary had no choice but to turn to him as well. Her smile, however, fell from her face, and the nod she gave him was decidedly frosty.

Charlotte moved toward the front door, the other girls

trailing along and happily discussing the prospect of shoes and hats and dresses, but Sir Royce took Mary's arm, holding her back.

"Do you plan on not speaking to me for the rest of our lives?" he asked in a low voice.

Mary made herself look at him. Royce was smiling at her, and she could not deny the sensation that twisted inside her at his smile. Why did he have to have that appealing cleft in his chin? And must his eyes be such a vivid green, like a leaf after the rain?

"Of course not," she answered in a cool tone. "No doubt we will have occasion to speak now and then. But it seems unlikely that we shall spend much time around each other in the future."

"Does it?" His eyebrows quirked up. "The Talbots are a close family."

"As I recall, you have little interest in being tied to the Talbots. Besides, you will marry according to your station, and our paths are unlikely to cross."

"Mary . . ." He sighed. "I understand your desire to punish me. I deserve it for my clumsy and unthinking remarks. But I did not mean to hurt you. I would not have done so for the world. Do at least give me some hope that eventually you will end my punishment."

"I don't know what you mean. I am not trying to punish you. I am merely speaking the truth, as you did. I have no liking for deception."

"Deception!" He frowned. "I did not deceive you."

"Of course. No doubt it was I who misunderstood. I am accustomed to simpler people. I took amusement and mockery for friendship."

Royce looked startled. "Mockery—no, Mary, you must not think that I—"

Embarrassed that she had revealed too much of her own hurt, Mary shook her head, giving him a quick, tight smile. "Nay. 'Tis silly to belabor the point. Excuse me."

She pulled her arm from his grasp and hurried to rejoin her sisters in the hallway. With a sigh, Royce followed her. He did not, as she had half feared, try to talk to her again. Merely bowing to her sisters, he gave Cousin Charlotte his arm, and they left.

Mary turned back to her sisters and was somewhat surprised to find all three watching her. She raised her brows questioningly. "Is something the matter?"

"I was about to ask you the same thing," Rose replied. "Is something wrong between you and Sir Royce? Has he offended you?"

"No. Of course not. There is nothing wrong." Mary turned away and started toward the stairs. If she had hoped to leave the others behind, she was disappointed, for all three girls followed on her heels.

"Then why did you avoid him?" Lily asked "You hardly said two words to him the whole time he was here."

"You didn't even smile at him," Rose added. "It was quite obvious."

"And just now, when he was talking to you, you looked . . . upset," Lily finished.

"The man can be annoying." It would have been a relief to tell her sisters about the conversation she had overheard. But it would serve no purpose other than to upset her sisters and set them against their new relatives. Mary did not want that. It was important, especially for the two younger girls, that they get along with the earl. Besides, the girls liked Sir Royce, and it seemed too cruel to tell them how he really felt.

So she said only, "I cannot remember what nonsense he was talking, but I am sure it was nothing important. You know how he is."

Rose shot her a doubtful glance, but Mary ignored it.

"Let us talk about something more interesting," she said as she went up the stairs toward their rooms. "Like our shopping trip with Cousin Charlotte."

Predictably, this topic quickly diverted her sisters' minds from Sir Royce.

"Isn't it wonderful?" Lily asked. "Just think—dresses and hats and shoes! Even gloves. I don't know how I shall contain myself, waiting for tomorrow to pass. Did you look at Cousin Charlotte's dress?" Lily let out a rapturous sigh.

"Well, I am sure the earl will not wish to buy us anything as beautiful as that," Rose told her. "It must have been terribly expensive, don't you think? But it would be wonderful to look not so dowdy."

"Clothes are all very well," Camellia admitted as Mary opened the door to the room she shared with Rose, and they all trooped in after her. "But I don't see why we have to have someone looking after us. We aren't children." She threw herself onto the bed and turned on her side to face them, propping her head with her hand.

"No," Lily agreed, sitting down on the trunk at the foot of the bed. "But it's clear that we don't know a lot of things we need to know in order to live here. Think of all the forks and spoons last night. Did you know what to do with them? I didn't."

"No, but it's silly to have that many. You need only one of everything." Camellia set her jaw. "You never saw Mama lay out so many eating utensils."

"Mayhap not, but I'll warrant she knew which one to use," Mary put in. "We aren't at home any longer, Cam. We cannot live the way we did there. If we are going to live here, we must change our ways. Learn how to do things properly." Mary might have decided not to reveal to her sisters what she had overheard, but she was determined that no one would have an opportunity to talk about the Bascombe girls in that way again.

"I refuse to turn into some dried-up old stick like those aunts!"

"I don't want you to," Mary shot back. "But I will not have anyone saying that you are not as good as they are." She fixed each of the other girls with a firm gaze. "Do you want to have people laugh at you because you don't know which spoon to use? Do you want to step on your partner's feet because you don't know the steps to a dance?"

Camellia grimaced, but she did not argue.

"We are going to go to this Season that Cousin Charlotte was talking about, and we're going to show them that we are not country bumpkins."

"I think the Season sounds like fun," Lily announced. "Cousin Charlotte was telling me that you go to ever so many parties and dance and talk and flirt, very discreetly, of course. And there are plays and opera and—"

"I don't care about all those things," Camellia protested.

"Maybe not. But Lily does. And I care about all of you having good and happy lives here." Mary swept her sisters with a determined gaze. "I want you to marry and have children and all the things that you deserve. You won't get any of that if you're immured in some house out in the country—which is, I warrant, where the earl will leave you if you can't learn to at least masquerade as a lady."

"Mary's right," Rose said. "I don't want to go to all those parties and have people staring at us and talking about us, either. But it seems to be the way they do things here. I don't want anyone to say that we couldn't do it. Do you?"

"No!" Camellia's retort was as swift as it was predictable.

Mary hid a smile. Rose had a way of finding just the right words to get Camellia and Lily to do something.

"Well, then," Rose continued, "you will have to listen to whomever the earl hires and do what she says."

"Oh, all right," Camellia agreed grudgingly. "I'll listen to her and learn to do things the way they do here. But I'm still going to be the same person."

"Of course you are." Mary gave Camellia a swift hug. "We are all going to be the same people."

Dinner that night was a much smaller affair, with only the Bascombe girls and the earl present. Fitz, the earl informed them, already had plans elsewhere, and he had not invited anyone, even Royce or the aunts. Noting that the earl had declined to don formal attire this evening, instead wearing the same clothes he had worn during the day, Mary could not help but soften a trifle toward him.

However, since the earl was not blessed with the ease of conversation that Fitz or Royce possessed and Mary and her sisters were still largely in awe of the man, conversation proceeded in a rather ponderous manner, with a great deal of time given to the weather and the details of the Bascombes' trip across the ocean. It was something of a relief when the meal ended, and the women were able to leave the table while Stewkesbury stayed for his customary glass of port.

The rest of the evening passed rather slowly as well. In their spare time at home, Lily had often read to the others aloud as they mended clothes or darned their stockings. However, Lily, thrilled by the size of the library here, had been very disappointed to find that none of the books in it were of the exciting sort she liked.

"Not one by Mrs. Radcliffe," she announced in an offended tone. "They're all history and philosophy and boring things like that!"

"Nothing with even a skeleton or two?" Rose teased. But

they all had to agree that none of the volumes would liven up their evening.

At home there had always been something with which one could occupy oneself—if not mending, then old garments to be torn into cleaning rags and bandages, or flour sacks to be hemmed into dish towels, or their few dishes of silver to be polished. But the silver salt cellar and serving utensils had been sold to help finance their trip, and they had brought only their best clothes, so there was nothing to be mended or disposed of. Mary had brought her knitting needles and crochet hook, but no yarn, which would have taken up too much space.

They searched fruitlessly through the drawing room for a game or even a deck of cards to while away the time, but found nothing, and after a time they decided to retire early.

The next morning Fitz returned to the house, looking slightly rumpled, as they were going down to breakfast, but he managed only a smile and a perfect bow before hastening upstairs to his bed. The earl breakfasted with the sisters, then informed them that after an hour or two in his study, he would be going to his club for lunch.

The girls, left alone, once again faced the prospect of a dull day.

"I know." Camellia leaned forward, her gray eyes lighting with interest. "Let's go exploring."

"Where?" Rose asked. "There's nothing but city out there."

"That's what we're going to explore."

Lily straightened, a smile beginning on her lips, but Rose looked doubtful. "But we haven't any idea where to go. What if we get lost?"

"Then we'll ask someone how to get back to this address," Camellia responded. "Anyway, it can't be that hard.

Mary managed to find her way all the way back to the inn the other day."

"That's true," Mary agreed. She had not enjoyed her walk through the city, but at the time she'd been worried about finding her way back and had not really *looked* at anything. "I got lost a few times, but I did finally get there. This time I shall pay more attention to where I'm going." She stood up, smiling at Rose. "It might be fun. At least it will be something to do."

There was still a frown creasing Rose's forehead, but she nodded, willing, as always, to go where her older sister led. They got their bonnets and gloves, for, Mary thought to herself, they were not such heathens as to go out bare-headed and barehanded. But as they trooped downstairs, they hesitated at the sight of the footman standing at the ready in the front hallway.

Mary suspected that the earl would not be best pleased at their expedition into the city alone, but, she thought, the servant would hardly try to stop the earl's cousins from doing what they chose. Holding her head high, she marched toward the front door, her sisters following in her wake like ducklings. To her relief, the footman sprang forward to open the door for her.

Mary gave him a regal nod. "If my cousin asks, tell him we have gone for a walk."

Their steps quickened as they went out the front door and down the steps to the sidewalk. They turned up the street, buoyed by the sudden rush of freedom. The day was warm, if a little gray, and there was a bit of breeze to stir the air. And while what lay about them might not be as scenic as the view of trees and winding road that they saw when they stepped out their door in Three Corners, it was filled with activity. Before they had gone one block, they had already seen two gentleman riding by on horses, a grand carriage rolling in the opposite direction, and two young women walking along at a far slower pace than the Bascombes, with a woman in a maid's uniform trailing along behind. The two young women cast a look askance as the sisters overtook them, and Mary was sure she heard a smothered giggle behind them as they walked on.

"There are so many buildings," Rose said, looking around her. "Everywhere you look. And so many people."

"I know!" Lily exclaimed, almost skipping as she walked. "Isn't it exciting?"

They reached an intersection, and a ragged young boy darted out to cross the street in front of the Bascombes, sweeping before him with a short broom. The girls regarded him in astonishment, and when he turned to them on the other side, an expectant look on his face, they gazed back at him blankly.

His face fell into a grimace. "Oi sherda known," he muttered, and hastened back across the street to perform the same ritual in front of an elegantly clad gentleman.

"What did he say?" Rose asked in confusion.

"I have no idea. I'm not sure he was speaking English."

The gentleman reached their side of the street and tossed the boy a small coin.

"I see! We were supposed to pay him something," Mary surmised.

"For what?" Camellia asked. "Stirring up the dust?"

"I think he cleans the street so one's shoes and hem don't get dirty. I saw some of these boys the other day, but I hadn't any idea what they were doing."

As they walked on, Lily kept glancing back at the intersection. Halfway down the block, she stopped, saying, "Look, he didn't do it for that man."

The sisters all turned. A large, broad-shouldered man lumbered across the street. He wore a cap on his head and a rough jacket, with trousers that hung loosely over his battered work boots.

"The boy knows he hasn't any money," Rose said. "He's a laborer of some kind, I would warrant, from the way he dresses."

"Then I am surprised the boy swept it for us," Mary retorted.

They continued along the street, looking around them with great interest. So fascinating was everything that they had walked for almost thirty minutes before Camellia remembered that she had not been paying close attention to where they were going. Neither, it turned out, had the other girls, and they stopped abruptly and looked around them.

"Well, at least we haven't wandered into a terrible area," Mary commented. "The houses are still quite nice and the streets broad."

"Perhaps we had better retrace our steps," Rose suggested, "before we get so far afield we cannot remember how to get back."

Reluctantly Camellia gave in, and they started back the way they had come.

"That's odd," Lily commented.

"What's odd?"

"That fellow who crossed the street after we did—the workman that the boy didn't sweep for. He's right there up the block."

The girls all raised their heads. There, just as Lily had said, was the large man. He was walking along, looking toward them; suddenly he stopped and swung around, staring for a moment at the door of the house next to him. Just as abruptly, he hurried across the street.

"Are you sure it's the same man?" Camellia asked.

"Of course I am. That cap, that jacket—and his hair was longish, too; I could see it hanging out beneath his cap."

"I think she's right," Mary agreed.

"Isn't it strange that he was still behind us?" Lily asked.

"You always think something sinister is going on," Camellia pointed out. "Remember when you were certain that Mr. Johnson had killed his wife because no one saw her for a week, then it turned out she had sprained her ankle and couldn't walk?"

"That was ages ago," Lily sniffed. "I was only fourteen. Anyway, all I'm saying is that it's peculiar that he was still behind us."

"Perhaps he's going to the same place we were," Mary suggested.

"But we weren't going anywhere." Rose frowned.

"Well, no, but it doesn't mean *he* wasn't."

"And we just happened to wander along the same route he was taking?" Rose retorted.

"Well, that does seem rather unlikely, but . . . what else could it be?" Mary asked reasonably. "Do you think he was following us?"

"No, of course not. It's just . . . odd."

As they trudged on, Lily glanced behind them periodically. Finally, as they stood on a street corner trying to remember which direction they had come from, Lily let out a little yelp.

"He's there!"

"What?" As one, the other three girls swung around to look.

"I don't see him." Mary scanned the length of the block.

"He ducked behind that lamppost when I saw him, but look, he's too big—you can see his arm."

"Let's go this way." Mary whisked her sisters around the corner and up the block.

A few yards up the street, a carriage stood waiting at the curb. Mary hurried past it, then pulled her sisters into the street a little way in front of the carriage and team. The girls turned, peering around the horses toward the corner.

"Here, what do ye think yer doing?" the coachman growled from atop his high perch. "Get away from them horses."

"We aren't going to hurt them," Camellia assured him. "We're only standing here."

"That's no excuse. These're the Honorable Mr. Pinkley Fanshaw's team, I'll have ye know—prime steppers, every one. I won't have ye fluttering about, scaring them."

"We aren't fluttering." Mary frowned at the man. "Would you please be quiet? You're causing a scene."

"*I'm* causing a scene!"

Whatever else he had to say, the girls did not hear it, for at that moment their pursuer came barreling around the corner.

Chapter 10

He stopped, scanning the block in front of him.

Camellia darted back onto the sidewalk and planted herself in the man's path, arms akimbo.

"Camellia!" Rose hissed, reaching for her, but it was too late.

"What do you think you're doing, following us?" Camellia demanded. The other girls, unable to stop their sister, hurried forward to stand beside her.

The man stared at them, opening his mouth then closing it. He swung around and took off at a run. Camellia started after him, but this time both Mary and Rose reached for her, grabbing her arms and pulling her back.

"Camellia! Wait! What do you think you're doing?" Mary asked.

"I'm going to find out why he was following us."

"Har!" A scornful laugh erupted from the coach seat above them. "Why would ye think a lout *wouldn't* be following ye?" the driver of the vehicle called down from his perch. "Four of ye, no better than ye should be, I warrant, traipsin' about, showing your ankles to all and sundry—it's a wonder ye didn't have more than one lad following ye."

Mary blushed to her hairline at his words, and the four

girls glanced down at their skirts. Perhaps they were a trifle shorter than most of the women's skirts, Mary admitted; after all, repeated washings had shrunk the cotton. But they did not fully expose their ankles, and, in any case, the girls' legs were concealed by half boots.

"How dare you!" It surprised Mary that it was Lily, not Camellia, who stepped forward to face the man, arms crossed, her face bright with anger. "We've done nothing wrong, and it certainly isn't our fault if that—that churl was following us. Can four women not walk through this city unaccosted?"

"That's right!" Camellia, never one to avoid a fight, moved up to stand beside her sister. "You're the one who should be ashamed, sitting in judgment like that."

"I should, should I?" The coachman climbed down from his seat, an action somewhat robbed of its dramatic effect by the effort it required for him to maneuver his rather too-well-fed body off the seat and down the side of the carriage.

"Camellia! Lily!" Mary plucked at Camellia's sleeve. "Please. We cannot get into an altercation here on the street." She could imagine the earl's reaction—and, she had to admit, he would have every right to be upset. The driver was excessively rude, of course, but even in Three Corners, getting into a shouting match with a stranger on the street was not the behavior of a well-brought-up woman.

But temper had gotten the better of both her younger sisters. Facing the red-faced coachman, their voices rose as they responded to his shouted imprecations. Passersby as far as half a block away were turning to stare. Even worse, Mary saw, the onlookers were drawing nearer. Soon there would be a crowd around them.

Hissing their sisters' names, Mary and Rose tugged at their arms, but the two girls dug in, struggling to stay as their sisters inexorably dragged them away. At that moment, two things happened: a small dog came bounding down the street, and a tall, thin man stepped out of the door of the nearest house.

The dog barked joyously, running in circles around the knot of arguing people, pausing now and then to jump first to one side, then the other and bark even more loudly, his stump of a tail wagging all the time.

The tall, thin man's response was less enthusiastic. "Wainsley! What the devil is going on?"

Rose and Mary, intent though they were on drawing their sisters away, could not help but stare at the man who came down the stairs. Mary presumed this must be the Honorable Mr. Pinkley Fanshaw, owner of the horses. And he was attired in clothes that would have no doubt have wrung a gasp of admiration from Royce's inebriated companion Gordon.

His long, narrow legs were encased in tightly fitting pantaloons in a pale shade of green, and his bright blue jacket, nipped in tightly at the waist, was padded out ludicrously at the shoulders and had tails so long they almost touched his ankles in back. The high hat that other gentlemen wore had become two inches taller on him and bowed out at the top so that, to Mary's untutored eye, it looked rather like a plant pot with a brim. A quizzing glass hung on a chain from one lapel, and in the other was a boutonnière so large that it put Cousin Gordon's to shame. His waistcoat was a paisley pattern of blue, yellow, and purple, and it sported an ornate watch with a golden chain weighted down by fobs. Rings adorned three fingers on each hand, and a large diamond winked in the folds of an intricately tied neckcloth. The starched points of his collar stood straight up, so high that he could not turn his head with spoiling them, so that when the man spoke to someone, he had to pivot his entire body to face the person. In his hand he carried a glossy black cane topped by a large gold knob.

He planted himself in front of the girls, posing with one hand on his cane, and repeated, "What the devil is going on here?"

The coachman bowed as low as he could, given the size of his stomach. "Mr. Fanshaw, sir, beggin' yer pardon. These girls were messin' about with yer horses, and—"

"We were not messing about," Mary felt compelled to interject. "We were simply standing there. It was your coachman who was rude to us."

The man turned and raised his quizzing glass to stare at her. Mary gazed back at him, startled.

Finally it was brought home to the man that his stare had left Mary unintimidated, and he dropped the glass. "I don't believe I was addressing you."

"No. I was addressing you." Mary wondered if perhaps the man was a bit dim. "I was saying that the behavior of your driver was quite rude. He began—"

At this moment the dog, apparently disappointed that the shouting had ceased, darted forward and leapt up in the air several times as if he were on springs. On the last jump, he planted his front feet on the pale green pantaloons of Mr. Fanshaw and left behind two long muddy streaks as he dropped to the ground.

Fanshaw's face turned tomato red and he let out an unearthly shriek, swinging his cane at the dog. "You cur! You wretch! You've ruined them!"

The dog easily dodged as Fanshaw lunged this way and that, trying to hit him with his cane.

"Stop!" Lily cried. "You'll hurt him! Don't hit that dog!"

In fact, the man had little chance of landing a blow, for the dog was much more agile than he and danced around the man, yapping happily. As Fanshaw whirled and stomped, brandishing his cane to no effect, the dog's gaze fell on the long tails of the man's coat, flapping enticingly. The dog darted forward and clamped his teeth into one of the coat-tails. He planted his paws and dug in, growling and shaking his head as he worried his prey.

This action sent the Honorable Mr. Fanshaw into a spasm of rage. Cursing and ranting, he whirled around and around, trying in vain to hit the dog. Firmly latched onto the tail of his coat, the dog spun with him, always out of reach.

"Damn you, Wainsley, get this mutt off me!" Fanshaw shrieked, his face so violent a shade of purple that Mary feared he might suffer a fit of apoplexy.

The coachman strode forward and kicked the dog, catching its hindquarters and sending it tumbling across the side-walk with a yelp of pain. Camellia dashed for the animal, scooping him up and facing the coachman pugnaciously, her arms wrapped protectively around it.

"Don't you dare touch him again," she warned, her eyes shooting a kind of fire that would have given a more intelligent man pause.

"You little hussy!" The coachman reached out and grabbed Camellia's arm, jerking her forward.

He raised his other hand as if to hit her, but Rose flung herself forward and wrapped both her arms tightly around his, holding it back. Even as he shook her off, Mary charged in, hands clasped together, and began to rain blows upon the man's head. Lily clawed at the hand he had clamped around Camellia's arm as Camellia tried to wrest free.

The crowd drew closer, entranced by the sight of a fop examining the tails of his coat and keening over the damagé done to them while a few feet away his hefty coachman shuffled around in a clumsy dance, warding off the blows of three young women with one hand while with the other he clung to the arm of a fourth. The dog squirmed out of Camellia's grip and landed on the sidewalk, where he proceeded to once again bark merrily at the combatants, now and then springing up in a paroxysm of joy.

It was into this scene that a gentleman strode, smoothly parting the crowd until he was standing at the edge of the inner circle. He stood for a moment, watching the struggle; then, with a sigh, he stepped forward, raised his cane, and brought it down sharply upon the coachman's head.

The burly driver staggered, blinking, and released Camellia's arm. She too stumbled backward and was steadied by a hand on her arm.

"Careful there," said the gentleman who had intervened in the scuffle.

Mary heard the voice and was swept by a wave of relief. "Sir Royce! Thank heaven!"

She turned to him, a smile breaking over her face. He swept her a bow, grinning, and in that instant she remembered that she thoroughly disliked him. A variety of conflicting emotions rushed through her, foremost among them an intense gratitude. But following directly on its heels was the humiliating knowledge that Royce had come upon her and her sisters engaged in a public brawl—a fight, moreover, that was being witnessed by a swelling crowd of people. She had been furious with him for calling her a hoyden the other night, but how could she deny his charge when here she was, wrestling with a coachman in the street?

"Well, I can see that you girls have gotten yourselves into another interesting situation." Royce's eyes danced.

Mary's lips tightened. She could not even try to make an excuse.

Lily was not so reticent. "It wasn't our fault," she cried, rushing over to Royce. "Truly it wasn't. We were just standing in front of his horses and—"

"'Ere, now, wot d'ye think ye're doin'?" The driver, recovered somewhat from the blow Royce had struck him, planted himself in front of Royce, regarding him in a bellicose manner.

"I was about to ask you the same thing," Royce replied coolly. "What were you doing to these young women?"

"Doin'! I weren't doin' nothing to 'em!" The coachman puffed up with indignation. "It were them what attacked me. And Mr. Fanshaw."

"We did nothing to Mr. Fanshaw!" Mary could not keep from joining in at this gross misstatement.

"That hound of yers did!" The driver pointed an accusing finger, and they all swung to look at the animal in question.

The dog was sitting on the sidewalk observing them with great interest, his stumpy tail wiggling back and forth. Royce gazed at him for a moment, then turned back to Mary. "You have acquired a dog?"

"No. He's not ours. He just came running up when he heard this man ranting and raving. And he did not attack Mr. Fanshaw. Well, not really." She glanced somewhat uncertainly over to where Fanshaw stood, still morosely examining the teeth marks in the tail of his coat.

The man's head came up at her words. "What do you mean? That wretched cur certainly did attack me. Just look at my pantaloons!"

"Yes, well, I'm sure you can clean them. And he did not mean to harm them," Mary replied impatiently. "He was merely excited."

"My coat is ruined!" Mr. Fanshaw stretched out his hand toward Sir Royce, shaking the end of the coattail in emphasis. "Look at these teeth marks! There's a rip, too. I cannot just clean this away. That dog ought to be done away with!"

"No!" Lily cried, and Camellia swept the dog up again, as if the fop might seize him and make good his threat.

"My good fellow, I am sure there is no need for that." Sir Royce clapped his arm around the man's shoulders in a friendly way. "Please, allow me to give you the name of my tailor. I am sure he can whip you up another coat to replace it."

As he pulled out his card case and extracted a card, Fanshaw ran an assessing eye over Royce's olive green jacket. "Weston?" he hazarded.

"Ah, I can see that you are a gentleman with a discerning eye."

"Always found his coats a bit plain for my taste."

"I am sure that Weston would welcome the chance to try something more daring." Royce smiled. "I fear that plain fellows like myself must make his work somewhat tedious. Tell him that I sent you, and he will have you fixed up as quick as you like."

"Sir Royce Winslow . . ." Fanshaw studied the calling card. "I believe I've met your cousin, Mr. Gordon Harrington."

"Of course you have."

"Splendid chap."

"Mmm. That's all settled then. I shall escort these girls home, and—"

"But what about the dog?" Fanshaw asked, frowning. "And these girls shouldn't be running about loose. They're a menace. They attacked my driver."

Sir Royce raised a quieting hand as the Bascombes all chorused a denial. "They will be taken care of, I assure you. Just up from the country, you see. Cousins . . . um, of my housekeeper. In desperate need of training, of course; I fear I'll have to insist that she send them back to Yorkshire."

"Ah, Yorkshire, is it? I thought they spoke oddly."

"Indeed." Royce tipped his hat to Fanshaw and sent a peremptory gesture to Mary and the others. "Come along, girls. We'd best get home. I shudder to think what Mrs. Hogarth will say to you."

Mary gritted her teeth at his high-handed tone, but she and her sisters fell in behind him. Lily turned to shoot a triumphant glance at the glowering coachman behind them, but Mary pinched her arm and she turned around.

"Now we're your servants?" Mary grumbled when they were a few yards away from Mr. Fanshaw and his driver.

Sir Royce chuckled. "Galled you, did that? I could scarcely tell him you're Stewkesbury's cousins; it'd be all over the city in half an hour. Four serving girls up from the country aren't worthy of gossip. Besides, it will ensure that Fanshaw won't remember you should you by some wretched chance meet him again someday. He would never recall a servant's face."

"He hardly looked at us anyway," Camellia stuck in. "All he cared about were his coattails. It's no wonder Pirate attacked them, the way the silly things were flapping about his ankles."

"Pirate?" Royce looked inquiringly at her.

"The dog. I think he looks like a pirate, don't you?"

Royce turned to consider the small animal in Camellia's arms. The dog appeared to be mostly terrier, white with black splotches beneath the dirt that begrimed him. A vaguely circular swath of black surrounded one eye, which did give him a piratical air—as did the scar that sliced up across his muzzle, pulling his lip up on one side in a sort of perpetual sneer. One ear pointed up, but the other, missing a piece at the top, drooped downward.

"I think he looks like a singularly unattractive dog," Royce replied. "Did you have to bring him with you?"

"I could hardly leave him there. That awful coachman would have killed him—well, if he had been able to catch him."

"No doubt Oliver will be delighted to have a dog about the place," Royce commented dryly.

"He will hate it, won't he?" Mary sighed. She knew her sisters. Camellia loved animals of all kinds, and Lily and Rose were both softhearted creatures. She hated to think what would happen if the earl wouldn't let them keep Pirate. "Oh dear. Perhaps we can hide the dog from him."

At that moment, Pirate took exception to a passing carriage and began to yap frantically at it. Royce cast Mary a speaking glance.

"He does have a tendency to bring attention to himself," Mary admitted. "But we will be here only a few days. Then we'll be in the country, and the earl won't have to see him. Or hear him."

"Or have him nip at his coattails," Royce added.

"Only if they flutter about." Mary giggled. "You should have seen that man whirling this way and that, trying to whack the dog with his cane, and his coattails twirling around."

Royce chuckled. "I think I understand the dog and Fanshaw, but why were you tussling with the coachman?"

"He kicked Pirate!" Rose told him, remembered indignation turning her cheeks pink. "And then, when Camellia snatched him up, the man was about to hit *her*."

Royce's brows rose. "You're joking. Obviously I should have thumped him harder."

"Yes, you should have," Lily agreed. "Only he couldn't hit Camellia because Rose grabbed his arm. Then Mary started to hit him, but he wouldn't let go, so I tried to pry his hand loose, but he was quite strong. I would have bitten his hand, but he had on those big driving gloves, so that would have been no use."

Royce choked back a laugh. "No. I fear not." They continued walking for a few moments in silence. "I am sure I must be a bit slow, but I still don't quite comprehend what his horses had to do with it."

"They didn't have anything to do with it," Mary told him. "I don't know why he kept blathering on about them. We didn't touch his horses. We were standing in front of them, that's all, because it was the best place to hide."

"Hide?" Royce's brows rose. "You were hiding?"

"Yes. Well, you see, we thought this man was following us."

"He *was* following us," Camellia interjected. "Because as soon as we turned that corner and hid, he came around it, looking about for us."

"*Who* was following you?" Royce kept determinedly to his point.

"I haven't any idea. We didn't know him. Well, we wouldn't, would we?" Mary asked reasonably. "We don't know anyone here."

"He was quite large and ferocious-looking." Lily gestured with her hands to show his height and breadth.

"He was large," Mary agreed. "Though in all fairness, I would not say he looked ferocious. We could not see his face really until he came around the corner, and then he just looked puzzled."

Lily sighed. "You haven't the slightest bit of drama in you."

"Do you have any idea why he might have been following you?" Royce asked carefully. "You didn't by chance do anything or say anything to him—"

"No," Mary said firmly. "We were never close enough to say anything. We just saw him walking a block or so behind us. Later on, he was still behind us. That's when we turned the corner and hid in front of the carriage, so that we could find out whether he was in fact following us. When we saw that he was, Camellia jumped out to ask him why—"

Royce let out a muffled groan. "Of course."

"But he turned and ran," Camellia put in contemptuously.

"Were you brandishing your knife, by any chance?"

"No." Camellia's brows drew together in irritation. "I didn't take it with me. I can see now that I should have. I didn't realize that it was so dangerous in the city."

"Mmm. Neither did I," Royce agreed.

"That dreadful coachman said that it was because our skirts showed our ankles." Lily stuck one foot out, peering down at the offending limb. "But I think he was just being rude. I don't think they're offensive, do you? It's not as if you can see them beneath our boots."

"Indeed not. I never find the sight of a lady's ankle offensive. I think 'tis far more likely that some lout, seeing four comely young women, unescorted, might have followed, thinking that he would try his luck at, um, making unwanted advances."

"To four of us?" Mary asked skeptically.

Royce shrugged. "Perhaps that is why he was trailing behind, in the hopes that you might split up."

"Well, really!" Mary grimaced. "If that isn't the outside of enough! Can we not even go for a walk in London without being accosted?"

"I would not think 'twould be a problem in the normal

course of events—as long, of course, as it is not one of you entirely by herself. But, if you will remember what Cousin Charlotte told you, your attire is, um . . ."

"Yes, yes, we realize that our clothes are unfashionable." Mary cast him a flashing glance. "Everyone has gone to great pains to point that out. But how does that attract louts such as this one?"

"It is, perhaps, not readily apparent that you are young ladies of quality. Now, if you had a maid walking with you or a gentleman escorting you, I doubt there would be any problem. I, for one, would be quite happy to offer you my services in that regard."

"So we are stuck inside unless we drag a maid along with us? Or get you or Cousin Fitz?"

"I think we should take Papa's rifle with us, like we do when we go berry hunting in the woods," Camellia offered.

"Sweet Lord." A spasm crossed Sir Royce's face.

"No, we can't do that," Mary said. "Everyone already thinks we're odd enough. I know it's a trial, but we'll be in the country soon enough." She turned to Royce. "We can walk there without any problem, I presume?"

"Of course." Royce frowned. "But you can walk here as well. Simply take a maid if you don't wish to wait for one of us men."

"With all the work they have to do?" Rose spoke up. "They wouldn't want to have to trail about after us as well."

Her comment left Sir Royce without words for a moment. Finally he said, "I think she might prefer to trail after you than clean the fireplace or dust the mantel."

"Yes, but she would still have them to do after she returned," Rose said with the air of one who spoke from experience.

"I would feel a fool, having a maid trudging along behind me," Camellia added.

"But what are we going to do?" Lily wailed. "It's terribly boring here."

"Boring? In the city?"

"In that house," Lily replied feelingly. "There is nothing to do. We've looked. There isn't a single interesting book in that whole huge library. No games. We couldn't even find a pack of cards. I almost wished for a few stockings to darn."

"Ah, now there I can help you." Sir Royce smiled. "I know where the games are."

"There *are* games?" The girls brightened a little.

"Yes, indeed. You should have asked Oliver's butler. He would have brought them to you."

"Oh, no!" Lily looked shocked. "We couldn't ask *him*. He doesn't like us."

"Has Hooper been rude to you?" Royce asked.

"No. But he never smiles. At all."

"Butlers never do," he assured her. "But it doesn't matter. You can find all the games you'd like upstairs in the nursery. And probably more entertaining books as well. We did not usually accompany our parents to London, but now and then we did, and the nursery was kept equipped, in any case. There is a card room, too."

"A room just to keep cards?"

"For *playing* cards. It has tables and chairs and all the necessary items. There are always those at a party who'd rather retire for a few hands of whist, particularly among the older set. It's the best way of getting Aunt Euphronia out of one's way, I can assure you. I will show you where it is. Ah, here we are."

The footman who opened the door looked so relieved he almost smiled as he greeted them. "His lordship will be pleased to hear that you have returned."

"Ah. Then Stewkesbury is here?" Royce said.

"He just returned from his club, sir. He was, um, a bit concerned about his cousins."

"I shall have to apologize to him for keeping them out so long, then, shan't I?" Royce handed the man his hat, gloves, and cane.

The footman, setting down Sir Royce's possessions, turned to take the girls' bonnets as well. The dog, nestled comfortably in Camellia's arms, took exception to the move and snarled.

"Good G—" The footman swallowed his words, but he continued to eye Pirate as he took the other hats. "I, uh, I'll just tell his lordship you are here."

"We'll be in the card room." Royce turned to Mary and her sisters and ushered them down the hall.

The dog, intrigued by his new surroundings, jumped down from Camellia's arms and trotted along with them, bounding out in front then returning, his stump of a tail wagging so hard that his entire hindquarters wriggled. When they reached the card room, he grew even more excited, running from one end to the other, leaping onto chairs and even on top of one of the tables.

"Ah, Royce. Ladies." The earl's smooth voice came from the open doorway. "I am glad to see that you have returned."

"Yes. I met your cousins talking a walk," Royce began, but Oliver held up a hand:

"Please, spare me whatever tale you have concocted."

"Tale?" Royce's eyes widened innocently. "Why, there is no tale; I simply was enjoying the girls' company so much that I fear we went a little far. I apologize if we worried—" He broke off as Pirate, spotting a new person, charged over to join them.

"Good God." Stewkesbury stared at the little dog, which

was now jumping up and down like a mad thing, wiggling and twisting. "What . . . is that?"

"Pirate!" Mary darted forward to grab the dog. "Blast it!" The animal leaped nimbly out of reach and darted away. "Camellia! Catch it!"

The two men watched as the girls gave chase, but Pirate, thoroughly enjoying this new game, ran here and there, bouncing off chairs and skidding across the polished floor, weaving in and out among the chairs and tables.

"I see you acquired a dog upon your walk," the earl commented.

"Your cousins rather took a fancy to the creature."

The earl cast a sideways glance at Royce, who opened his mouth to attempt an explanation of the dog's presence among them.

"No." The earl shook his head. "I don't want to know."

Raising two fingers to his lips, the earl let out a piercing whistle that had the effect of stopping everyone in the room. The girls turned, and Pirate raced back, once again flinging himself into the air in a frenzy before the earl. Mary dreaded what the earl would have to say.

"You!" Stewkesbury fixed the dog with a stern gaze and snapped his fingers once. He pointed to the ground. "Stop. Sit."

To the amazement of everyone, Pirate promptly plopped his hindquarters on the floor and gazed up at Stewkesbury, his tongue lolling out of his mouth in a fatuous grin.

The earl gazed at the animal for a long moment. "That is perhaps the ugliest dog I have ever had the misfortune to meet."

"He's quite bright," Camellia offered. "And see how well he minds?"

"Quite." The earl pressed his lips together tightly.

"Well, he cannot stay here unless he has had a thorough washing."

The Bascombes, who had all sagged in disappointment at the first part of his sentence, immediately erupted in an explosion of thanks. Stewkesbury, shaking his head, held up a hand and began to back away.

"And when you have done that, I would like to see all of you in my study."

He turned and left the room. The girls glanced at one another.

"Oh dear." Mary reached down and scooped up the dog. "I fear we are in for a scolding."

"At least we get to keep Pirate," Camellia pointed out.

"Yes." Mary looked down at the creature in her arms and had to chuckle. "A mixed blessing, no doubt." She handed him over to Camellia. "Here, go find a tub or something to bathe him in. I will be there in a moment."

The other three girls trooped out of the room, and Mary turned back to Sir Royce. During the walk home, she had talked with him easily enough. It had been hard to hold on to her anger, given his rescue of them, and the presence of her sisters had made it seem more natural. But now, standing here alone with him, she felt suddenly awkward.

"I-I wanted to thank you for what you did back there. With Mr. Fanshaw and the coachman and all. And for pretending to the earl that you had been with us much longer than you were."

Royce shrugged. "It was little enough."

"No. It was quite a bit. It's the second time you have rescued us—no, the third time, really, since you brought us here to meet our cousin when I could not get in to see him."

He smiled. "Yes, well . . . I shall have to keep my armor

polished. Never know when you'll need a knight again." He paused, then moved closer to her. "Mary . . ."

He was standing so close that she had to tilt back her head to look into his face. She could smell the subtle scent of him, and it stirred something deep within her. She could not help but remember the way his lips had felt on hers, the pressure of his hand upon her waist, the strength of his arms around her. What did it say about her that, even knowing his disdain for her, she could still think with longing of that kiss? Could still wish, deep down, to feel it again?

"I am truly sorry for what I said the other night," he told her, his eyes warm as they looked into hers. "And I am even sorrier that you should have heard it. I was annoyed with Oliver and his high-handed ways, and I spoke without thinking. I would not have hurt you for the world."

Royce was far too easy to like, she thought. And, as she had found out this afternoon, it was difficult to remain angry at him, especially when he said something that made her laugh, or smiled in that way he had with the corners of his eyes crinkling up, or, as he was doing now, looked deep into her eyes, so that it felt as if he could see into the very depths of her.

Mary shifted away from him. "I know," she said, choosing her words carefully, "that you would not have said what you did had you known that I was listening."

However angry she had been, Mary did not think that Royce would knowingly have hurt her. But that did not change the fact that he believed what he had said. Royce frowned, obviously aware of the lack of full forgiveness in her words.

Mary went on quickly, "You need not continue to seek my forgiveness. They say one will not hear good about oneself if one listens outside doors. I should not have intruded upon your conversation with your stepbrother. Besides"—she shrugged—"given the situation you found us in this afternoon, I can hardly claim that your description of us was wrong or unfair. How can I blame you for speaking the truth? My sisters and I are not, I fear, suitable wives for Englishmen. I do not envy this governess's task of molding us into proper ladies."

"Do not allow her to change you too much."

Mary gave him a speaking look. "Do you wish us to remain unwed?"

"You would not remain unwed. Believe me. There will be any number of men who will fall at your feet." He moved closer to her, looking down into her face. "Some man will find himself falling into those blue eyes, and all will be lost. He'll want nothing but to be with you, to whisper into your ear, to kiss your cheek, your brow, your lips. . . ."

He leaned closer. Mary stared at him, wide-eyed, unable to look away. Unable, indeed, to move or even breathe. His words touched her like a physical caress, and she could feel her body tightening in response.

Abruptly, Royce turned away. "Many men will want to marry you."

"Just not you." Mary realized as soon as she spoke how her words sounded, as if she wanted him to marry her. She tried desperately to think of something that would somehow change her words.

But Royce seemed not to notice any awkwardness. "No. Not I. I have no intention of marrying anyone."

"Ever?"

He shrugged. "I see no reason to. There are those who have to marry. Oliver, for instance. He will doubtless search until he finds the perfect woman to give him heirs and excel as the Countess of Stewkesbury. I have little interest in either heirs or my duty."

"Some people have an interest in falling in love." Mary wasn't sure why his adamant words annoyed her, but she found herself wanting to argue the point.

"Love is for fools."

Mary stared at him. "How can you say that?"

He shrugged. "I've seen enough of those afflicted with it. My mother was very much in love with Oliver's father. So in love that they had little interest in the rest of us. All that mattered was their grand passion. Of course, there were also the jealous scenes, the tears and the tantrums, the remorse. And before you knew it, they were back in each other's arms, madly in love."

"My parents were in love, and they were not like that. They were happy with each other—and with us."

"Then you are a lucky woman, and your parents were lucky as well. It is not the normal state of things."

"I am not sure your view is either." Mary paused, studying him. She could not help but wonder if there was more to his vehement dislike of love. There had been something so bitter in his eyes when he said that love was for fools. However, she felt sure that whatever it was, she would not get it out of him today.

"So . . ." she said lightly, "I am not the only female you have no wish to marry?"

A half-smile touched his lips. "True. There are any number of females I do not intend to marry."

"At least I am not alone."

"What about us? Do you forgive me? Are we friends again?"

"Were we friends before?" Mary asked.

"You wound me. After I have rescued you two—nay, three times? And we are not friends?"

Mary laughed at his mock indignation. "All right. Yes, we are friends."

The truth was, she wasn't sure what they were. There was still, she knew, an ache deep in her heart from what he had said the other night. Yet she believed him when he told her he had not meant to hurt her. She enjoyed his company. It would be pointless to try to maintain an icy aloofness with him.

But was it friendship when each time you saw a person, the first thing you thought of was kissing him?

Chapter 11

After Royce left, Mary went in search of her sisters. It did not take long to find them, as they were all roaming the upstairs hall, whistling and calling, "Pirate!"

Mary let out a groan. "What happened? Did you lose him?"

"Mary!" The others brightened when they saw her. "Have you seen him?"

"No. I thought you were bathing him."

"We were," Lily told her.

"Though I can tell you he didn't like it by half," Camellia confided. "My dress was completely soaked. Lily was supposed to dry him while I put on a different dress." She looked pointedly at her younger sister. "And she let him go."

Lily rolled her gray-green eyes. "I didn't *let* him go. He escaped. He's terribly slippery," she confided to Mary.

"That's why I told you to hold on to him," Camellia reminded her.

"All right, all right." Rose raised her hand wearily. "We have been through this before. It doesn't matter. Pirate is gone, and we have no idea where he is."

"Oh, dear." Mary shuddered at the thought of the damage the small dog could cause in this elegant household.

"Well, we must find him quickly. The earl expects us in his study."

The four young women hunted diligently, but they could find no sign of the small dog. Finally, giving up, they went downstairs. While Mary dreaded what Pirate might do before they found him, she dreaded even more keeping the earl waiting. The door to the earl's study stood open and he was at his desk, a ledger book open before him. He glanced up as Mary and her sisters stopped in the doorway.

"Cousins." He stood up and started around the desk. "Please, come in."

He went around them to close the door as the girls moved forward to stand somewhat uncertainly before his desk, glancing around at the heavy, dark masculine furniture.

"Pirate!" Camellia exclaimed.

Her sisters whirled to glare at her, and Camellia pointed to the small black-and-white dog stretched out on his side on the floor in a square of late-afternoon sunlight streaming through the windowpanes. Pirate opened his eyes and lifted his head at the sound of his name. "He's here! Look."

"Yes," the earl agreed. "He came in some time ago, looking like a fox with the hounds after him."

"We bathed him," Camellia explained.

"So I gathered." The earl glanced over at the dog. "I must say, it hasn't improved his appearance markedly." Oliver gestured toward the chairs arranged in a conversational grouping near the windows. "Please, sit down."

He waited politely for them to be seated, then took the remaining chair. Pirate, who had gotten up and trotted over to greet the girls, now lay down beside the earl, resting his head on the toe of the earl's boot.

Stewkesbury followed their shocked gazes. "Yes, he seems to have taken an unaccountable liking to me."

"I-I'm sorry," Mary told him. "I—is he bothering you? Would you like us to take him away?"

The earl waved his hand negligently. "'Tis no problem. As you will be leaving for the country soon, it won't last long."

For a long, awkward moment, the four girls and the man regarded one another silently. Finally, he began, "If I recall correctly, Cousin Charlotte is taking you shopping tomorrow."

Mary's heart sank. Was he going to take away their shopping trip because of the scrape they had gotten into today? She didn't dare look at her sisters. Lily especially would be crushed.

"It occurred to me," the earl went on, "that you would need pin money. Charlotte, of course, will have the bills sent to me, but there will surely be small things like ribbons and candies and such that you will want to purchase yourselves."

His words were such a surprise to Mary that she could not speak. Clearly her sisters were equally astonished, for all of them simply sat there, gaping at him. Oliver rose and went to his desk, took out a stack of notes, and handed several to each girl. Mary stared at the money. She was not sure exactly how much a British pound was in comparison to American money, but she rather thought that it was worth more. And five of them—for each sister!—seemed a great deal to spend on ribbons and candy.

"But, sir," she said at last. "Surely this is too much."

The earl regarded her with faint surprise. "I wouldn't think so. Perhaps I should consult Charlotte. I fear I haven't much experience with outfitting young ladies. But I would expect there are a number of things you might wish to purchase on your own, and it is, after all, for the whole month."

"The month!" Rose repeated in amazement.

"Yes. I think it should be adequate for that, but if it is not, we can discuss it later."

"But, sir . . ." Mary looked at him with some distress. "We cannot accept this." She ignored Lily's surreptitious pinch. "I never thought—I didn't dream—that is, we did not intend to be such a burden to you. I did not realize what it would be like here."

"I am afraid I don't understand."

"We expected to find our grandfather, and it seemed only natural that he would take in his grandchildren. But you are only our cousin. It hardly seems fair to expect you to support us. And I assumed that we would do something for our grandfather in return for our upkeep, not just batten on him."

"Do something?" he repeated blankly.

"Yes, you know, *work*. Help clean or cook or tend the garden—something to help earn our keep." At the earl's astounded expression, she went on quickly, "I realize now that that is not possible. But I never meant for you to feed us and clothe us and have servants do everything for us."

"But you are Talbots. What else would I do? Had my grandfather known of your existence, he would have done these things for you. He should, quite frankly, have made provision for you in his will. As he did not, I am duty-bound to provide for you."

"I understand that. And we are very grateful, believe me. But surely you are not duty-bound to provide for us in so grand a way. I think that we must give this back."

The earl regarded her for a moment. "My dear cousin, I have a certain reputation to uphold. If my cousins were to go about the city penniless and dressed in rags, I would be subject to public ridicule. I should be labeled miserly, mean—or worse, they would say I could not afford to dress you properly, that I was run off my legs. Surely you do not wish to be the cause of my public humiliation?"

"No, of course not. But—"

"No, no." He held up his hands. "There are no 'buts.' I know London. I would be pilloried by the gossips."

"Because you did not give us pin money?" Mary asked with some skepticism.

He shrugged. "A title carries a great deal of responsibility."

Mary had the distinct impression that she was being manipulated by the earl, but she realized that it was rather ludicrous to continue to argue, especially when he obviously considered the amount of money negligible. "If that is what you wish, of course. Thank you. It is very kind of you."

"As for earning your keep, I believe you will find it sufficient work learning all you need to know to make your debuts next Season," he went on. "However, if you wish for something more to do, it occurs to me you might want to look through your mother's things while you are at Willowmere."

"Really?" Mary glanced at her sisters, then back at the earl. "There are still some of her things there?"

"I imagine so. Such items are usually packed up and stored in the attic. There are items up there from generations ago. Grandfather was hurt and angry, but I do not think he would have gone so far as to toss out all her possessions."

"Thank you." Mary beamed at him. "Thank you so much."

The earl had done a great deal for them, more than she would have ever guessed he would. But this, she thought, this opportunity to get a glimpse of her mother's early life, was more valuable to her than any amount of clothes or money.

*   *   *

Not long after breakfast the following day, Cousin Charlotte returned to Stewkesbury House, trailed by a slight middle-aged woman carrying a small bag.

"Hello, cousins," she called gaily as the butler showed her into the morning room. "I have brought Miss Ransom, the wonderful seamstress I was telling you about. Lady Vivian is going to meet us here, so I thought I would have Miss Ransom measure you while we wait. Then we can go buy the cloth for her to sew up into your new frocks."

The sisters trooped up to Mary and Rose's bedroom, where, to their surprise, Miss Ransom made them all strip down to their chemises. Pulling a tape measure, a pad, and a stub of a pencil from her bag, she proceeded to measure them from top to toe, all the while jotting down notes. It was the better part of an hour before she declared that she had ample information and Charlotte sent her on her way.

"Now we shall wait for Vivian," Charlotte said as they settled again in the morning room downstairs. "With luck, she won't be terribly late."

"Is she usually late?" Lily asked.

Charlotte shrugged. "Vivian is never 'usually' anything. But she does follow her own sense of time."

Fitz strolled into the morning room, and after a few min-utes the earl joined them, Pirate trotting at his heels. The dog made a grand tour, greeting everyone with a great deal of wriggling and jumping. Then he returned to the earl and plopped down beside him. As seemed to be his habit when he was not tearing about, he stretched out on his side and fell instantly and soundly asleep.

Charlotte, who had eyed Pirate's entrance and prog-ress about the room with some astonishment, said at last, "Stewkesbury . . . don't tell me you have acquired a dog."

"Not my dog," he informed her.

"We found him on the street yesterday," Camellia offered. "So we brought him home with us."

"Indeed. But how—"

The earl shook his head. "I suspect it's better not to know. That way when the constable comes knocking on my door, I shan't have to lie."

Lily's protest that there had been nothing illegal about their acquisition of Pirate was interrupted by the butler, who entered and said with great dignity, "Lady Vivian Carlyle, my lord."

"Vivian!" Charlotte exclaimed with delight, rising to her feet.

"Lord help us," the earl muttered with a good deal less enthusiasm, also rising.

A woman with deep auburn hair swept into the room on the heels of the butler. She wore a walking dress of emerald green, and a black velvet heart-shaped bonnet framed her face, dipping romantically in the center almost to her forehead and lushly lined with pleated silk. A feather of the same vivid green curled across the middle of the hat from the back. On any other woman, the dramatic bonnet might have stolen the viewer's eye, but on this woman it served merely as a backdrop to one of the most beautiful faces Mary had ever seen.

Vivian Carlyle's eyes were large and wide-set in a perfectly proportioned face, and they were of a shade of green as arresting as her dress. There were those who said (though never in public) that Lady Vivian's mouth was a trifle too large and her jaw a bit too strong for true beauty, but such minor imperfections were not noticeable to Mary and her sisters. Nor were they, as some genteel people were, put off by the woman's open, candid gaze and air of confidence.

"Hallo, Stewkesbury, don't look so nervous," Lady Vivian said, offering her hand to the earl in response to his bow. "I shan't be here long. We have a day's worth of shopping ahead of—" She glanced down and saw the dog, which had risen and padded along after the earl and now stood gazing up at Vivian with interest. "Good Lord. Oliver, is that *your* dog?"

The earl glanced down at Pirate. "I am beginning to think so."

"Well." Vivian looked from Oliver to the dog and back again. "Clearly you must have hidden depths."

The earl cocked a sardonic eyebrow at her. "If they are represented by that dog, I dread to think what they might be."

Vivian laughed and turned to greet Charlotte and Fitz. Last, she went to Mary and her sisters, holding out her hand and saying, "And you must be the Bascombes. Charlotte has told me so much about you. I'm pleased to make your acquaintance."

Charlotte introduced each of the sisters to Lady Vivian. After a few moments of polite chitchat, the women bade good-bye to Fitz and the earl and left on their mission. Lady Vivian's smart hunter-green barouche waited in front of the house, drawn by four matched grays, its leather top folded back to allow the ladies to see and be seen. A liveried footman jumped forward to fold down the step and hand the women up into the vehicle. It was a bit of a squeeze, but fortunately the barouche was roomy as well as luxurious, and the women were slender.

"Now," Charlotte said as the carriage rolled away from the curb, "you must tell me about this dog and how he came to be following Stewkesbury about."

"Yes, do," Lady Vivian urged. "I was never so surprised as I was to see the earl with that, that . . ." Words apparently failed her, and she had to laugh.

Lily, by consensus the best storyteller, began to relate their experiences with the coachman, the dog, and the Honorable Mr. Pinkley Fanshaw. By the time they reached New Bond Street, Vivian and Charlotte were laughing so hard they cried.

"Oh my." Charlotte dabbed her handkerchief to her eyes. "What I wouldn't have given to have seen that man whirling about with the dog hanging on to his coattails!"

"Do you know Fanshaw?" Vivian asked.

"No, do you?"

"A little. If you knew him, you would be even more delighted at the thought of his dance with Pirate. He's a terrible fop; no absurdity is too outrageous for him."

"He sounds like Cousin Gordon," Charlotte commented.

"Worse. At least Gordon Harrington has the excuse of being eighteen years old. Fanshaw is approaching forty and still has the sense of a goose."

The barouche pulled to a stop, and the footman sprang down from his seat to assist them out. Mary followed the others, glancing around at the busy commercial area. As far as the eye could see, there were shops on either side of the street.

"Where are we going?" she asked.

"Grafton House first," Charlotte replied. "One has to get here before eleven or it's horridly crowded; one can hardly find a shop assistant to help."

Such was not the case now, Mary saw. Although there were more customers inside than she had ever seen in a store before, a clerk was immediately by their side, bowing and offering his assistance. Mary had the suspicion that even had they come at the height of the day's business, someone would have rushed forward to help Lady Vivian.

Neither Mary nor her sisters paid any attention to the shop assistant, however, for they were gazing about them in wonder. On every side were row upon row of bolts of cloth, some rolled up and set in large shelves, others standing on cabinets or atop the shelves, the material hanging off them in a luxurious fall of color. Even in Philadelphia, Mary had not seen so large a store devoted almost entirely to fabrics. On wooden counters that ran down either side of the store, clerks rolled out bolts of cloth to show their customers or to measure and cut lengths. Most of the customers strolled about, gazing at the materials, or stood at the counters, but the assistant whisked out stools for Vivian and Charlotte, settling them at one counter and eagerly fetching down whatever cloth they wished to examine.

At first Mary and her sisters wandered through the store, almost stunned by the wealth of fabrics—elegant silks and satins, plain flannels and wools, linens, velvets, brocades, dimities, muslins—but Charlotte soon called them back and they settled down to the task at hand. Soon they were choosing cloth after cloth from a dizzying array.

When, after a time, Mary glanced over at the stack of fabrics that had been measured and cut and set aside for them, she was astonished at its size. "Oh my, we have purchased too much, surely."

"Nonsense," Charlotte assured her. "We have just begun. There are four of you, after all, and you need . . . well, everything."

"The earl has been most generous to us. But . . . are you sure he will not mind?"

Vivian, on the other side of Charlotte, let out a little hoot of laughter. "Stewkesbury? He'll scarcely notice it's gone. He inherited a fortune from Lord Reginald, and everyone knows he's done nothing but increase it. He doesn't gamble; he doesn't throw it away on horses and carriages and clothes; he rarely even sets up expensive *chères-amies*—" She stopped abruptly and cast a guilty look at

Lily and Camellia, who were regarding her with great interest. "That is to say, the man lives a remarkably plain life for one in his position."

"Are you talking about mistresses?" Camellia asked, looking astonished.

"I'm sorry," Vivian said quickly. "I spoke out of turn. I had forgotten, you see, that you are only girls—oh dear."

"I wouldn't have thought of *him* having a mistress," Camellia went on. "I can hardly imagine him taking off his neckcloth."

Her words surprised a giggle out of Charlotte, who clapped a hand to her mouth, and Vivian began to laugh. "I feared *I* had been too blunt."

"Camellia . . ." Rose gave her sister an admonitory look. "That's exactly why he's making us have a chaperone who's also a governess."

"No, really?" Vivian asked.

Mary sighed. "Yes. He says we aren't ready for polite society. I fear he's right."

"I find you perfectly delightful," Vivian responded. "However, 'tis probably true that you need to curb your tongues around many of the *ton*. Still, a governess—I'm not sure that is exactly the sort of chaperone you need." She shrugged. "Of course, if Oliver's made up his mind, there's no changing it. He always was an excessively stubborn man, even back when I used to visit Charlotte at Willowmere."

"You and Cousin Charlotte have been friends a long time?" Rose asked.

"Longer than either of us care to recall, I imagine." Lady Vivian cast a droll look at her friend. "Lord Humphrey— my father's younger brother—lives at Halstead House, not far from Willowmere, and I used to visit him and my aunt in the summers when I was a girl. My mother died when

I was born, and I had only brothers, so Papa thought it good for me to have my aunt's influence. I loved Halstead House. And since Charlotte and her mother were often at Willowmere after the Season ended, I had a bosom friend there as well, which was even more wonderful." She smiled at the Bascombes. "You have no idea what it's like, growing up with all brothers. I envy you; I always wanted a sister so."

Mary could not imagine growing up without her sisters—and without a mother as well. "I'm very sorry," she said impulsively, reaching out to lay a hand upon the other woman's arm. "It must have been very hard for you."

Surprise tinged Vivian's face. Then she smiled dazzlingly. "How kind of you." She squeezed Mary's hand, then turned toward her friend. "You know, Charlotte, I believe I shall visit my uncle again now that the Season is winding down. Perhaps you and I could drive up there, say, after Lady Cudlington's ball? It would give us all a chance to visit—and to discuss our plans for next Season."

Charlotte agreed, smiling. Later, when Lady Vivian had wandered off to examine a bolt of dark maroon brocade, Charlotte told the girls, "You have won Lady Vivian over."

"She is very nice," Rose said. "'Tis easy to like her."

"Yes, but it's hard for most to see past the fact that she is a duke's daughter. There are a few whom she has known for years and years to whom she is close. But most people are interested in her more for her position or wealth than for Vivian herself. It's a pleasant surprise to her *not* to be treated like a Carlyle. It's even rarer for someone to understand that her life has not been perfect."

"I wasn't trying to win her over," Mary protested.

"I know. So does Vivian. That's why she likes you. Now,

let's choose between these two sprig muslins, Lily, and we must leave. There's a great deal left to be done."

They soon discovered that Charlotte was not exaggerating. When it came to shopping, their affable cousin was all business, and she ushered them from store to store, buying a mind-boggling array of products. They visited a glover, a shoemaker, a hosier, a plumassier (a diversion made for Lady Vivian, who wished to find a certain feather for retrimming one of her bonnets), and a milliner. They bought fans; they bought reticules; they bought buttons, handkerchiefs, lace, and ribbons. Having always worn stockings they knitted themselves, the Bascombes were elated to find ones made entirely by machine. Mary bought several pairs of cotton stockings, and she could not resist a pair or two of silk hose with cotton feet. But she could not bring herself to go so far as Lily and purchase a pair of silk stockings with embroidery at the ankles, meant to be worn with an evening gown. Rose bought a beautifully knitted shawl and derived almost as much pleasure from paying for it herself as she did from possessing it. And Lily, when they passed Hatchard's, had to go in and get a book. Mary, watching as Lily found not one but two novels she could not live without, reflected that Lily's money was perhaps not destined to last an entire month.

Still, Charlotte informed them, their labors were not done. Their last visit was to be to a mantua maker. When Camellia protested that they had just bought a wealth of fabrics for the seamstress to make up into dresses, Charlotte simply shook her head.

"Those were but day dresses. You must have an evening gown or two. Even in the country, one dresses for dinner."

There was some discussion between Vivian and Charlotte as to which modiste to see, for Vivian, it seemed, relied entirely on the skills of Madame Arceneaux, but Charlotte, who frequented several mantua makers, held that Mademoiselle Ruelle, while not as exquisite in her taste perhaps, turned out a dress in a shorter time.

In the end it was Vivian who won the day, saying flatly, "Trust me, Charlotte, Madame Arceneaux will have the dresses done on time. The prospect of making eight evening gowns, with the bills to be paid by someone as punctual as Lord Stewkesbury, would make her finish them in half the days."

So they went to Madame Arceneaux's shop, a small but elegant establishment on Oxford Street. Madame herself came sweeping out of the rear of the shop to greet Lady Vivian, and when she heard what was required of her, she set her assistants hopping with a few snaps of her fingers. The girls were whisked away to once again be poked, prodded, and measured, but any weariness or annoyance was swept away when they sat down with Charlotte, Vivian, and the modiste herself to look through books of drawings of possible dresses. It was, the Bascombes agreed, annoying that they could not choose anything but white, for all were drawn to the sea greens and pale yellows favored by Charlotte or the more vivid emeralds and royal blues that Vivian fancied. However, they were soon immersed in discussions of fabrics, overskirts, necklines, fichus, lace trim, and the like, and the sameness of color was quite forgotten.

By the time they were through, each girl had managed to choose two new evening gowns, and Madame Arceneaux was positively beaming with delight—not least because Lady Vivian, while waiting, had discovered that she could not live without a gold-and-white–striped gossamer evening dress with a stomacher front and a blue jaconet muslin morning dress ornamented by long sleeves *en bouffants,* while Charlotte had become equally enamored of a pelisse in brown levantine silk. All returned to Stewkesbury House well pleased with their day.

Unfortunately, the Bascombes had no sooner bid goodbye to their new friends and gone inside than their spirits were lowered by the earl, who stepped out into the hall and said, "Ah, there you are. Glad you've returned. Come in and meet your new companion."

The girls exchanged a look, but followed him obediently into the drawing room. "Allow me to introduce you to Miss Dalrymple," the earl went on with what Mary thought was far too much satisfaction. "She has agreed to accompany you to Willowmere and instruct you for the next few weeks."

He turned toward the woman sitting on the sofa. She was square and dour, with dark brown hair pulled into a severe knot atop her head and thick dark eyebrows that ran straight across her forehead, almost meeting in the middle and giving her the look of a perpetual frown.

After spending a half hour in the woman's company, Mary decided that perhaps the look was less a result of Miss Dalrymple's unfortunate brow than of her cheerless personality. During that same period of time, Miss Dalrymple corrected the posture of each of the sisters at least once, reproved Camellia for her unrefined language, and held forth on the superiority of the British female to that of any other country. By the time she departed, Mary was wondering how she would keep her sisters from rebelling. Indeed, she thought that she might be inclined to lead the revolution.

After the governess left, the earl put the final cap on their misery by saying, "Fortunately, Miss Dalrymple is available to work right away, so the day after tomorrow you will be able to leave for Willowmere."

Mary's heart sank. As she and her sisters trooped dejectedly up to their rooms, Lily expressed what all of them were thinking: "I don't want to go to Willowmere with that awful woman!"

"She's horrid." Even Rose, usually the most easygoing of creatures, agreed. "It will be nothing but 'do this, don't do that.'"

"And no friends. I was looking forward to seeing Cousin Charlotte and Lady Vivian again," Lily said.

"*I* was looking forward to going to Astley's Amphitheater." Camellia scowled. "Cousin Fitz said he would take us. He said they have the most amazing spectacles, where they stage replicas of famous battles."

"And the Tower. Sir Royce said he would show us the Tower." Lily gave a shiver of delight. "Where Anne Boleyn was beheaded, and the little princes were murdered. And Traitor's Gate."

"I'd rather see the horse riding," Camellia said flatly. After a moment's consideration, she added, "But the Tower sounds very exciting, too."

"Anything would be more exciting than being stuck way out in the country with Miss Dalrymple." Mary was as disgruntled as any of them. What she would not have admitted to anyone—what, indeed, she wished were not true—was that she was filled with disappointment not for any of her sisters' reasons but because she would no longer see Sir Royce every day or, indeed, at all.

It was the height of foolishness, she knew. Even if she had thawed toward him a great deal yesterday, it did not mean that they were friends. Certainly they were not, could not be, anything more. Yet when she thought of not seeing his eyes light up or his lips curve into a smile or his eyebrow rise in that cynical, amused way for weeks, even months to come, her life at Willowmere seemed unbearably dull and dark. And the fact that she felt that way left her decidedly irritated.

That evening at dinner, however, all the sisters were some-what reconciled to their imminent departure when Royce and Fitz, upon learning of the haste with which the Bas-combes would be leaving London, suggested that they spend the next day pursuing one of the adventures the two of them had promised. Camellia and Fitz preferred the horses and spectacle of Astley's to the history and romance of the Tower, but they were outvoted.

Accordingly, the next morning the six of them set out from Stewkesbury House, armed with a guidebook and looking, according to Fitz, like proper gawkers. However, it did not take long for both Fitz and Camellia to be caught up in their visit to the Tower, listening with the others to the Yeoman Warder's grisly tales of the presumed murders of Edward IV's two young sons by their uncle Richard of Gloucester or the terror of the young Princess Elizabeth when she was taken into the Tower through Traitor's Gate and fell to the stairs, weeping, refusing to budge, afraid that she would enter the Tower and never leave, like her ill-fated mother, Anne Boleyn.

"I don't think I would have wanted to be a princess," Rose said. "It sounds more frightening than romantic."

"I have to say it seems easier to elect a president than to go about killing one's relatives in order to be king," Mary agreed.

"It's not so much the way we do things anymore," Royce said mildly.

Lily rolled her eyes. "Honestly, sometimes I wonder if I'm really related to the rest of you. How can you be so pro-saic? Doesn't your heart just squeeze in your chest when you think of that poor Lady Jane Grey—younger than I am, made queen and then in a week or so, all of that is lost, and she's sent to her death?" She paused dramatically, her hands clasped together at her heart.

A snort from Camellia followed her speech. "Come on, Sarah Siddons. I want to go down and see the lions."

"Oooh, I want to see that, too. But we mustn't forget the jewels." Lily followed her sister down the stairs, happily chattering.

Mary was the last in line as they descended the winding staircase. As they emerged into the courtyard, she glanced across the yard. And there, at the base of one of the towers, stood Cosmo Glass.

Chapter 12

Mary stopped and stared. How could her stepfather be here?

As suddenly as she had seen him, the man turned and walked away, melting into a knot of people. Mary broke from her frozen state and hurried toward him, but when she reached the place where he had been standing, she could see him nowhere. Cosmo was a short man and difficult to see in a crowd. But there—just turning the corner of the building—surely that was his sandy-colored hair, thin and worn too long.

Grabbing her skirts in one hand, she trotted across the yard and slipped around the corner. A long green path of grass stretched before her, running between a wall and the side of the castle, with a tall iron gate at the end of it. There was no one in sight, and Mary hesitated. Had he come this way? And could it really have been Cosmo?

She started across the grass, moving quietly. There was a recess in the building ahead. Mary slowed as she reached the corner. Placing one hand on the stone wall, she leaned forward.

"Mary!"

She jumped and whirled around. Sir Royce hurried toward her, scowling.

"Where the devil did you go?" He came up beside her and took her arm. "I turned around, and you were gone."

Blast! Well, if that *had* been Cosmo, no doubt he was long gone. Mary jerked her arm away. "I was not aware that I had to report my movements to you."

He grimaced. "I'm responsible for you. You can't expect me to let you go running loose wherever you want."

"It may surprise you to learn that I managed to take care of myself for twenty-five years without your guidance."

"And I'm beginning to think that it's a wonder you survived."

The two of them glared at each other. Then Sir Royce heaved a sigh. "Devil take it." He opened his arms, palms up in an exculpatory gesture. "I'm sorry. I am not usually so . . ."

"Overbearing?" Mary suggested sweetly.

His mouth twitched. "Yes. Overbearing. I just—I'm not accustomed to having to keep an eye out for anyone. It frightened me when I couldn't find you. London can be a dangerous place—much more so than you realize, I fear. The area around the Tower is not exactly Mayfair. You could get into far worse trouble than you did the other day—through no fault of your own," he added hastily.

Mary had to laugh. "That was very diplomatic of you."

He grinned. "I'm learning. I may be slow, but . . ." He shrugged. Stepping back, he glanced around. "What are you doing here anyway?"

"I, um, thought I saw one of the ravens," Mary offered, referring to another of the Tower's legends. "I wanted a closer look, but I must have frightened it off."

"They're nothing special, really, just ravens."

"They sound special to me if the monarchy will crumble if they disappear."

"Not likely; I believe they clip their wings to make sure they stay around." He moved forward. "Did it go around here?"

"I thought so," Mary said, quickly following him. It suddenly occurred to her that if Cosmo had ducked around the corner of the building, he might still be there; there might not be an exit. And she had no desire for Sir Royce to come face to face with her stepfather.

She was relieved to find that she and Royce were all alone in a sort of alcove. Mary glanced around. "Well, I must have been mistaken." She turned back to Royce. "No doubt we should rejoin the others."

"No doubt." He was looking down into her face, and there was a certain light in his eyes that made Mary suddenly feel warm and a little fidgety.

She turned away. It was ridiculous to feel this way—uncomfortable in Royce's presence, yet at the same time wanting quite fiercely to remain there. "I . . . um . . . I should thank you for coming to look for me. I am not entirely naïve; I know there are dangers in a huge city like this. I should not have snapped at you."

His eyebrows soared. "Are you feeling quite right?"

Mary gave him a quelling look. "Don't spoil it. I am attempting to be more proper. Our new chaperone told me twice yesterday that I didn't act in a proper manner."

"No! I can scarcely credit it."

"There is no need to be sarcastic."

"Lily regaled me with her opinion of your new chaperone. If she is indeed as Lily described her, I tremble at the thought of the days ahead."

Mary sighed. "I do as well. Perhaps Miss Dalrymple will improve upon further acquaintance. She may have been trying to impress the earl with her competence."

"Perhaps."

Mary glanced at him. "I wish I could believe that."

"You could speak to Oliver," he suggested.

"No. I fear it would only confirm his opinion that we are difficult and unruly. In truth, I have not yet given her a fair trial. Besides, we have to learn those things. I quite see that we cannot live here and remain the way we are. We would be an embarrassment to the earl."

"I am sure he would not wish you to be . . . hounded or changed into something other than you are."

She sent him a glinting look. "Really? I had quite the opposite impression. At any rate, I rather doubt that Miss Dalrymple will be able to run roughshod over us."

"No. I foresee battles."

"At least you will not have to witness them." Mary forced a smile.

"I expect to be quite close to the front lines. Indeed, I may get hit by a stray ball."

"What?" Mary looked at him, puzzled. "What are you talking about? We are going to be at the earl's house in the country."

"Willowmere. Yes, I will be too. I am escorting you there."

"What?" Mary clamped her lips together to hold back a smile. "You—I thought that you would be staying here."

"I have brought you thus far. Surely you don't think I would abandon you now." He continued in a more practical vein, "Oliver has business to finish in the city. I, on the other hand, am quite free."

"But we don't need anyone at all." The very fact that his presence among them lightened her spirits perversely compelled Mary to argue against his coming. "We have a companion, and we will be in Stewkesbury's coach."

"It is always easier to have a gentleman along to arrange things," Royce countered.

"We are quite capable of arranging things on our own."

He quirked an eyebrow. "Hoping to get rid of me?"

"No," Mary answered honestly. "No, of course not."

"For I find that I am quite looking forward to being with you." He took a step forward, reaching up to brush back a strand of her hair.

Mary flushed, embarrassingly aware of the way her heart sped up at his touch. She wished that she could think of some tart rejoinder to disguise her physical reaction to him.

"Your new bonnet is very attractive."

"What? Oh. Thank you. Cousin Charlotte and Lady Vivian took us shopping yesterday." Mary cursed inwardly at her prosaic response. Why was it impossible to think when Royce stood so close to her?

"It has come a trifle askew, however." Royce reached out and, before Mary could move, deftly untied the wide ribbons and pulled it from her head. He started to reposition it, then stopped, gazing down into her eyes.

Mary's heart slammed against her rib cage.

"There is only one problem with it," he murmured as he leaned closer. His voice was almost a whisper. "It makes it far too difficult to kiss you."

She knew she should turn, should run away. Instead she went up on tiptoe, meeting his lips as they settled on hers. Sensations flooded through her, warming and arousing her. Every inch of her skin was suddenly, breathtakingly aware. She could feel the soft fabric of her dress against it, the tantalizing brush of a breeze, the heat that poured from his body so close to hers.

Royce's mouth was soft and warm upon hers, his lips searching, opening her mouth to his questing tongue. Mary trembled, her hands going up to clutch his lapels, holding on to the only sure thing in her suddenly tilting world. His arms went around her, pressing her into him. She could feel the hard length of his body all the way up and down hers, pressing into her softness. She slid her hands up and around his neck.

She realized that she was kissing him back, her lips moving against his, her tongue meeting his in a sensual dance. Desire twisted through her, curling down into her abdomen, setting her whole body tingling in a way she had never known before.

He tore his lips from hers, moving down her throat, and she let her head fall back. His lips were like velvet on the tender skin of her neck, and she shivered, lost in a wash of unaccustomed hunger, the world around her fading into nothingness.

Royce froze, then straightened, his arms falling away from her. Mary staggered and looked up at him in surprise and confusion. In the distance, she heard Camellia's voice calling her name, and her brain cleared in an instant. She had been standing here in a public place kissing Royce like a wanton! Like a common lightskirt!

She jerked her hat out of his hand and shoved it onto her head, hastily tying the bow beneath her chin. Her fingers went to her lips, pressing against the tender flesh. She hoped the others could not tell from the look of them exactly what she had been doing. Whirling around, she rushed out of the alcove. Her sisters and Fitz were standing at the end of the grassy strip, fortunately facing away from her. Mary started toward them.

"There you are! I'm so glad to see you!" she cried. "I seem to have gotten lost." Hurrying up to them, she linked her arm through Rose's. "I'm sorry. Have you been looking for me?"

"Yes. Royce set off to look for you," Fitz explained. "And now he appears to have disappeared as well."

"I am certain he will turn up sooner or later," Mary said cheerfully, walking away and pulling Rose with her. "Why don't we go to the menagerie? No doubt when Sir Royce can't find me, he will join us there."

"No doubt." Fitz's eyes lingered on her face for a moment; then he turned. "On to the lions and tigers, ladies."

"Mary! Slow down," her sister said, half laughing. "You are practically dragging me."

"Oh." Mary glanced at Rose and obediently slowed down. "I'm sorry."

"Is something the matter?" Rose asked in a low voice. "You seem . . . shaken."

"What? No. I . . ." She considered for a fleeting moment telling her sister what had happened with Royce, but quickly discarded the idea. She had always told Rose everything, but this was too fresh, too raw. Mary glanced behind them. They were several feet ahead of Camellia and Lily, with Fitz strolling along in the rear. Turning back, she whispered, "I thought I saw Cosmo."

"What!" Rose looked at her in alarm, her face turning a deathly white. "Here? Are you sure?"

"No. He was so far away, I couldn't be sure. I went after him to get a better look, but . . ." She shrugged. "I lost him."

"You think he followed us here?" Rose gripped Mary's arm so tightly it hurt.

"It seems absurd. Why would he? And if he had, why wouldn't he make his presence known? He wouldn't be content with following us about, going to the Tower and such. Besides, how would he know where we were?"

"He might have known the earl's name," Rose pointed out. "Mama could have told him at some point. If he tracked us down to Philadelphia and found out what ship we sailed on, he would have known we were bound for England— probably for Mama's relatives. Why else would we come here? Even if he didn't know the earl's name, if he came as far as London, he could have picked up our trail again. I feel sure they would have remembered us at the inn—even more so because the Earl of Stewkesbury sent his servants to collect our trunks."

Mary frowned. She had successfully concealed the reason for her agitation, but she was beginning to wish she had not brought up the other matter. "But to have followed us so quickly?"

"If you will remember, our ship was delayed by storms in the Atlantic. He could have left several days later and gotten here when we did. He might even have arrived before us."

"But why? What could he hope to accomplish?"

"He wants me to marry Mr. Suttersby."

"He cannot make you. He can't even make you go back to Pennsylvania. We are free women and of age."

"Not Camellia and Lily."

"He's not their guardian." Mary thought with relief of Fitz's words to her the other day. "The earl is. And the earl would not allow Cosmo to take them. I am certain of that. None of them would—not Stewkesbury nor Sir Royce nor Fitz." She smiled. "Just think, Rose, we are not alone now. We have family who will help us."

Rose's brow unfurrowed, and she offered Mary a weak smile. "Yes, I suppose you are right."

"I'm certain I am. It probably was not even Cosmo I saw, just someone with a fleeting resemblance. And if he does show up at the earl's door, he will receive a welcome that's even less warm than the one I got." Mary chuckled at the thought and squeezed her sister's arm. "That is as far as he'll get. We won't even see it, for tomorrow we're leaving for Willowmere. We shall be miles and miles away. Cosmo won't have the slightest idea where we are."

Rose relaxed, her arm falling away from Mary's. "Yes, of course." She smiled, more naturally this time. "We will be far away and quite safe."

"Exactly. Quite safe," Mary repeated. Behind her she heard Royce call Fitz's name, and she turned to look back casually. Royce was striding toward them, tall and relaxed, moving with easy grace.

She might be safe from Cosmo Glass at Willowmere, she thought, but how was she going to avoid the danger that was Sir Royce Winslow?

The party set off from Stewkesbury House right after breakfast the next morning. It was a relief to Mary to find that Sir Royce would be riding his horse. She had spent much of the previous evening wondering how she would act naturally, confined in the carriage with him, when every time she looked at him she was reminded of the soul-stirring kisses they had shared the afternoon before.

The earl walked out of the house to hand them up personally into the carriage and bid them good-bye. Pirate trotted along beside him and sat down alertly at his feet, watching with interest as the girls climbed one by one into the carriage, but he made not the slightest effort to jump up after them.

"Pirate?" Camellia leaned out of the carriage. "Are you not coming with us?"

Beside her, Lily let out an inelegant snort. "Don't be daft, Camellia. It's clear he's adopted cousin Oliver."

The dog tilted his head, regarding them with bright interest, but he made no move. The earl looked down at him, then up at the girls. "I, ah, think that perhaps Pirate is a city dog, not meant for the country."

Pirate let out a sharp bark, his rear end wriggling as he wagged his stump of a tail, and the girls all had to laugh. A footman jumped forward to close the door, and Stewkesbury gestured to the coachman. With a call and a slap of the reins, the carriage lurched into motion, Sir Royce riding alongside. Mary glanced back at the house they had just left. The earl was standing on the front steps watching them, the scruffy dog nestled in the crook of his arm.

Mary's eyes went to Royce, and she could not help but admit that he cut a fine figure on horseback. His tall, broad-shouldered frame showed off well atop the dark bay, and he moved with the instinctive grace of one who had been riding almost from birth. It was a pleasure to watch him.

With an inner sigh, she pulled her eyes away. It was foolish to spend her time this way. Better by far to be thinking about how to deal with the feelings that bubbled up inside her whenever he was around—or, even better, how to stop feeling anything at all.

"Young ladies do not lean out of carriage windows," Miss Dalrymple said, reaching over to rap Lily sharply on the knee.

"But how can I see anything?" Lily protested.

"There's nothing out there a young lady needs to see." Leaving Lily gaping at her, she turned her attention to Camellia. "And pray do not point, Miss Camellia. Only the vulgar point."

Without pause, Miss Dalrymple went on to remind Rose that a lady did not slump, even in a carriage, and to admonish Mary for not addressing the earl properly as they said good-bye. She then closed the curtains and lectured the girls on the behavior expected of young ladies. Fortunately, before long Miss Dalrymple stopped talking and began to nod, and within a few moments she was napping.

After that, the journey was more entertaining. The girls reopened the curtains and watched the scenery pass by, chatting in low voices so as not to awaken their chaperone.

They stopped at an inn along the way for a late luncheon and to rest the horses. Royce opened the carriage door and gave each of the women a hand to help them down. Mary's stomach quivered a little, and she wished there were some way to avoid putting her hand in his, but she knew that there was not. Steeling herself, she laid her hand on his palm, and his fingers closed around hers, hard and strong. She looked down into his face. He was gazing back at her, his expression relaxed and polite. There was nothing in his face to indicate that anything had happened between them the day before.

Surely, Mary thought, she could be as unconcerned as he was. She suspected that he had had a great deal more experience at it than she, but Mary had no desire to let him see that. Her smile to him was polite and perfunctory, and she felt rather pleased with herself. But as she walked into the inn, she could not help but notice that her fingers still tingled from the contact. And she could not pretend to herself that being around him left her unaffected.

It was wonderful to be out of the carriage. No matter how well-sprung it was or how comfortably cushioned its seats, rolling along over the road for hours left them all cramped and stiff. The girls also welcomed the cold collation laid out for them in the inn's private dining room. However, it was rendered far less pleasant by Miss Dalrymple's admonitions on correct table manners and proper conversation.

Mary, forcibly quelling her temper as she worked through the meal on her plate, raised her head to find Sir Royce's gaze on her. His eyes danced with amusement as Miss Dalrymple, having covered such social solecisms as speaking too loudly or out of turn or at too great a length—a taboo Miss Dalrymple herself obviously felt no compunction about breaking—was now droning on about what one should discuss.

"No one wants to hear a young girl talking about herself," she announced. "Nor should she choose matters that are intellectual. One does not wish to acquire a reputation as a bluestocking, after all. Weather is always a pleasant topic, and an inquiry about another's health rarely goes amiss.

And, of course, you must always remember to compliment the decoration of the table and the quality of the meal."

"The weather?" Mary raised an eyebrow at the woman. "We are supposed to talk of nothing but the table, the weather, and everyone's health?"

The older woman turned a disapproving eye on Mary, but before she could speak, Rose jumped in. "It sounds a trifle dull."

"Better to sound dull than to appear forward or inappropriate." Miss Dalrymple pursed her mouth primly.

"But, surely, Miss Dalrymple," Royce said, casting a glinting look in Mary's direction, "there must be some occasion when an intelligent conversation is warranted."

Miss Dalrymple's dour face broke into an almost coy smile. "Now, Sir Royce, everyone knows that in order to keep up an intelligent conversation with a gentleman, a girl need only follow his lead."

The Bascombes all gazed at their chaperone blankly. Finally Camellia asked, "You mean, let him do all the talking?"

"Oh, no, you must offer a few words of pleasant agreement now and then in order to convey that you are listening."

"Well, if that isn't the stupidest thing I ever heard!" Camellia exclaimed.

Miss Dalrymple's brows drew together ominously, but before she could say anything, Sir Royce turned to her with not even a quiver of expression to betray that he had heard Camellia's words and said, "I believe I once met a gentleman named Dalrymple in Exeter. Are you by any chance related to him? Gerald Dalrymple, I believe his name was. A banker."

"Oh, my, no. I come from a long line of clergymen and scholars, Sir Royce." Miss Dalrymple practically preened under Royce's attention. "My father held a living at Warnham, near the Shelley estate. Poor man—such a trial of a son."

Mary finished her food rapidly and shot Rose a significant look, nodding toward the door. Rose stood up from the table as Mary did. "Pray excuse us. Rose and I want to take a walk before we get back on the road."

"Wait for us," Camellia cried, and she and Lily crammed a last bite in their mouths, then jumped up to follow their sisters.

Miss Dalrymple looked as if she would protest, but with a glance at Sir Royce, she smiled instead and settled down to finish the meal with him. The sisters hurried down the hall and out the rear entrance of the inn, tying on their bonnets as they went. Behind the inn a narrow path led off toward the right, and Mary started along it, her sisters trailing after her.

"That woman will drive me mad!" Camellia ground her teeth in frustration.

"Perhaps it will not be as bad once we are at Willowmere. Here we are stuck with her every second, but there, surely, we will be able to escape now and then," Rose reasoned.

"I'm not sure one could escape her long or often enough to make it bearable," Mary grumbled. "Lord, what a tyrant that woman is. If we have to behave exactly as she wishes, I fear we will never manage to be ladylike."

"Thank heaven we have Sir Royce with us." Lily giggled. "Have you seen how she looks at him? He is quite clever at drawing her ire away."

The girls continued to chatter as they walked. Mary, however, was uncharacteristically silent. Something was wrong, she thought. She had an odd, uneasy feeling, a vaguely vulnerable sensation across her back. She stopped, glancing around her. There was no one in sight, either in the garden or along the path. Her gaze went to the inn. She could see no one at any window. Yet she felt as if someone was watching her.

She glanced to her right, where a copse of trees lay a little distance ahead. It was dark among the trees. If someone was there, it would be difficult to see them. She wondered if she was being foolish, letting her imagination run away with her because of the odd incident at the Tower yesterday.

"Mary? What's wrong?" Rose turned to look at her.

"Oh—nothing, really. I felt . . . I don't know . . . odd." The other girls had stopped, too, and they looked puzzled. Mary had not told the others what had happened the day before. It seemed pointless to worry them, especially when she was not sure she'd actually seen their stepfather. She gave them a faint smile and shook her head. "Just a mood. Come, we'd best get back to the inn. They'll be wanting to leave, I imagine, and we don't want Miss Dalrymple lecturing us on being tardy."

"All right." Rose frowned, but refrained from pointing out that they had been gone only minutes.

The girls began to walk back to the inn. Mary remained alert to any sign of movement around them. She saw nothing, but she could not keep from casting an encompassing glance behind her as she went through the door. As she turned back, Rose shot her an inquiring look. Mary replied with a faint shrug and a grimace.

She was overreacting, she told herself. It was merely an odd feeling, a momentary shiver that she would normally have disregarded. Had she not seen a man who looked like Cosmo Glass yesterday, she would have thought nothing about it at all. There had been no one in the woods or anywhere around the path. Indeed, it was likely that she had not even seen her stepfather yesterday. He would not have followed them to London, and even if he had, he would have immediately tried to get money out of their new relatives, not skulked around watching them. Her imagination had simply run away with her. Still, she could not help but be glad they were traveling with Sir Royce.

The carriage ride that afternoon was much the same, except that Mary's weariness and boredom seemed to arrive even earlier. Finally, they pulled into the courtyard of another inn and disembarked. Everyone was tired and ready for bed, so they ate quickly. Mary did not feel particularly sleepy, but she could see that her sisters were flagging—and Miss Dalrymple was practically snoozing over her plate.

Rose went to bed almost as soon as they climbed the stairs to their room, and she was asleep within a few minutes. Mary puttered about quietly, but with Rose asleep, there was little to do, so she soon climbed into bed. It took some time for her to go to sleep, but she must have dozed off, for a noise brought her awake. Mary turned her head and saw a man silhouetted against the moonlight that streamed in through the open window. Terror seized her throat.

The man was turned away from her, walking slowly and carefully toward the window. He was huge and strangely misshapen. In the next instant, Mary realized that the bed beside her was empty and that the intruder was carrying Rose away over his shoulder.

Chapter 13

Mary screamed at the top of her lungs and jumped out of bed. "Royce! Royce! Help!"

She ran toward the intruder, and he whirled, startled. He wore a cap pulled low on his forehead and his collar was turned up; a dark half-mask obscured most of the rest of his face. He turned and ran the last steps to the window and flung his leg over. Mary threw herself at him, grabbing for her sister's arm.

"Rose!" She wound up clutching the man's jacket instead and pulled on it for all she was worth, again yelling Royce's name. The man let out a curse and jerked away from her.

She stumbled back, then righted herself and lunged forward again. There was the sound of a door crashing open down the hall, followed by running footsteps. The intruder shrugged Rose's limp form from his shoulder and shoved her at Mary. Mary staggered backward under Rose's sudden weight and crashed to the floor. The back of her head hit the bedpost with a blinding pain, and suddenly everything went dark.

"Mary! Mary! Wake up!"

She was aware of being held, a muscular arm around her shoulders, her head leaning against something hard and warm. It felt good and somehow reassuring, especially the rhythmic thumping beneath her ear. She was being jiggled, and next there was a sharp little sting to her cheek.

"Blast it, Mary! Wake up!"

She opened her eyes, and a man's face swam above her. Her stomach lurched, and she quickly closed her eyes again.

"Mary! Thank God. Come on, now, open your eyes again and look at me. It's Royce."

Royce. She smiled to herself. In the next instant, full consciousness came back to her, and she remembered everything.

"Oh! Rose! Is she here? Is she all right?" Mary opened her eyes and struggled to sit up.

"She's right here on the floor beside you. Don't exert yourself. I think you've had a nasty crack on the head. What the devil happened? Why is the window open?"

"The man! He was taking her—he was taking her out the window." She sat up despite Royce's advice, and though her head throbbed painfully, she no longer felt woozy.

"The devil!" Royce released her and stood up, going to the open window. He leaned out, looking in both directions. "There's no sign of him." He turned to Mary. "Are you all right by yourself? I want to take a look outside."

"Yes, I'm fine. Go."

He left the room, and Mary sat where she was, trying to gather her scattered thoughts. She reached one hand up to her head and felt around gingerly. With a wince, she brought her hand down. There was a sticky liquid on her fingers, and she realized that the wound must have bled.

She turned to her sister, lying in a crumpled heap on the floor beside her. "Rose? Rose, can you hear me?"

Mary tugged at Rose's shoulder. She was lying on her side, but Mary's tug rolled her onto her back. Mary smoothed the tangle of her hair back out of her face. Rose's eyes were closed, her face still. For one terrified instant, Mary thought her sister was dead, but then she saw the slow rise and fall of Rose's chest.

Mary shook her shoulder. "Rose! Wake up!"

What was the matter with her? Mary had been knocked unconscious, yet she had come to. Why was Rose still asleep? And how could she have slept through everything that had happened? She moved her fingers over her sister's scalp, but she could find no bump. Rose did not even stir.

Mary struggled to her feet and lit the candle on the dresser. She found her handkerchief and dipped it in the washbowl, then returned to kneel beside her sister and bathe Rose's face with the cool cloth. As she did so, her mind raced. Who was that man? And why was he trying to steal Rose?

Her thoughts went first to her stepfather. But the intruder had been far too large—Cosmo was a narrow, wiry man only a few inches taller than Mary. The man who had flung Rose over his shoulder had been much taller, perhaps even as large as Royce. Mary frowned as she wrung out the cloth and dipped it in cool water again. Her head ached, and her thoughts were fuzzy.

"Rose. Sweetheart, please wake up. What is wrong with you?" She took her sister's wrist and found her pulse. It seemed slow but still strong. She patted Rose's cheek as she called her name.

Rapid footsteps sounded on the stairs, and a moment later Royce entered the room. "I could find no one. I walked all around the inn, but there was no sign of anyone."

Mary turned to him. "Did you slap me?"

"What?" He stopped and stared at her blankly.

"Earlier, before I came to. I think I felt you slap my cheek."

Royce grinned and came farther into the room. "A loving tap, that is all. I was trying to wake you." He set the candle he was carrying on the dresser and came over to kneel beside Rose. "She still has not awakened?"

"No. I think he must have knocked her out, though I cannot find a lump."

"Who knocked her out? I still have no idea what happened."

"I woke up a little while ago; I think I heard a noise. And I saw a man carrying Rose. I screamed and jumped out of bed and ran at him. He was trying to climb out the window with her. I grabbed him, and we struggled. Then I heard you coming. And he threw Rose into me, and we both fell. I think I must have hit my head on the bedpost."

"I don't understand. Someone came into your room and was trying to *take* your sister?"

Mary nodded. "I know. It sounds mad. But that is what happened."

"Who was it?"

"I have no idea. But that is not what concerns me now. Rose won't wake up, no matter what I do."

"You think he hit her on the head?" Gently Royce lifted Rose's head and felt around her scalp. "I don't feel a knot."

"Neither did I." Mary looked at him worriedly. "What should we do?"

"To begin with, let's get her off the floor." He scooped Rose up and laid her on the bed, and Mary followed to pull the covers up to her sister's shoulders.

Mary stood for a moment gazing down at Rose, then she suddenly stiffened, raising her head. "Where is everyone?"

"What?" Royce looked at her.

"Where are Camellia and Lily? And Miss Dalrymple, for that matter. I was screaming at the top of my lungs. Clearly I awakened you."

"And another chap at the end of the hall. He helped me

search the grounds, though I think he believed you had had a nightmare."

"Oh, God." Mary whirled and ran out of the room, Royce at her heels.

"Perhaps they stayed in their room," Royce offered.

Mary shot him a withering glance as she flung open the door to the other girls' room. "Hiding? Those two?"

"I see your point."

Royce had had the presence of mind to snatch up the candle as he left Mary's room, and he lifted it as they walked into Lily and Camellia's chamber. Two forms lay in the bed, and as they drew closer, they could make out the two sisters, both sound asleep.

Mary and Royce looked at each other. Royce held the candle so that the light shone directly on Camellia's face; she continued to sleep peacefully. On the other side of the bed, Mary shook Lily's shoulder. When there was no response, she shook it even harder. Finally, Lily frowned in her sleep, muttered something, and turned over.

"They've been drugged. It has to be." Mary turned to Royce in dismay. "Or poisoned! What shall we do?"

Royce bent over Camellia, so close that Mary thought in astonishment that he was about to kiss her, but he only sniffed once or twice and straightened. "I've smelled that before. It's laudanum."

Mary relaxed a trifle. "Thank heavens. That is . . . you do not think they could have been given too much?"

He looked again at the girls. "They don't seem to be having any trouble breathing."

"True. And their color is good." She paused. "But how could they all—it must have been in our food tonight!"

Royce nodded. "I can think of no other way so many of us could have been drugged."

"But who—how—"

"There must have been some dish that all the others ate that you and I did not. Or something we did not drink."

"I had no pudding. Rose did, but I'm not sure about the others."

"I had none of that, either. And I didn't eat the soup."

Mary nodded. "Nor I. I ate a spoonful or two, but the turnips made it bitter—" She stopped, her eyes widening. "Do you think it was that? Perhaps that was why the soup was bitter."

"It's quite possible."

"What should we do about them?" Mary asked, turning back to her sisters.

He shrugged. "I think we will have to let them sleep."

"I suppose so." It made Mary uneasy to leave her sisters in this state, but she had no idea how to wake them. Nor did there seem any purpose in doing so. "I will look in on them again later."

"We'd best check on Miss Dalrymple. Do you know which chamber is hers?"

"The one on the other side of mine." Mary led the way down the hall and knocked on the woman's door.

There was no answer, and she knocked again more loudly. Finally, Mary opened the door and put her head in. She could make out the chaperone's form on the bed, and the room was filled with the sound of her stentorian snoring.

Mary sighed and closed the door. "She apparently is in the same condition."

As they turned away, the landlord came huffing and puffing up the stairs. A voluminous dressing gown was wrapped around his ample form, and a nightcap covered his bald head.

"Sir. Miss. Is there some problem? There was a complaint about the noise, you see, though I'm sure there must be an explanation. If I could be of help to you—"

"A fellow broke into Miss Bascombe's room and tried to abduct her sister," Royce told him bluntly.

The man's jaw dropped. "I . . . I . . . I beg your pardon? Are you sure?"

"Of course I'm sure. I have a large bump on my head to prove it," Mary replied somewhat crossly.

"There is also the problem that several people in our party were drugged here tonight," Royce added.

This statement had the effect of rendering the man speechless. His eyes bulged, and he wheezed out a few incomprehensible noises. He waved his hands in front of him as if frantically wiping something.

"No, no, I assure you," he said at last. "Drugged? How could they be? We would never—no one in this establishment would do such a thing! I swear it."

"It must have been put into our dinner," Mary told him.

"No. No. Impossible. My wife herself cooked your meal. My daughters brought the trays to your parlor."

"Then it would seem that it must have been done by one of them." Royce took a step closer to the man, who immediately backed up, his eyes widening in alarm.

"No! No, I swear it. Why would we wish you harm? Perhaps they were not drugged. Perhaps they are merely . . ." He trailed off helplessly.

"We cannot awaken them. I smelled laudanum on their breath."

"Perhaps they, um, took it themselves. For pain or—or they felt ill."

"All four of them?" Royce asked skeptically. "It seems most unlikely."

"We don't even have any laudanum." Mary looked the landlord in the eye. "You might not have thought it would do any harm. Just a little something to make a person sleep soundly. Perhaps someone paid you?"

"No!" The landlord's head swung toward her, and he looked even more disturbed, if that was possible. "Never. This inn has an excellent reputation. I would never do anything to damage that. Not for any amount of money."

"Then how did the laudanum get into the food?" Royce asked.

"Perhaps it did not happen at the inn. It was earlier."

"We were in a closed carriage for several hours before we got here. It had to be done at supper." Royce crossed his arms and regarded the man.

The landlord wilted, reluctantly admitting that the food, after preparation, was set on trays on the far side of the kitchen, waiting for the man's daughters to take it up to the guests in the private dining room. So, apparently, were the pitchers of cider and milk. It had been a busy evening, and it was possible that the food had sat there for some minutes.

"So anyone could have walked by and dropped something in it?" Royce asked.

"Not anyone! We would have noticed a stranger in the kitchen, surely." In the next instant, the landlord realized that this contention once again made him culpable, and he quickly backtracked. "Well, perhaps . . . that is to say, it was quite busy. My wife might not have noticed someone in that corner of the kitchen. It is right by the hallway. Someone could have nipped down the hall from the public room and dropped it in."

Mary sighed. "I suppose there is nothing we can do about it now."

Royce nodded and dismissed the landlord, who reiterated his assurances that nothing of this sort ever happened here. As the man trudged off down the stairs, still muttering to himself, Royce turned to Mary.

"Let's get you to your room. I want to take a look at that head wound. We should have tended to it long ago."

"It was not the most pressing issue," Mary pointed out, but she let him take her arm and propel her back into her room.

Inside the bedchamber, Mary checked on Rose, who was still sleeping, peacefully unaware of the turmoil about her. Royce dampened a washcloth and beckoned to Mary.

"Come here by the light." He took her arms, turning her so that he could look at the wound. "You're going to have a nasty bump. It cut the scalp as well."

He parted her hair gently and held the wet cloth to the wound. Mary scarcely noticed the sting. She was far more aware of the feel of his fingers on her head. Royce's breath ruffled her hair; his body was large and warm behind her. Suddenly she could think of nothing but the fact that he was standing so close to her. It occurred to her for the first time that she was in her bedchamber, inches away from a man—with nothing more than a thin cotton garment covering her.

A shiver ran through her, and her nipples hardened against her night rail. Had he noticed? Had his mind, too, turned to their physical closeness? Was he thinking now how alone they were, with everyone else fast asleep?

She could not help remembering that Royce, too, was not fully dressed. He had obviously yanked on only his breeches and shirt and come running when he heard her call, his shirt hanging loose and open at the top, exposing a V of his chest and a hint of his skin beneath, the dark circles that were his nipples.

Royce rested his other hand on her shoulder as he tended to her head. His hand was warm, and Mary could not help but remember his hands on her when he kissed her. She thought of his fingers gliding over her shoulder, caressing her, and her skin prickled. He moved, his hand sliding over a fraction to cup the curve of her shoulder.

She sensed him shift behind her, and his hand fell away.

He cleared his throat. "Um, I think that is as clean as I can get it." He moved to the washbasin and rinsed out the rag. "We should put something on it—I shall go ask the landlord if his wife has any sort of ointment."

"I have something." Mary reached for the bag that sat at the foot of her bed, acutely aware of how little she was wearing and of the way her breasts, free of the restraint of her chemise, swayed as she moved.

She cast a surreptitious glance at Royce as she dug through the bag. His eyes, she noted, were not on her face but on her body. She flushed as she pulled out the small jar and held it toward him.

"Here. 'Tis only a home remedy, but it helps wounds heal, I've found."

He stepped forward and took the jar, his fingertips grazing hers. Mary could not suppress another shiver.

"Cold?" he asked.

Mary nodded, not daring to look at him. She hurried to the chair beside her bed and picked up her dressing gown, quickly slipping it on. She turned back to Royce as she tied the sash.

There was something in his heavy-lidded gaze that took her breath away. Her hands trembled on the bow she was tying. She curled her hands into fists and dropped them to her sides to hide the movement.

He walked over to her, and Mary looked up into his face. His eyes were dark and mysterious in the dim light, pulling her in. "Turn around so I can put this on you."

"What? Oh." Mary tore her eyes away and pivoted so that her back was to him.

"You have no idea who the intruder might have been?" he asked, carefully pushing her hair away on either side of her wound. His fingers slid through her hair, and the locks twined around them and fell away.

"I—um—not really." Mary struggled to conceal the breathlessness in her voice. The nape of her neck lay bare, and she felt vulnerable and exposed—and tingling with anticipation. "I could not see his face. He wore a cap pulled low and a mask over much of his face. What I could see did not look familiar." She considered telling Royce about Cosmo, but she was reluctant to bring him up. It could not have been Cosmo, anyway; the man was too large.

Royce gently touched the cool ointment to her head, his finger gliding over her scalp, soothing the pain—and at the same time sending a spark sizzling through her veins.

Mary closed her eyes and swallowed hard. "We don't know anyone in England; we have only been here a few days. How could we have made any enemies?" She concentrated on ignoring the delicate touch of his finger upon her scalp, forcing herself to think about Rose and her attempted abduction.

"I don't know." Royce's voice sounded rougher, deeper, and there was a changed quality to his breathing. His hand skimmed over Mary's hair as he pulled it away. "There. 'Tis done."

"Thank you." Her voice was shaky. She did not want to turn around and look at him, afraid that something of her inner turmoil would reveal itself.

"My pleasure," he told her, and she felt the low rumble of his voice all through her. He was so close that their bodies were almost touching. She could feel his heat through her clothing.

He leaned closer, murmuring, "When you needed help tonight, you called out to me."

He was right. She had not even thought about it. His name had jumped immediately to her lips. "There was no one else, was there?"

"The landlord. Other guests. But you called my name."

He touched the nape of her neck, trailing a forefinger down the length of it. Mary sucked in her breath, unable to hide her reaction.

"You are so lovely . . ." Royce bent and pressed his lips to the tender skin of her neck.

Mary shivered. "I do not think—"

"Good. Don't think." His voice was thick.

Royce's hands went to her shoulders, turning her around, and Mary could not find it in her to resist. She tilted her face to look up at him. His eyes were dark and fierce in the dim light, his skin stretched taut across his cheekbones. For an instant, they stood gazing at each other, immobilized by the desire storming through them.

He bent toward her, his face looming closer, until Mary closed her eyes on a soft sigh. Then his mouth was on hers, swift and hungry, and there was nothing else in the world.

Chapter 14

Royce's arms went around Mary, pulling her up to him. His mouth consumed hers; his hands swept over her, following the soft curves of her body beneath her clothes. Impatient, he went to the tie of her dressing gown and yanked it undone. His hand slipped beneath the robe, roaming over the body that was now separated from his touch only by a thin nightgown.

Mary jerked in surprise at the feel of his hand moving over her stomach and hips, but she did not draw away. The sensations rippling through her were far too pleasurable. His fingers skimmed over her torso, moving up to touch her breasts. Her nipples tightened almost painfully in response, and something deep inside her warmed and opened in a pleasurable aching. Her arms rose and twined around his neck.

His mouth left hers, kissing her cheek, her ear, her throat in a leisurely journey that stoked the fire in her abdomen. His lips were like velvet, caressing the tender skin of her throat as he tasted and explored. Mary let out a soft groan, shaken by the hunger he aroused in her. She was restless and eager, driven by feelings she had never known before, and at the same time was filled with a luxurious lassitude, unable to move or even think beyond this moment.

Royce toyed with her nipples through the soft cloth of her nightgown, arousing them to hard, thrusting points, and with each movement, as if connected by a cord, the ache between her legs grew and throbbed. Mary squeezed her legs together, realizing with shock that she wanted to wrap them around his body.

He made a low noise deep in his throat and seized the lapels of her dressing gown, shoving it back and down her arms, dropping it on the floor. Sinking his fingers into the fleshy mounds of her buttocks, he pulled her into him, molding her against the hard ridge of his desire. Mary felt his flesh quicken and pulse against her. Her breath rasped in her throat. She looked up into his face and saw the raw desire stamped there. He bent to kiss her again, and she went up on tiptoe to meet him.

At that moment, Rose made an unintelligible noise and turned over in the bed.

Mary froze, suddenly aware of the world around her. She was wildly kissing Royce, letting him touch her intimately—indeed, reveling in that touch—and all the while her sister was lying in bed only a few feet away!

She pulled back and saw the same realization dawning in Royce's face. He muttered a curse and turned away, running his hands over his face. Quickly, Mary wrapped her dressing gown around her again and jerked the sash tight. Her face felt flushed—partly from embarrassment and partly from the desire that still pounded through her. She could hardly bring herself to look at Royce.

"I beg your pardon." Royce did not look at her. A muscle jumped in his jaw. "My behavior was inexcusable." He marched to the door and opened it, then turned back. "Lock your door—and that window." He hesitated, then finally, with a stiff nod, said, "I shall see you tomorrow morning."

He turned and left. Mary stood for a moment, staring at the blank door. She could not seem to move or even think. Finally, she went to the door and turned the key, then checked the window to make sure the latch was in place.

Slowly she sank onto the bench at the foot of the bed. She pressed her fingers to her lips, still tingling from Royce's kisses. What had she done? What had she been thinking? And how in the world was she going to face Royce again?

The group that assembled the next morning around the breakfast table was a sluggish one—all of them bleary-eyed and quiet, their movements a trifle slow. Even Miss Dalrymple was not her usual self, not even correcting the girls once.

Mary, her eyes smudged dark with lack of sleep, came into the room last. She cast a quick glance around the chamber, her eyes lighting immediately on Royce, then just as quickly flitting away to each of her sisters. She slipped into her seat and was grateful to have a cup of coffee poured for her instead of the ubiquitous tea.

As she sipped it, she studied the others once more. Rose yawned, her eyes dull, her gestures listless. Even Lily, usually full of chatter, was silent, toying with her food. Anger welled in Mary. She might be a little sleepy—she'd had the devil of a time trying to fall asleep again last night—but at least she was not suffering from the effects of a narcotic. Clearly the dose had been large—the man could have seriously harmed one of them. What if one of her sisters had simply not awakened from her sleep?

She brought her cup down with a snap. "Do any of you remember anything about last night?"

Everyone but Royce turned a blank stare upon her.

"What do you mean, Mare?" Camellia frowned at her. "About supper?"

"No, about the enormous din I created screaming." Several mouths dropped open. "You were drugged. And someone tried to abduct Rose."

A babble of questions followed this pronouncement, and Mary went through the story in more detail—leaving out everything that had happened after she and Royce returned to her bedchamber. There was a long moment of silence after she finished.

"I cannot believe we missed the whole thing!" Lily cried rather petulantly.

"I know. The only excitement in days, and we were sound asleep," Camellia added in disgust. "I wish I had had a crack at the man."

"Yes, your gun might have come in quite handy," Royce offered, a twinkle in his eyes. "I presume you sleep with it under your pillow."

"Don't be daft." Camellia sent him a scornful look. "It was in my bag, not even loaded." She brightened. "I shall take it out now, though, and carry it with us. Do you think there's a chance he will try again?"

"Camellia!" Rose exclaimed. "Don't even say such a thing!"

"Well," Miss Dalrymple said with the air of one making a pronouncement, "I must say, I have never had this sort of thing happen at any of my other places of employment."

"I daresay," Royce agreed mildly. "No doubt the earl would have been reluctant to hire you if kidnappings had been a regular occurrence at your places of employment. However, I suspect that you might as well get used to such things now."

Miss Dalrymple goggled at him.

"Who do you suppose it was?" Lily asked. "Do you think

it was like the wicked Duc de Montclair, and he saw Rose from afar and lusted after her?"

Miss Dalrymple let out a gasp. "Miss Lily! Mind your language."

Wrapped up in her story, Lily went on, "Maybe he saw you in London, Rose, and he followed us here, and then he stole you, intending to have his way with you."

"Honestly, Lily, you and Camellia act as if you're glad someone tried to carry me off!" Rose glared at her sister.

"No, of course not. But you must admit, it's the most exciting thing that's ever happened to us." Lily fell silent, looking somewhat chastened.

Rose turned to Mary, a question in her eyes, and Mary knew she was thinking about Cosmo, just as she had. Mary gave her a subtle shake of her head, and Rose said nothing.

"I know who it could be!" Lily exclaimed, snapping her fingers, her momentary constraint vanished. "That man who followed us the other day! You said that the man last night was large, and so was he."

"That's true," Mary agreed, looking thoughtful.

"Perhaps he followed us the other day because he was . . ." Lily cast a glance at Miss Dalrymple. ". . . interested in Rose. Maybe he's been watching us, trailing us, just waiting for an opportunity to take her."

Royce shrugged. "Perhaps. Or maybe someone staying here caught a glimpse of her and decided to abduct her. I checked this morning, and none of the guests fled the inn in the middle of the night. But the intruder clearly did. There are footprints in the mud below your window, and they led out to the road." He paused, then continued, "Whoever it was, I hope that after last night's failure, he will have given up. Still, I think it would be a good idea to take some precautions."

Camellia nodded. "I'll take my pistol in the carriage."

"I never imagined that I would say such a thing, but I think that would be a good idea. The driver usually has a gun on long trips, and I shall tell him to have the groom carry it at the ready. No doubt it will be unnecessary, but better to look foolish than to have to face Oliver and tell him I lost one of his new cousins along the way. Now, it is still some distance to Willowmere. Traveling at a comfortable pace, we would have to stop again tonight at an inn, which I am reluctant to do. Therefore, I intend to make a small detour. My own estate, Iverley Hall, is not far off the route we will take. I think the extra distance is worth it to spend the night where I know we will be secure." He cast a look around the table and, seeing no protestations or questions, gave them a nod. "Good. Then I will leave you lovely ladies to pack your things while I talk to the coachman."

"I like him," Camellia announced as the door closed after Royce.

"Me too," Lily agreed. "It must have been terribly romantic, his running in to rescue you like that." She heaved a sigh.

"I wouldn't know," Mary replied dryly, "since I was unconscious at the time. When I woke up, he was slapping my cheek."

"Slapping you!" Miss Dalrymple repeated, aghast. "No, no, I will not believe it. A perfect gentleman—"

"Oh, not like that," Mary told her, annoyed. "Just . . . you know . . . trying to wake me up." She demonstrated on her own cheek.

"It is best if you don't mention it at all." Miss Dalrymple shook her head disapprovingly. "A gentleman should never enter a lady's bedchamber."

Mary rolled her eyes. "Even when she screams for help?"

"If word got out, it could ruin your reputation," the chaperone countered, rising to her feet. "Now, I am going to get ready to leave, as Sir Royce suggested, and I expect you girls to do the same."

As soon as Miss Dalrymple left the room, Camellia rounded on her two older sisters. "All right. What aren't you two telling us? Don't deny it; I saw that look between you earlier. You know something more than you're letting on to Sir Royce."

"Mary saw Cosmo the other day," Rose said.

"What?" Lily's voice rose. "And you didn't tell us?"

"I wasn't sure it was him," Mary protested.

"You could have told us anyway! You never tell us anything."

"We aren't children anymore," Camellia addded.

"I know. I'm sorry. I would have told you, but Sir Royce and Fitz were there, and then when we got home, we were so busy. I didn't think it was important, anyway."

"All right," Camellia said somewhat begrudgingly. "Never mind all that. Where did you see him? Did he talk to you?"

"No. I saw him at a distance. That's why I wasn't sure it was him. It was at the Tower, when I left the rest of you. I thought I saw him some way off, and I went looking for him, but I lost him. And then . . ." She shrugged, a blush rising in her cheeks as she remembered what had happened after Royce found her. "Anyway, I just saw him for a moment, and it wasn't up close. I could have been imagining things."

"You didn't imagine what happened last night."

"No. But that man couldn't possibly have been Cosmo, he was far too big. Besides, even with a mask, I think I would have recognized Cosmo."

"Is that why you didn't tell Sir Royce either about seeing him?" Lily asked.

"Yes. I knew it couldn't be Cosmo. And I just . . ." Mary sighed. "I don't know. I never told the earl or any of them about Cosmo. I'm not sure why. Maybe I was afraid it would make Lord Stewkesbury more suspicious of us. Or perhaps I was simply embarrassed. Cosmo Glass is not the sort one wants to admit knowing."

"That's true enough." Camellia nodded. "I wouldn't have told them either."

"Besides, whether it's Cosmo or someone else, all any of us can do is keep an eye on Rose and make sure that nothing happens to her." Mary looked at Rose. "Unless you would rather I tell Sir Royce?"

Rose shook her head and offered a wan smile. "No. I'd just as soon no one here even heard of the man. You're right. I just need to be careful."

"We'll *all* be careful."

It was late afternoon when their carriage pulled into a long driveway, cool and green with overarching trees lining the way to a regal block of a house. Made of red sandstone, it glowed in the mellow light of the sinking sun. Sets of mullioned windows glittered across the front, and both ends were anchored by sturdy square chimneys, with another pair rising from the center. Somehow both stately and warm, the house had a welcoming air about it, and Mary felt at once that they would indeed be safe here.

"What a wonderful house!" she exclaimed as she swung out of the carriage, taking Royce's proffered hand to step down.

He smiled, and his hand tightened briefly around hers. "Thank you. I think so. Welcome, ladies, to Iverley Hall."

A butler emerged, his smile letting Mary know at once that this man was a far cry from the earl's Hooper. He was followed by a middle-aged woman, smoothing down her apron and beaming. After the inescapable greetings, introductions, and instructions, the middle-aged woman, who turned out to be Mrs. Appleby, the housekeeper, led the sisters to their rooms herself, apologizing all the way because only a few of the rooms were ready for visitors.

"We wasn't expecting the master for three or four weeks yet," she confided in Mary. "Usually, Master Royce is good about letting us know when he's coming and whether he's bringing guests—" The housekeeper stopped, looked horrified. "Not that I'm complaining, you understand, miss. I'm sure he would have sent word if there'd been time."

"No doubt he would." Mary smiled at the woman. "It was a sudden decision. I am sure he has full confidence in your housekeeping." She cast a glance around. "It is clear that the house looks lovely, even in Sir Royce's absence."

The older woman pinkened in gratification. "Thank you, miss, it's good of you to notice. We do our best, we do. It's always grand when Master Royce comes home."

"I noticed how pleased everyone was to see him."

"Oh, yes, he's a good man. He was raised proper, you see. When Lady Barbara married again after Sir Alan died and took the little master off to Willowmere with her, we were afraid that we wouldn't see him again. That he'd be grown before he came back. We weren't even sure we wouldn't all be turned out and the house shut. But the old earl said no—it was him that ran everything, even about the boy. And he said that Master Royce must know his property and the people here. He kept the staff, and he'd come here three or four times a year. He always brought Master Royce with him. Wanted us all to know him and the other way around." She smiled and sighed, shaking her head fondly. "That boy loved coming here—mind, I think 'twas more he liked that it was just him and the old earl when they visited. Master Royce was that fond of the man. Well, he could hardly remember his own father, and his grandfather passed on before he was born."

She stopped in front of a room and took a breath. "Ah, here I am, talking your ear off, and you'll be wanting to have a rest and wash-up 'fore supper, I warrant."

"Oh, no—I mean—well, yes, of course, I would like that. But it's been most enjoyable talking to you." Mary smiled. This friendly, warm woman was poles apart from any of the servants at Stewkesbury House.

Mary's bedchamber was smaller than the one at Stewkesbury House, but quite comfortable and pleasantly, if not as elegantly, furnished. Relaxed by the surroundings, Mary was able to take a short nap after she washed up from the journey. When she awoke, she put on her best dress for dinner and went to look around the house before supper. As she strolled through the hallway downstairs, looking at the portraits lining the corridor, a masculine voice sounded behind her.

"Felonious-looking lot, aren't they?"

"Hello, Royce." Mary turned to face him.

He, too, was dressed for dinner, though he had eschewed formal attire, as the Talbots had the last few nights. As always, the sight of him caused her heart to leap traitorously. She could not help but think of what had passed between them last night, and a blush stole up her throat. She wondered if he thought of it, too—or perhaps it was so commonplace a thing to him that it had slipped his mind.

To cover her sudden nerves, she said lightly, "I would have said that they were quite pious, actually."

"Not from what I've heard." He came to stand beside her, gazing up at the large oil painting before them. "That's the first baronet, got his title from Queen Elizabeth. I believe he was something of a corsair, but as he stuck to stealing from Spain, the Queen didn't mind. He bought this place from the Iverleys—who had sadly gone into decline—and changed into a lord of the manor."

"Is this his wife?" Mary asked, going on to the next painting, which depicted a woman with strawberry blond hair and a high ruff rising behind her head.

"The second. The first one, it's said, jumped off a tower when he gave up the sea. Couldn't face the idea of his being home all the time. She never lived at Iverley Hall. But Lady Margaret here outlived her husband by a good many years and ruled the place with an iron hand—and, apparently, a great deal of skill, for she increased the family fortunes her grandson inherited. Her son was something of a cipher, and she remained in virtual control of the place even after he reached his majority."

"You're very familiar with them all."

"Indeed, yes. Lord Reginald insisted I learn about my land and family. He said I should not become a stranger to my own people just because my mother had married a Talbot. He was right, of course; he nearly always was—though clearly he made a mistake in cutting himself off from his daughter." He cast a sideways glance at her.

Mary smiled. "Thank you for saying that. Mama never talked about him, except that once when she told us about their falling out. I could not judge what sort of man he was; I could not even tell for certain how she felt about him. But you sound as though you were quite fond of him."

He nodded. "I was. I am still. He could be an irascible old devil and difficult to deal with. There was hell to pay if one crossed him. But he followed the same rules he laid out for others. He wasn't an affectionate sort. An approving nod was usually the best you could get from him. But he spent far more time and trouble on a lad who had no real claim on him than most others would have. He was much more a father to me than my own."

Mary smiled, thinking how his words echoed those his housekeeper had spoken earlier. Obviously the woman had been on the mark with her assessment of Sir Royce.

"What about your stepfather?" she asked. "Oliver's father?"

Royce shrugged as he turned away, walking with her along the hall. "He was a good enough sort. But neither he nor my mother was there a great deal. They preferred the bright lights of London to the solitude of Willowmere. Oliver and Fitz and I saw them infrequently, usually only for a month or two in the dead of winter—or when they were under the hatches and had to spend a while in the country to repair their finances."

"I'm sorry." She tried to imagine growing up as he had, rarely even seeing his parents. Her life might have lacked the financial advantages his had, but she preferred the close, loving family relationship she had known.

"Oh, they were never at *point non plus,*" he said, misunderstanding her words of regret.

Mary glanced at him, but he was looking away from her, and she wondered whether he had purposefully taken her statement to be about something he found easier to discuss.

"The old earl ran the estate," Royce continued, "so Lawrence could only borrow on his prospects, and my mother's father had tied up her money so tightly that they could get nothing but income from it. Obviously, everyone knew how poor they were at managing their finances. The old earl was forever on at them about it. I think he was actually a bit relieved when Lawrence died before him; he feared that his son would dissipate the fortune before Oliver got hold of it. Grandfa—I mean, Lord Reginald managed my lands and money as well so that Lawrence and my mother could not make a hash of that either." He grinned at her, taking the sting out of the words. "Come, let me show you around the house. There are better things to be seen than these stuffy old ancestors."

He held out his arm, and Mary took it. His closeness made her fingers tremble, and her breath came faster in her throat. Her head was filled with thoughts of his kisses and caresses, and her body tingled all over again.

Even now, as they strolled through the hallways, Royce pointing out this room and that, smoothly chatting about the house and his life, Mary wished that he would stop and take her in his arms and kiss her. It would be wrong, of course; she was well aware of that. There was a bevy of reasons for them to stay at arm's distance. Unfortunately, the force pulling her to him was far stronger than the logic holding them apart.

Did he feel the same way? No, she told herself. She was foolish to let herself even consider the possibility. He was attracted to her, certainly, but for a man like Royce Winslow, their kisses last night would have been something quite minor. He had probably indulged in many such moments.

He led her finally out onto the terrace, which looked down upon a garden that was delightfully unregimented, flowers growing in profusion and narrow paths winding among them with few borders between.

"It's a charming house, Sir Royce. I cannot imagine that Willowmere could be any nicer."

Royce chuckled. "You should wait until you have seen Willowmere. I suspect you will change your mind. Iverley Hall is dear to me, but it is far less grand."

"Grandeur does not always appeal," Mary replied.

"Very diplomatic of you." Royce turned to her.

They were so close that Mary could see the ring of darker green on the outer edge of his irises. Her throat grew tight, the pulse leaping in it. Royce wanted to kiss her; she could see it in his eyes, in the softening of his lips. Her entire body tingled with the memory of the kisses they had shared the night before.

He should not kiss her, she knew. She should not want him to. What had happened last night had sprung from the excitement of the moment, from the bizarre situation in which they had found themselves. Now, cooler, calmer heads must prevail. Yet somehow she could not move, could only stand, poised and trembling, as if on the brink of some precipice.

Royce turned away abruptly. "We should go back inside."

"Of course." Mary drew a shaky breath and walked back with him to the door, careful not to take his arm again.

Chapter 15

When they drove away from Iverley Hall the following morning, Royce took two extra grooms with him, one ranging ahead of the carriage and the other lagging behind. Mary noticed that both men had pistols tucked into their belts.

The journey was shorter than on the first two days, taking only six or seven hours, and the sisters found the landscape more interesting. Yesterday, as they approached Iverley Hall, Mary had noticed that the peaceful English scenery had become—well, somehow larger. Blue-tinged hills appeared in the distance, and today they traveled into them. Vistas spread out before them, now often dotted with beautiful dark lakes. Mary remembered that Oliver had called it the Lake District. There was an aura of grandeur to it, almost of wildness.

In the middle of the afternoon, Sir Royce dropped back by the carriage to tell them that they were turning into the park surrounding Willowmere. The sisters all crowded to the windows, despite Miss Dalrymple's protestations, leaning out to catch a first glimpse of the house that would now be their home.

The carriage rolled through a long avenue of yews, emerging at last on a green expanse of lawn, with a house sitting in the middle like a jewel in a setting. Willowmere sprawled over the ground, three stories tall and spreading in every direction, far larger than Royce's home. It lacked Iverley Hall's symmetry, for it had clearly been added onto several times, with towers and wings pushing out here and there; yet the overall result was somehow pleasing. Built of yellowish stone, it reflected a welcoming glow in the afternoon sun. The stone had discolored irregularly, so that it seemed permanently shadowed in places, and ivy almost completely covered one wall. Trees and shrubs softened the edges of the building, and gardens spread out from either side.

"Oh my," Lily breathed.

Mary glanced at Miss Dalrymple and saw that even she was wide-eyed as she gazed at the house.

"Quite a sight, isn't it?" Royce leaned down to talk to them through the carriage window. "Don't worry. It's much more comfortable than Stewkesbury House. You'll soon feel at home here."

Mary wasn't sure about that, but she had to admit that the house was lovely. Still . . . there was something about the smaller, squarer Iverley Hall that she preferred.

At least the staff here were not as stiff as those at Stewkesbury House—or perhaps, Mary thought, it was just that she and her sisters had learned not to act in the ways that shocked them so. Since the earl had sent a message informing them of the girls' arrival, the servants had had time to prepare, and each girl was shown to her own room. Mary's bedchamber lay on the west side of the house, overlooking a garden that fell in levels to an expanse of green. Beyond that lay one of the inky pools of water, called tarns, that were scattered about the countryside. A small wooden gazebo lay at the edge of the tarn. The pond was fed by a stream diverted from the nearby river, and a narrow stone bridge arched the stream, looking like something out of a fairy tale.

Mary left the window and took a slow visual turn of her room. The maid had called it the iris bedchamber, and indeed the wallpaper was patterned with delicately drawn flowers. The drapes and bedcover echoed the deep blue of the irises, and a dark golden wingback chair by the fire offered a welcome accent. The furniture was neither as dark nor as heavy as the pieces in her room at Stewkesbury House, which pleased Mary as well. Perhaps, she thought, it would not be so bad here after all.

That hopeful idea was doused the following day, however, when Miss Dalrymple set out in earnest to train the Bascombe girls into proper young ladies. First she tested their skills in the various arts required of a girl about to make her debut, marching them into the music room to play the piano and sing, then taking them to the nursery for a bit of watercolor and charcoal drawing. It did not take her long to discover that none of the girls had the slightest ability to draw and had not, indeed, ever picked up a paintbrush. Their musical skills were almost as horrifying to her, for while all four girls could carry a tune and Camellia, at least, had a nice, clear voice, only Lily could play the piano, and her skills were limited to a few rollicking popular songs.

When they moved on to sewing, Mary had higher hopes, but she soon found out that Miss Dalrymple was not impressed by the girls' ability at such prosaic things as making dresses or mending rents or tears. What she wanted was fine needlework like embroidery.

"But making a frock is more useful," Mary pointed out. "Rose is an excellent seamstress. She makes nearly all our dresses. We help with the seams, of course, but the fine work is hers."

"Don't!" Miss Dalrymple raised both hands, her eyes rounded in horror. "Don't ever tell anyone that! It will positively ruin your chances."

"Why? I would think it would be a good thing to be able to make one's clothes."

"You might as well tell everyone you can chop wood or scrub the floors."

"Well, we can, though I was never very good with an axe."

Miss Dalrymple looked for a moment as if her eyes might roll back in her head. She dropped into a chair and fanned herself furiously to regain her poise. "I haven't the time to teach you all the skills you lack. We will concentrate on the most important. You cannot hope to 'take' if you cannot dance."

"We can dance," Lily protested.

"I do not mean a jig." The older woman sent her a withering glance. "I mean the quadrille, the cotillion, the country dance, and the waltz. These are the essential dances for every ball, and until you have mastered them, it would be an absolute disaster to take you to even a county assembly."

The girls began a daily routine of deportment lessons after breakfast, followed by a luncheon with Miss Dalrymple that was primarily an exercise in table manners and in learning the names and uses of a dizzying array of utensils and dishes. Next came instruction in music and singing, ending finally with a dance lesson in the small ballroom. It was, Mary thought, a testament to their teacher's grim character that she managed to turn even normally pleasurable things such as singing and dancing into boring drudgery.

At first the girls danced with each other, but when Miss Dalrymple realized that the girls were dancing the men's steps even when they should be following the women's, she called in Sir Royce to serve as their partner. Royce was agreeable, as he usually proved to be, and his presence greatly enlivened the lessons. He was an excellent dancer, and even Mary, who had up until now declared herself hopeless on the dance floor, found it easy to follow the steps. Moreover, he kept up such an easy, effortless flow of chatter that she found herself paying more attention to his voice than to the movement of her feet, and, amazingly, before long she was able to sail through an entire dance without any stumbles or missteps.

The country dances were the easiest for the girls, for they closely resembled the reels that were popular at home. The quadrille and the cotillion, with their numerous couples and intricate patterns of steps, were more difficult, and it was almost impossible, with their small group of participants, to replicate what an actual dance would be like. But it was the waltz that captured their attention.

"Now, the waltz," Miss Dalrymple began, her mouth pinching up, "has not always been considered proper. A few years back you would not have found it approved at an assembly in the country, and it was not introduced into Almack's until ten years ago. Indeed, I am not convinced that it is the sort of dance that a young girl should be allowed to do. In particular, I have grave misgivings about teaching it to a group of girls who are, well, less than genteel in so much of their manner."

She fixed the girls with a grim look to drive home her point.

"However," Miss Dalrymple continued, "it has become so popular that a young lady cannot be considered ready to enter society unless she can waltz. Therefore, we will learn the steps. But remember that I expect you to execute them with the utmost grace and dignity, staying always an arm's length from your partner and engaging in only quiet, refined conversation. And do not forget that you must never dance more than two waltzes with the same gentleman in one evening unless he is your fiancé or husband. And if you should be so fortunate as to receive a voucher for Almack's"—the downward turn of the governess's mouth clearly expressed her own doubts regarding the matter—"you must not waltz until one of the patronesses has given you permission and presented you with a suitable partner."

"That sounds excessively silly," Camellia told her.

Miss Dalrymple's face pursed up as if she had bitten into a lemon, but Sir Royce forestalled her reply by saying, "Yes, isn't it? However, Miss Dalrymple is quite correct. The patronesses at Almack's can make or break a young woman entering society. The place is deadly dull, and the food is barely adequate; Lady Jersey runs it like a martinet. Yet nothing is as highly valued as a voucher to Almack's."

As was usually the case, Mary's sisters, even Camellia, were quick to accept Sir Royce's word as law, and they promised solemnly that they would not ruin their social futures by waltzing at Almack's without permission.

When Royce took Mary into his arms to demonstrate the waltz, she realized at once why the dance had been considered scandalous. "Arm's length" seemed entirely too close. Forced to look up into his face, she could feel the heat from his body, smell the scent of his shaving soap and cologne. Her hand was cupped in his, and his other hand rested on her waist. It was as near as she could come to being held by him in public. Her cheeks pinkened with embarrassment. What if her feelings were written on her face?

Something flickered in Royce's eyes—a momentary mirroring, perhaps, of her own thoughts—but was quickly gone. His expression became aloof, the smile vanishing. His voice and look were impersonal as he guided her into the steps of the dance, and Mary frowned at him in irritation. Her annoyance made her forget her embarrassment, however, and it was easier to follow the steps. By her second time around the floor, she was able to relax and follow him almost naturally.

"There, that's better," he said in a low tone.

"I beg your pardon?" Mary set her face in the expression Miss Dalrymple had been urging on them for days as the correct response for dampening pretensions. Mary was not entirely sure what constituted "pretensions," but she decided that Royce's attitude of indifference was reason enough to make the face.

"Well done," he murmured. "If you can respond to a compliment in that fashion and dance the waltz without a misstep, you are practically assured of success."

"Don't be absurd. I don't know what you're talking about. I certainly recall no compliment."

"I expressed approval because you had stopped thinking about yourself and were simply enjoying the dance."

"I wasn't enjoying it."

He quirked an eyebrow. "Then we must continue to practice until you do."

"And I cannot imagine why you thought I was thinking about myself."

"I could see it on your face. I fear you will have to learn to school your expression if you hope to make it through the choppy waters of the *ton*." He leaned closer and murmured, "I could see, for instance, that when I put my hand on your waist, you were thinking of the other night."

Heat flooded Mary's cheeks and she would have stumbled, but his grip tightened and kept her moving through the steps with only a minor stutter.

"You think entirely too much of yourself," she retorted.

"No doubt. Still, I know that is where your thoughts were. Mine were as well."

"Indeed? You looked as if you scarcely knew me."

He chuckled. "Would you have had me leer at you? I think that would hardly have helped you through the dance."

"Of course not. You are talking nonsense."

"Am I?" His eyes glinted down at her, and Mary could feel a familiar and most unwelcome heat stealing through her body.

With a grimace, she pulled away from him. Miss Dalrymple, who had been pounding out the waltz beat with her palm on the piano top, stopped and glared at Mary.

"Miss Bascombe! A lady does not simply stop in the middle of a dance."

"I didn't feel like continuing," Mary replied crossly.

"That is of no importance. One should press on until the end of the dance. After that, of course, you may plead a headache and ask to be returned to your chaperone. But one must not interrupt the dancing."

"Oh, for goodness' sake, we are just practicing!"

Miss Dalrymple's bosom swelled with indignation, and Mary was reminded forcibly of a pouter pigeon.

Before she could speak, Sir Royce stepped between them, saying, "I fear it was my fault, Miss Dalrymple. I was teasing Miss Bascombe, and it quite distracted her. You must blame me."

Mary watched Miss Dalrymple somewhat sourly as she simpered at Sir Royce. It was most annoying the way the woman, so rigid with them, positively melted if Royce so much as smiled at her.

"Now, Sir Royce, isn't it just like you to take the blame?"

"Mmm. He's a perfect gentleman."

Miss Dalrymple frowned at Mary. "Sarcasm is not beguiling, particularly in a young person."

"I wasn't trying to be beguiling," Mary shot back. "Really, Miss Dalrymple, must we be charming and sweet our entire lives? Is there no time when we are allowed to be ourselves?"

The older woman pursed her lips. "Not if you expect to land a husband. No man wants a wife who cannot keep a civil tongue in her head. Isn't that right, Sir Royce?"

He, for once, was at a loss for words. "Um . . . well . . ."

"I am quite aware of Sir Royce's standards in a wife." Mary sent him a single, flashing glance. "Fortunately, I would not think to look for such a paragon of a husband as Sir Royce."

Even her sisters looked amazed at Mary's caustic tone. Miss Dalrymple drew her breath to deliver a lecture, and suddenly Mary felt as if she would explode if she had to listen to one more word from that woman.

"Excuse me," she said shortly. "I fear I am not good company this afternoon."

With that, she whirled and ran from the room. Behind her she heard Miss Dalrymple sharply call her name, then Royce's calming murmur.

Mary rushed down the hall and out the back door, afraid that one of her sisters might take it into her head to come after her. Mary did not feel like talking to anyone, even Rose. She had made a fool of herself, she knew. She did not care what the annoying Miss Dalrymple thought, but her siblings would not understand why she had spoken so slightingly about Royce. Indeed, she was not sure she understood it herself.

Mary crossed the terrace and went down the steps into the garden. She had walked through much of the garden that lay close to the house, but today she headed toward the lower garden, where the plants grew in wilder profusion, leading to the small orchard and beyond that a meadow. Perhaps a longer walk would help her work out why she had grown so irritated with Sir Royce. She had forgiven him for what he'd said that night to the earl. Nor was she angry about what had happened between them at the inn. That had been as much her fault as his, the result of the excitement of the moment, the bizarre situation in which they had found themselves.

But, she realized, he had been able to move on, seemingly to forget about the passion that had flared between them. He could be at ease, even flirt with her in his old, meaningless way, whereas she found her mind returning again and again to those few minutes, reliving the kisses and caresses. Indeed, if she was honest with herself, she knew that she wished she could experience those things again! It was absurd. Pointless. And that, she knew, was the crux of the problem, the basis for her irritation: she wanted something—someone—she could not have.

Mary raised her head and glanced around, faintly surprised to find how far she had come. Somehow she had wandered onto a path lined on both sides with thick green hedges that grew higher than her head. Where was she?

She turned in a circle. She could see only the curving hedges about her. Finally, with a shrug, she started forward again. She was bound to emerge from the hedges at some point, and once she could see the house again, she would be able to find her way back.

After a few more minutes, Mary came upon an intersection of paths. She paused, wondering whether to turn left or right. The hedges grew high in either direction until they curved out of sight. What was this place? As she stood there, she heard a rustling noise on the other side of the hedge.

"Hello?" she called, turning toward the noise. Perhaps one of her sisters had come looking for her, and the two of them were wandering about only a few feet from each other. "Is someone there?"

She was met with a profound silence. Yet somehow, she knew there was someone on the other side of the hedge. She took a few steps, her ears alert for the slightest sound, and again she heard something—had that been the crackle of twigs breaking?

Mary stopped, poised and waiting. From beyond the hedge came only silence. But she was certain now there was someone . . . something there. It was not the quietude of emptiness, but the heavy, brooding hush of an enforced stillness.

"Who's there?" she asked sharply. "Answer me!"

Was that breathing she heard? Mary was too aware of her pulse thudding in her ears to be certain. A faint scent teased at her nostrils, tugging at her memory. The smell of pipe smoke, underlaid with whiskey . . . Cosmo.

There was a small, sharp crack. Mary whirled and ran back the way she had come. She didn't know what path she had taken, so she could not retrace her steps. She simply ran as fast as she could, her heart pounding. She turned right or left on impulse, praying that her choices would not lead her straight to the person on the other side of the hedge. Finally she wound up in a bower where rosebushes grew in sweet-smelling abundance along climbing trellises that arched over the path. And there, at the end of the flowery tunnel, the garden opened up. She flew down the path toward it.

A man's form entered the bower, silhouetted against the light so that she could see only the dark outline of him. With a shriek, she stopped abruptly, sliding on the fallen petals beneath her feet.

"Mary?" The man started forward.

"Royce! Oh, Royce!" Mary ran to him, too relieved to even think of propriety.

At her obvious distress, he broke into a run. Mary threw herself at him, wrapping her arms around his neck and holding on tightly.

"Mary! What happened? What's the matter?" Royce's

arms went around her, pressing her to him. "Are you all right?"

Mary nodded and clung to him, luxuriating in the feeling of being safe. But gradually she became aware of the intimacy of their situation. Her body was flush against Royce's all the way up and down; she could feel his hard bone and muscle pressing into her softer flesh. His strength and warmth surrounded her.

If anyone saw them like this, it would be scandalous. And on the heels of that thought came another: if she remained in his arms much longer, she would be all too likely to raise her head to kiss him. She shuddered and stepped back.

"Are you cold? Here." He peeled off his jacket and settled it on her shoulders. "Now, tell me what happened."

"I—it was probably nothing." With Royce standing beside her, her fears of a moment ago began to seem foolish and exaggerated.

He raised a skeptical eyebrow. "You came running at me like the hounds of hell were after you. Don't tell me that you ran away like that from nothing."

Mary felt a flush steal up her throat. "Well, yes, I did think—but there wasn't really any—I was probably just being silly."

"Why don't you tell me what happened, and then we'll decide whether it's silly?"

Mary sighed. "Very well. I was walking, and I wasn't really watching where I was going. I was, well . . ."

"In a high dudgeon?" he suggested.

She smiled faintly. "Yes, that is a fair description. I am sorry that I was snappish with you. I—Miss Dalrymple fairly drives me mad. But that is no excuse—"

"It doesn't matter. What happened as you walked?"

"I wound up between very high hedges, and I realized

that I was lost. So I stopped, trying to decide which way to go, and I—well, I heard a noise."

"What kind of noise?"

"Nothing frightening, really. Just a rustling, as if someone had brushed against the other side of the hedge or was walking through leaves or—I'm not sure what, but it sounded as if there was someone there. So I called out, thinking they could help me find my way back. I thought perhaps it was a gardener or one of my sisters, come looking for me. But there was no reply. So I started forward again, and I heard something more, or I thought I did, and I called out again. No one answered, but I—it just felt as if there was a person on the other side of the hedge. That probably sounds foolish, but—"

He shook his head. "No. I know the sensation."

"A twig snapped, and I took off running." She was not about to get into the topic of the scent she had smelled or its relation to her stepfather. "I didn't know where I was going. Then you came along." Mary shrugged. "I am sorry that I threw myself at you. You must think me hysterical."

"Believe me, you have never been around a hysterical woman if you think that. Let's go back to where you were and see what we can find."

"It was probably only nerves," Mary warned, but she fell in beside him as he started off in the direction she had come.

"I have never met a woman less prone to 'nerves.'"

"I shall choose to take that as a compliment."

Royce grinned at her. In the dappled shadows of the bower, his eyes were the color of dark green leaves. "Oh, it is."

She found herself smiling back. "Still, upon reflection, 'tis likely that it was only an animal, if it was anything."

"When you called, did you hear it scurry away?"

"No. There was complete silence. I was listening very hard."

"Don't you think most animals would have run from the sound of a human voice? And a dog would have barked or growled or tried to join you, surely."

"Then perhaps a gardener."

"Why wouldn't a gardener answer when you called out? I can't think why anyone would not have answered you—unless they were someplace they should not be."

They had reached the high hedges, and Mary led him back through them as best she could. "What is this place?"

"A maze. It was built generations ago and became rather overgrown. We used to play here as boys, and after Oliver inherited, he had it restored to its former condition. There's quite a lovely little pond at the center."

"Here, I think." Mary pointed to the hedge on the right. "It was just about here that I heard the noise. I walked that way a few steps before I turned and ran back."

Royce studied the hedge for a moment, glancing in both directions. "Come with me. I think I can find my way to the same spot on the other side."

Mary followed him, growing more convinced by the second that she had imagined the whole incident. It was absurd. Wasn't it? Particularly absurd was the thought that it might have been Cosmo. She could not smell that scent now. And even if it had really been there, how could she be sure that it was the smell of Cosmo's tobacco? The tobacco was not his alone; doubtless many other men put the same blend in their pipes, or something close to it.

"I think this is just about opposite where you were." Royce looked down, his eyes carefully sweeping the area.

Mary joined him in his search, though she was not sure what she expected to find. Beside her, Royce stiffened, pointing to the ground right beside the hedge. "Look."

Mary's eyes followed the direction in which his finger was pointing. There in the slightly damp earth was the impression of a shoe.

Royce's tone was grim as he went on, "Someone *was* here."

"But why?" Mary asked in a hushed voice. "Why would someone have stood here and said nothing?"

"That is what I intend to find out."

"This print could be from some other time, not necessarily this afternoon." She tried surreptitiously to sniff the air. Was there the faintest trace of something smoky? She could no longer be sure.

"I don't think so," Royce told her. "The print looks fresh to me, not dried out. Nor was it made by a gardener. It is clearly a gentleman's shoe."

"Oh." Mary looked again at the print. He was right. It was not the broad outline of a boot, but the slender, more fitted form of a shoe made for a gentleman. "Do you think . . ." She looked up at him, hating even to express the thought.

"That it's the same man who tried to abduct your sister?"

Mary nodded.

Royce paused thoughtfully, then said, "It seems unlikely. After all, it has been several days since that incident, and we are miles away. He would have had to follow us all this way, staying out of sight the whole time."

"Yes, it seems far-fetched."

"I will speak to the gardeners," Royce went on, "see if any of them have spotted someone lurking about. I'll send one of the grooms into the village to ask around, find out if there have been any strangers staying there since we returned." His voice hardened. "And I'll make bloody sure that the grounds are patrolled more carefully. There will be a full complement of gardeners out here every day. You and your sisters will have no cause to feel unsafe. Though I would prefer it if you did not walk alone this far from the house again. Stick to the upper gardens."

"Surely that's not necessary," Mary protested.

"Probably not. But just this once . . . humor me." He turned, offering her his arm. "Now, would you care to see the rest of the maze?"

Mary smiled. "That sounds very nice."

The hedges continued high on either side, curving sometimes and at others running in a straight line. Royce made each turn without hesitation, though Mary grew more and more lost as they went along.

"I hope I never wind up here alone. I should doubtless starve to death before I found my way out."

"It's not that bad once you've learned it. But it does serve to keep out strangers."

They came out at last upon a tranquil circle, surrounded on all sides by hedges except for the single opening. Inside the circle lay a pond, still and soothing. Lily pads floated in it, and two large goldfish swam lazily through the water. Completing the pleasant picture, two stone benches sat on either side of the pond. Entering the circle was like stepping into a cool green room. Mary felt separated from the rest of the world, and her earlier fright seemed distant, even foolish.

"It's beautiful," Mary breathed, walking up to the pond.

"I'm glad you like it." Royce came to stand beside her. "Would you like to sit for a while?" He gestured toward one of the benches.

They settled onto the bench side by side. After a moment, Royce said, frowning, "I had thought to give you and your sisters riding lessons, but perhaps I should not if someone is lurking about."

"What? No, you mustn't change your mind," Mary protested. "Camellia would love to ride. We should all enjoy it—if nothing else, it would get us out from under the gimlet eye of Miss Dalrymple."

He chuckled. "That is certainly a consideration."

"Please . . ." Mary put her hand beseechingly on his arm. "We don't know that the footprint belongs to anyone wishing us harm. The more I think about it, the sillier it seems. And you will be with us when we are out riding, in any case. Say you will do it."

Royce turned and looked down at her. His eyes darkened. "How can I refuse when you ask me like that?"

Mary went still, her heart suddenly in her throat. For one long moment, everything seemed to stop. Mary was aware of the soft brush of the breeze against her cheek, the faint plop of a small frog as it leapt into the water, the shaded cool here at the heart of the maze.

Then Royce was bending to her, his arm sliding around her waist, and Mary melted into him. His mouth was warm upon hers, his arm like iron around her. They could have been miles from anyone, wrapped in a cocoon of heat and hunger, all awareness of anything besides themselves and this moment falling away. His hand moved over her, caressing her through her clothes, moving almost lazily over her back and hip and up again to smooth over her breast.

Her body flamed to life beneath his touch, the fire gathering deep in her abdomen. With a groan, he pulled her over onto his lap. With his arm around her back, he kissed his way down her throat, nuzzling and nipping at the side of her neck. His hand roamed over her front more urgently now, cupping her breasts and teasing the nipples through the cloth until they stood up hard and hungry, straining against the thin material.

Mary was aware of an ache between her legs, an eager yearning. She wanted him, hungered for him in a way she did not fully understand. She slid her hands over his shoulders and up his neck, tangling them in his thick hair. She felt him quicken beneath her, and instinctively she moved her hips and was rewarded with his harsh indrawn breath.

He breathed her name, his breath hot against the skin of her chest. His mouth moved downward until it reached the neckline of her dress and he nuzzled down into it, seeking the soft, quivering flesh of her breasts. Mary gasped and moisture pooled between her legs.

Abruptly Royce let out an oath and raised his head. He stared down into Mary's face for a long moment, his eyes dark in the shaded surroundings. His face was taut, the skin stretched over his bones, his mouth full and dark from their kisses.

"Bloody hell. You are a dangerous woman, Marigold Bascombe."

He stood, scooping her up and setting her on her feet in one smooth motion. "I think it's past time we returned to the house."

Mary could manage only a nod as Royce turned and led her out of the maze.

Chapter 16

Unsurprisingly, it was Miss Dalrymple who put a damper on Sir Royce's plans. The girls, she said, shocked, could not possibly ride without riding habits.

"Why?" Camellia protested. "We can wear what we have."

"It would never do." Miss Dalrymple shook her head. "Riding habits are specially made, with extra material to fall down over one's, um, limbs. It would be unladylike—indeed, quite scandalous—to mount a horse wearing a day dress."

No matter how much the girls argued, the chaperone was adamant, and this time Sir Royce came down firmly on her side.

"I'm sorry, ladies, but Miss Dalrymple is right. I shall write Charlotte and tell her to have riding habits made up as well. Don't fret. The horses won't go anywhere."

"No, but I shall die of boredom," Camellia grumbled as they left the small ballroom and made their way upstairs.

They had finished their dance lesson and the rest of the afternoon was their own, for Miss Dalrymple was fond of taking a daily nap. The first few days they had spent their spare time exploring the sprawling house and its grounds.

"Now what will we do?" Lily asked. "We've gone all over the house. And Royce said we can't go to the maze. It scarcely seems fair that you got to see it."

"I know." Mary schooled her face to show nothing, though at mention of the maze she felt a twinge of warmth steal through her. "I have an idea. Remember what Cousin Oliver said about looking through Mama's things?"

Her sisters brightened at this thought, and they went in search of one of the maids to show them the entrance to the attic. The maid's reaction to such a request was an astonished stare, and she scurried away, quickly returning with the housekeeper, Mrs. Merriwether.

"That would be the north attic, my lady," Mrs. Merriwether said. "The more recent things are stored there. I'll have a footman go up and find whatever you wish."

"Oh, no, we want to go ourselves," Mary assured her. "If you could just direct us to the right place?"

"But, my lady . . ." The older woman looked doubtful. "There's little ventilation and light in the attic. And though we clean it regularly, it tends to be dusty. Your clothes will suffer. It will be much easier to have the trunks brought down."

"That's quite all right." Mary was becoming more adept at fending off the servants' efforts to arrange their lives. "We'd like to explore the attics. It will be fun."

If the housekeeper thought this an odd bit of fun, she was too well trained to express it. She simply smiled politely and instructed the maid to take Mary and her sisters to the attic.

Following the maid, they climbed the back stairs to the top floor, where the servants lived. Another narrow staircase led to a small door. Opening the door, the maid, Junie, led them into the attic and held up a kerosene lamp to give them a better look at their surroundings. The attic was an enormous room that must have covered most of the north wing of the house. A few windows running along the east wall provided light, revealing a collection of boxes, trunks, and furniture interspersed with a number of odd objects including a dress form, a sled, and even a grotesque umbrella stand made out of an elephant's foot. The place was as dusty as the housekeeper had warned. Mary could understand why; the room was so large that even Willowmere's staff would be hard-pressed to keep it clean.

"The newest things start here and go back that way," Junie told them, pointing. "Mrs. Merriwether said Lady Flora's things would be back a little ways. A lot of this is old stuff belonging to 'the boys,' as she calls his lordship and the others. She was working here when they were just lads, you see." The girl looked around the room, then gamely asked, "Would you like me to pull out anything for you, miss?"

"No, we'll manage," Mary assured her, and received a smile of relief in return.

The maid offered her the lamp and left, and the girls began to explore. Mary didn't mind the dust or even the occasional cobweb. Sifting through the jumbled castoffs of many years was the most enjoyable thing they had done since they'd arrived.

"This is so much fun!" Lily exclaimed, opening a trunk and pulling out a military-style jacket, cut along small lines. "Who do you suppose this belonged to?"

"One of 'the boys,' I'd warrant," Rose said, coming over to examine it. "Can you imagine the earl wearing this?"

"Only if it's a general's uniform," Mary responded dryly. "Look, there's a toy musket!"

They dug down through the trunk, pulling out and replacing balls and cricket bats and sacks of marbles, along with a collection case of butterflies.

"I wonder whose trunk this is," Rose mused. "Maybe these things belonged to all three."

Mary lifted the lid of a smaller brown trunk beside it. Clothes belonging to an older, larger male were packed away in it. Mingling with the scent of camphor was a faint trace of men's cologne. It teased at Mary's nose, reminding her of Royce—not exactly the cologne he wore now, but somehow similar. She wondered if the trunk belonged to him, and it occurred to her that it was impolite to snoop through his things. Still, she could not resist pulling out a bundle of folded papers stuck down beside the clothes. The pale blue paper carried a more feminine scent, and the stack was tied with a dark blue ribbon. Mary turned over the bundle and there on the front of the folded paper was written "Royce" in a looping feminine hand.

Love letters, she thought, and her curiosity sharpened. Mary smoothed her thumb across the aging ink. She dearly wanted to see what lay inside. But that, she knew, was far too grievous an invasion of Royce's privacy. With reluctance, she put the bundle back in the trunk and closed the lid.

"Look!" Rose cried a few feet away from her. "Dresses! Maybe we're getting back to Mama and the aunts."

She and Camellia pulled out a couple of jackets, both velvet, one in brown and the other a dark green. They were cut along clean, even severe lines, with no frills or furbelows, and large metal buttons marched down the front of each. The collars and lapels had a mannish look, though the size and shape of the jackets clearly indicated that they had belonged to women. There were skirts in matching colors, full and trailing, as well as hats, small and saucy in style.

"They're riding habits!" Lily pulled out a blue jacket, this one rather military, with a stand-up collar and a small shako-style hat.

The girls exchanged excited looks.

"We could wear these!" Camellia's eyes shone. "Then that old fussbudget couldn't keep us from learning to ride."

"Even their boots are here at the bottom." Lily dug out a pair of boots and bent over to compare them to her own feet. "Do you think they might fit us?"

"I'll make them fit me," Camellia retorted.

"We could alter the dresses—well, I mean Rose could."

"Of course I could." Rose examined the jacket in her hands. "The material is in good condition. And there are four of them."

"Let's take them downstairs," Camellia urged. "We can start on them tonight. I'll help you, Rose—pull out stitches or pin, whatever you need."

The girls repacked the trunk and dragged it over to the door, then returned to open another one. A wedding dress was carefully packed between sheets of tissue and laid in it, along with a number of other articles of clothing, and the girls agreed that the wedding clothes clearly marked it as one of the aunts' possessions since their own mother had eloped. But when they opened the next trunk, the familiar scent of attar of roses wafted up. Mary's throat closed, and tears started in her eyes.

"Mama!"

"It has to be." Reverently, Rose reached into the trunk and took out a folded dress. "Look! It's a child's dress."

Pink embroidered roses dotted the white cotton dress, matching the pink ribbon sash, both faded over the years. Rose turned to lay it aside, then stopped, glancing around. "No. Mrs. Merriwether was right. We shouldn't take the things out up here—they'll get dirty."

Mary nodded. "We'll set it aside to be taken downstairs, too."

They had just dragged this trunk over to the door when it opened to reveal Junie, who had come to remind them that it was drawing close to time for dinner. Mary and her sisters would have liked to continue hunting, but as it was obvious the light was fading, they abandoned the project for the day, requesting that a footman fetch the two trunks they'd selected down to their rooms. There would be ample time, after all, to explore the rest of the attic.

That evening after supper, they excused themselves early and went upstairs to work on the riding habits. They found, much to their relief, that little needed to be done. The habits were not a perfect fit, but they were close enough; and though all the boots were a trifle small, the girls were able to cram their feet into them, which they thought would do well enough since they would be riding, not walking.

The next day they began their riding lessons. Camellia quickly established herself as the best pupil on horseback, though all of them found it easy to learn under Royce's relaxed tutelage. As Mary had thought when Royce suggested the plan, it was wonderful to get out of the house— not only to get away from Miss Dalrymple, but also simply to be outside. Mary realized how very cooped up she had been feeling only when they were outside doing something active.

After a beginning session in the stable yard, they rode out, skirting the gardens, and crossed a meadow. All the while, Royce kept an eye on their riding form, but Mary noticed that he also managed to maintain a careful watch on the area around them. They made their way through a stand of trees and emerged on an old track running alongside a low stone wall.

Lily pointed toward a hill in the distance that dominated the countryside around it. "What is that?"

Atop the hill stood some sort of structure, though it was difficult at this distance to tell exactly what it was.

"Beacon Hill," Royce replied. "It's the tallest point for

miles around. As its name suggests, in ancient times they lit fires there to rouse the countryside."

"But what is that building?"

"Ruins of a Roman fort. It's an interesting spot for a day's excursion. Perhaps one day we can go there when you are more accustomed to riding. We can take a basket of food and make an all-day affair of it. Would you like that?"

"Oh, yes." Lily was starry-eyed. "It sounds terribly exciting."

"I'm not sure how exciting it is. . . ."

Mary laughed. "Don't you know that ruins are always exciting?"

"Yes, just think of the possibilities!" Lily gazed off into the distance, as if watching something none of the others could see. "The people who have lived and died there—smugglers, rebels . . ."

Royce chuckled. "I'm not sure we have much in the way of smuggling. Or rebellion."

"Don't spoil the story," Mary told him.

"Of course. I beg your pardon." Royce pulled a serious face.

Riding lessons took up most of their afternoons, but the next week the sisters took the opportunity of a rainy afternoon to explore the attic again. Finding three more trunks they thought belonged to Flora, they dragged them to the attic door to be carried down. They had just descended the stairs themselves when they saw Mrs. Merriwether making her way along the hallway toward them.

"I'm so glad you have finished. I did not care to disturb you, but you have a visitor. Lady Carlyle has come to call."

"Vivian?" Mary asked, astonished. "But we just saw her in London."

Mrs. Merriwether smiled. "Not Lady Vivian. 'Tis Lady Sabrina who has come to call. She is married to Lady Vivian's uncle, Lord Humphrey Carlyle. They live at Halstead House, not far from here."

"Then she is Lady Vivian's aunt?"

"Oh, no—" Mrs. Merriwether paused, then said, "Well, yes, I suppose she is, but one does not think of her as such. Lady Sabrina is Lord Humphrey's second wife."

When Mary stepped into the drawing room, she saw at once why the housekeeper had trouble thinking of Lady Sabrina as Vivian's aunt. The woman sitting on the sofa chatting with Miss Dalrymple could be no more than thirty-one or thirty-two years of age. With light blue eyes, blond hair, and a pale ivory complexion, she was also the epitome of the cool English beauty.

Though the sisters had stopped in front of the hall mirror to smooth their hair into order and brush away the dust that had settled on their clothes, Mary felt at once awkward and disheveled at the sight of Lady Sabrina's pale perfect looks. She braced herself for the same sort of cold reception that they had received from their aunts.

However, to the girls' surprised delight, Lady Sabrina stepped forward, smiling, and shook each girl's hand as Miss Dalrymple introduced them. "How nice to meet all of you. I have been eager to see you, but I made myself wait a few days to allow you to settle into your new home. But it is so lonely here in the country that I simply could not hold back any longer."

The girls sat down, relaxing under the sweet warmth of Lady Carlyle's smile. Mary glanced around and noticed that Sir Royce was not in the room. Firmly she pushed away her disappointment.

"But where is Sir Royce?" Lily asked, and Mary felt a spurt of relief at finding that she was not the only who noticed his absence.

Miss Dalrymple shot Lily an admonitory look, but Lady

Sabrina gave a musical laugh, saying, "I am sure that he ran off at the sight of a caller. Men are like that, aren't they? Women's chats bore them silly."

Mary had trouble believing that many men chose not to visit with a woman as attractive as Lady Sabrina. Still, she could not help but feel warmed by the idea that Sir Royce was apparently not drawn to the beauty.

"Now, you must tell me all about yourselves," Lady Sabrina went on. "Miss Dalrymple was explaining to me that you are Lady Flora's children and you have come all the way from the United States! It sounds exciting."

It was not hard to talk to her, and soon the girls were chattering away. Mary was glad that her sisters did not bring up the subjects of taverns, guns, or wild Indians, apparently as eager as Mary not to shock or offend their pleasant visitor.

"It's wonderful to have neighbors again," Lady Sabrina told them as the tea cart was trundled in and Miss Dalrymple began to pour. "It has been so boring these last years, with only bachelors at Willowmere."

"Does not Lady Vivian come to visit? She is your niece, isn't she?" Camellia asked. "We met her with Cousin Charlotte in London, and she seemed very nice."

Lady Sabrina let out her charming little laugh. "Yes, she is. So amusing, is it not, that I should be her aunt, when we are of an age? We were bosom friends, you know, when we were young. I lived nearby with my grandparents. Alas, my grandfather, the admiral, is long since gone, as is my dear grandmother." She sighed. "What fun we had. Dear Vivian and Charlotte. I fear neither of them comes to our little village as often as they used to."

"They talked about visiting after the Season is over," Mary offered.

"Did they? But how delightful." Sabrina's face brightened.

"I must have a ball. Introduce you to the countryside. How does that sound?" Scarcely waiting for the girls to voice their approval, she swept on, "Miss Dalrymple tells me that the earl and his brother will be joining you soon. With Charlotte and Vivian, that will make a very fair number. But, of course, you must promise to call on me long before that."

It was agreed that the Bascombe sisters would call upon Lady Sabrina the next week; after that, the women settled down to a thoroughly satisfying discussion of the ball she intended to host.

After Sabrina left, Lily exclaimed, "What a nice woman! I am so glad we met her. And isn't she pretty? She looked just as I imagined Lady Jessamine did in the *Count of Otrello*."

"Yes, she was most agreeable. She did not make the slightest comment about our clothes." Mary looked down at her skirt. "I noticed right after we walked in that I had a streak of dust above my hem, but she didn't even look askance at it."

"It was exceedingly generous of her to take an interest in you." Miss Dalrymple rose to her feet and looked around at each of the girls as she drove her point home. "The Carlyle name is one of the most distinguished in the country. I was surprised by her tolerance, but clearly she is a most gracious and refined woman. You should look to her as an example. The rest of this week, we shall work on appropriate topics of conversation when you call on her."

With that parting shot, Miss Dalrymple exited the room. Camellia let out a heartfelt groan and sprawled out inelegantly in her chair. "All I can say on the matter is, thank God Lady Carlyle isn't cut from the same cloth as Miss Dalrymple."

"Yes." Rose nodded. "I do look forward to visiting her. I only wish . . ."

"What?" Mary turned to look at her sister.

"That those clothes Cousin Charlotte ordered for us would get here!"

"Me too!" Lily chimed in. "Wasn't Lady Sabrina's dress divine?"

The girls trooped out of the room, happily discussing the wonders that would await them when their new dresses arrived.

Mary was surprised when Royce did not join them for dinner that evening—and more disappointed than she would have admitted to anyone, including her sisters. She also felt quite irritated that she was disappointed.

"Dinner is a much duller affair without Sir Royce present," Rose said, echoing her thoughts.

Mary shrugged. "I enjoy having the opportunity to be alone with my sisters."

Rose gave her an odd look, and Lily goggled openly, but said only, "Where do you suppose he is? Do you think he's sick?"

"He seemed well enough at lunch," Camellia answered. "I bet he went down to the village. To the tavern, probably."

Miss Dalrymple sent her a reproving look. "It is scarcely your place to be questioning Sir Royce's whereabouts. Besides, it is little wonder that any man would chafe at constantly being in the company of young women."

"You mean he's bored by us?" Lily asked, her mouth turning down.

"No, of course not," Mary hastened to assure her sister, shooting a grim look at Miss Dalrymple. "I am sure Sir Royce likes us. But no doubt he would enjoy other company as well. Other men to drink with, for instance."

"One cannot expect a gentleman to spend all his time with us ladies," Miss Dalrymple went on pedantically. "That is simply the way of things. Men have other interests . . . often things of a lower nature."

Lily eyed the older woman with some fascination. "What things?"

Miss Dalrymple frowned. "It is scarcely appropriate for us to speculate on them. A well-brought-up young lady does not ask where a gentleman is going or why."

"Then how is she supposed to know?" Camellia asked reasonably.

"There are a number of things that it is better that a lady not know." On that foreboding note, Miss Dalrymple applied herself once again to her fish.

After supper, they retired to the smaller, less formal drawing room as they usually did after the meal, but here they found themselves even more at a loss without Royce's presence. Without him there to countermand her, Miss Dalrymple managed to quash every interesting topic of conversation, as well as any suggestion of a more lively activity than playing a quiet hand of whist.

When at last Miss Dalrymple decreed that it was the proper time for young ladies to retire, the sisters trooped up to bed without a single demurral. Mary went into her bedroom and started to undress. However, after she had finished her evening's toilette, she was still not sleepy. It was lonelier here, she thought, not sharing a room with Rose.

For a moment she hesitated, then slipped next door and softly opened Rose's door to peer inside. It was dark and Rose was already in bed, so Mary withdrew and returned to her own bed. After a few minutes of tossing and turning, however, she got up and belted on her dressing gown to go down to the library for a book. Lily had declared the books here only minimally more interesting than the ones in the London house, but perhaps a nice dull tome would put her to sleep.

Mary eased out into the hallway, not wanting to awaken Miss Dalrymple, who considered a good night's rest one of the cornerstones of a young lady's preparation for the rigors of a Season and had countless stories of one young lady or another who had suffered a breakdown in the midst of her come-out because of exhaustion brought on by the constant round of parties and social events. There was no sign of life from Miss Dalrymple's room.

Mary glanced in the other direction, toward Royce's bedchamber. No light showed beneath his door, and she wondered if he had not yet returned home. Had he indeed gone down to the tavern, as Camellia had surmised? Was he still there? Was he flirting—or worse—with some tavern wench?

She told herself that she did not care. If he preferred an evening at the tavern to one with her, it was perfectly all right. She had no claim on Royce, and she refused to be jealous. But she could not deny a stab of pain beneath her heart at the thought of him flirting with another woman. Was it all the same to him whether he flirted with her or with some girl in a tavern?

Mary pushed that lowering thought out of her head as she tiptoed along the corridor and down the stairs. Her candle provided enough light to see where she was going, but she noticed when she reached the first floor that the sconces were still burning along the corridor leading to the library. At the end of the hallway, light spilled out of a doorway.

She stopped outside the library, looking down the hall. The light came from the smoking room, and she had no doubt that Royce was there. Mary hesitated, knowing that she should get a book and return to her room. But a small voice in her head urged her toward the smoking room. If she was honest, wouldn't she admit that she had come downstairs less to get a book than to see if Royce had come home?

Abandoning the library, Mary continued to the open doorway. As she had suspected, Sir Royce was inside, sprawled in one of the heavy leather wingback chairs, his booted legs crossed negligently at the ankles, a bottle of port on the floor beside the chair and a glass in his hand. His dark gold hair was mussed, and his jacket was off, his cravat gone, and the top tie of his shirt undone.

"Marigold Bascombe." Royce grinned and pushed himself to his feet, wobbling a little as he swept her a bow.

"Sir Royce." Mary took a step into the room, setting her candle down on the small table near the door. "I was getting a book from the library, and I saw your light."

"My good fortune. Come in, sit down. Would you like a drink? No, that would not be proper, would it? Perhaps I could find some ratafia." He glanced around vaguely.

"That's quite all right. I'm not thirsty."

"Neither am I." He grinned, plopping back down into his chair. "But that detail doesn't stop me from drinking."

"I can see."

"Oh, dear. Do you disapprove, Miss Marigold?"

"Please stop calling me that ridiculous name."

"But it is your name," he pointed out. "I rather like it."

Mary rolled her eyes. "You're drunk."

"You *do* disapprove." He fetched up a lugubrious sigh.

Mary could not repress a chuckle. He looked adorably boyish with his hair mussed, a lock curling down across his forehead and falling into his eye. She could picture him as a boy, clothes torn, hair every which way, in trouble for having gotten into some scrape or another.

"Why should I disapprove?" she countered. "Miss Dalrymple assured us that it is the natural order of things for a gentleman to eschew ladies' company in order to spend time in a tavern, drinking and indulging in the sort of 'low' pursuits men are drawn to."

He let out a crack of laughter. "Did she now? Exactly what 'low' pursuit was she accusing me of?"

"I'm not entirely certain. I think she had a broad range in mind. The important thing was that it was not a young lady's place to question where a gentleman went or what he did. It is better, you see, not to know."

"Then I should keep it from your delicate ears."

"Hah! Personally, I would like to know. Indeed, I deserve to know, for I can tell you that supper was excessively dull with only Miss Dalrymple for company."

"I am honored that you consider me a livelier companion than Miss Dalrymple." He paused, tilting his head to one side and studying her. "Truth be told, I did go to the tavern. It's the hub of all activity in the village. I have sent my grooms there to see if any stranger has been seen in the area since we arrived—just to make sure that your mysterious intruder at the inn had not followed us. But the locals might not talk to outsiders like my grooms, so I decided to ask them myself."

"Oh." Mary had not considered this possibility, and she found that his explanation raised her spirits. "Then it was not because you have grown tired of the company of women?"

"That, my dear, would be the last thing I would grow tired of." Again his endearing smile flashed across his face.

"I had thought you merely wanted to escape a boring social visit," Mary teased. "But when I saw Lady Sabrina, I realized that surely that must not be the case."

Something flickered in his eyes and was gone. He rose, finishing off his glass of port, and set it on the heavy sideboard that held the decanters of liquor. "I have known Lady Sabrina for a long time. I fear I have become inured to her charms. Yours, on the other hand, are far harder to resist." He turned and leaned back against the sideboard, crossing one foot negligently over the other. "How is it, my lady, that I keep finding myself alone with you in a state of dishabille?"

"Oh!" Mary looked down at herself, and a blush heated her cheeks. "I-I should not have come here. I confess, I am not used to living in this sort of situation."

"Neither am I. However, I cannot pretend to regret the way fate continues to throw us together. I am not that much of a gentleman."

Mary lifted her gaze to his face. His words were light, but the look in his eyes was far different. There lay darkness and desire, the smoldering of a barely banked flame. An answering hunger stirred deep in Mary's abdomen. She glanced away quickly, swallowing.

"I should leave." Her voice came out a trifle shaky, and she dared not look again into Royce's eyes.

She started to turn away, but in that instant Royce moved, crossing the space between them more quickly than she would have thought possible. His hand wrapped around her arm, and Mary looked up at him, startled. His eyes were heavy-lidded, so dark they were scarcely green, and desire was etched upon his features.

"No," he said huskily. "Leaving is the last thing you should do."

Chapter 17

Their mouths met and clung as he released her wrist and wrapped both arms around her. She could taste the lingering hint of port wine upon his tongue as they kissed again and again, feverishly. When his mouth at last left hers, it was to kiss his way across her face to nibble at her ear.

"I've been dying to do this ever since that night at the inn," he murmured, the feather-light brush of his breath setting up shivers all through her. "It's been sheer hell, being with you, seeing you at Iverley Hall—in my home, at my table, imagining you in my bed." His mouth trailed its way down the side of her neck, tongue teasing at the delicate flesh, his teeth nipping at the cord of her throat. "And here, every night, knowing that you are just down the hall . . . I cannot sleep, thinking of walking those few steps. Coming into your room."

Mary let out a shaky sigh, arching her head back to allow him easier access to her throat. His words set her aflame almost as much as his kisses. She murmured his name and ran her hands up his arms, tangling her fingers in his thick hair. The textures of him aroused her—the soft lawn shirt, the muscle-padded skin of his neck, the silken way his hair slid through her hands.

She could not begin to express the sensations coursing through her, the sensual bombardment on every level—even the sound of his harsh breathing was enough to make her tremble. And when his hands began to move over her, slow and sure, she shuddered with the force of her desire. When he had kissed her that night at the inn, Mary had felt passion awakening in her in every nerve, every sense, every muscle. But tonight . . .

Tonight the sensations did not surprise her. She had some knowledge of the pleasure that would come from the stroke of his fingers, the brush of his lips. Half expecting that knowledge to lessen the force of her responses, to her astonishment she found that anticipation only enhanced the feelings. She waited for the pleasure, the tingling rushing hunger, sure that it could not have been as amazing as she remembered and marveling when she found that it was even more so.

His lips were soft upon her skin; his teeth scraped and nipped. His tongue traced hot, damp designs upon her flesh. Mary trembled, wanting more even as she thought that she might shatter under the tension. Heat pierced her abdomen and spread outward.

Royce's mouth reached the neck of her nightgown, and he growled out an irritated oath. Straightening, he jerked at the sash of her dressing gown and it opened, the sides of the robe falling apart. Light sparked in his eyes as he spread the garment wide to reveal her slender body clad only in pristine white cotton. The scoop neck revealed little more than her collarbone and the pale expanse of her upper chest, but the round orbs of her breasts pushed out against the gown.

His gaze never left her body as he grasped the lapels of her dressing gown and slid it down her shoulders and arms. Her breasts quivered at the subtle movements of her body, and her nipples thrust against the thin material. His fingers went to the ties of her night rail and they fell apart one by one, revealing a wider swath of white skin with each undone ribbon.

Mary watched the subtle reactions that played across Royce's face as he looked at her. His eyes glittered as the color rose in his skin. His mouth widened and softened, and his breath came harsh and fast in his throat. Watching him, she felt passion pooling ever more hotly deep within her.

The inner curves of her breasts were framed by the open neck of her gown, and Royce reached out to trace his index finger along each slope. Mary pulled in a sharp breath, heat burgeoning between her legs. It seemed to her that she could feel each tiny groove and ridge of his fingertip upon her sensitive skin as he moved with almost unbearable slowness down one breast and up the other.

Opening her gown, he slipped his hands inside, covering her breasts. Mary blushed and closed her eyes, no longer able to hold his gaze. She was not sure whether she flushed from embarrassment or from desire, for her body was flooded with excitement at his touch. She was aware of a surging desire to feel his hands all over her, to have him explore and touch and arouse her. Her nipples tightened, pressing into his palms, and her knees began to tremble until she wondered if she would be able to continue to stand.

Mary grasped his shirtfront to steady herself. She could feel the heat of his skin searing through the cloth and the pounding of his heart in his chest. She wanted to touch him as he touched her, learning all the textures of him, all the planes and angles and valleys. Unable to resist, she slid her hand inside his shirt and moved it slowly across his chest. His flesh quivered beneath her touch, suddenly afire. She glanced up into his eyes, and the fierce heat she saw there made her pulse leap. He watched her, his gaze unwavering, even challenging, as his hands continued to caress her breasts.

Drawing a shaky breath, Mary let her fingers roam across his flesh, tangling in the softly curling hairs of his chest, pressing into the firm pad of muscle beneath his skin. She trailed her fingers down the hard line of his breastbone, then spread her hand to glide across the ridges of his ribs. His breath rasped in his throat, but he did not move as she inched her way upward, finding at last the flat hard buds of his masculine nipples.

Recalling what he had done with her at the inn, she gently pinched the nipple between her thumb and forefinger and was rewarded by a small, soft noise. Smiling a little, she toyed with him, teasing and caressing, stroking and squeezing gently.

"Your mouth," he whispered. "I want to feel your mouth on me."

Mary glanced up at him, her lips rounding into a startled O. But she knew even through her surprise that she wanted to do as he asked—that, indeed, putting her lips to his skin was what she had been aching to do from the moment he started kissing her.

He saw the self-satisfied little smile begin to curve her lips, saw the intent blossom in her eyes, and his own face flared with hunger. He released her and took a step back, reaching down to pull his shirt up over his head and fling it to the floor. Mary moved in close, spreading both her hands across his waist. She slid them slowly up his body and, as she did so, bent and placed a flutter of a kiss on the center of his chest.

The shiver that ran through his body was all the response Mary needed, and she continued to travel up his chest with ever more lingering kisses. Remembering how he had aroused her as he kissed her neck earlier, she began to ply her tongue and teeth as well. His flesh was hot and faintly salty to her exploring mouth, and each quiver or groan she elicited from him ratcheted up the level of her own desire.

He grasped the open edges of her nightgown and pulled sharply, and the garment split down the front seam with a loud rip. Mary gasped and looked up at him. Royce's face was suffused with hunger, and his eyes were almost black. Heedless of what he had done to her night rail, he shoved it off her, exposing her to his voracious gaze. His hands moved down her body, gliding over her breasts and stomach and around to her hips.

Mary trembled, sure that her legs were going to give way. Then he moved his hand between her legs, and she let out a noise of astonishment and delight. It seemed as if the whole world suddenly stopped, narrowing to the delicious sensations blossoming there. She had never dreamed of anything like this, never thought of a man touching her there, never would have imagined that it could feel this way.

He bent to kiss her, his mouth hot and demanding, opening her lips to his plundering tongue as his fingers continued to work their magic, opening and separating the folds of her flesh, stroking across the sensitive skin with supreme delicacy.

Mary dug her fingers into his arms, quivering under the intensity of her feelings. He pulled his mouth from hers, leaving her gasping at the loss as he bent and picked her up, laying her down on her dressing gown. Stretching out on his side next to her, he began to kiss her again, his fingers trailing across her stomach and abdomen and up and down her thighs, teasingly traveling almost to the hot center of her desire, then gliding away until Mary was almost sobbing with need.

He kissed his way greedily down her throat and came at

last to rest on her breast, his tongue circling first one nipple, then the other, as his fingers kept up their teasing dance. Mary moved restlessly beneath him, lost in the pleasure of his hands and mouth, even as a fierce need built up within her. She wanted to again feel his fingers on her there, where desire was now pooling, where a growing emptiness ached for more. She wanted—Mary wasn't certain any longer just what she wanted, only that she was filled with want. Indeed, she seemed to be nothing but want.

Royce's mouth fastened upon her nipple, pulling it into the hot cave of his mouth, and at the same moment his fingers sought out the slick center of her heat. Mary moaned, digging her heels into the floor and arching up against his hand.

He suckled at her breast, and every movement of his mouth shot a white-hot spear of desire to the very center of her being. At last, growling low in his throat, Royce moved between her legs, fumbling at the fastening of his trousers. He looked up at her face—and froze.

"Bloody hell!" The oath broke from his lips, and he rolled off her, sitting up and burying his head in his hands.

Mary rose on her elbows, staring at him in dismay. Her entire body was simmering, and the insistent throbbing between her legs made her want to cry out in frustration.

"Royce?" she asked, her voice coming out in a croak.

"Get dressed." His voice was tight and hard, and he still did not look at her.

"But why—"

"Just do it!" His voice cracked like a whip. "Just put on your gown and run back to your room and thank your lucky stars that I am not completely drunk."

Mary blushed beet red. She felt suddenly small and exposed. Scrambling to her feet, she picked up the dressing gown on which she had been lying and wrapped it around her, tying the sash with a jerk. Grabbing the ruined night rail, she wadded it into a ball and ran from the room.

In her bare feet she made little noise as she dashed down the corridor and up the stairs to her room. Ducking inside, she locked the door after her and leaned back against it, gasping for breath, her legs shaking.

What had she done? What would he think of her?

Mary groaned and sank to the floor, cradling the bundle of her torn nightgown against her chest. She did not know how she would ever be able to face Royce again. At least he had the excuse that he had been drinking. But she had been perfectly sober and clearheaded—and still she had behaved like a wanton!

She should be in tears, she told herself. She should be crying in shame and distress. Yet she could not. And as horrified as she was at her behavior, she could not deny the tremors of desire still running through her. Her blood pounded in her veins, and her skin was so sensitive that she was supremely aware of even the touch of her dressing gown on her naked skin.

What she had done was reprehensible. And yet . . .

Mary let out another groan and sank her fingers into her hair, pressing her fingertips into her scalp as though she could stop the thoughts running rampant in her head. She had enjoyed every moment of what had happened downstairs. Her entire body had come alive beneath Royce's kisses and caresses. If he had not stopped, she was sure that she would not have done so. And if he were to come into her room right now, she knew that she just might fall into his arms all over again.

She also knew, however, that there could be nothing between her and Royce. He had made that perfectly clear. And to give herself to him would be the worst decision she could make. She would be ruined. Disgraced. That truth was drummed into every young girl's head from the moment she blossomed into a woman.

Mary had always wondered why everyone was so insistent on this lesson. Avoiding the sin of lust had seemed easy enough to her; she had never once been tempted to do any more than kiss a man. But now she understood. Pleasure offered a slippery slope indeed. She would have to be far more careful in the future if she intended not to go sliding right down it.

And that meant staying away from Royce. With a sigh, Mary rose to her feet. That shouldn't be too hard; at the moment, he was the last person she wanted to see. She felt sure her face would turn crimson the next time she saw him. She could not bear to imagine what he must think of her. He had regarded her as a hoyden before; now he must think her a hussy as well.

Bundling the nightgown into a ball, she strode over to the trunk at the foot of her bed and opened it, then stuffed the ruined gown down under the folded blankets. She could not let the maids catch sight of it. It would be impossible to explain the enormous rip down the front.

With that task done, she drew her other night rail from the dresser drawer and pulled it on, then climbed into bed. She should try to sleep, she knew, if she did not want to look tomorrow as if she had stayed up all night.

When Mary awoke the next morning, she looked just as she had feared—dark circles under her eyes and a weary set to her mouth. She considered staying in bed and pleading sick. Looking at herself in the mirror, she did not think anyone would doubt her.

However, if she was too sick to join her sisters, they would all come trooping up here, full of questions and sympathy. That was the last thing she wanted. No, it was better to go downstairs and subject herself to Miss Dalrymple's lessons. Her sisters would be too busy with their own dislike of the tasks before them to think overmuch about Mary's lack of spirits.

She was relieved to see that at least she was too late for breakfast, so she rang for the maid and asked for a tray of tea and toast. When she was done with her meager breakfast, she put on the best face she could and went downstairs to face the others.

She was greatly relieved to find that Royce was not with her sisters and Miss Dalrymple, but she found it even more difficult than usual to pay attention to Miss Dalrymple's explanation of the proper forms of address for all titles. Her mind kept wandering to the night before and whether Royce would try to avoid her today just as she was avoiding him. How low had his opinion of her sunk?

Royce did not join them for lunch, but when it was time for their dancing lesson, he appeared in the small ballroom as he always did. Mary's heart sped up when she saw him, and she glanced quickly away. She was tempted to hang back and let him dance with the others, to say that she had turned her ankle. But that was not her way, and she did not consider it long.

When it was her turn to dance, she strode forward, and though she was certain that the color in her cheeks was higher than normal, she looked straight into his face. She might be embarrassed about what she had done last night, but she refused to let him see that. He bowed and led her out onto the floor. At least, Mary thought, they were not practicing the waltz today. She did not have to feel his hand on her waist or stand so close to him. She had only to face him as they moved and from time to time put her hand on his arm. That was difficult enough, with her insides quivering like jelly.

Royce's expression was polite, but more remote than she had ever seen. There was no twinkle in his eyes, nor a smile at the corner of his mouth. Indeed, Mary thought, he was doing an admirable imitation of the earl. His coolness did away with the last of her nerves. Did he have the audacity, she wondered, to be angry with her?

He seemed much more himself as he moved on to dance with her sisters. Mary watched them, her irritation growing as he laughed and talked with Rose or Lily. She knew, deep down, that she was being unfair to expect him to be at ease with her when she had felt such trepidation at facing him. But she could not help but fear that she had lost his friendship, that he would never again act the same with her.

When the lesson was over at last, Miss Dalrymple retired to her room for her customary nap, and Mary's sisters headed out the door as well. As Mary started after them, Royce reached out a hand, not quite touching her arm.

"Mary, if I could have a word with you. . . ."

Mary stopped and turned to face him, her stomach sizzling with nerves. Royce's jaw was set. If possible, he looked even stonier than he had earlier.

"I must apologize for my behavior last night," he said, his voice formal and as stiff as his back. "What I did was reprehensible."

Mary stood silently, not sure what to say. Was she supposed to agree? To forgive him? To admit that it was as much her fault as his? She was certain that she should not reply with the first thought that sprang to her mind, which was that last night had been the most exciting thing that had ever happened to her.

"I sincerely regret what I did," he went on, clasping his hands behind his back. "If I could take it back, I would."

Mary was aware of a pain somewhere in the area of her heart. "Pray, do not trouble yourself. It was not your fault."

"But it *was* my fault. I behaved like a cad. Oliver would have my head if he knew about it, and rightfully so."

"Oliver!" Mary's eyebrows went up. "Just what, may I ask, does Oliver have to do with it? I don't recall him being in the smoking room with us."

"No, of course not. I only meant—well, you are his cousins, under his protection. And he placed you in my care. I should have been protecting you, not engaging in drunken debauchery." A muscle in his jaw twitched, and he swung away, beginning to pace. "I am not the most noble of men, I admit that freely, but I do not normally go about seducing innocent young girls. Especially when they are placed in my care."

"Would you stop staying that? You make me sound as if I were a—a basket of eggs, or a child."

Royce grimaced. "Blast it, Mary, can you not even accept an apology without arguing? Obviously you are not a child, but I am older than you and more experienced. You are new to this world. I should be warning you about the dangers that men present to you, not *be* one of them. I was in my cups, and I lost control."

The burning irritation that had been growing in Mary's chest burgeoned at his words. He had kissed her, caressed her, indeed, *ripped* her gown from her, and was his excuse that he had been driven mad by her beauty or that his lust for her had carried him past all gentlemanly restraints? No. His reason was that he was drunk!

"And what was your excuse that night in the inn?" Mary snapped. "You were not drunk then, as I recall."

He stared at her, his mouth opening, then closing. Color flared along his cheekbones. Finally, tightly, he said, "It will not happen again, I assure you."

"Good!" Mary crossed her arms in front of her, her eyes fierce.

Royce sketched a brief bow toward her. "If you will excuse me . . ."

He turned and strode away. Mary threw a parting shot after him, "Don't worry. I shan't carry tales to your precious Oliver."

Royce checked for an instant and turned to shoot her a fulminating glance, then continued out the door.

Mary wished she had something she could throw. But everything in this house was far too expensive to demolish in a fit of temper. She felt foolish and petty, her emotions raw. If she were a real lady, she supposed, she would have been furious with him for kissing her, and she would have welcomed his apology. Nay, she would have demanded it.

It wasn't that she wished him to act as if he had done nothing wrong. It wasn't that she disliked his being a gentleman. It was just . . . well, couldn't he have said one little thing about how wonderful it had felt to kiss her? Couldn't he have offered her a compliment or two instead of regrets?

No, she told herself, because clearly he had not felt those things. He wished it had never happened. He hated having lost control. They had almost made love only because he was too drunk to know what he was doing.

Mary set her jaw. She could feel tears pricking at her eyelids, but she willed them back. She would not cry about this. It would be too humiliating. Turning, she made her way upstairs. She found Rose in the sitting room, sewing a ruffle back on the hem of one of Camellia's gowns.

"Where are the girls?" Mary asked, sinking down onto the settee beside her sister.

"They were squabbling—I'm not even sure about what—and finally I lost my temper and told them to go fuss at each other somewhere else." She lifted her face and gave Mary a wan smile. "I fear I am not the most pleasant company today."

"You too? It must be going around." Mary sighed and leaned back, stretching out her legs and crossing them at the ankles in a way that she knew would have earned a rebuke from their chaperone. That thought perked up her spirits a bit. "But I cannot imagine that you were unduly cross. You are the most angelic of creatures."

"I'm not." Rose shook her head. "I snapped at Junie this morning. I don't understand why she must try to do my hair! I hate having people fuss over me."

"I know. Even when you are sick, you like to be alone. Which is, believe me, far more appreciated than demanding to be babied and taken care of all the time."

Rose half smiled. "I suppose. But I know that is Junie's job, and I should not be so sharp with her. I don't think a maid's lot is a happy one, especially here. At least at home, the cook and Josie and Annie lived at their own houses. Here, they all have to live in those tiny rooms upstairs. They get up before us and go to bed after us. And no one ever thanks them."

"They look at you as if you're crazy if you do," Mary pointed out.

Rose chuckled. "That's true. Maybe I feel sorrier for them than they do for themselves." She sighed. "I certainly didn't show her any kindness by barking at her, though. I just feel—don't you feel so hemmed in here?"

Mary looked at her, astonished. "Hemmed in? But this house is enormous. We each have our own bedchamber, and it's twice the size ours was back home."

"No, I don't mean that. I mean all the people around. Everybody watching you. I know that inside they're thinking I shouldn't be here, that I'm not really a lady."

"You are far more ladylike than the rest of us. If you aren't like the other British misses, what does it matter?" Mary shrugged. "I'd far rather have you as a sister than some limp girl who would say and do everything Miss Dalrymple wants us to."

"I know you would." Rose smiled at her. "You're right; I'm foolish, I know. Everyone would say that we have landed in a pot of cream. We have a beautiful place to live, all the food we could possibly want, a whole set of new clothes. I feel like an ungrateful wretch. . . ." She paused, looking down at her hands lying idly on the gown. "But, oh, Mary, don't you ever feel homesick? Don't you wish you could go back?"

"No. Actually, I haven't felt homesick a bit. I mean, I miss Mama; sometimes I think about her, and I can't help but cry. But I don't miss Three Corners or Cosmo or the tavern." Mary frowned in concern. "Do you? Rose, are you unhappy here?"

"Oh, Mary!" Rose raised her face, her cornflower blue eyes swimming with tears. "I do miss it! I miss—" She raised her hand to her mouth, and great tears spilled out of her eyes, rolling down her cheeks. "I never realized I would miss him so much!"

Mary goggled at her. "Miss *who*? Rose, never tell me you miss Cosmo."

Rose let out a watery little chuckle and swiped at the tears on her cheeks. "No! Not Cosmo. I'd never miss Cosmo in a hundred years. I meant Sam."

"Oh. Sam Treadwell. But I thought you said . . ." Mary paused, trying to remember exactly what it was her sister had said about the young man who had courted her back home. "When we talked about him at the house in London, you said you weren't pining for him."

"I'm not. I don't." Rose sighed again. "At least, I don't want to. But I didn't—I didn't realize it would be so hard. I didn't know how much I would miss him. I keep thinking about the way he smiles and wishing I could see his smile again. He has the most wonderful brown eyes, and when he looks at me"—Rose hugged herself and gave a little shiver—"it makes me feel tingly all over."

"Do you love him?"

"I don't know." Rose let her arms drop to her sides. "I'm not sure. When I think about spending my life with some other man, I can't imagine it. But with Sam, all I can think about is being with him always. Am I terribly silly?"

"No! No, you aren't silly at all." Mary hesitated. "Did he—did you ever kiss him?"

Her sister's cheeks turned pink. "Mary!"

"You did kiss him, didn't you! You sly thing, why didn't you tell me?"

Rose shook her head. "I couldn't. It was—I don't know, it was so wonderful and . . . and . . . special. I just wanted to hug it to myself. Besides, I was afraid you might . . . I don't know, think less of me."

"No, of course not. I would never think anything bad about you. When did he kiss you? What happened?"

"It was one day when I was walking to Nan Sutton's house, and Sam came riding down the street. He'd been to Philadelphia on business, he said, and, oh, he looked so grand riding along." Rose's eyes shone with the memory. "He got off his horse and walked with me. I walked right past Nan's house just to stay with him. He took his horse into the stable, and there was no one else about. He reached out and took my hand, and then he kissed me." She blushed again. "He kissed me twice."

"Did you—did you never want it to stop?" Mary asked.

Her sister glanced at her, startled. "No, no, I didn't. But how did you—Mary, who have *you* been kissing?"

"Royce." She wasn't about to reveal how much more than kiss she and Sir Royce had done, not after Rose's shy confession of two stolen kisses. "But you must promise not to breathe a word to Lily or Camellia; they would tease me about it unmercifully. And if they said anything to Sir Royce . . . "

"No, oh no, I will not say a word; I swear it. But, Mary, do you love him?"

"No, of course not." Mary shook her head sharply. "There's no question of any of that between us. He had been drinking, so one can hardly hold a man to anything he does then. Indeed, he apologized mostly politely this afternoon." Mary's expression hardened. "He told me he wished it had never happened."

Rose stared at her. "Really?"

"As good as. He said he would take it back if he could, or something like that. Obviously he regrets it."

Rose reached out to take Mary's hand. "Do you?"

"Honestly?" Mary looked over at her sister and shook her head. "No. I don't. I thoroughly enjoyed it. Well, now I have blackened my soul, haven't I?"

"Don't be silly. I just told you that I kissed Sam and wished it hadn't stopped. If your soul is black, so is mine."

Mary smiled a little. "At least we shall have company."

Rose squeezed her hand. "Are you sure you don't have hopes in that direction?"

"Marrying Sir Royce?" Mary chuckled and shook her head. "No, dear sister, do not worry your head over that. I am not pining away for him. I will admit it wounded my pride a bit to hear how much he regretted what passed between us, but that is easily enough recovered from. Marriage, especially to one of these prickly British gentlemen, does not appeal to me. I have the lowering presentiment that I shall wind up a spinster—and no doubt a trial to all my happily married sisters, who will be too kind not to let me impose myself upon them."

"Nay, I fear we shall be spinsters together. Lily and Camellia will have to take us both in," Rose retorted. "Or perhaps we shall just remain a trial to our cousin the earl."

"Now, that's an idea." Glad to see her sister's spirits lifted, Mary smiled and picked up Rose's sewing bag. "Let me help you with the mending. I find I have a great desire to jab in a few pins."

Chapter 18

The Bascombe sisters were in the music room with Miss Dalrymple the next day, struggling over their notes and chords, when the butler ushered in Lady Sabrina.

"Lady Sabrina!" Miss Dalrymple sprang from her seat with surprising nimbleness and hurried forward. "What an unexpected pleasure. Girls, girls, do come and say hello."

Her words were quite unnecessary, for the sisters were rising to greet the other woman with evident pleasure.

"I hope I have not interrupted anything important," Lady Sabrina began politely.

"No, indeed." Miss Dalrymple beamed. "The girls were brushing up on their skills at the piano."

This enormous understatement earned stares from all four of the girls in question, but Lady Sabrina merely smiled and nodded, apparently accepting Miss Dalrymple's words. Mary could only think that Lady Sabrina had not heard Camellia's hesitant plinking on the keys as she walked down the hall.

"Then I hope they will not mind if I steal them away for an hour or two."

"No," the girls chorused eagerly, and Lady Sabrina laughed.

"'Tis not very exciting an expedition I'm proposing," she told them. "You must not get your hopes up."

"Excitement is a relative matter, my lady," Mary said. "I feel sure we will enjoy it."

"I had planned to call on the vicar's wife today, and it occurred to me, why not take you with me? It will make the duty far more enjoyable for me, and you can meet some of your neighbors. The squire's wife often calls on Mrs. Martin on Tuesday afternoon, so with any luck, I will be able to introduce you to her as well."

"What a marvelous idea, my lady." Miss Dalrymple's smile broadened, if that was possible, and she nodded for emphasis. "Marvelous indeed. So kind of you to think of them." She turned, leveling a basilisk gaze on her charges. "I am sure they are very grateful."

For once, it was easy to agree with their chaperone, especially for Mary, as the trip with Lady Sabrina would take them away from their dancing lesson. Though she had been civil, if a trifle frosty, when she saw Sir Royce at breakfast that morning, Mary had no desire to spend the afternoon close to him again.

The girls scurried off to get their hats and gloves, glad that at least these items of their apparel would not be unfashionable, if not perhaps up to the standard of Lady Sabrina's attire. As they came back down the stairs, Sir Royce stepped into the entry.

He checked for an instant as his eyes landed on Lady Sabrina, then came forward and executed a polite bow. "Lady Sabrina. I had not realized that you had come to call."

"Hallo, Royce." Sabrina held out her hand to him. "Are you so formal now? You once called me just Sabrina."

"That was many years ago, my lady." Royce's expression was even more remote than the one he had directed at Mary the day before. "Before you were married."

"Ah, but I have not changed." Amusement touched Sabrina's light blue eyes.

"I fear I have."

Mary and Rose exchanged glances at Sir Royce's short response, which bordered on rude, and Lily rushed to fill the awkward silence: "Lady Sabrina has kindly offered to take us with her to call on Mrs. Martin."

"Has she?" Royce shot an assessing glance at the sisters, lined up in hats and gloves, ready to leave. "But what of your lessons?"

"I am sure you will not mind being relieved of that task, Sir Royce," Mary told him. "You will have the rest of your afternoon free."

"Sir Royce is teaching us to dance," Lily offered in an aside to Lady Sabrina.

"Is he now?" Lady Sabrina's eyes twinkled. "I am sorry indeed to interfere with that. Perhaps I should stay and help."

This offer was met with a chorus of protests, and Lady Sabrina agreed, laughing, to stay with her original plan. She turned to Sir Royce. "There, you have escaped. But I must warn you that I am sending you and your cousins an invitation."

"They are not my cousins."

"To the ball?" Lily asked, ignoring Royce's interjection.

"No. That is some time away. Far too long, I decided. I am inviting you to Halstead House for dinner next week. I do hope you will come."

"We should love to," Mary assured her.

"I am not sure whether I will be free—" Sir Royce began.

Sabrina cut him off with her silvery laugh. "But I have not told you which day!"

Royce's jaw tightened. "I am sure the girls will be delighted to attend."

"But you must come as well. Humphrey will be quite disappointed if you do not. And the girls must have an escort."

"Of course." Sir Royce sketched a bow to her and turned to Mary and her sisters. "If you will wait until tomorrow, I will take you to call on Mrs. Martin. Then you need not impose on Lady Sabrina."

"It is no imposition." Sabrina looked puzzled. "I welcome the company."

"I would prefer it." Royce sent a significant glance at Mary. "It would be safer."

"Safer!" Lady Sabrina laughed. "Really, Royce, what do you think is going to happen? It isn't as if there are highwaymen riding the roads here."

"We will be fine, I'm sure, in Lady Sabrina's carriage," Mary told him flatly.

His lips thinned, but Royce said only, "Very well. I shall send one of my grooms along, if you don't mind."

He strode off, leaving Sabrina staring after him in astonishment.

"You must not mind Sir Royce," Lily told her.

"That's right. He's been cross as a bear for two days," Camellia added.

"Oh." Sabrina waved the matter away with one elegantly gloved hand. "I pay no attention to Royce. I have known him almost since I was in short skirts and braids."

When they had settled into the carriage, Royce's groom sitting on the high seat beside the coachman, Sabrina turned to the sisters with a smile and confided, "I had an ulterior motive in inviting you today. It is often deadly dull calling on Mrs. Martin, and I thought your presence would make it much more enjoyable. I hope you will forgive me."

The girls assured her that they were happy to relieve her boredom, especially since she was relieving theirs.

"My purposes were not entirely selfish," Sabrina went on. "It will be easier for you to meet the vicar's wife with someone else along to ease the way. She is a good woman, of course, and quite intelligent. Her father was also a clergyman, you see, and a well-known scholar, so she is very well educated. She speaks three languages—aside from ancient Latin and Greek, of course, and she is able to converse with the earl and Lord Humphrey on all the philosophers. I vow, sometimes I think I am back in the schoolroom when she and Mr. Martin begin to lecture."

"My goodness," Lily said inadequately.

"You must not let her intimidate you. She is not unkind, but she does not always realize that the rest of us have not had the grounding in the classics that she has. That is why I thought it might be easier to meet her with me along to smooth the path, so to speak. I am accustomed enough to her now that she does not frighten me."

"What about the other lady, the squire's wife?" Rose asked in a subdued voice.

"Ah, yes, Mrs. Bagnold." Sabrina's eyes twinkled. "She feels, perhaps, that she is a bit above the simple country folk. Her grandfather, as she is fond of saying, was an earl, and even though her father was only the youngest of five sons, she is very conscious of her noble bloodlines. She can be . . . well, a trifle stuffy. Of course, she is always quite agreeable to me, since Lord Humphrey's brother is a duke, but Mrs. Martin is as low down the social scale as she cares to associate. Since you are the earl's cousins, that will be no problem."

Mary cast a look at Rose. It seemed they were going to be faced with another pair like their aunts. "I'm glad that you will be there, my lady."

"Please, call me Sabrina. We are going to be great friends, I can tell. Don't worry. I promise we shan't stay long. Remember, don't be nervous. They cannot bite, after all—and I shall be there to help you if they do."

Mary's enthusiasm for the trip had been dampened considerably, and the girls were uncharacteristically silent when they pulled up in front of the vicarage, a two-story brown brick building next to the square-towered Norman church. The house itself had a gloomy air, Mary thought, dark and overgrown by ivy and shrubbery. She suspected that Lily was probably already making up some scary tale about it.

A maid showed them into the parlor of the vicarage, where two middle-aged women sat. One was as tall and spare as the other was short and plump. Mrs. Martin turned out to be the almost gaunt woman, slightly stoop-shouldered, with sandy hair streaked by gray. Her face was long and thin, and her forehead seemed creased in a per-petual frown. She wore metal-rimmed spectacles, and the light glinting off the glass concealed her eyes, which made it difficult to read her expression. Squire Bagnold's wife looked to be the older of the two, for her hair was almost entirely iron-gray beneath her matronly cap. Her face was round, with a short nose and large round eyes, giving her an incongruously babyish air.

Both women offered the barest of smiles, and it seemed to Mary that Mrs. Bagnold's gaze bordered on wary. Lady Sabrina introduced the Bascombes, saying, "They are Lady Flora's daughters. Perhaps you remember her. She was the present earl's aunt."

"Yes, I remember." Mrs. Bagnold did not appear pleased by the memory. "Pert young thing. Lord Reginald was quite fond of her, as I recall—a fine man, the late earl. Reminded me of my own grandfather, the Earl of Penstone."

Sabrina cast a laughing glance at Mary, and Mary had to

press her lips together not to smile. Obviously, Sabrina knew her neighbors well.

"Not that Lord Oliver isn't a good man," Mrs. Bagnold continued. "But not the same as the old earl and my grandfather. Their like will never be seen again."

"Indeed." Sabrina put on a pleasant expression.

The conversation continued in a halting manner, for neither Mrs. Martin nor the Bascombe sisters contributed much to it. Most of the time, the discussion was about people and places that Mary and her sisters did not know, though Lady Sabrina gamely pulled it back time and again, saying with an apologetic smile, "But we are forgetting our guests from America. They have never met Lord Kelton. . . ." Or Mrs. Hargreaves. Or the Countess of Brackstone.

Mrs. Martin sent the maid for tea and cakes. It was a relief, in a way, for it gave Mary something to do with her hands and an excuse not to speak when some chance remark was directed her way. However, she worried that she would commit some ghastly faux pas, such as spilling her tea on the rug or taking too large a bite of one of the little cakes. Ordinarily, she was not constrained by fear of taking a social misstep, but Miss Dalrymple's training had left her certain of only one thing—that she was woefully ignorant of the social niceties. She did not want to embarrass Lady Sabrina by displaying that ignorance.

After a time, even Sabrina ran out of conversation, and a long silence fell upon the group. Mary could feel Rose growing more and more tense beside her. She also knew from experience that the longer a silence lasted, the more likely Camellia or Lily would feel compelled to break it. Desperately, she cast about for something to say, but her mind was a blank.

Finally, in a rush, Mrs. Martin said, "Are you interested in reading, Miss Bascombe?"

"Lily is," Camellia piped up.

"Indeed?" It was hard to tell behind the spectacles, but it seemed to Mary that Mrs. Martin's expression warmed a trifle as she turned toward Lily. "Then you must be enjoying the library at Willowmere. It is quite extensive."

"Yes, it is," Lily agreed, looking unaccustomedly nervous.

"What sorts of things do you like to read?"

Mary's fingers curled into her palm until the nails were cutting into the skin. Lily would reveal her reading tastes, and this highly educated woman would make a slighting remark or give her one of those frozen-in-horror glances of which Aunt Euphronia was a master. Then Camellia—and Mary herself—would feel compelled to come to Lily's defense, and the visit would turn into one of their usual disasters. Only this time Lady Sabrina would be dragged into it as well, after all her kindnesses to them.

"Um, novels," Lily replied softly.

"Indeed?" Mrs. Martin's eyebrows lifted. "How interesting. I am fond of them myself."

"Really?" Lily perked up. "Cousin Charlotte took us to Hatchard's—"

"Such a lovely place." There was now definitely warmth in the older woman's voice, and Mary felt the clutch of tension in her stomach begin to ease.

Then Lily went on, "I bought *The Mask of the Corsairs* by Mrs. Preston."

As soon as she uttered the words, Lily went pink and closed her mouth. She cast an apologetic glance at Mary and quickly turned her eyes back down to her lap. Mary felt a pang at seeing Lily abashed, and a warming anger began to rise in her.

"I have not read *The Mask of the Corsairs*," Mrs. Martin said, breaking the silence. "But I cannot imagine that it could be any more exciting than *The Lady of Mirabella*, Mrs. Preston's second book and, in my opinion, her best."

Lily's head snapped up, and a brilliant smile spread across her face. "Oh, yes, I agree. It is my very favorite book. Do you like Mrs. Radcliffe, too?"

"Of course." Mrs. Martin was smiling now, her cheeks tinged pink with excitement. "Perhaps you would care to see my library. It is not nearly so fine as that at Willowmere, but I have several books I think you would like."

"Yes, thank you! I would love to see it." Lily bounced to her feet, barely remembering her teacup in time to set it aside on a low table.

Mrs. Martin stood up, taking Lily's arm and leading her out of the room, talking animatedly. Mary cast a surreptitious glance at Rose and Camellia, then at Lady Sabrina, all of whom wore the same expression of amazement. It was all Mary could do not to laugh.

"Well, I'm glad Miriam has found someone who likes to read those books," Mrs. Bagnold commented. "I haven't the faintest liking for them myself. Not much of a reader, really, but when I do read, I like something practical. The squire, of course, doesn't hold with reading at all."

"How is the squire?" Sabrina asked sweetly, recovering from her shock. "I haven't seen him out riding lately."

"His back's been bothering him again, poor thing." For the first time, Mrs. Bagnold's voice softened, and she shook her head. "Pain shooting down his back. He can hardly walk, but he can hardly sit still either. Can't bear to get up on a horse."

"I'm so sorry. Has Dr. Berry been to see him?" Sabrina asked.

"The man's useless. All he ever wants to do is cup him

or purge him." Mrs. Bagnold's mouth was set in grim lines. "That's what killed my grandfather, I'm convinced."

Emboldened, perhaps, by Lily's success with Mrs. Martin, Camellia said, "Maybe you could help, Mary." She turned to the squire's wife. "My sister is quite good with herbs and such."

"Indeed?" Mrs. Bagnold rested her rather imperious gaze on Mary. "Is that true, young lady?"

"I—well, yes, I've always nursed my sisters in their illnesses. I know some folk remedies."

To her surprise, Mrs. Bagnold nodded. "My nurse was a healer, I remember. There were those who whispered she was a witch, but that was nonsense, of course. She could always make a tea to help with your headache or stomachache." She paused, then asked, "What would you suggest?"

"Does the pain run low in his back like this, and down into his leg? Or is it all up and down his back?"

"Exactly like you said. Low in his back and down his leg."

"Old Mr. Benton used to have that sort of pain. Poultices of bishopsweed helped him. It's also called goutweed. Just boil the leaves, wrap them in a cloth, and put it on his back. Don't let it burn him, of course."

The older woman looked at her for a long moment. "Fancy that. Bishopsweed, eh?"

"Yes, ma'am."

"Well, you seem to have a head on your shoulders. Bit of the old earl in you, I can see."

"Um, thank you." Mary wasn't quite sure how to respond, but her answer seemed to satisfy Mrs. Bagnold, who turned back to Sabrina and launched into a discussion about Lord Humphrey's horses that left Mary in the dark and even, after a time, brought a line of annoyance to Sabrina's smooth forehead.

It was some time before Lily and Mrs. Martin returned, Lily happily cradling several books in her arms. Lady Sabrina rose almost immediately, making her good-byes, and led the girls out to her carriage.

"Can you believe that?" Lily asked, her face flushed with excitement. "Mrs. Martin lent me three of her books, and she said I could borrow more when I finished. She has all Mrs. Radcliffe's books and several more that I have not even heard of. I told her I would bring her the two I bought in London, and she seemed most appreciative."

"Who would have thought that the vicar's wife liked to read your books?" Camellia marveled.

"Who indeed?" Lady Sabrina remarked rather sourly.

Lily and the others glanced at her in surprise, and Sabrina sighed. "I am sorry, dear. That sounded quite petulant, didn't it? But when I think of all the times that I have sat and listened to her talk about Homer and Chaucer and Aristotle and such, when all the time she's reading novels of romance! One never knows, does one?"

Sabrina leaned her head back against the luxurious leather squab behind her, closing her eyes.

"Are you all right, Lady—I mean, Sabrina?" Mary asked.

"Yes, my dear, quite all right." Sabrina opened her eyes and smiled. "I must apologize. I should have brought you to see the vicar's wife some other day. I fear facing both of them together was too much. I find it's even given *me* a headache. I hope Mrs. Bagnold was not too overwhelming."

"She's not nearly as bad as our aunts," Camellia told her candidly.

"She seemed fond of her husband," Rose added.

"I don't think that Mrs. Martin is cold," Lily said. "I think she is actually shy. That's probably why she doesn't talk much. But when we were alone in her library, she was very pleasant."

"It is so nice, the way you are all able to see the bright side of things." Sabrina's tone was cheerful, but Mary could hear the underlying strain in her voice, and she knew that Sabrina's headache must be causing her a good deal of pain.

Impulsively, Mary laid her hand on Sabrina's arm. "It was good of you to introduce us to them. You have made it much easier for us to get on here."

"I am so delighted." Lady Sabrina's lovely smile was somewhat brittle.

Knowing that their new friend was tired, Mary hustled her sisters out of the carriage and into the house. Lily was disappointed, as she had been about to show Lady Sabrina the books Mrs. Martin had lent her, but she quickly recovered and was content to pass the treasures around among her sisters. She also regaled Sir Royce with the tale of their adventure that evening at supper, finishing with the candid revelation that she had never thought that a preacher's wife could be so nice.

Sir Royce's lips twitched a little, but he answered gravely, "Indeed, I have often found them a trifle frightening myself."

"It was very good of Lady Sabrina to introduce us to them," Rose added.

"Was it?" Royce's smile was sardonic.

"But of course." Mary lifted her chin a little challengingly. It seemed almost as if Sir Royce wanted to thwart their friendship with Lady Sabrina. The notion made no sense, and she could only put it down to his general bad temper of the past few days. "It is bound to be of great benefit to us to be introduced as her friends," Mary went on reasonably. "As you are well aware, we do not always make the best impression upon the people we have met in England."

"You seem to have made friends readily enough with Lady Sabrina," he pointed out sourly.

"I fail to see why that should be any concern of yours," Mary shot back.

"It's not, of course." He set his wineglass down sharply. "I was simply concerned about your safety. I would have thought you would be, too."

Mary's amazement was mirrored in her sisters' stunned expressions around the table. "I beg your pardon. I fail to see how it is in any way unsafe to visit Lady Sabrina."

He let out a grunt of humorless laughter. "Yes, you would." He cast a glance around the table and sighed. "The devil take it." He stood up, tossing his napkin aside. "I must ask you ladies to excuse me. I find that I am in no humor for company tonight."

Royce started toward the door, then turned. "I would ask, though, that you inform me next time you decide to take a jaunt away from Willowmere."

He walked out the door, leaving the other occupants of the room staring after him.

"Well!" Camellia lifted her eyebrows. "I wonder what's bothering him."

"It is not our place to question Sir Royce's behavior," Miss Dalrymple began sententiously, and Camellia rolled her eyes at Mary. "However, I imagine that it begins to grate on a young gentleman to be idling away his time in the country, looking after a set of girls."

"If he finds it so boring, why doesn't he leave?" Mary snapped.

Miss Dalrymple drew in a horrified breath. "He could not do that. A gentleman would not leave you four unprotected. He feels duty-bound to wait until the earl or Mr. Fitzhugh arrives."

"We aren't children. We don't need someone watching over

us all the time." Mary glanced around at her sisters. "We managed to take care of ourselves well enough until now."

Miss Dalrymple sighed. "It is precisely that sort of remark that I fear will make it hard for any of you to make a suitable match."

"Maybe we aren't interested in 'suitable' matches." Camellia scowled.

"Hardly surprising. However, it is your duty to the earl." Satisfied that she had ended that particular rebellion, their teacher turned her attention to the pastry tray.

Mary, seeing the fire that sparked in Camellia's eye, kicked her under the table.

"Ow!" Camellia shot her an aggrieved look, but she subsided, and they finished the meal in silence.

The next morning Miss Dalrymple sent a note that she was feeling indisposed, much to the Bascombe sisters' relief.

"I hope she is not feeling too ill." Rose glanced at Mary guiltily. "But I cannot say I'm sorry to be free of her for a day."

Camellia was less sympathetic. "She probably wouldn't be sick if she hadn't had the fish, ham, *and* roast beef last night, not to mention three pastries and two jellies."

"The question is, what are we going to do with our free day?" Lily asked.

They spent the morning in the attic, and by the time they sat down to a luncheon of cold meats and cheeses, they had found two more trunks filled with Flora's things and had them brought down to the sitting room. After lunch, however, Camellia declared that they should go exploring.

"I could show you the maze," Mary volunteered. She had told Royce she would not take them there, but at the moment she did not feel particularly inclined to follow his edicts. "Though I fear we would get lost there by ourselves."

Camellia grimaced. "Somewhere farther than the lower garden." She leaned against the window frame, staring out disconsolately. "I know! What about that little lake?"

"The tarn?"

"Yes, the one beyond the gardens. It would be a nice walk, and there's some sort of little house down there."

"A summerhouse." Mary nodded. "I saw it, too." She went to the window to look across at the small dark lake and the round folly that stood beside it.

"We could have a picnic," Lily suggested. "We could get Cook to put those little tea cakes in a basket, and we could have tea by the lake."

"What about Sir Royce?" Rose stood up. "He wants us to tell him if we leave."

"Don't tell me you've decided we can't get on by ourselves, too," Camellia said in disgust.

"No, of course not. But—"

"But nothing," Mary interjected. "If we tell him, he'll insist on going along or sending some grooms or something, and it will spoil the whole thing."

"I suppose." Rose, too, looked out the window a little wistfully. "But what about that man at the inn?"

"I doubt that he is still hanging about."

"But there was that time in the garden—"

"Mary didn't even see anybody," Camellia protested. "They just found a footprint, and what does that prove? Anyway, she said he smelled like Cosmo, and the four of us can take care of Cosmo."

"Of course we can," Mary agreed. "The fellow at the inn ran away when I screamed, and whether it was really Cosmo in the garden or not, he didn't do anything even though I was completely alone."

"We can take Papa's pistols, and Camellia can bring her knife," Lily volunteered. "What about the rifle?"

After some discussion, they agreed that the rifle was not necessary, given that they were taking other weapons and it was rather heavy as well. So they dug out the case of pistols and loaded them, concealing one in Camellia's pocket and the other in Lily's. They picked up a blanket, put on their sturdier walking boots and old bonnets, and made their way downstairs. It took little persuasion to get the cook to fix up a small basket of cakes and a jug of water for them. It was more difficult to convince her that they did not require a footman to carry the basket.

Mary felt a qualm as they exited the side door, carrying their basket, jug, and blanket. She knew she should not encourage her sisters in a scheme that would ignite Sir Royce's wrath. But she was tired of living as they had since coming to Willowmere, staying about the house all day, drilling on a seemingly unending list of nonsensical things. She had had enough of being told what to do. It would be fun to get outside for a while and do something new and unexpected.

And when Royce started to lecture, as he undoubtedly would, she would explain that she had been entirely responsible for the expedition and deflect his anger from her sisters onto herself. She felt sure that Royce would be all too ready to do that anyway.

They went west from the house, bypassing the gardens and cutting through the arm of trees that extended south from the woods, then crossing the sloping meadow beyond. The tarn was as darkly beautiful as it had appeared from the house, and the little bridge that arched over the narrow end provided a picturesque touch. They explored the summerhouse first. It was little more than a round room, with a circular bench that ran most of the way around it. Whatever furniture had once been there had been taken away, and since the archways were shuttered and even nailed closed, it afforded no view of the lake except through the open doorway.

They decided to spread their blanket on the bank of the tarn instead. They took out the cakes and ate them, chatting and laughing, and later, having put their things back in the little basket and shaken off the crumbs, they lay back, desultorily talking as they watched the puffy clouds float overhead, the sound of the water gently moving in their ears.

Mary had just drifted off into a doze when there was a snap and a stifled screech from Lily. Mary's eyes flew open and she sat up just as a man broke out of the nearby shrubbery and ran straight for them.

Chapter 19

Instinctively Mary bounded to her feet. Lily screamed as the man grabbed Rose's arm, and Rose swung her fist at him, but her blows fell ineffectually on his arm. Mary could hear Camellia cursing as she pulled out the pistol, and she knew that Camellia was concerned about firing at the man with Rose so close. Mary grabbed up the picnic basket and swung it with full force at his head. It landed not on his head but on his shoulders, and it cracked apart, sending him staggering back a step.

Lily threw the earthen jug, hitting the assailant high on the back. He let out a roar and swung around, his grip on Rose loosening. Rose flung herself to the ground, and Camellia seized the opportunity to fire a shot. The man's cap flew from his head, and he let out a yelp and turned, his eyes round with astonishment. Lily was already digging the other pistol out of her pocket.

The man turned and ran for the woods. Camellia, the better shot, took the pistol from Lily's hand and raised it. Bracing it on her arm, she squeezed off another shot. The attacker staggered, grabbing his arm, then ran as if the hounds of hell were after him.

"Rose!" Mary flung herself down beside her sister. "Are you all right?"

Rose nodded, sitting up and rubbing her arm where the man had grasped it. "I'm fine. I'll have bruises there tomorrow." She let out a giggle of nervous relief. "I won't be wearing any short sleeves for a while."

"Blast it!" Camellia dropped the pistol into her pocket. "I missed him twice."

"You hit him with that second shot," Lily replied a little breathlessly, sinking down to the blanket with her sisters. "I saw him clutch his arm."

"Yes, but I aimed for his back, which was a broad enough target."

"He was running, and it was at some distance. You got his cap the first time."

Camellia picked up the hat in question, turning it over in her hands and examining it. "Went clean through it," she commented, sticking her finger in first one hole, then the other. "Hope it put a crease in his skull as well."

Mary began to laugh. "Did you see the look on his face?"

Lily joined in. "I know! I bet he never thought a bunch of girls was going to pepper him with shot."

"What about when you tried to crown him with the water jug?"

Soon all four were hooting with laughter, holding their sides and rocking, letting out another howl whenever they recalled some other moment. But their heads snapped up at the sound of something crashing through the shrubbery, and they turned toward the narrow path leading from the gardens to the tarn. In another instant, Royce hurtled into sight on the path. He was jacketless and hatless, and he carried a large stick in his hand as he bore down on them at full speed. Gradually he slowed, then stopped as he took in the picture of the four girls lounging on the blanket before him.

"What the devil is going on? I heard shots." His words came out in pants.

Mary looked at the broken branch in his hand. "So you were going to fight him with a stick?"

He grimaced and tossed the branch aside. "It was the only thing at hand. I'd already left the house when I heard the shots. I was coming because they'd told me you had taken it into your heads to go picnicking at the tarn." He scowled blackly.

"I was the one who fired," Camellia said, hauling out a pistol to show him. "He didn't have a gun. At least, I didn't see one. I hit him once, but he got away."

"So you *were* attacked!" His expression grew even more thunderous.

"Yes. I think it was the man from the inn," Mary told him. "He was quite large, and he grabbed Rose, but we fought him off. Then Cam shot him. Twice."

Her voice trailed off as Royce's face turned to stone. The girls glanced at one another. Finally Camellia stepped forward, holding out the cap in mute offering to Royce. At that moment a gardener and one of Royce's grooms came running into view. When they saw the group before them, they stopped, holding their sides and bending over to catch their breath.

Royce took the cap from Camellia without a word, but his eyes never left Mary's face. Mary squared her shoulders. "Don't blame them. It was my fault."

"I have no doubt of that," Royce retorted.

"That's not true. We all wanted to come," Rose protested, and Lily and Camellia echoed her words.

Royce shot the others a single flashing glance. "Get your

things and go back to the house." He turned. "Jarrett. Giddings. Take these girls straight home. Do not let them out of your sight."

"Yessir." The two men approached the sisters and waited. When the girls did not move, they cast an anxious glance at Royce, then at the sisters.

"Miss . . ." The gardener tugged at his cap and stepped back.

"We're not leaving Mary." Camellia folded her arms pugnaciously.

Before Royce could speak, Mary told her, "No, go. I'll be fine."

"But—"

"Trust me. It will be much better if Sir Royce and I have our discussion in private."

All three of her sisters looked from Mary to Royce.

"The devil take it!" Royce burst out. "I'm not going to hurt her!"

Mary nodded encouragingly. "Go on."

With a few last reluctant looks, the three young women trailed off, followed anxiously by the groom and the gardener. Mary watched them go, then turned back to Royce.

"Shooting at kidnappers," he said almost conversationally, bending over to pick up the blanket. His gaze fell on the food basket, its side bashed in. He gave it a nudge with his foot. "Cracked this over his head, I imagine."

"I tried. He was too tall."

Royce let out a strange dry laugh. "Of course you did." Savagely he kicked the basket, sending it flying. "Bloody hell, Mary! Have you no sense?"

Mary flinched at the sudden movement, but quickly regained her composure. "I assume that is a rhetorical question."

"I told you to stay in the house!" He whirled to glare at her.

"No, actually, you did not; you said to tell you before we left on a jaunt," Mary corrected him. She knew that she was goading him, but something in her wanted to continue doing it, to send his seething temper soaring. She was ready, almost eager, for the explosion. "But that is neither here nor there. We aren't children to be ordered around. You cannot tell us what to do and expect us to blindly follow your commands."

"Are you mad? What does it matter? We're talking about your lives here!" He strode over to her, color high on his cheekbones, his eyes bright. "You could have been killed! Don't you care? Doesn't it matter that your sisters could have been killed too?"

Mary sucked in a harsh breath, an answering anger surging up in her chest. "Don't you dare say that! I have looked after my sisters all our lives. Nothing matters more to me than they do."

She pivoted and marched away. He hurried after her, catching up to her in front of the summerhouse. He grabbed her arm, jerking her through the door into the privacy of the small structure.

"Then why in the bloody *hell* did you run out here with them?" He was still carrying the blanket, and he flung it down on the floor of the round room, letting out an oath. "Don't you realize what might have happened? He could have hurt you, kidnapped you. He could have murdered you all!"

"I sincerely doubt that." Mary faced him, her hands on her hips. "If you will notice, none of those things happened. We considered the possibility that he could be around here, but it seemed unlikely." She ignored the snort of derision he let out. "We took reasonable precautions. It was daytime, and we were on the alert. There were four of us. It's difficult for one man to kill four people. Even if he'd had a pistol in each hand, he would have had to reload."

"So you're only risking two of your lives."

"Don't be ridiculous. We took our pistols, and Camellia is an excellent shot. *She* shot *him*. Twice. If you were more interested in catching him than in braying about your authority over us, you might send some men to search the area where he ran away. There are probably traces of his blood that could be tracked."

"Braying about my authority! Bloody hell, woman, do you think I care about my authority? About my control over you?"

"That certainly seems to be what's concerned you the last day or two—where we go, when we go, who we go with. We're supposed to ask your permission before we escape the prison of that house. We can't walk except in the upper gardens. Lady Sabrina kindly offers to take us somewhere, and you object. What is any of that about except your desire to rule everyone?"

"You could have been killed! When they told me where you had gone, I started out here to make sure nothing happened to you. Halfway here, I heard screams and shots. I thought you had been killed. I was afraid that when I got out here, I'd find your lifeless body lying on the ground. And you accuse me of being worried about my authority!"

He took two steps and grabbed her by the arms, staring down into her face with burning eyes. "Damn it, Mary, you will drive me mad."

Mary stood her ground, staring back at him. She could feel the heat radiating from him and see the fire in his eyes. It matched the flames that danced in her own chest, the frustration and anger that made her blood sizzle through her

veins. She wanted to lash out, to hit him, to scream, to . . .
Her eyes flickered down to his mouth.

In the next instant, she was crushed against his chest,
his arms like iron around her, his lips sinking into hers in a
bruising kiss. They melded together, lips fused and bodies
pressing into each other's all the way up and down. Mary's
fingers dug into the back of Royce's shirt, balling up the
material in her eager fists. She wanted, wildly, to sink into
his flesh and merge with him, to lose herself in him.

Royce's hands went to her hair, pulling it loose from its
pins and sending it cascading down, filling his hands and
tumbling over her shoulders. Sinking his fingers into the soft
mass, he kissed her until she was breathless.

Mary was falling into the vortex of his passion, spinning
and tumbling, and she clung to Royce as the only steady
thing in this suddenly chaotic world. He kissed her again
and again as his fingers made their way down the back of
her dress, undoing the row of buttons. Her dress fell open
and his hands slid inside, roaming over her back, her skin
separated from his questing fingers by only the thin lawn of
her chemise.

He trailed kisses down her throat, murmuring her name,
and her dress slid from her shoulders, catching at her wrists.
Impatiently, Mary pulled the sleeves over her hands and let
the frock drop to the floor. Royce raised his head, his eyes
darkening as his gaze drifted down her.

His breath rasped in his throat as he took the bow of her
chemise and tugged gently. The ribbon slipped undone, the
top of the chemise sagging open. Mary watched him, her
own eyes gleaming with the same intensity as his. The desire
in his face filled her with satisfaction, even joy; she wanted
to see the fire of passion consume him.

Without stopping to think, she grasped her loosened
chemise and pulled it off over her head, tossing it aside. A

blush crept into her cheeks at being thus exposed to him, but Mary stood her ground, tilting her chin as she gazed up at him. Royce's eyes widened as he took in the sight of her bared breasts, and his nostrils flared as if he could not draw enough air.

Almost reverently, he curved his hand over her breast, caressing the satiny skin and lingering over the hard button of her nipple.

"You are so beautiful," he murmured, his eyes following the movements of his hands over her pale flesh. "Marigold . . . you are lovelier than any flower could ever hope to be."

He bent, surprising her, and spread the blanket out on the floor. Then he swept her up in his arms and laid her down upon it, going to his knees beside her. Untying the drawstring of her petticoat, he drew it from her. He slid off her slippers and stockings, his long fingers lingering over her skin as he moved the plain, practical lisle stockings down the length of her legs. He paused now and again to press his lips upon some entrancing bit of skin he had just revealed, and Mary jerked in surprise even as another tendril of heat uncurled in her abdomen.

His gaze still on her, Royce stood and divested himself of his clothes. Mary watched, both embarrassed and entranced. She gazed at the wide breadth of his chest, the lines of muscles and bones, the softer plane of his stomach, the blond hair that V-ed down his chest and led from his navel down to the proud, pulsing staff between his legs. She glanced away, blushing fiery red.

Mary was not entirely ignorant of what went on between a man and a woman, as many gently reared girls were. She had, after all, spent some of her early years on a farm, and they had lived in a small town, never far from the land and animals, so that she had picked up a general knowledge of how the young came into being. Moreover, she had often enough had to help out in the tavern serving drinks, and though the daughters of the tavern owner were generally treated with more respect than the ordinary tavern wench, Mary had heard enough of the men's talk and jokes to figure out the basics of the marital act.

Still, she had never before actually seen a naked man— much less one in a state of arousal—and it was a startling sight. But not, she realized as her eyes crept back to look at Royce again, an uninviting one.

He kicked his clothes aside and lay down beside her, propping himself up on one elbow. He gazed at her for a long moment, his hand gliding slowly over her body, sending shivers through her. Mary closed her eyes, basking in the pleasure and heat, loving the faint roughness of his hand on her skin. Her senses were heightened, alive to every new feeling that swept through her.

He bent to kiss her, his mouth moving against hers in a slow, delicious fashion, enticing and arousing her. All the while, his hands stroked and caressed her, exploring the curves of her body. Mary twisted, a small moan escaping her. Royce smiled and began to kiss his way down her body, skimming over the tender skin of her throat and tracing the line of her collarbone, his tongue delving into the delicate hollow. His lips moved ever downward, crossing the quivering orbs of her breasts, coming at last to the nipples. His tongue circled one hard button of flesh, caressing, then lashing it with tiny strokes before his mouth settled on the bud, sucking gently.

As his mouth worked on her breast, his hand slid down her body, caressing her stomach and hips and legs. With each movement he drew closer and closer to the juncture of her legs, until finally his fingers slipped between her thighs. It did not startle her as much as that night in the smoking room, but the sensation, she found, was even sweeter.

Expertly he stroked and teased until she groaned, her legs moving restlessly apart.

Mary swept her hands over his arms and shoulders, wanting to touch him everywhere, her fingers digging in helplessly whenever he brought her to some new height of pleasure. She was panting, her skin slick with sweat, and deep inside need coiled, tight and desperate, aching for release. She could feel the hunger in Royce as well, in the harsh rasp of his breath, the taut contraction of his muscles, the dampness of his skin.

"Please . . ." she murmured.

His answer was a groan. "God help me, I have to have you."

He moved between her legs, slowly, gently probing at the tender flesh, moving up until he met resistance. He hesitated, his eyes going up to hers.

"No. Don't stop."

He thrust inside her, and Mary let out a small gasp at the slice of pain. He went still, burying his head in the crook of her neck. She could hear his breath rasp in and out of his throat, but he remained motionless until she relaxed. Then he began to move within her again, and the last whispers of pain receded before the need gathering and pushing inside her. Rhythmically he stroked in and out, and with each movement, the hunger, the urgency within her grew.

He filled her in a way she had never imagined, as though there had been an empty ache inside her that she had never known existed. Yet there was something more, something eluding her, beckoning her, and she felt as if she were running, reaching for it, just beyond her fingertips.

Suddenly the elusive feeling exploded within her, and Mary tightened all over, arching up against Royce, waves of pleasure washing through her. Royce cried out, muffling the noise against her neck, and thrust into her hard and fast. For an instant they were joined completely, lost in some mindless dark realm of utter pleasure, their souls seemingly as entwined as their bodies.

Mary floated in a seemingly timeless moment, gradually becoming aware of the heavy weight of Royce's body across her and the scratchy blanket beneath her back, the hardness of the wood floor beneath that. Her heart slowed its triphammer beat, and she smiled, luxuriating in the tingling pleasure that hummed all through her body. She thought dreamily of lying here in Royce's arms for the remainder of the afternoon. He would kiss her neck and caress her arms, whisper sweet words in her ear—

Royce rolled from her and let out a groan. "Bloody hell. What have I done?"

Mary's mind cleared sharply. She was suddenly very aware of her nakedness, and not in the pleasant way she had been a moment before. She glanced over at Royce, who had sat up and was bent away from her, hands plunged into his hair. She gazed at the smooth expanse of his back, the broad shoulders and knobby line of his curved spine. She would like, she thought, to trace that outcropping with her tongue all the way up to his neck, to taste the salty warmth, feel the satiny texture of his skin over the stony hardness of bone beneath. But the chill starting in the pit of her stomach as the silence grew quickly vanquished that urge.

Instead, she sat up and groped for her clothes. How had they managed to get so scattered?

"God, Mary, I'm sorry. I don't—I should never—"

"Please," Mary broke in, her voice tight as a coiled spring. She should have known; it had been foolish to think that Royce would react any other way. "Spare me your regrets."

She had already pulled on her chemise, leaving the ribbons untied, and now she stood up, stepping into her pantalets, then her petticoat. Her stockings she balled up and thrust into the pocket of her dress, thinking with some bitterness that she always seemed to be stuffing away articles of her clothing around Royce.

"Mary, no. Wait." He turned to see her dropping her dress over her head.

She put it on backward, knowing it would take too long to fasten the buttons behind her. She had to get out of here now, before the tears that were threatening at the back of her eyes overflowed.

"We have to talk." He came to his feet.

"No. We do not." Mary thrust her feet into her half boots, not taking the time to button the sides, and rushed out the door, fastening the remainder of her dress as she went.

"No, wait!" He started after her, then stopped in the open doorway, remembering that he was utterly naked. He turned back, cursing.

Mary flew across the ground, taking the route Royce had come through the gardens. Misery lent speed to her feet and she tore down the path, desperate to reach the safety of her room before Royce, with his longer legs and greater speed, could catch up. Tears streamed down her face. She refused, absolutely refused to let the man see her cry over him.

She had had the most beautiful, thrilling experience of her life, and all Royce could offer was apologies and regrets!

Luck was with her, and she met no one on her way. Opening the back door, she slipped inside and up the back staircase. There was no one in the hall, and she ran along it to her room. Closing the door softly behind her, she turned the key and sank onto the floor, gasping for breath. And, finally, she let the sobs come.

Mary was not sure how long she sat there, knees pulled up to her chin and her head resting on her arms. She heard footsteps in the hall and a soft knock on her door, then Royce saying her name in a low, urgent whisper; he even rattled the doorknob. She set her jaw and said nothing. After a moment, he strode away, and she heard a door down the hall close with a sharp crack.

She leaned her head back with a sigh and rested it against the door. She would have liked to crawl into bed and not come out for the rest of the day—but Mary Bascombe did not give up or give in. And she certainly did not hide in her room feeling sorry for herself. She also would have liked to pour out her heart to someone, but she could not tell Rose, her usual confidant. It would shock Rose—who had been too shy to mention the kiss Sam Treadwell had given her!—down to her toes. Even worse, Rose would probably go running straight to Royce and give him a piece of her mind, even demand that he marry her sister now that he had committed the sin of deflowering her.

Mary allowed herself a small smile at the thought of Rose shaking her dainty finger in Royce's face as she rang a peal over his head. But that, of course, was the last thing Mary wanted. She didn't need a husband, certainly not Royce. She would be fine; she didn't need his apologies. And she would just have to get by without putting her troubles on her sister.

As she sat there, it struck her that the second floor was awfully quiet. She did not hear her sisters in their rooms or in the sitting room down the hall. And on the heels of that thought came another—she could hear the faint sound of voices drifting up from downstairs. A moment later, she heard the lower rumble of a masculine voice. She stood up and cautiously opened the door a crack.

A woman's laughter, not one of her sisters', floated up gently, followed by Fitz's voice.

Cousin Fitz was here! And he had obviously brought someone with him. No doubt her sisters were down there, chatting with them. Mary closed her eyes and let out a sigh. The last thing she needed was to have to meet people and be polite. But, she realized, it actually offered a perfect opportunity. With Fitz and the others around, it would be far more difficult for Royce to talk to her in private—or to make some sort of a scene. She had to face everyone sometime, and this was probably the best chance she could have.

Quickly Mary undressed and washed, then put on a fresh frock and pinned up her hair. She stood for a moment, doing her best to put the past few hours out of her head, then sallied forth. Following the sound of voices, she made her way to the drawing room, where she found her sisters sitting and chatting with Lady Vivian Carlyle and Cousin Charlotte. Fitzhugh Talbot stood before the fireplace, one arm propped negligently on the mantel.

He turned and smiled. "Cousin Mary! How happy I am to see you."

He came forward to bow over her hand in his carelessly elegant way. Mary greeted him with real pleasure and turned to Charlotte and Vivian, seated together on the sofa.

"I am so glad to see you. I had not expected you so soon."

"London was growing boring," Charlotte told her gaily. "Then we found out that Fitz was coming up before Oliver, so we decided to join him."

"Although I fear poor Fitz was none too pleased." Lady Vivian smiled slyly, cutting her eyes over at Fitz. "With us along, he had to come in a carriage and leave his curricle for Oliver to drive. I am surprised he didn't refuse to bring us."

"Nonsense. I would prefer to escort two lovely women anyway. But, Mary, where is that brother of mine? Your sisters told me the two of you were taking a stroll about the garden."

Mary did not dare glance at her sisters. "We were. . . ."

"Do not tell me that he abandoned you. Surely even Royce is not so graceless."

Mary could not help but smile. It was impossible not to like Fitz, and even harder not to relax in his presence. "No, he did not abandon me. I fear 'twas the other way around."

Fitz grinned. "Was it, now? Well, I am sure it served him right."

"Indeed, it did," said a masculine voice, and they turned to see Sir Royce entering the room.

Mary noticed sourly that he looked as neat and calm as ever.

Royce bowed to Charlotte and Vivian, then reached out to shake Fitz's hand. "I'm glad you are here."

"As am I."

"The earl did not come with you?" Mary kept her eyes on Fitz, not glancing at Royce as he joined his brother at the fireplace.

"No, Oliver still had some business to attend to in the city. I had grown quite weary of London, though. It sounded much more amusing to spend time with my new cousins than to hang about in London watching Oliver meet with his man of business and his solicitors."

"We are very glad you did," Lily told him emphatically. "Now we will have another dance partner. It will make it ever so much easier."

"Yes, and you will have a far better one as well," Fitz

teased, casting a laughing glance at his older half brother. "Royce has two left feet, I understand."

Royce raised his brows. "I am accounted an excellent dance partner."

"Not as good as I am."

"And you are such a humble man as well," Mary said with a laugh.

"One cannot be humble about some things," Fitz tossed back. "When it comes to dancing or making a bow, I would challenge any man."

"It would be less maddening if it were not true," Royce conceded.

The butler, Bostwick, appeared at the doorway, hovering until the occupants of the room turned toward him. "The trunks have arrived, my lady," he said, bowing to Charlotte. "Where would you have me put them?"

Charlotte's face lit up. "The clothes!" She turned toward the girls, her eyes sparkling. "Where would you like to have your new clothes taken?"

Lily sprang up with a barely stifled shriek. "Our new dresses? You brought them with you?"

"Yes. The wagon with the trunks was slower than we were, but apparently it has arrived. Shall we send them up to your bedchamber, Lily, and sort them out there?"

"Yes, oh, yes!"

Charlotte laughed and gave a nod to the butler. Turning back to the men, she smiled, looking only slightly less merry than the Bascombe sisters. "If you gentlemen will excuse us, I believe a higher duty calls."

"Ah, yes, the goddess of fashion. I can hear her now." Fitz grinned. "We shall be quite devastated without you, of course, but we understand. And I shall look forward to seeing what you wear down to dinner tonight."

"We shall choose the prettiest ones just for you," Lily promised.

Mary was swept with relief as the women rose. She exited the room with the others, leaving Royce and his brother together.

"A drink to clear the dust of the road from your throat?" Royce asked, starting for the door.

"God, yes. A cigar would be nice as well. I always forget what a devilish long drive it is from London."

"No doubt that's why you rarely come." Royce strolled with him down the hall to the smoking room and crossed to the liquor cabinet.

He thought of Mary in this room with him the other night, remembering the sight of her pale body as the nightgown gave way in his hands. And beneath him this afternoon in the summerhouse. Determinedly, he pushed the thought of her out of his mind as he poured his brother a drink.

"I am glad you came up early." Royce offered Fitz the box of cigars. "I have put the servants on the alert and brought two of my grooms from Iverley as well, but I'm glad to have the best marksman in England in the house."

Fitz shrugged. "Oliver and I thought I should come, after the letter you sent. Sounds as though it was a good idea, given what my cousins were just telling me. Did someone really try to kidnap Rose again?"

"Apparently. I wasn't there. I had told them not to go anywhere without telling me, but of course they went charging off on their own as soon as their chaperone came down ill. Blasted woman."

"Yes, it was rather inconsiderate of her to fall sick."

Royce gave him a sour look. "Easy for you to make light of it. You aren't the one who has to attempt to keep them in order."

"Is it that great an ordeal?" Fitz asked, his blue eyes laughing.

Royce let out a short bark of humorless laughter. "One must explain to them that they cannot simply go wandering down to the stables to look at the horses or chat with the stableboys, as apparently they were wont to do at the tavern back home. Or why the servants take it amiss when the girls start helping the footmen move the furniture. The dancing lessons are fine, but every day there is a new quarrel with Miss Dalrymple. She is a tiresome woman, I admit. But I cannot always side with them against her, and Miss Dalrymple is usually right, although God knows I wish she could find a more felicitous way of telling them how to behave. And that she could overlook some of their minor transgressions."

"They are wild?"

"Not wild, exactly. Simply . . . accustomed to more freedom than an English lady. Miss Dalrymple is correct; their ways will probably get them into trouble. Yet one cannot want to see them . . . suppressed."

"I think the Bascombes would be devilish hard to suppress." Fitz paused, then added carefully, "You seem to have become fond of the American girls."

"Fond?" Royce's brows soared, and he let out a chuckle. "I don't know that I would have described it quite that way, but . . . yes, they are amusing. Life is never dull when they are about."

"And is there one in particular whom you find 'amusing'?"

Royce shot his brother a cautious look. "I'm not sure what you mean."

"I mean that it appeared to me just now that when you entered the room, your eyes went straight to Cousin Mary. And there was more in your gaze than when you looked at anyone else."

"Lady Mary and I are . . . I find her . . ." Royce glanced around, then set his glass down with a thud. "Truth be told, I plan to marry her."

"What!" Fitz leaned forward in his chair. "Are you serious? You are going to marry the girl?"

"Of course I'm serious. But she's furious with me right now—and rightly so."

"You gave her a bear-garden jaw over their going off alone?" Fitz ventured. "The girls told me you looked black as thunder and held her back to have a few words with her. They were all for going down to the tarn to rescue Mary, but I managed to talk them out of it."

Royce looked at his brother for a long moment, then said, "Not exactly. Well, I mean, yes, that is part of it." He began to pace. "She thinks me overbearing. And I have not—well, the truth is, I seem to regularly lose my head when I am dealing with her." He turned, giving Fitz a tight smile. "Perhaps I should get your advice before I ask her. You are always a hand with the ladies."

Fitz, who had been watching Royce with great interest, shrugged. "I know nothing about proposing, I can tell you that. I am careful to stay away from any talk of marriage. As well as from young ladies. I prefer to pay my addresses to actresses or opera dancers or genteel widows—"

"Or married women," Royce interjected with some sarcasm.

"Only those with complaisant husbands. I don't fancy being embroiled in a duel. After all, I could scarcely shoot the fellow, but I have little desire to delope and then find the man is a good shot."

"That would present a problem."

"The important thing is, I choose women who know what they are about, who are interested in a romance that is mutually enjoyable—not some young girl who wants your heart laid at her feet and your ring upon her finger."

"On the other hand, marriage is precisely what I'm interested in."

His half brother studied him with a certain fascination. "I had not heard of this before."

"There is the estate, after all." Royce made an offhand gesture. "One has to think about the matter of heirs."

"Ah, yes. The estate. Heirs. It all makes sense now." Fitz swirled the remaining liquor around in his glass, watching it intently.

"And I am of an age to marry now. Time to settle down."

"Quite. You are, in fact, approaching middle age."

"I am quite aware that you are making jest of me." Royce looked at his brother.

"What? I?"

Royce grimaced. In the past he would have told his brother everything. He could not remember ever holding back about any problem concerning a woman. He had few qualms about revealing his own transgressions—in fact, he would have loved to confess his guilt, to admit how rashly he had acted, how he had tossed aside all honor in the heat of his hunger for Mary. It would be a welcome catharsis. But this time, he could not tell even Fitz. This involved Mary's honor as well as his own.

Royce turned away. "Anyway, that is neither here nor there. What we need to concern ourselves with right now is this madman who keeps trying to steal Rose."

"The girls tell me they saw his face today and have no idea who he is—although they are inclined to believe that he is the man who followed them in London. Did you know about that?"

"Yes." Royce sighed. "I thought nothing about it at the time. They went walking alone one day, and they tend to, um, draw attention to themselves. I assumed it was some chap who thought the worst of them. He ran when Camellia confronted him."

"It seems bizarre that he would have been so taken by Rose that he followed her out of the city and has tried to abduct her twice."

"I agree."

"Course, some men are dashed loose screws. And Rose is a remarkably attractive woman."

Royce nodded. "She is a beauty—though I would say that Mary is the better-looking of the two." He was turned away from Fitz and did not see the amused glance his half brother sent him.

"Do you think it could be someone who has followed them from America?" Fitz asked.

Royce turned to look at him. "That seems even more un-likely than following them from London."

"It is a good distance. But at least he would be acting upon more than a chance sighting of Rose on the street."

"I suppose so. But wouldn't the girls have recognized him?"

"If they are telling you the truth."

"What a devious mind you have." Royce crossed his arms, considering the matter. "The Bascombes may dress their stories up a bit, but I don't think they would lie. Mary got a bump on the head the night the fellow tried to take her sister, and the other girls were clearly drugged. And I heard screams and shots this afternoon as I was going toward the tarn. It seems an elaborate ruse, especially since the result will be more of the restrictions they dislike." Royce sighed. "I thought I had the situation well in hand after the incident in the garden."

"What incident? There was something else?"

Royce told him about the fright Mary had had in the maze. Fitz, listening to the description of the footprint, frowned.

"But that footprint would not fit the man the girls say tried to abduct Rose just now," Fitz pointed out. "They said he wore a cap and rough clothes."

"Yes. I've seen the cap; it does not seem to go with the gentleman's shoeprint. Which is a trifle worrisome."

"You think there could be two of them?" Fitz's voice rose skeptically.

"Frankly, I didn't see how there could be *one* of him. I sent my grooms to the village, even went there myself to ask a few questions. No one has seen a stranger around lately. Certainly no one's been at the inn or renting a cottage. Oliver's gamekeeper said that once or twice he's found evidence of a campfire in the woods, but that could be travelers camping off the road, or a poacher." He shrugged. "I've instructed the gardeners to watch out for the girls and to stay around whenever they are in the garden. I have the gamekeeper's men patrolling the perimeter of the grounds, and at night there is a guard outside the house."

"I would think that would have been enough to scare away even the most determined abductor."

"I thought so as well. Until this afternoon."

"It doesn't seem practical in the long run to continue keeping such a heavy guard on the girls."

"I agree."

"And my cousins appear to be chafing at the restrictions imposed upon them."

"That is putting it mildly."

"Then I suppose we'd better figure out who this fellow is and why he's after Rose." Fitz tossed back the rest of his drink and stood. "Camellia said that she winged the fellow. So I suggest that while we still have enough light to see, you and I go back to the area where he fled and look for a trail of blood."

A feral smile touched Royce's lips, and he too set aside his drink. "Let's go."

Chapter 20

The footmen were bringing up the trunks by the time the women reached Lily's room, and Mary and her sisters went straight to pulling out the marvelous goods within, while Vivian and Charlotte looked on with indulgent smiles. The girls began to spread the clothes out over the bed, then all other available spaces as well.

"Cousin Charlotte! These cannot all be ours!" Mary exclaimed.

"Of course they are," Charlotte answered with a smile. "There are four of you, after all, and you must have day dresses and evening dresses. Riding habits—Royce told me to include those. Except for the riding habits, it's what you chose in London, the bare minimum, I assure you. For your come-outs, you must have a great deal more."

"I cannot imagine how." Mary looked around at the frocks scattered all over the room.

"It looks like so much more here than in the drawings," Rose agreed softly. Not only were there dresses in varying degrees of elegance, but there were also slippers, nightgowns, cloaks, pelisses, and underclothes of the softest cotton and lawn.

"Jewelry?" Rose exclaimed, opening a small box and turning toward Charlotte, astonished. "You bought us jewelry?"

"Just a few pins and earbobs and such," Vivian assured them. "You must have some, after all."

Charlotte looked around at the Bascombes. "Do you not like them?"

"Of course we like them!" Mary replied.

"We *love* them!" Lily corrected, bouncing over to hug her cousin, then Vivian. "You are wonderful to do so much for us."

"We can scarcely have you going about looking like raga-muffins, can we?" Charlotte grinned. "It would, after all, reflect badly on the family."

·"Then I suppose it is our duty to look as elegant as we can." Mary smiled.

Vivian pushed aside some of the clothes on the end of the bed and perched on it. "Now, you have to try them on so Charlotte and I can see how glorious you look."

It did not take any persuasion to convince the girls. Mary went straight to one of the evening dresses she had chosen. The narrow white silk gown was slightly lower in the waist, as was the new fashion, so that it hinted at the slenderness of the body beneath it. The neckline was lower than on any dress Mary had ever owned, exposing the tops of her white breasts—and her bare shoulders as well, for the short puffed sleeves started on her upper arms just below the points of her shoulders. The overskirt, trimmed around the bottom by a single ruffle of blond lace, was draped and held in place with satin rosettes of the same subtle honey color, exposing the pale golden and white-striped under-skirt below.

Mary knew that it was sheer vanity, but she could not help turning this way and that in front of the mirror. This, she thought, was what she would wear downstairs this evening to supper. Let Royce see her in this!

"You must wear that tonight." Vivian echoed Mary's thoughts. "With a gold ribbon wound through your curls. And, I think, this cameo."

She held up a gold chain from which hung a white cameo against a brown background. Mary let Vivian clasp the necklace around her neck, and her eyes glowed as she gazed at her reflection.

"Perfect," Charlotte agreed.

Mary tried on several more, including a dimity round dress with a pale blue pelisse that matched the tiny pattern of the fabric, not to mention another evening dress in white and soft pink. She could not find any that didn't make her lips curve up into a smile, but the white and champagne evening gown remained her favorite. Prue, the upstairs maid who took care of Mary's clothes, had been trying to arrange her hair as well, ever since they'd arrived. Tonight, Mary thought, she was going to let Prue do it.

As the girls worked their way through the clothes, Vivian and Charlotte returned to the subject of the girls' confrontation this afternoon.

"Were you terribly frightened when he ran at you like that?" Charlotte asked. "I should have been terrified."

"It was scary," Rose admitted. "But then, I am always the biggest coward. I'm sure Camellia was not."

"No, he was frightening," Camellia admitted. "He was very big. And I hadn't expected him to appear."

Mary nodded. "I didn't think we would ever see him again."

"That's why it took me so long to get the gun out of my pocket," Camellia went on. "By then he had Rose, and I couldn't get a clear shot."

"It's wonderful that you can shoot," Vivian told her. "Would you teach me?"

Camellia looked at her, surprised. "Really?"

"Yes, really. It seems a much more useful skill than most I possess."

"I am sure Miss Dalrymple would not say so," Lily put in. "No doubt you can play the piano and sing and paint. I bet you even know French."

"Enough to buy a dress in Paris," Vivian answered with a laugh. "Or converse with the cook. But I can tell you that if you were ever stopped by a highwayman, he would not be overcome by a song or a phrase in French."

"Have you ever been stopped by a highwayman?" Lily asked, her eyes round—as much, Mary suspected, with envy as with horror.

"No," Vivian admitted. "But if I were, I'd rather pull out a pistol than my purse."

Finally, as the fashion parade slowed, Vivian sighed and said, "I am sorry not to see the others' reactions when you come downstairs tonight, but I should be going."

"But you must stay for dinner, surely," Charlotte protested.

Vivian smiled. "I fear it would be most unkind, even for me, to roll up to Halstead House this evening after everyone has gone to bed. Fear not, I will return often to visit. Constant companionship would not suit Lady Sabrina or me."

"Does she not like Lady Sabrina?" Lily asked Charlotte after Vivian had gone.

Charlotte turned to her, somewhat surprised. She hesitated, then said carefully, "Lady Vivian and Lady Sabrina are, um, rather different in character."

"Lady Sabrina said that they used to be great friends."

Their cousin shrugged. "Yes, they did. Many years ago."

"I don't much like Lady Sabrina," Camellia announced.

"What?" Her sisters swung around to stare at her.

"Since when do you not like her?" Lily asked.

"I thought you found her charming," Rose added, puzzled.

Camellia shrugged. "I didn't mean that I *dis*like her. I liked her more at first. But last time . . . I don't know. She seemed disappointed that the vicar's wife and the squire's wife liked us."

Mary stared at Camellia for a moment, frowning. "I think Lady Sabrina did not feel well. She had a headache."

"I am sure you must be wrong, Camellia." Rose looked troubled. "She has been most kind to us."

"Well, you shall have ample time and opportunity to discover exactly how you feel about Sabrina," Charlotte told them. "In the meantime, I think we had best get these things sorted and given to the maids to put away. It's almost time to dress for dinner."

As Mary had suspected, Prue, happy to at last dress Mary in clothes that befitted a lady, was almost ecstatic when Mary suggested that she also arrange her hair in the manner Lady Vivian had suggested. It took her far longer to dress than Mary was accustomed to—and was more than she was willing to do on a daily basis. But the results, she couldn't help but think, were worth it.

Mary was unable to suppress a certain smug satisfaction when she entered the anteroom where they all gathered before the evening meal and Royce looked at her, then straightened, staring as if he had never seen her before. Mary gave him a regal nod before she strolled over to join Fitz and Lily in conversation.

She could feel Royce's eyes on her throughout the meal. She managed to refrain from returning his gaze most of the time, though once she could not help but turn her head toward him. His green eyes were intent on her, and when their gazes met, something sparked in his eyes that sent an answering shiver down her spine. Quickly she turned her gaze back to her meal, waiting for the tremor of sensation to subside.

After the meal, she was careful to sit between two of her sisters on the sofa in the drawing room, so that when the men rejoined them after their port, there was no possibility of Royce conversing with Mary alone. Whatever he had wanted to discuss this afternoon—probably another lecture about how wrong the whole incident in the summerhouse had been and how much he regretted it, with added declarations that he would make sure it never happened again—she did not want to hear it tonight.

However, Mary was well aware of how single-minded Sir Royce could be, so she had little hope that he would simply abandon the idea of a conversation. It did not surprise her, therefore, when the following morning Sir Royce jumped up to follow her out of the breakfast room as soon as she had finished her meal.

Reaching out to take her arm, he said without preamble, "I would like to speak with you in private."

Mary's heart began to thump. His face was remote and deadly serious; she felt almost as if she did not know him. She grabbed at the first excuse she could think of. "I'm sorry, but it's time for our lessons with Miss Dalrymple."

"I'm sure she would not object to our taking a stroll about the garden first."

It was pointless, Mary knew. She had to face him sometime. She might as well get it over with. It would be awful; already her insides were churning, but she hoped she would get through it without giving way to tears.

"Of course." Mary smiled stiffly. "Pray let me get my bonnet."

When she returned with her hat, Sir Royce was waiting at the bottom of the stairs. He led her down the hall and held open the back door for her. Mary swept out onto the terrace and trotted down the steps, tying on her bonnet as she went. She did not look at him, and she was relieved that he did not offer her his arm as they walked along in silence. She tried to think of some commonplace topic, some pleasantry, but her head was too filled with memories of the day before. She could not keep out the sight of his face, suffused with desire, or forget the feel of his chest beneath her hand, the taste of him upon her tongue . . .

She picked up her pace.

"I had not realized we were in a race," Royce commented dryly.

"I like a brisk walk."

"Clearly. But I have something to say to you, and I have no desire to chase you down the path shouting at the top of my voice."

"Then perhaps you should not have asked to go for a walk."

"Mary, please . . . I know you are angry with me, and you have every right to be. But allow me the opportunity to—to do what I can to set it right."

Mary stopped, surprised, and turned to him. "I am not angry."

"You should be. I—my actions were reprehensible. I behaved like a cad. I have no excuse."

Mary's face burned. "There is no need to apologize. You were not the only participant."

His eyebrows rose, and a smile tugged at the corner of his mouth. "I should have known that you would not respond in the typical way."

"I am sorry if I am not sufficiently well-bred. No doubt you would prefer it if I collapsed with the vapors, but I am afraid I have no idea how to do that and I would feel perfectly ridiculous attempting it. What happened, happened, and it seems to me that the best thing is to simply go on and—and forget it."

"I am afraid I cannot do that," he responded gravely. "I crossed a line, and I must apologize for that."

"Very well. I accept your apology." Mary nodded at him and turned away.

"Wait. I have not finished."

She pivoted back. "What else is there to say?"

"Here. Let us sit down." He led her to a stone bench.

"All right." Mary sat down, eyeing him warily.

Royce sat beside her, then rose and walked a few steps away, turned, and came back. "I, um, I had a speech prepared, but it sounds unbearably foolish now as I think of it. I—Mary, will you—that is, well, I am asking you to marry me."

Mary stared at him, at first barely comprehending what he had said. For an instant, joy surged up in her, and her heart began to pound. She envisioned marrying him, living with him, spending the rest of her life by his side, her nights in his bed. The rush of yearning that sprang up inside her startled her. But a moment later, her pragmatic self took over. She was not the lady of a manor; she was plain Mary Bascombe.

"Why are you asking me?" she said, suspicion in her voice.

He gaped at her. "Why? I think it should be obvious."

"Not to me. Are you doing this to salvage my reputation? Because it's the gentlemanly thing to do after . . . what happened yesterday?" She could feel a flush rising up her throat into her face, and she glanced away. "I assure you, there is no need. I will not reveal it."

His face registered shock. "I don't feel impelled to marry you because someone might find out about it—though, of course, it's vital to your reputation that it remain a secret.

I could not do other than marry you after . . . after taking your innocence as I did."

"Is that what you call it?" she said dryly.

"What the devil is that supposed to mean?" He scowled at her. "I am a gentleman. Perhaps the men you are accustomed to seduce and abandon innocent young girls, but I am not that sort of man."

"Do not worry." Mary sent him a flashing glance. "I absolve you of all blame. I take full responsibility for my actions. I am a grown woman, not a child, and I was well aware of what I was doing."

He stared at her. "What are you saying?"

"I think it is clear enough. I do not expect you to propose marriage. I have no intention of chaining you to me for life because of a single mistake. An accident of fate." Mary stood up, her color high.

"I would not call it an accident," he retorted. "However spontaneously it transpired, I was fully aware of what I was doing. And of the consequences."

"The consequences—I take it you mean the punishment of marrying me."

"No! Blast it, you have the most damnable way of twisting things. It is not a punishment. It is, rather, the logical result of what we did."

"What we did is not enough upon which to base a marriage."

"It is not the only basis for the marriage. Merely the precipitating factor. There are numerous reasons . . ."

Mary folded her arms and regarded him skeptically. "Indeed. What are they? And don't you dare tell me that not offending Lord Stewkesbury is one of them."

"What? No. It has nothing to do with Oliver." Royce scowled. He paused for a moment, gathering his thoughts. "Well, obviously, there is an attraction between us. I think we would deal well together, both in and out of bed. I have an adequate income; I can support you in a pleasant style, and I am not ungenerous. You have seen Iverley Hall and found it commodious, I believe. At present I rent only a few rooms in London, but, of course, during the Season, we can lease a house in Mayfair or even purchase one, if you find you enjoy the social whirl."

"My. You present an excellent case for the benefits marriage would provide me," Mary said crisply, trying to keep a rein on her temper. "I cannot help but wonder why *you* should wish it."

"A beautiful wife is something any man would wish for," Royce replied stiffly. "A connection to the Talbot family is a good thing. The old earl would have been pleased to see it."

"That is why you wish to marry me?" Mary stared. "To please my grandfather?"

He hesitated, then went on, "Perhaps. Partly. He—he was very good to me, and I know he would have been happy to have me actually in the family. He spoke with regret about the split between him and his daughter. I am sure he would have provided for you and your sisters had he known of your existence. But since he did not, yes, he would want Oliver and Fitz and me to do our best for you."

"Well, you may be perfectly happy with marrying to suit the old earl, but I, sir, am not." Mary's eyes flashed.

"I am not marrying to suit the earl; it is only one of the factors that—"

"Please, spare me any more talk of your 'factors.' I have heard more than enough. Your vision of marriage is a trifle cold-blooded for me."

"Marriage usually is," he retorted.

"Love doesn't enter into it?"

"I have no intention of marrying for love. I don't believe

in love or in throwing one's life away for the elusive prospect of it. A man fancies himself in love and wakes up with a wife who makes his life a living hell for forty years."

"If that is your view of marriage, it seems to me that you should not marry at all," Mary shot back. "Certainly, I have no interest in being locked into such a marriage."

"Come, Mary, I would not have taken you for a romantic miss."

"No, clearly you take me for a woman who is so desperate for a husband that she will accept even the most spiritless and insulting of proposals. I am sorry to disappoint you, but I am not in so bad a case. What I gave you yesterday I gave freely, out of my own desire, not to blackmail you into wedlock. I have no interest in marrying a man for his income or because I like his house! Even less would I do it because some hardheaded, hard-hearted old man whom I never met would have wanted me to. I am a practical woman, but that doesn't mean I am bloodless. I saw my parents, and however little they had and however 'poor' a marriage they made, they were *happy*. They loved each other. I could not settle for anything less. When I say yes, it will be to a man who cannot live without me—not one who has to talk himself into it. Least of all one who proposes simply because he is a 'gentleman.' "

Mary whirled and strode back to the house, leaving Royce staring after her.

Mary charged up the stairs, fueled by the heat of her fury. She could not join her sisters in their daily deportment lesson feeling the way she did now. She could scarcely talk or even breathe, she was so filled with anger; one idiotic rule from Miss Dalrymple would probably make her erupt.

As she passed the small sitting room, however, she saw that Rose was there alone, sitting before one of the trunks they had hauled in. The trunk was open, with a few things piled in front, and Rose was bent over a book. She looked up and smiled when she heard Mary at the door.

"Good! There you are. Miss Dalrymple gave us the morning off since you were walking with Sir Royce—it is amazing how much more amenable she is now that Cousin Charlotte is here. Charlotte just suggested to her that we take the lessons another time, and Miss Dalrymple smiled and agreed, as though she were the most reasonable woman in the world."

"You are going through Mama's things?" Mary asked as she walked over to her sister. She was surprised at how calm her voice sounded.

"Shh. Don't tell the others. I said I'd wait. Camellia and Lily are still downstairs at breakfast with Cousin Charlotte. Charlotte is a late riser, and you know how Lily loves to dawdle over her coffee. But I couldn't resist taking a peek. Look, it is Mama's diary." She showed a small leather-bound book. "Nothing very remarkable—she was only ten, I think, according to the date on it. Just things that she ate or walks with her sisters or her studies. Imagine—her governess was already making her walk with a book on her head, just as Miss Dalrymple does with us." Rose chuckled. "She hated it. Camellia will be happy to hear that."

"How nice." Mary tried to swallow her agitation as she knelt beside her sister. She took the small book and smoothed her hand across the old leather cover.

Rose frowned and reached out to touch Mary's hand. "Sweetheart . . . what's the matter? You seem upset."

"Do I?" Mary tried to smile, but the effort was feeble.

"Yes. What happened? Miss Dalrymple said she saw you walking into the garden with Sir Royce. Was he lecturing you again? Did he make you unhappy?"

Mary jumped to her feet, hardly noticing that the diary

tumbled from her hands onto the floor. "Oh, Rose! He asked me to marry him!"

Her sister gaped at her. "He—he what?"

"He asked me to marry him. I have never been so astonished in my life."

"What did you say?" Rose asked in a weak voice.

"I told him no, of course."

"You did?"

"Did he really think that I was so plain, so dowdy, so utterly unattractive that I would leap at the chance to marry anyone?" Mary demanded, spreading her arms wide.

"No! Mary, he never said that!"

"Well, no, he did not. But only a person in those straits would have accepted his proposal. He said that we 'would deal well together.' "

"Oh my."

"Exactly. He pointed out that he had a 'pleasant income' and that I liked his house. Can you imagine? As if I would marry him because I enjoyed Iverley Hall! He also assured me that we could get a house in London because he's 'generous.' Of course, for him the advantage would be doing something that would please the old earl. And being connected to the Talbots."

"Mary, how awful!" Rose jumped to her feet and put her arms around Mary.

Warmed by Rose's ready sympathy, Mary hugged her sister hard. It made the huge, tight knot in her chest lessen even though tears sprang into her eyes. She pulled away, dashing the drops from her eyes. "I refuse to cry about it."

"Perhaps he did not mean it the way it sounds," Rose offered helpfully. "Maybe he is merely infelicitous in his way of talking."

"He is certainly that." Mary sighed. "Thank you for throwing that rope to a drowning woman, but no, I fear it is a perfectly accurate expression of his feelings for me. It was the coldest, most bloodless proposal that was ever made."

"Did he—did he say nothing about love?"

"No, not a word." Mary's voice rang with bitterness. "He did not say once that he could not live without me or—or that my eyes shone like stars. Or even how proud he would be for me to become Mrs. Sir Royce, or whatever they call it."

"I'm so sorry."

"He thinks I'm unmarriageable, that's what it is. That no one will have me because of my lack of decorum, my country bumpkin behavior, my deplorably American manners!"

"That is why he's marrying you?"

"No, he's marrying me because he's a gentleman!"

"What? Mary, I don't understand."

Mary stopped, realizing suddenly where she had gone in her ire. She crumpled a little. "Oh, Rose . . . I have not told you all. I didn't want you to hate me."

"Silly. I couldn't hate you."

"No, *you* probably could not. But I know you will think less of me." She sighed, then squared her shoulders in her usual way. "I told you that he kissed me."

"Yes . . ."

"Yesterday, at the summerhouse, when he was so mad at me—"

"Mary!" Rose gasped. "Do not tell me Sir Royce forced you!"

"No! Goodness, no. It was nothing like that. It was mutual. But there were certain liberties taken."

"You mean—"

Mary nodded, blushing to her hairline. "As Royce so circumspectly put it, my 'innocence' is gone."

"Mary!" Rose sat down with a thump in the nearest chair.

"You do hate me. I'm sorry. I shouldn't have told you, but I couldn't keep on pretending."

"No, of course I don't hate you. I'm glad you told me. It's just so startling I scarce know what to say."

"I was rather stunned by it myself." Mary sank down in the chair next to her sister.

Rose reached out to take her hand. "Mary, tell me . . . what was it like? Was it awful? Frightening?"

"It was . . . wonderful." A reminiscent smile curved Mary's lips. "'Tis almost enough to make me agree to marry him. I felt—I felt—I've never felt anything like it. When he touched me, I felt alive all over, as if I was dancing inside. I felt beautiful and twitchy and absolutely sizzling."

"Oh my." Rose's eyes brightened as she watched her sister's glowing face. "Maybe you *should* marry him."

"How can I marry a man who doesn't love me? Who asked me because he felt obligated?"

After a moment, Rose asked softly, "Do you love him?"

"No." Mary's answer was swift and decisive. "I-I thought perhaps I might . . . have feelings for him." She remembered with a swift stab of pain that moment when she had felt joined with Royce, so much a part of him that she scarcely knew where she began and he left off. "But now I see that it was purely physical lust. The sort of thing they warn us about. That is all. We—there is no love between us."

Rose sighed, frowning. "Then you must not marry him. How could you have a happy marriage without love?"

"How indeed?" Mary echoed tonelessly.

There was the sound of voices down the hall, and Mary turned to Rose anxiously. "Please, don't tell Lily and Camellia."

"Of course not. I won't tell anyone. I promise." Rose patted Mary's hand.

"Thank you."

"Mary! You're back!" Her younger sisters entered the room, followed by Charlotte. "Good. We can start looking through Mama's things. Can Cousin Charlotte join us?"

"Of course." Mary smiled at their cousin. "Although you may find it a bit boring."

"Oh, no, I think it's all quite fascinating," Charlotte assured her. "Mother never told me about Aunt Flora before, but since you arrived, she has said quite a bit. She feels terrible about what happened. At the time, she wouldn't have defied their father, but she regrets losing her sister."

They began to rummage through the trunks, finding mostly old clothes, but also a cloth doll with a china head, somewhat battered, and a miniature tea set with a chipped teapot. There were old composition books, filled with childish notes and essays. The diaries they found were all those of a child, filled with scrawls about lessons, meals, and, primarily, her sisters. Lily read these aloud, adding her own dramatic inflections, as the others rummaged through the trunks, and everyone laughed to hear the accounts of Phrony's bossiness or Cyn stealing Phyl's lemon drops or the four girls conspiring to play a trick on their governess.

"I should hold this over Aunt Euphronia's head," Charlotte declared. "The next time she tells me my boys are wild as March hares, I'll remind her about the frog in Miss Carpenter's bed."

"Oh, look!" Rose brought out a wooden box and opened it. A mirror was attached inside the lid, reflecting the little figures of a man and a woman dressed in clothing from the past century, their hands held up to touch as they dipped toward one another.

"It's a music box! How sweet." Charlotte reached over and wound the key. The figures sprang to jerky life, turning in a minuet.

"It's her jewelry box." Rose set it down and began to take

out the objects tucked away in the satin squares—two rings that were too small to fit anyone but a child, several filigree buttons, a couple of pairs of earrings, a glittering brooch shaped like a vase of flowers, a tortoiseshell bracelet, and a pendant portrait of a gentleman in a white wig.

"Children's things and paste," Charlotte said, picking up the brooch and looking at it. "A girl her age would not have had many valuable items, and no doubt she took with her the few she did." She turned to the portrait on the pendant. "This is the old earl, her father."

"How sad." Rose ran a thumb across the pendant. "She must have been so angry with him she didn't even want his picture. I wonder if she regretted it later."

"Here are some letters." Camellia pulled a small stack out of another trunk. The letters were bound by a dark green ribbon, which Camellia tugged open. "Lady Cynthia Talbot. They're all addressed to Aunt Cynthia here at Willowmere."

The girls glanced toward Charlotte, who looked puzzled. "My mother? But she told me she never received a letter from Aunt Flora. She said she wished she had known where she was, that she would have offered her help."

"They haven't been opened." Camellia handed the missives to her.

Charlotte turned the top letter over, frowning as she examined the unbroken seal and the address. "I suspect Aunt Euphronia or Lord Reginald must have kept them from Mother. I don't think she would have ignored all these. Perhaps the first one, out of respect for her father. But Mother is much too softhearted not to have even read any of them." Charlotte thumbed through them, counting. "There are eight. Aunt Flora must have decided then that Mother had cut her off, too. How sad." She echoed Rose. Charlotte raised her head. "May I take these to my mother? I know she would like very much to see them. I truly don't think she knew of their existence."

"Of course. Take them. They were written to her, after all." Mary glanced at her sisters for confirmation, and they nodded.

Charlotte tied the letters again and set them aside as the girls continued with their exploration. Mary opened the last trunk, which was filled primarily with clothes. Lying on the top was a small leather case bound with ribbon. When she untied it, the case folded open to reveal several sheets of paper. She drew in her breath sharply as she looked at the angular writing.

"Papa! This is Papa's handwriting." Quickly she scanned the letter. "He's asking for our grandfather's forgiveness. Oh my, this must have cost him dearly." Tears sparkled in her eyes. "He says that he should bear full responsibility for their elopement, that Mama did not wish to go against her father, but Papa talked her into it. Which is absolutely not true!" Mary added fiercely, looking up at her sisters.

"Of course it isn't," Rose agreed. "Mama said she was furious with her father, and she was determined to elope."

"But Papa wants our grandfather to forgive Mama. He talks about his three little girls—Lily, you must not have been born yet—and he says how sorry he is that they will grow up without knowing their family. Listen: 'I do not ask for your aid. Though our lives are not the sort which Flora and I knew in England, we are too happy to wish for any-thing other than what we have. My wife, however, feels the loss of paternal love, and I would ask that you write and as-sure her that your face is not turned against her.' "

Mary handed the letter to Rose, who read it with Lily and Camellia leaning over her shoulders.

"It doesn't say when it's written—I mean, not the year, only the day and month," Rose pointed out.

"I know." Mary nodded. "The return address is Littleboro, Maryland. I remember living there. Papa opened a school. We moved when I was seven or so."

"What else is in there?"

Mary looked down at the case in her lap. "It's a letter, several letters, in fact, from someone in Baltimore. He seems to be a solicitor." She thumbed through them. "He is corresponding with Lord Reginald about a search for Mr. Miles Bascombe. Here he says that he has gone to Littleboro, and he itemizes the expenses he incurred. This is the final letter. It is dated July 10, 1806. He says he cannot locate our father and his family in Littleboro, Maryland, or any of the surrounding towns. 'I cannot in good conscience,' " Mary read, " 'continue to accept your fees for my services, as I am unable to fulfill your wishes.' "

Mary looked around at her sisters. It felt as though something had lightened in her chest.

"Our grandfather was looking for us?" Lily asked.

"Of course he was!" Charlotte beamed. "I knew he could not have remained stiff and unbending all that time. Grandfather was not a bad man."

"But he waited too long to write Papa, and by then we were gone." Tears pricked at Mary's eyelids. "He tried to contact us. He wanted to know us."

"Maybe he would even have wanted us to come here," Lily offered.

Mary nodded. "For the first time, I feel a bit as if we belong here."

With a choked noise, Charlotte leaned over to hug Mary. "Of course you do. You have always belonged here."

Chapter 21

Lady Sabrina's dinner party was two nights later, and the entire group at Willowmere attended. Mary was relieved to learn that Royce and Fritz would be riding their horses. She had spent the better part of two days avoiding Royce, and the last thing she wanted was to be closed up in a carriage with him. She could tell, from the frequent glances Royce sent her way, that he wanted to talk to her again. Mary had little doubt that he intended to again press her to marry him—which was precisely why she made sure to seat herself between two of her sisters every evening in the drawing room after supper.

Tonight the sisters wore their finest evening dresses, eager to show them off to Lady Sabrina. Lily could hardly sit still, but kept shifting in her seat and leaning over to twitch aside the carriage curtains and glance outside.

"Honestly, Lily," Camellia grumbled the fourth time Lily did so. "It's too dark to see anything out there anyway."

"I know. I keep hoping we'll see the lights of Halstead House soon. How long do you think it takes to reach it?"

Charlotte smiled patiently. "It won't be long, I'm sure."

The next time Lily reached over to take a peek, she let out a little squeal. "There it is! It's grand."

The other girls now shot to the windows to get a glimpse. Halstead House, ablaze with lights for its visitors, was indeed a great mansion, almost equal in size to Willowmere and far statelier in appearance—though to Mary's mind it lacked Willowmere's more haphazard charm. Made of dark gray stone, it was built in a perfectly symmetrical E, and the lawn in front of it was laid out with the same precision, walkways crossing it in a perfect X, a single walk bisecting it from the curved drive to the front door. Liveried footmen stood on either side of the entrance, and one sprang forward to open the carriage door while the other opened the front door for them, bowing as they passed.

They were shown by the butler through a grand entry, two stories tall and floored in black and white marble, to an anteroom decorated in cool sea green and white. Lady Sabrina, serene and cool in ice blue, a choker of large white pearls around her neck, awaited them upon a bench in the center of the room. Several feet away stood Lady Vivian, vivid in a dark gold dress that showed off her milk-white shoulders and elegant swanlike neck, chatting animatedly to a slightly stoop-shouldered older gentleman with graying hair.

Sabrina's eyes opened wide when Mary and her sisters entered the room. She rose with liquid grace, coming forward to greet them. "My dears, how absolutely lovely you look." She shook her head as she clasped Mary's hand between hers, leaning forward confidingly. "Isn't it amazing what a London frock will do for one?"

Warmly she greeted the girls by name, then turned to the others. "Charlotte, Fitz, I am so glad you and our dear Vivian were able to come up so soon. And Royce . . ." She smiled slowly. "I am delighted you decided to join us." She held out her hand and he bowed over it, then released it, stepping back and turning toward Vivian and the older man as they approached the guests.

"Sir Royce. Talbot." The older man shook their hands, his manner reserved.

"My dear, allow me to introduce you to the earl's cousins." Sabrina smiled sweetly at him. She went through the introductions, confirming that he was, as Mary had suspected, Lord Humphrey Carlyle, Sabrina's husband and Lady Vivian's uncle. Almost as an afterthought, she turned toward Vivian. "Oh, and, of course, you know Lady Vivian."

"Of course." Vivian swept past Sabrina, smiling brilliantly and giving each of the Bascombes a warm greeting. "It is wonderful to see you again. How very handsome all of you look. You will take London by storm next Season."

"You are going to London next year?" Sabrina turned to the sisters in surprise. "Well . . . how delightful. I am sure that you will handle it just fine. The main thing to remember is not to let the old matrons frighten you. Or at least," she added with a dimpling smile, "do not let them see you are afraid."

"You needn't worry about that," Vivian assured her. "I think you'll find there is little that frightens the Bascombe sisters. In any case, I will be there to help smooth their way. I intend to sponsor them next Season."

"Really."

"Yes. I am planning a ball to introduce them all."

"At the duke's town house?" Sabrina's smile wavered a fraction.

"Of course. Only the grand ballroom there would be adequate. It will be the event of the season."

"I am sure you know what is best, dear." Sabrina turned to Mary. "I must confess I found Carlyle Hall quite overwhelming the first time I was there." She tucked her arm through Mary's and began to lead her away from Vivian and the others, leaning her head closer to say in a low, confiding voice, "Our dear Vivian, of course, grew up in the house. She does not understand how the rest of us might feel when confronted with such grandeur. Why, even this house has such a grand air that one cannot quite feel at home in it, can one? Willowmere, I fear, must seem the same to you."

"Willowmere is rather large," Mary hedged, for she liked Willowmere. She knew that she probably would have found it more intimidating if she had not first stayed in Stewkesbury House in London. Though Willowmere was larger, it was less formal, from its wayward sprawl of buildings to its friendlier servants, and it had a lived-in feel, with comfortably worn furniture and the marks that showed generations had inhabited the house.

Mary noticed that the rest of the party had drifted after them and was again grouped around Mary and Sabrina.

"You must not worry," Sabrina went on. "I am sure that you will become accustomed to Willowmere. At least Halstead House is not so gloomy as it used to be. I redecorated several rooms, including this one, soon after Lord Humphrey and I were married."

"Yes, this room once had a Jacobean carved walnut doorway into the dining room," Lady Vivian said brightly. "Of course one *would* wish to get rid of that old thing."

Sabrina let out a little chuckle. "I fear Vivian is much attached to the house as it was; she still has not forgiven me for my changes. The doorway was lovely, of course, but so massive and dark." She turned toward Royce. "You remember it, don't you, Royce?"

"I cannot say that I do, my lady."

A moment of dead silence followed his terse remark, then Fitz stepped into the conversational breach. "Your renovations are as charming as yourself, Lady Sabrina."

Sabrina bestowed her glowing smile on Fitz. Mary, glancing at Fitz, noticed that his return smile did not reach his eyes, and it only then occurred to her that Fitz's compliment could be taken in an entirely different way. She glanced back at him sharply, but he was already turning away and she could not see his expression. Did Fitz not hold Sabrina in high regard?

Mary frowned. It was scarcely remarkable that two such attractive women as Sabrina and Vivian, both used to being the center of attention at any gathering, would have some clashes, particularly when they were residing in the same house. But she could not help but wonder why men, especially such flirtatious men as Sir Royce and Fitz, might not like a woman as lovely as Sabrina.

Lord Humphrey escorted his niece, the highest-ranking woman in the room, into the dining room, which left it to Fitz to offer his arm to Sabrina, and Sir Royce to take in Charlotte. Mary and her sisters trailed along behind them. As they took their seats around the table, Mary noticed that, breaking with the usual ranking, Sir Royce and Fitz had been placed in the midst of the women on either side, the whole group arranged near the head of the long table.

"I apologize for the unevenness of the table," Sabrina said. "I tried to think of some unattached gentlemen I could invite to even it out, but I could not. So you must forgive me for setting you two gentlemen amongst us. I could not help but feel it would add to the conviviality." She turned to smile at Royce, seated on her left. "We all know each other so well, 'tis almost like family, is it not?"

"A number of us are related to each other," Royce admitted. "And others are no kin at all."

He looked across the table at Mary, and she felt a blush begin to spread along her cheeks. *Drat the man!* The way he affected her was most annoying. Even now, just looking at him, she could feel the visceral tug of attraction. She remembered his thick hair sliding between her fingers, his hands on her skin, her body surging with pleasure beneath him.

Mary lowered her eyes to her plate, embarrassed by her physical reaction. Women were not supposed to be this way, were they? To feel such need, to hunger for a man—not for his love, but for his body? She could not help but think that if she agreed to marry him, such pleasure would be hers almost any time she wished. Lovemaking would be sanctioned; indeed, it would be expected, at least until an heir was born. But she could not marry just for pleasure. A marriage entered into solely for passion would not last; it could not. She knew that ultimately it would not make her happy.

Talk flowed around her. Fitz and Vivian were both expert conversationalists, and whenever the evening showed signs of flagging, they brought the discussion to life with a bit of gossip or news from London. Mary added little to the conversation, and even Lady Sabrina seemed rather reticent through much of the evening. Mary could see the way Sabrina's eyes lit up whenever the talk turned to London and the Season, and she remembered the times that Sabrina had mentioned her boredom here in the country. It must be hard for her, Mary thought, married to someone much older than she and mired on this rural estate.

The dinner seemed interminable. Far more formal than the evening meals served at Willowmere, it went on for course after course. Mary, full after the fish course, the rest of the time just pushed her food around on her plate—though she did note, with a small upsurge of pride, that she knew which utensil to use with every dish.

It was a relief when Sabrina finally stood up, signaling for the women to leave the men alone with their port. They made their way to what Sabrina called the assembly room, a long chamber with several groupings of chairs and sofas, as well as a large burnished mahogany table in the center.

"Come, Mary," Sabrina said, once again linking her arm through Mary's. "Let us take a stroll around the room."

Mary smiled and walked with her along the perimeter of the large room as Vivian and Mary's sisters seated themselves on a sofa and chairs at one end.

"I enjoy having a friend again," Sabrina told Mary with a sweet smile. "Life is lonely here, with no one my age about. It's nice to have someone to talk to."

"I am glad you consider me a friend. I cannot imagine how awful it would be to have no female to talk to, accustomed as I am to living with my sisters."

"I hope the dinner was not too awkward."

"No, it was quite pleasant," Mary lied. She had not enjoyed it, but that had not been Sabrina's fault.

"Royce was . . ." Sabrina sighed. "Well, I had hoped that with time he would get over his bitterness. That we might be friends again. Obviously he could not. He was so hurt."

Mary looked at the other woman, her curiosity rising. "You and Sir Royce were friends?"

Sabrina turned to her, her eyes opening a little wider. "Do you mean—you did not know? No one told you?"

Mary shook her head. "Know what?"

"Sir Royce and I were once desperately in love."

Mary stared at Sabrina. She felt as if her heart had suddenly plummeted to her feet. "What?"

Sabrina nodded, her face wistful. "We were very much in love. But it was one of those sad stories—my parents did not like the match. And the earl was against it as well."

"Why—when—I'm sorry, I had no idea," Mary finished weakly. She wished that she were anywhere but here. Her head whirled with the news, but she struggled to conceal her shock. She could not let Sabrina guess that she had any feelings for Royce.

"I am surprised you did not hear it from the servants or Charlotte," Sabrina went on. "It was quite the story around here. Of course, it has been ages now. We were both too young, no doubt. Perhaps our parents were right. But at the time, it hurt a great deal."

"What happened?" Mary suspected that Miss Dalrymple would tell her that her question was rude, but she could not keep from asking.

"My family's lineage is quite good—my mother's cousin is an earl, and my father is the son of a baron. However, they had no fortune, and it was necessary that I marry well. They refused to let me marry Sir Royce."

"But I thought Royce was—"

"Royce's fortune and name are quite adequate. But my parents were in dire straits; they needed much greater wealth. And Lord Humphrey sought my hand as well."

"They forced you to marry him?" Mary asked, appalled.

"No, they were not so brutal. But they forbade my marriage to Royce, and I could not go against them."

Mary could not envision being in love with one man and marrying another, no matter what one's parents wanted, but she held her tongue.

As though she guessed Mary's thoughts, Sabrina released a small sigh. "No doubt you think me poor-spirited. You would have answered them with that bold American defiance. But I could not be responsible for my family's ruin. Perhaps it is different where you come from, but here, among people like us, one marries as one's family wishes. Lord Humphrey is a good man, a kind man; he has been the very model of a husband."

Mary thought of her own mother's defiance of her father's wishes. She thought it was not so much an indication of one's nationality as of one's nature.

"I cannot regret what I did," Sabrina went on softly, her eyes sparkling with tears. "But I do regret hurting Royce. He was so angry at me. He wanted me to refuse to do as they wished. We should run away to Gretna Green, he said. But I could not—the scandal would have made my family's problems worse. I feared Royce would create a dreadful scene, but the old earl and Oliver shipped him off to one of the Talbot holdings in Scotland. I hoped that in time Royce would forgive me, that he would find wedded happiness, too. But he has never married."

Of course he had not.

It was all clear to Mary now. Everything Royce had done made sense—dreadful, appalling sense. No wonder he was short, even rude to Sabrina. It was too painful for him to be around her. He blamed her for breaking his heart. He had loved Sabrina; indeed, his feelings for her had probably never died.

"I-I am sorry to hear about . . . your past sorrow," Mary said, groping for the right words. She wanted only to get out of here, to rush home, to hide in her room and try to absorb this news. Why had Royce told her none of this?

"You are kind." Sabrina squeezed her arm affectionately. "It is such a relief having someone in whom I can confide."

Mary smiled noncommittally, hoping she would not have to hear any more confidences. Sabrina, as though sensing her mood, strolled back to the other women. Mary slipped into the space between Rose and Camellia on the sofa.

The men rejoined them soon, and after that the evening wore down quickly. It was clear that Royce was impatient, and even Fitz made little effort to keep the conversation going. In the carriage on the way home, everyone was quiet, even the usually voluble Lily and Charlotte. Mary closed her eyes and leaned her head back against the seat, her thoughts boiling. She went over everything that had happened between her and Sir Royce, viewing it this time from the vantage point of her new knowledge. No wonder he had told her he did not expect to fall in love. He was already in love with a woman whom he could never have. What did it matter to him whom he married?

At least she had not accepted his proposal, which made Mary feel a little less a fool. Still, she could not help but burn with resentment. How could Royce have asked her to be his wife without revealing his past with Sabrina? Granted, he had made it clear that he would never love Mary, but that was not the same thing as admitting that he loved another. Mary could not imagine that any woman would want to marry a man who yearned for another woman he could not have; certainly she had no desire for such a marriage.

Pleading a headache, Mary went straight to bed when they got home, never once glancing in Royce's direction. She could not bear to have the maid fussing over her, so as soon as Prue had helped her out of her evening gown, she sent her to bed, telling her that she would deal with her hair herself.

Flinging herself down on the chair in front of the vanity, she yanked the pins from her hair, tugging her curls so painfully that her eyes watered. Frankly, she would have liked to cry; it would be easier to give way to a fit of sobs. At least then she could purge some of the emotion churning inside her. But tears came no more easily than sleep, and by the time the sun was first streaking the sky the next morning, she was still tossing and turning in her bed.

She managed to sleep for a few hours, awakening after breakfast had been served. She was happy enough to have nothing but tea and toast brought to her room, where she intended to spend the rest of the day. Let Miss Dalrymple fuss all she wanted, Mary thought. She refused to face Sir Royce yet.

Mary considered going through some of the things in her mother's trunks again. They had not read all the diaries. Or perhaps she could investigate the nursery, looking for books and such that had belonged to Flora. Neither of those prospects aroused her interest. The thought of the trunks reminded her of the attic, however, and the stack of letters addressed to Sir Royce that she had found. Could those have been love letters from Sabrina? The possibility tugged at her, and she itched to go up into the attic and retrieve the bundle.

It would be wrong, she thought, a terrible invasion of Royce's privacy, and she must not do it. But it was difficult to deny the urge, and her mind returned to it often as she ate her toast and got dressed. Finally, to distract her wayward thoughts, she decided to take out the ripped nightgown that she had hidden in the trunk more than a week ago and repair it.

Going to the chest at the foot of her bed, she groped under the blankets to bring out the wadded-up gown. It was only after she closed the lid of the trunk that she realized that something had seemed odd. Opening the chest again, she looked thoughtfully at the contents. Then it struck her—the case in which she had carried her papers was not wedged between the blankets and the wall of the chest.

Frowning, she dug into the trunk and felt around the inner walls, searching for the small leather satchel. She even thrust her hand under the blankets and between them, just in case some maid had shoved it out of the way. She was certain she had put the satchel in that trunk, but just to make sure, she rifled through all her drawers and even searched the bottom of the wardrobe. The case was nowhere to be found.

Stuffing the nightgown into her sewing bag, Mary rang

for Prue. The maid had not seen the leather case, but she looked again in all the places Mary had tried, even getting down on hands and knees to look under the bed.

Next, Mary went in search of her sisters, whom she found rather easily by following the sound of their laughter to the library downstairs. She stepped inside and saw her three sisters sitting around one of the tables with Fitz and Royce. Mary came to an abrupt halt, her gaze going to Royce. In her puzzlement over the missing satchel, she had not considered that she might run into Royce. She turned hot, then cold, and her tongue seemed to cleave to the roof of her mouth. Fervently she wished that she had never entered the room, but she could hardly leave now.

Finally she managed to tear her eyes from Royce and turn to Rose. "What are you doing?" she asked as she glanced around suspiciously. "Where is Miss Dalrymple?"

"Shh." Fitz held an admonitory finger to his lips. "We have given her the slip."

"Cousin Fitz is teaching us faro," Camellia told her with a grin.

"Yes, and I am inclined to believe Cousin Camellia has sadly misled me about her lack of knowledge of the game," Fitz added. "She is, I fear, a Captain Sharp. As you can see, she has vastly reduced my fortune." He waved at the pile of buttons before him.

"I can see you are in drastic circumstances." Mary sent him a dry look. "I hope you are not leading my sisters astray. Will Miss Dalrymple disapprove of this?"

"Have you not heard?" Lily piped up. "Anything Cousin Fitz does is perfect as far as our Miss Dalrymple is concerned. He has replaced Sir Royce in her affections."

"I am quite downcast over the matter." Royce smiled in a way that Mary felt all through her. "You needn't worry. Faro is a perfectly acceptable game for ladies of the *ton*."

Mary refused to smile at him in return. It was beyond irritating that she could feel as angry and hurt as she did and still be affected by his smile.

"Come and join us, Mary," Rose offered. "We can add another person."

"No," Mary refused hastily. "I am doing some, um, darning." She ignored the eyebrow that Royce raised in polite disbelief.

Lily wrinkled her nose. "I hope you are not going to ask us to join you."

"No. The thing is, I noticed that my satchel is missing. I cannot find it anywhere, and I wondered if one of you might have taken it."

Five similarly blank faces gazed at her.

"The case that had our papers in it," Mary explained.

"Why would I want that?" Lily asked, puzzled.

"I don't know why anyone would, but you girls are the only ones who are likely to have borrowed it."

Her sisters agreed that they had not taken the case. Indeed, it was clear that they had not thought of it since they had taken up residence in the earl's house.

"The case is missing?" Royce asked, frowning. "Are you certain?"

"Yes. Prue and I looked all over my room, and we could not find it anywhere. I cannot imagine where it could have got to."

"Do you think it was stolen?" Fitz asked.

Mary looked at him, startled. "Stolen? Why would anyone steal it? It had nothing of importance in it, only the deed of a farm that belonged to our father and a bill of sale for the wagon and horses he bought from old Mr. McCready. The earl took out the things that were valuable—our birth certificates and the marriage certificate, the letter our mother wrote—and locked them in his safe in London."

"Perhaps whoever took it didn't know that," Royce offered.

"Are you serious?" Mary looked from one man to the other. "You actually think it was stolen?"

Fitz shrugged. "Probably not. It seems unlikely a thief would break in here and steal only that."

"True." Mary thought of the many valuable objects that lay around this house—a leather case would not compare to some of the candlesticks and vases, let alone things like silver epergnes and tea services or the gold and enamel box on the mantel of this very room.

"Still . . . there must be some reason it is gone," Royce said. "Some very peculiar things have transpired the last few weeks. When did it go missing?"

"I don't know." Mary sighed. "It could have been anytime since we've been here. I tucked it in the trunk when we first arrived, and I haven't paid any attention to it since. It was only by accident that I noticed it today."

"I will have Bostwick check with the servants. Perhaps one of them picked it up and put it somewhere."

Mary nodded and started to turn away. At that moment Miss Dalrymple's voice came trumpeting down the corridor. "Girls? Where are you? It is time for your music lesson."

Camellia let out a groan, but the girls rose to their feet. Fitz stood up with them, promising gravely to draw their chaperone's fire.

Mary started to follow the others out of the room, but Royce rose, saying, "Mary—stay a moment."

Mary did not look at him. "I should join my sisters."

"I will make your excuses to Miss Dalrymple later." He came around the table.

Mary's only hope of escape was to beat him to the door, but she refused to sink to the indignity of racing him. She faced him, squaring her shoulders. "I can think of nothing else to add about the satchel."

"I had not intended to discuss the missing satchel." Royce closed the library door and returned to her.

Mary glanced toward the closed door. "That is a trifle indiscreet, is it not?"

"Perhaps. But I do not think that either of us would wish to have our conversation heard by everyone in the house."

"All right." Mary crossed her arms over her chest, almost as if she could hold in the emotions roiling within her. Trepidation, anger, resentment, hurt, jealousy all warred for supremacy, and she would hate for Royce to glimpse any of them. She wished she had not impulsively come down here. "What did you wish to discuss?"

"Our marriage."

"There is no marriage."

"There has to be." Frustration stamped Royce's features. "Blast it, Mary, face the truth. Your reputation, your very future are at stake. You must marry me."

Mary's brows rose. "I *must*?"

"Damn it, Mary, stop acting this way. What is wrong with you? Surely you realize what it would do to your good name—"

"To hell with my good name!" Mary's eyes burned as her arms fell to her sides, hands clenching. "I told you that I would not marry a man who doesn't love me. Even less would I marry one who loves someone else!"

He stared at her. "What?"

"Lady Sabrina told me your story last night." Mary noted with a painful satisfaction that Royce's face shut down at the mention of Sabrina's name.

"No doubt that was entertaining for both of you. What did Sabrina say?"

"She told me that the two of you were in love, but her parents refused to let her marry you, that they pushed her to marry Lord Humphrey. You urged her to run away with you, but she refused."

Royce rolled his eyes. "I see she is still a liar."

"You deny it, then?" Mary strode closer, her head high. "You did not love her?"

The muscles in Royce's cheek jumped, and his eyes blazed with an unholy light. For a moment Mary thought that he would not answer her.

But then, turning away, he growled, "Yes! Yes, I did love her. However, the events did not unfold precisely as she says." He pivoted back. "Her parents did not refuse to let her marry me. It was her decision, not theirs. Sabrina liked me well enough, but her primary interest was money. No, I am wrong—she had two interests, money and position. She thought I had enough of both until Lord Humphrey began to dance attendance on her. She kept me dangling for a while until he came up to the mark. When he made an offer, she cut me loose—with that sweet smile and an artful tear, of course."

Mary winced at the sarcastic tone of his last words. Nothing, she thought, could have said more clearly that the wound in him had never healed. He still carried Sabrina in his heart.

"That is why you didn't join us when she came to call, isn't it? Why you didn't want to go to her dinner last night? You could not bear to see her."

"No, I did not want to see her. I should be quite happy never to see her again. I cannot think why that should concern you."

"You asked me to marry you, and you don't think that the way you felt about her, the way you *still* feel about her, is any concern of mine? You don't think a future wife might care to know that you love another woman? Your arrogance is astounding. You don't even think of a wife as a person, just another possession you set somewhere in safekeeping! Something without feelings or understanding or pride."

"What? No! I don't believe that at all. Have you gone mad? I've never done anything to suggest I think that way of you. Or of my wife."

"Then why did you not tell me about her? Why did you not say your heart was given to Sabrina?"

"Because it is not! Bloody hell, Mary, but you twist my words. I admitted that I loved her—twelve years ago. I do not love her now."

"No? You were so hurt by the reminder of her and all she meant to you that you got drunk the night she came to call on us. You went to the tavern and drank, and then you came home and sat drinking and brooding about the woman you loved and lost."

"I went to the tavern to get information, to find out if anyone had been seen about town. I drank because I was being convivial, trying to loosen tongues."

"You just happened to choose that particular night to do it?" Mary raised a skeptical brow. "You kissed me that night. You kissed me because you were drunk and I was here and she was not!" Mary stopped, unable to go on for fear tears might spring forth. She would not let him see her cry over him.

"No! That isn't true!" He took a long step forward, his eyes blazing.

"Isn't it? You drank too much, trying to forget her. Then you used me as a substitute for the woman you really wanted."

"If you believe that, you're a bloody fool." Royce took her by the shoulders, his fingers digging into her. "*You* are the one who has run me mad the past few weeks. Can't you see that? It is you I think of every night in my bed. It is you who makes me lie awake, sweating, wanting you so badly it is all I can do to keep from going down the hall into your room.

Sweet heaven, Mary—it is your lips, your breasts, your soft white flesh that I crave. That I cannot live without . . ." He clamped his lips closed, staring down at her, his green eyes blazing with frustration and heat.

Mary gazed up at him, speechless, her mouth rounding in a startled O. The raw passion of his words stirred her, turning her insides warm and aching.

"Blast it, Mary, all I desire is you." He stared at her for a moment more, his face stamped with an undeniable hunger. Then he swooped down to kiss her.

Chapter 22

Mary trembled, struggling to remain unaffected by his kiss, by the whirlwind sweeping through her. But she could not deny the hunger that sprang into life as soon as he touched her. His lips plundered hers, claiming, demanding, and she could not resist.

She flung her arms around him, pressing her body into his, eager to feel once more his strength, his power, his hard flesh digging into her softness. She shuddered as his hands moved over her, molding her to him intimately, curving over her back and buttocks. Memories of their lovemaking poured through her, mingling erotically with the sensations he evoked in her now. His fingertips dug into her fleshy cheeks, lifting her up and imprinting her with the hard length of his maleness. He rubbed her against him, and she could feel the quiver and throb of his desire.

His mouth devoured her, taking her in an imitation of the way his body wanted to, and one hand came up between them to cup her breast. Her flesh was supremely sensitive, as if every nerve in her body were on the surface of her skin, reacting to the slightest movement. He slipped his hand down the front of her dress, impatiently shoving past the material that kept him from what he wanted. He caressed her bare skin, his finger teasing at the hard fleshy nub of her nipple, and Mary felt moisture flood between her legs. She trembled, afraid that at any moment her knees might give way and she would simply ooze down to the floor, a melting puddle of desire.

But his other arm was like iron around her, holding her up. He lifted his head and gazed down into Mary's face. With an inarticulate noise, he bent to kiss her throat. Making his way down the tender column, he kissed and nibbled, using lips, teeth, and tongue, driving her desire ever higher.

He cupped her breast in his palm and bent to take her nipple into his mouth. Gently, firmly, he suckled her, his tongue curling around her nipple, stroking it with velvet heat. Hunger pulsed in Mary. She felt empty, aching to be filled by him, and she remembered the glorious sensation as he had pushed into her, stretching her, making her his. She wanted to feel that again, to know him, to hold him, to wrap her entire being around him, and she shook with the tension and the need.

"Mary . . . please . . ." he murmured, kissing the soft flesh of her breast, his hand sliding in between her legs, cupping her. "Let me. . . ."

His fingers moved insistently, arousing her through the cloth of her dress, and she could feel the need building within her, spiraling toward an explosion of pleasure. Mary could feel her awareness dimming and contracting, focusing solely on throbbing hunger. It was coming; she felt as if her being was reaching for it.

"Sweet." His voice was low and thick. "My sweet Marigold. My wife."

Mary stiffened, cold reason returning in a flash. She jerked away. "No!" Her body still pulsed with desire, her skin quivering, but she ignored the sensations.

"Mary!" Dazedly, Royce took a step forward, reaching toward her.

"No." She jumped back, hastily pulling up her dress to cover her naked breast. "Stop. You cannot win every argument this way. I told you before—I am not going to marry you." Mary whirled away.

"That's not why—" He cursed roundly and started after her. "Damn it, Mary, you *will* marry me."

She turned, her eyes bright, her color high. "If you believe that, then you don't know me at all."

For the next few days, a quiet war raged between Mary and Royce. None of the other inhabitants of the household understood it, but it was inescapable. When Royce entered the room, Mary found an excuse to leave. If being together was unavoidable, such as at dinner, the air between them was frosty, their questions perfunctory, their answers short and clipped. Mary did not ride with the others. Royce, on the other hand, was apt to stride out of the house frequently, a grim look on his face, and set off for a long solitary ride. And if anyone tried to broach the subject of this sudden animosity with either participant, he or she was met with a cool stare and a denial that anything untoward was going on. Only Rose understood the cause of the strife, but she remained as silent as Mary.

The icy tension prevailing at Willowmere was broken when the earl's carriage came rolling into the yard a few days later. Word spread throughout the house, and everyone came to greet the new arrival. Oliver strode in, his disreputable-looking mutt trotting at his heels, and shrugged out of his many-caped driving coat. As he handed it and his gloves to the footman, the Bascombe sisters appeared in the hall, followed by their chaperone.

Lily let out a squeal, "You have brought Pirate!"

With a sharp bark, the dog darted over to the girls and proceeded to go through his entire repertoire of leaps and twists, all the while yapping joyously.

"I tried to leave him behind." Oliver looked at the cavorting animal. "But the household staff begged me to take him, and I couldn't refuse. He has broken two lamps, three vases, and a fire screen since he arrived at Stewkesbury House. And the shoes he's chewed through are too numerous to mention. I didn't mind losing the slippers Aunt Euphronia gave me, but I was damned fond of that pair of boots."

Mary chuckled. "One wonders you haven't put him out, then."

"Oh, I could not do that. It's far too entertaining watching Hornsby try to hide everything from the animal. So far Pirate has proved slyer than my valet—a not inconsiderable feat." The earl allowed a small smile as he came forward. With a snap of his fingers to Pirate, the dog fell silent and sat down, the stump of his tail still wagging. Oliver bowed over Mary's hand. "Cousin." He repeated the gesture with each of the girls, then turned to his brother and shook his hand. "Fitz."

"Good to see you," Fitz greeted him. "I trust you brought my curricle unmarred."

Oliver sent him a dry look. "I think I can manage a curricle. Yours is well-sprung, but your grays tend to pull to the left."

Fitz let out a snort of disbelief. "More likely the hand guiding them."

"Royce." The earl shook his stepbrother's hand last, his eyebrows raised in inquiry. "Any news?"

Royce shook his head. "Nothing since I wrote you. It's been quiet this week."

The earl nodded and turned toward his cousins. "Ladies,

if you will excuse me, I should wash away the dust of the road. I'll see you at tea?"

The Bascombes assented, turning reluctantly to go back to their lessons. Royce, however, stepped forward.

"Oliver . . . if I could have a few moments of your time?"

Mary cast a sharp look at the two men. Stewkesbury regarded his stepbrother in faint surprise.

"I have something of particular import I wish to ask you," Royce continued.

"Of course. Let us go to my office."

Mary watched them walk away, her mind racing.

Oliver and Royce strode down the corridor in silence, but as soon as they entered the earl's office and closed the door, Oliver turned to Royce with a frown. "What's happened? I thought you said there had been no other trouble."

"No, it's nothing like that. It is, in fact, another matter on which I wish to speak with you. I . . ." Royce paused, looking uncomfortable.

"Yes?" Oliver asked, his interest thoroughly roused now.

"I am asking for your cousin's hand in marriage. Mary's, I mean."

For an instant longer the earl stared at him; then a wide smile broke across his features. "But that's splendid! Yes, yes, of course, you have my permission. But, Royce, how did this come about? I had thought you—"

He broke off at a short but forceful rapping at the door.

"A moment," the earl called before turning his attention back to Royce.

However, the knocking sounded again, more vigorously this time. "Stewkesbury! Sir Royce! I wish to speak to you."

"Cousin Mary!" The earl, not noticing Royce's apprehensive expression, opened the door, smiling. "How very propitious. Royce has just been telling me the good news."

"Has he indeed?" Mary shot a scalding glance at Sir Royce.

"I asked Oliver for his permission," Royce told her, facing her squarely. "I told you I planned to."

"I assumed that was what you were doing when you whisked him off." Mary crossed her arms over her chest and regarded both men with disfavor. "And I presume *you* gave him 'permission.' "

"Yes, of course. I hope you will both be very happy." Oliver smiled at her.

"No doubt we will be, but not with each other." Mary glared at the earl. "I'm sure it occurred to you no more than it did to him that *I* had anything to say in the matter."

The earl's eyes widened, and he glanced from Mary to Royce and back. "I'm sorry. Did I speak out of turn? I assumed that Royce had paid his addresses to you—"

"Oh, yes, he *told* me about his plans to marry me, if that's what you mean. And I told him the same thing I am telling you now: I have no intention of marrying Royce. Now or ever. So make all the merry little plans you want. Just do not include me."

Mary turned on her heel and stalked out the door, leaving both men staring after her.

"Well." Stewkesbury pivoted to look at Royce. "I believe your wooing of the lady has left something to be desired."

Oliver closed the door and returned to lean against the front of his desk, legs stretched out in front of him and crossed at the ankles. He regarded Royce quizzically.

Royce ground his teeth. "You needn't look so smug. *You* should try dealing with Mary. She is the stubbornest woman on earth. She refuses to admit that marrying would be the best course for both of us. And now she's taken it into her head to become bosom friends with Lady Sabrina!"

"Sabrina!" All traces of amusement fled from the earl's face. "I see."

"I doubt that very much." Royce turned and saw the look on Oliver's face, a mingling of sorrow and pity. Waving a dismissive hand, he grumbled, "No, do not play that tune with me. This has nothing to do with Sabrina."

"Doesn't it? Your decision to marry seems to have sprung up very suddenly."

"I am not trying to substitute Marigold for Sabrina! Blast it, man, you are as bad as Mary."

"She knows about Sabrina?" Stewkesbury's eyebrows vaulted upward.

"She knows Sabrina's rather biased story. Mary believes she and I were madly in love and Sabrina's parents refused to allow her to marry me. I tried to explain what really happened. I told her how I feel about Sabrina, but she would not listen."

"What do you feel?" Oliver asked quietly.

"Nothing—except for an urge to be around her no more than is absolutely necessary. It was the best thing you ever did for me when you packed me off to Scotland before I made an even worse fool of myself."

"As I remember, you did not think so at the time. I believe you called me a mindless tool of my grandfather's. Also a stiff-necked prig, incapable of either passion or empathy."

"Well, you are those things, but you were right about Sabrina. I was lucky to escape marrying her."

Oliver smiled faintly, studying his stepbrother, then asked, "Are you sure you want to marry my cousin? I would welcome it, you know, but I do not want you to feel obligated. I wasn't serious when I suggested that. You must know that I already consider you family, no matter whom you marry."

"I know." Royce's eyes met Oliver's briefly, then pulled away. "That isn't why I'm doing it. It makes sense. I think the old earl would have been pleased."

"But surely that is not enough for a marriage."

Royce scowled. "I hope you are not about to indulge in a bag of moonshine about love and eternal devotion. I would think you, of all people, would understand a rational approach to marriage. It is a good match. She won't have to endure the nonsense of her come-out. She's past the age of most of the girls, and besides, she's bound to say or do something that will set up some old biddy's back. Once she's married, her sisters will be accepted more easily, too. You know that. Mary and I will suit very well—once she gets over this silliness."

Oliver crooked an eyebrow. "I cannot imagine why she has not succumbed to such blandishments."

Royce grimaced, then had to chuckle. "I know. I know. I have handled it badly. I don't know why I've been such a fool. Mary seems to have a knack for bringing out the very worst in me."

"Odd, then, that you should want to marry her."

Royce scowled at the other man. "Oh, the devil take it." He turned and started out of the room. At the doorway, he paused and pivoted to look at Oliver. "But I *am* going to marry her."

That evening after dinner, when the three men rejoined the women in the drawing room, Royce made his way over to Mary, who was sitting on the sofa beside Lily. Mary ignored him as he strode toward them, but when he stopped in front of her, there was nothing she could do except look up at him, doing her best to keep her gaze one of cool inquiry.

Bowing to the women, Royce smiled with none of the

stiffness or rancor that had been in his expression the past few days. Looking at Lily, he said, "I have come to ask your sister to take a turn around the room with me. Do you think she will accept?"

Lily let out a little laugh. "I fear I cannot answer for her, Sir Royce. You know she is exceedingly independent."

"You can both stop speaking as if I were not here." Mary found she could not summon as cross a tone as she would have liked. It was much easier to be angry with Royce when he was in a black mood. But when he smiled like that, his green eyes dancing as if at some private jest, everything in her wanted to smile back, to do whatever she could to keep that smile on his lips. "I am quite capable of answering your question myself."

"Yes, but I fear what your answer might be," Royce retorted. "I am not a man who likes to be refused."

Mary cocked one brow at him. "I am well aware of that."

"Still, I must risk it and hope you will not trample on my heart. Will you take a turn around the room with me?"

Mary sighed. "How can I refuse such pretty words? My sister would lecture me mercilessly."

"Indeed, I would," Lily agreed, smiling at Royce.

Mary arose and laid her hand upon the arm Royce extended. They started to stroll around the edge of the large drawing room. Charlotte was playing the piano this evening, and her lively tunes, a welcome change from Miss Dalrymple's slow, often somber selections, created enough noise that it was possible to speak privately as long as they kept their voices low.

"You are a complete hand," Mary told her companion. "Trample on your heart indeed. You knew that Lily would take your part."

"Of course. I am not as foolish as I often act."

His words hinted at an apology, Mary thought, and she glanced up at him. He was looking straight ahead, and she studied his profile, taking in the curve of jaw and cheek, the straight line of his nose, the sweep of his lashes. She was aware of a strong desire to draw her forefinger down that profile, skimming his forehead and nose down to his lips.

Mary pulled her eyes away. They strolled on, silence stretching between them. Mary commented on the pleasant weather they had had today, and Royce agreed. Royce then remarked how nice it was to have Charlotte playing for them instead of Miss Dalrymple, and Mary nodded.

Finally, when Mary was beginning to wonder if their entire promenade would be spent on platitudes, Royce said abruptly, "I have no wish to be at odds with you."

"Nor I with you."

"I miss our conversations."

"I do as well." Mary glanced at him again. This time he turned and looked down at her, a smile curving his lips. Her heart seemed to roll in her chest.

"I hope you will forgive the way I have acted the past few days. I do not take disappointment well, I am afraid."

"Mmm." Mary made a noncommittal noise, trying not to smile.

"But I see now that I have been trying to bully you into marrying me, and that is hardly what I want. I cannot *make* you agree to become my wife. And I do not wish to drive you away by trying to do so."

"I-I am glad." Mary was aware of something oddly like disappointment at the thought that Royce was abandoning his pursuit of her. She was glad, of course. She did not want to be angry at him or constantly at odds. But she could not deny a pang of regret. However little she liked his idea of an arranged marriage, she could not help but wonder what it might have been like to be his wife.

She cleared her throat. "I would like for us to be . . . friends."

"I am determined that we should be so."

"Well, then . . . it is good that we have had this little talk." Mary glanced around. They had circumnavigated half the room and were now drawing near the sofa where Lily sat. As they turned in her direction, Mary said, "You will doubtless be glad in later years that you made this decision."

"I certainly hope so."

Mary gave him a tight smile. "You will count it your good fortune that you did not marry me."

"I never said I wasn't going to marry you."

"What?" Mary's eyes widened as she stared at him. "But you just told me—"

"I said that I was not going to bully you into marrying me. I didn't say that I had any intention of giving up on your becoming my wife." Royce stopped in front of the sofa where Lily sat. He turned to Mary.

"But how—I mean—"

He let out a little chuckle and leaned in closer. His breath tickled her ear, sending a shiver through her, as he whispered, "My dear girl, there are other methods of persuasion."

Mary simply stared at Royce as, with a bow, he picked up her hand, pressed his lips softly to the back of it, and, with a last, glittering look, walked away.

Mary's sisters went riding the next afternoon, but Mary did not go with them. She told herself that she stayed at home because she did not wish to be around Royce. However, deep down, she knew that there was another reason. She had been unable to get the packet of letters she'd found in the attic out of her mind, and lying awake last night, considering Royce and what he had said, she could not help but think that if only she could look at those letters, she would have a better idea of what Royce and Sabrina had meant to one another. Had it merely been the youthful first love that Royce indicated it was, something he had recovered from long ago? Or was it the love of a lifetime, as Sabrina had hinted and Mary suspected to be true?

As soon as she heard her sisters head downstairs, Mary sprang to her feet and slipped out into the hallway. Glancing up and down to make certain no one was about, she walked quickly along the corridor and up the back staircase, making her way to the attic door. It did not take her long to locate the trunk, and she hovered over it for a minute, torn. But as much as she told herself that looking at Royce's letters was wrong, she knew that she had not come up to the attic simply to turn around and go back down. Finally, with a sigh, she opened the chest.

There was the bundle of letters, lying on top. Mary picked it up and untied the ribbon, then sat down on the floor, careless of the dust on her skirts, and laid the letters in her lap. Setting her candle on the flat lid of the trunk beside her, she picked up the top letter with fingers that trembled slightly and opened it.

"Darling Royce . . ." it began. Mary turned over the page, her eyes going to the signature at the bottom: "Yrs. forever, Sabrina."

They were from her. He had taken Sabrina's letters and notes and carefully bundled them together, storing them away to keep forever. In all the years since, he had never come back and thrown them away. Tears stung Mary's eyes.

There was another letter among them, written in a different hand on different paper. When Mary examined it, she saw that it was a letter from Royce to Sabrina. She wondered whether he had never sent it or whether she had returned it to him. Slowly Mary unfolded the letter and began to read.

My Aphrodite,
I called upon you again yesterday, and again
your maid turned me away. I waited beneath your
window, hoping you would come to look out at me,
but you did not appear. I have told myself that you
do not withhold yourself from me voluntarily, that
your parents demanded it of you, that it is they
who force you to marry a man old enough to be
your father. Oliver has assured me that is not the
case, and I have refused to believe him. But when
I saw you in town this afternoon, unchaperoned,
with only your maid to accompany you, and you
walked away from me without a word, leaving my
heart trampled in the dust, I knew that it had not
been Oliver who lied.

The letter went on in this manner for a time, declaring his despair over the announcement of Sabrina's impending marriage to Lord Humphrey before descending into a bitter diatribe against Sabrina's faithlessness:

Do the vows we made to each other mean nothing to
you? When you told me that you loved me and wanted
to marry me, were you lying as you spoke, or did you
decide only later to make your word worthless?

He spoke of his intention to leave for Scotland, as Oliver and the old earl had arranged, and then finally, as if he could not hold them in, words of love poured forth again. He remembered the way she had looked when he had first seen her, describing her in loving detail. He recalled the things they had said and done, the way his heart beat faster whenever he saw her.

Tears welled up, blinding her, and Mary closed her eyes, letting the tears roll down her cheeks. His words had the passion and emotion of a young man, but they also carried the deep conviction of love. Could anyone who had loved so deeply, cared so much, really come to feel nothing for the person who had captured his heart?

Hastily, Mary folded the letter and put it back with the others, retying the bundle. She could not bear to read any more. She wished that she had never given in to the temptation to read it at all. Picking up her candle, Mary thrust the packet of letters back into the trunk and left the attic. She returned to her room, but she soon found that she did not want to be alone with her thoughts. So, after changing into one of her new sprig muslin day dresses, Mary made her way downstairs, hoping that she would find Charlotte also at loose ends.

She realized her mistake when she ran into Royce at the bottom of the stairs, talking to Charlotte.

"What are you doing here?" The words were out of her mouth before she realized how rude they sounded. She cast a quick, apologetic glance at Charlotte. "I mean—that is—I thought you were riding with the girls, Sir Royce."

"No, I let them go out with the grooms this afternoon. I was discussing some business matters with Oliver."

"Oh." Mary cast about for some excuse to leave, but Charlotte was too quick for her.

"Come with us," her cousin said, linking her arm through Mary's. "We were just about to join Oliver in the drawing room."

Her afternoon was going from bad to worse, Mary thought, as she smiled perfunctorily at Charlotte and followed her into the smaller drawing room at the front of the house. Now she would have to sit and make polite conversation with a number of people, including the very man she least wanted to be around at the moment.

When they entered, Fitz was apparently regaling his brother with the details of a new team of horses he was considering buying.

"But didn't you just buy a team last year?" Oliver said mildly.

"Yes, of course, but these bays are magnificent. You'd have to see them to understand."

Oliver smiled faintly. "Yes, I am sure that I would." He glanced toward the others as they entered, and Pirate, snuggled next to the earl, raised his head and let out a yip of greeting.

"You will have to excuse Pirate," Oliver told Mary. "He just finished chasing a number of squirrels back into their trees on our walk, not to mention sparrows into the sky, and he is too tired, I think, for his usual dance of joy at seeing you."

"Royce," Fitz said, "you've seen Parkington's team, haven't you? Aren't they worth the price?"

"I daresay," Royce agreed casually, going to stand by the fireplace and hooking his arm on the mantelpiece. "If one needed a new pair."

"You are as bad as Oliver," Fitz told him with a grimace. "But I *will* need a new pair, you see, when I purchase that high-perch phaeton I've a mind to get."

Oliver let out a groan. "Another vehicle?"

"You make it sound as if I have a fleet. And don't"—he held up a hand as if to ward off his brother's next remark—"don't start counting them, as you did that time with my pistols."

Both Oliver and Royce smiled at his remark. "As I remember, you sufficiently discouraged me at the time."

"It was only a black eye," Fitz told him unrepentantly. "And you thoroughly deserved it."

"You hit Lord Stewkesbury?" Mary was startled enough to ask without pausing to think about the rudeness.

"Oh, yes." Fitz shrugged carelessly. "Course he wasn't Lord Stewkesbury then. It was once when he was down from Oxford. He was a terrible bore, always prosing on about one thing or another."

"Only because you ran wild here when Royce and I were gone," Oliver shot back.

"I was the old earl's favorite, you see," Fitz said in an aside to Mary, grinning. "They were always jealous."

Before his two brothers could start on their versions of the story, Bostwick appeared in the doorway, announcing the arrival of Lady Vivian Carlyle. Both Charlotte and Mary bounced up to greet Lady Vivian.

"Forgive me for calling on you again so soon," Vivian said to the earl. "But I think that if Lady Sabrina and I had remained together another half hour, there would have been blood on the drawing room floor."

"You are welcome at Willowmere anytime." Stewkesbury stood up and bowed formally. "Though I feel sure that your visit with Lady Sabrina will become more harmonious once you have, um, grown accustomed to one another again."

Vivian let out a little laugh. "Really, Stewkesbury, I know you believe in maintaining a courteous front, but it is a sin to lie, remember. Sabrina and I have never gotten along, and we all know it. There's no reason to pretend otherwise."

"I see you are the same as ever," the earl responded dryly.

Again Lady Vivian chuckled. "As are you." She turned toward Mary. "Lord Stewkesbury remembers all too well when Charlotte and I were schoolgirls together. He was at Oxford then, I believe, and he found us most provoking. I used to visit a great deal, you see; I was very fond of my uncle and aunt—Uncle Humphrey's first wife. Charlotte and I would giggle and run through the halls of Willowmere."

"And play ghastly tricks on everyone," Royce added good-naturedly.

"Primarily on me," the earl countered, but he unbent enough to smile. "What hoydens you were. And you encouraged them, Royce."

"Me!" Royce looked indignant. "It was Fitz who aided and abetted them. I was merely an innocent—" He stopped suddenly and looked around. "Did you hear something?"

For a moment everyone went still, looking at him curiously. Then came a faint, high cry, the sound of a woman's voice in the distance. Mary leaped to her feet and ran to the window. She had heard her sisters' voices too many times not to recognize them even at this remove.

A strange sight greeted her eyes. Riding toward the house were her sisters and two grooms. And though her sisters were obviously yelling toward the house, they were not riding with any urgency. In fact, their horses were walking. One mounted groom was leading a second, riderless horse. In his other hand he held a pistol. Next to him the second groom was mounted on a horse with Camellia up behind him, her arms around him. Her hat had come off, and her dark blond hair was loose and streaming down her back. Lily and Rose brought up the rear, and Mary saw that each of them carried a pistol as well.

"What the devil!" Royce exclaimed. He and the others had quickly followed Mary to the window. "Something's happened to Camellia!"

Chapter 23

"I would say it's the groom who's in trouble." Mary turned and started toward the door. "It's Cam holding *him* on the horse."

She ran down the hall and out the front door, then across the small formal lawn, the others rushing after her. By the time Mary reached the driveway, the riders were only a few feet away.

"Mare! Thank God you're here!" Camellia called. "Somebody come get Teddy down."

The other groom sprang down from his horse. His face was stark white, the freckles standing out across his nose and cheeks. When he saw Lord Stewkesbury, he looked as if he might faint. He jerked off his hat and began to jabber. His accent was so thick and his speech so rapid that Mary had trouble understanding him, but the gist of it seemed to be profuse apologies and lamentations.

"Geoff!" The earl's voice cut through his babbling. "Enough. Help us get Teddy down, and then we'll hear what happened."

The groom fell silent and followed the three men over to Camellia's horse. They lifted the injured man down and laid him on the ground. His eyes were closed, his face even paler than Geoff's, and he did not stir except for a grimace and a groan when they pulled him from the horse.

"Now, what the devil happened?" Oliver demanded.

"I'm sorry, my lord, I'm sorry. I never saw him—all of a sudden, there he were, and he were shootin' at us." Geoff's speech had slowed down enough that Mary could catch most of what he said, though he still shifted nervously on his feet, twisting his cap between his hands.

"You were shot at?"

"There was nothin' we could do, I swear. I'm sorry, my lord."

"Oh, for heaven's sake." Camellia pushed past the trembling man. "Someone fired at us. Then he rode straight toward us."

"Teddy was shot?"

"No—at least, I don't think so. I didn't see any blood."

"She's right. There's no blood." Mary had knelt beside the injured groom as soon as they laid him down, and she was carefully examining him for signs of injury.

"When the man fired at us, Teddy's horse reared," Lily explained. "And Teddy fell off. That's how he got hurt."

Rose picked up the story. "So Camellia jumped off her horse and picked up Teddy's pistols and started shooting at the man. And he rode away."

"I wish I'd had a rifle." Camellia looked regretful. "Pistols haven't enough range. I don't think I hit him at all. And I only had the two shots. I started to take Geoff's pistols and go after him."

"But we decided we should get Teddy back instead," Rose put in.

"Anyway, we needed the shots we had left in case he came after us again," Camellia went on. "We didn't have any powder and balls to reload, so Geoff's guns were all we had."

"My pistol's just for show," Lily offered. "It's empty. Rose and Geoff are carrying Geoff's guns."

"Next time we ride out, I think we should all carry pistols," Camellia declared.

"Next time!" The earl had been gazing at the girls, thunderstruck, and now his brows rushed together in a scowl. "There'll be no next time."

The girls immediately set up a protest.

"What!"

"No!"

"That's not fair!"

"Quiet!" Stewkesbury snapped, and though he raised his voice only a little, everyone fell silent. "You could have been killed today. Next time his aim might be truer."

"I don't think he was shooting at us," Rose said. "I didn't see him fire the first shot, but the second time, he fired his pistol into the air. I think he was trying to scare us, perhaps hoping to dislodge us from our seats."

"Rose is right," Camellia agreed. "He was much too far away to hope to hit anyone, using pistols—especially since we were moving targets. I think he was trying to capture Rose again. Just like last time."

"And you think I intend to allow him to try that again?" Oliver asked quizzically.

"But if we always ride out together and we're armed . . . "

The earl rubbed his hand over his brow. "We will talk of this later. Geoff, take the horses to the stables and send one of the other grooms for the doctor."

"There's no need for that," Mary spoke up from where she knelt on the grass beside the fallen groom. "He's come around, and I cannot find any lumps or cuts on his head. I think he fainted rather than hitting his head. Probably from the pain. His shoulder is dislocated."

Everyone except Mary's sisters simply stared at her. Finally, the earl said, "And why, then, should we not send for the doctor?"

"There's no need to make him wait that long in pain. I can fix it."

"Of course you can," Royce murmured.

"If you gentlemen will but pick him up and set him on that bench—and be sure to fully support his arm."

The three men lifted the groom carefully from the ground and carried him over to a stone bench at the edge of the driveway. While Royce and Fitz held the boy firmly in place, Mary stepped up, taking the weight of his arm in both her hands. Talking all the while, she positioned the arm just so, then with one swift movement, thrust it up and into the socket.

Charlotte let out a small noise and fainted. Beside her, Lady Vivian managed to catch her and ease her down to the ground.

"Now, if someone will get me some cloth, I can bind his arm so it's immobile." Mary turned around and caught sight of her cousin on the ground. "Oh my. What happened?"

"Fainted, I'm afraid." Vivian looked up and grinned. "She's always had a bit of a weak stomach."

"Mmm. So has Teddy. I don't suppose you have any smelling salts?"

"No, but I'm sure Charlotte must. Respectable ladies rarely travel without a vial." Vivian cast a glinting look up at the earl. "And do not remark on what that says about me, Oliver."

The earl merely raised his brows expressively and turned toward the house. "Bostwick!" He raised a hand and gestured.

Mary looked toward the house and saw that a group of servants had clustered there on the lawn, watching goggle-eyed. The butler now separated himself from the others and hurried forward to get Stewkesbury's instructions.

As they waited for Bostwick to bring the supplies, Royce began to question Camellia and the others about their attacker. "Could you see his face? Was it the same man who tried to abduct Rose the other times?"

Camellia shook her head. "No. He had on a mask and a hat pulled low, so I couldn't really make him out. But he was much smaller than the last man."

"Are you sure?" Stewkesbury asked. "If he was on a horse, he wouldn't have looked the same."

Camellia sent him a level glance. "The other man would have looked big on a horse or off. Believe me, it wasn't the same man. This one was no larger than Geoff." She pointed at the unhurt groom, who had hung around, watching with awe as Mary fixed Teddy's shoulder.

Mary touched Rose's arm, pulling her away from the crowd and whispering, "Was it Cosmo?"

Rose shrugged and answered in the same low voice, "I don't know. He was about Cosmo's size, but truly, we could not see his face. It could have been anyone. But, well, it's not like Cosmo to come charging at a person with a gun, is it?"

Mary nodded, accepting the truth of that. There was still nothing to show that their stepfather was involved. Surely there was no harm in not telling the earl and Sir Royce about him.

Charlotte was already beginning to come around when both bandages and smelling salts arrived, but Vivian waved the vial under her friend's nose anyway, as Mary efficiently bound the groom's upper arm tightly against his body, then fashioned a sling for him. When she finished, Mary turned to find the others watching her. Charlotte had regained her feet and was standing with Lady Vivian's arm around her waist for support.

"How did you know what to do?" Charlotte asked in amazement.

Mary shrugged. "Where we lived, there wasn't always a doctor around. You learn to deal with the smaller things."

"Smaller," Charlotte repeated in a choked voice.

Lady Vivian looked at Mary and her sisters, smiling, her vivid green eyes glinting in the sun. "I am really very glad you girls moved to England."

Stewkesbury let out an inelegant snort. "Of course you are." He turned to the Bascombes. "Ladies, there will be no riding until this madman is caught. Royce. Fitz." He jerked his head toward the house.

The other two men nodded and followed him inside.

"Where are they going?" Rose asked as the women trailed after them into the house.

"Setting up search parties, I imagine," Charlotte said, leading them into the drawing room and ringing for tea. "Oliver is furious."

"Really?" Mary asked in amazement. "How can you tell?"

Vivian laughed. "If he expressed it, he wouldn't be Oliver—or, I suppose I should say, he wouldn't be the earl."

"He'll have them scouring the countryside," Charlotte promised.

"I wouldn't have thought he would care that much. I mean, he barely knows us," Camellia commented.

Charlotte glanced at her in surprise. "You don't know Oliver. It isn't affection—not that he dislikes you," she added hastily. "And I am sure that he will come to hold you in great regard as he gets to know you better." At the girls' disbelieving looks, she went on, "At any rate, it doesn't matter. The fact is, you are Talbots, and he is responsible for you."

"It's an insult to him that someone attacked us," Camellia said.

"Yes," Vivian agreed. "But more than that, it makes him absolutely determined to keep you safe. You are under his protection. You are his family, however little you know each other."

"And no one threatens his family," Charlotte added.

Mary nodded. "I understand. I just would not have thought it of him."

"Don't underestimate Stewkesbury," Vivian told her. "That is always a mistake. After all, he had the good sense to turn down Sabrina."

"What?" Mary turned to her, eyes rounded.

"I am sorry. I forget that you are fond of her. I should not expose you to my bias about the woman. No doubt I should say nothing about Lady Sabrina. Or I should preface my remarks by saying that my opinion is prejudiced by the fact that she took the place of my very dear and delightful aunt, who had been in her grave only three months when Sabrina started her pursuit of my poor, befuddled, grief-stricken uncle."

"Yes, that is a most unbiased statement," Charlotte agreed with mock gravity.

Lady Vivian shrugged. "I cannot pretend to like the woman. And while in theory it is all very well to say that one must say nothing rather than something ill of anyone, I cannot help but think 'tis better to warn those who do not know her that the coin of Sabrina's friendship is—well, perhaps not false, for she does truly like to have people about to admire her—but it certainly first and foremost is for the benefit of Sabrina."

"I told you I didn't like her," Camellia put in triumphantly.

"Do not turn away from her on my say-so," Lady Vivian said. "As I said, I am not impartial where Sabrina is concerned. But give your friendship to her with care."

She broke off as a footman brought in the tea tray, and they spent the next few minutes in the ritual of pouring and distributing tea and cakes. All the while, however, Mary's head was buzzing with what she had just heard. As soon as the servant left, Mary turned to Vivian.

"But it was Royce, not Lord Stewkesbury, was it not?" Mary asked. "I mean, Sabrina told me that she and Sir Royce were in love."

"She had his heart in her hand, that much is true," Charlotte agreed.

"But she tried to interest Stewkesbury first," Vivian said. "He was the heir, obviously, and he is a handsome man. Always was. As I remember, I had something of a *tendre* for him myself." She let out an amused chuckle.

"You did?" Charlotte set her cup in its saucer with a rattle. "I never knew that!"

"Well, I could hardly confide in you, could I? You were his cousin. I mean, I thought he was a terrible prig, of course, but I think one reason I played so many tricks on him was simply that I wished he would notice me." She laughed again. "Anyway, Oliver would have nothing to do with Sabrina. She told me so herself." Vivian took a sip of her tea, then sighed. "Obviously, I must expose my own youthful idiocies. I was still a gawky girl at sixteen, all legs and teeth and hair that looked as if someone had started a fire on my head. I was terribly flattered when Sabrina made overtures of friendship to me."

"I remember. I was jealous about all the time you spent with her," Charlotte agreed.

"I was a fool," Vivian replied dispassionately. "I didn't see how unlikely it was that a girl three years older than I and already out, the beauty of the surrounding countryside, would want to be friends with me. Nor had I learned the valuable lesson that a duke's daughter is prey to all sorts of people eager to be one's 'friend.' Only in this instance, it was my uncle, not my father, who interested Sabrina. My aunt had died not long before, and Sabrina saw an opportunity in Uncle Humphrey. Through me, she would have a way into his house, his confidence. She could offer a sympathetic and soft white shoulder to cry on. Then, of course, she could offer other things to soothe his heart and make him forget his sorrow. Within weeks, she dropped Sir Royce and married my uncle."

Vivian sighed, then shook her head. "There, now, I have run on far too much, I fear. You girls will think me a spiteful old hag."

They began to talk of other things, but Mary did not say much. Her mind was too busy going over their encounters with Lady Sabrina, seeing them in a new light. Had all of Sabrina's concerned statements actually been subtle attempts to create the fear and intimidation and inadequacy that she had been telling them not to feel? It seemed bizarre, but Mary had to admit that the woman's comments had always reminded them that they were not dressed properly or that their manners were not acceptable or that they did not know enough. Had she taken them that day to visit the vicar's wife in the hope that Mrs. Martin would dislike the Bascombes? Camellia had suggested as much the other day. Mary found herself reluctant to believe it, but she was honest enough to admit that her reluctance sprang primarily from the fact that it hurt to think that Sabrina had only been manipulating them.

Clearly, Vivian's view of Sabrina matched the description of her that Royce had painted. If they were right, then Sabrina had lied to Mary about marrying Lord Humphrey because her parents demanded it; it had been Sabrina's own desire for wealth and status that had made her jilt Royce. But whatever Sabrina's motives in breaking it off with Royce, the result had been the same: Royce's heart had been broken, and he had decided never again to trust or to love. The letter Mary had read this afternoon had only emphasized that fact.

A few minutes later, when Vivian said her good-byes and rose to leave, Mary jumped up and walked with her to the front door. "Lady Vivian . . . might I have a word with you?"

Vivian turned to look at her, her vivid green eyes curious, but her polite tone revealed neither curiosity nor surprise. "Of course. Shall we sit down on one of the benches in front?"

Mary smiled gratefully, and they walked out the front door and down the steps to the small expanse of lawn before the driveway. Lady Vivian's carriage stood waiting, the footman ready to open the door, but Vivian showed no sign of impatience. She made a brief gesture to the footman before she walked over to one of the stone benches that stood a few feet beyond the front door. When she and Mary were seated, she turned to Mary, politely waiting.

Mary felt suddenly awkward. "I'm sorry. I—no doubt I am being too forward. Miss Dalrymple usually says that I am."

"Miss Dalrymple. Pffft." Vivian made a dismissive gesture. "A small-minded woman; I cannot imagine what possessed Stewkesbury to hire her. Just tell me what you wish to say. If I find it too forward, I don't have to respond."

"That's true." Mary smiled. "The thing is . . . I am not accustomed to British gentlemen. I don't know how to judge their words. Their actions."

"Are we talking about Sir Royce?" Vivian asked.

"How did you know?" Mary's eyes rounded in amazement. "Is it that obvious?" Her hands flew up to her cheeks, which were suddenly burning.

Vivian chuckled. "No, don't worry. I would like to say I

have a special eye for these things, but, well, it's pretty clear that if you are having man trouble and two of the men here are your cousins, it is the one who is not who is probably the fellow in question."

Mary laughed. "I suppose it is. Well, subtlety aside then . . . you know Sir Royce far better than I. And you know all about him and Lady Sabrina. Do you think—do you think that he could ever forget her?"

Vivian raised her brows a trifle. "Is he still pining for her? I would not have thought it."

"He says he does not love her. And, indeed, I don't think he yearns for her. It's more . . . the opposite of that. He avoids her, and his words about her and what she did are harsh."

"Mary, I know that you like Sabrina, but—"

"No, it's not that I think he should not be angry at her. I see, I think, what she has been doing."

Vivian looked at her, head tilted to the side. "Then why is it a problem that Royce dislikes her intensely? If you care for him, I would think you would be glad."

"Because it is such a strong feeling. It is not love, but the opposite coin of love. It fills him up. It occupies his emotions. She remains the most important woman in the world to him, even if his feelings toward her are rancorous."

"Ah, I see what you mean. You worry that he is obsessed with her, that he cannot love you as long as he remains full of feelings about Sabrina, even anger and dislike."

"Yes." Mary smiled with relief. "Exactly. He has asked me to marry him."

"He has? That seems a strong indication that he is over Sabrina."

"One would think. But he was careful to let me know that he would never love me or any woman. Our marriage would be one of mutual advantage. That is all."

"I see." Vivian was silent for a moment. "That is the sort of marriage many people I know have. My own parents married for that reason."

"Were they happy?"

Vivian shrugged. "I don't know. My mother died when I was a baby. My older brothers and my father don't talk of such things. But from the gossip I have heard . . . no, I don't think they were very happy."

"My parents were. They loved each other a great deal. That is what I would like to have. But Royce keeps asking me to marry him, and it tempts me even though I know he does it only because he is a gentleman."

"Indeed?"

"Yes." Mary blushed, realizing that Vivian would guess at least in part what must have happened between her and Royce. "He is doing it because of my reputation, which is most kind of him, but I—I don't want a marriage like that."

"Let me be forward now." Vivian took Mary's hand and looked into her eyes. "Do you love Sir Royce?"

Mary's blush flamed even brighter. She wished she could lie to Vivian, but there was something about the other woman's penetrating green gaze that made it very difficult to do so.

"I don't know!" Mary's words came out in an anguished rush. "I sometimes fear that I do! He is witty and yet quite kind really, and while, yes, he called me a hoyden, he doesn't really seem to mind it. At least, he never appears to be embarrassed. Perhaps it would be different in public."

"I think he is the sort of man who is the same at home as he is in public."

"He likes my sisters. And he didn't tell the earl the full circumstances of how we came upon Pirate. He would have kept the whole episode a secret, actually, but the dog . . ."

"It would be difficult to keep that dog a secret."

"And, well, when Royce walks into a room, it's as though I light up inside."

"Ah." Vivian nodded wisely.

"Have you ever felt like that?"

"A time or two. At least to some extent."

"Is that love?"

"I'm not sure I am the best person to ask. I have always wondered a little about the feeling myself. There are those who would tell you that I am quite cold."

"You?" Mary's face mirrored her shock. "No, I cannot believe that."

"One has many disappointed suitors when one is the daughter of a duke. But I don't think that I have ever felt the kind of love your parents had. Would I defy my family and run away across the ocean and live without servants and position and wealth? I haven't found the man yet whom I would do that for." She paused. "Would you do that for Royce?"

"Yes." Mary was surprised at her own answer. "I mean, well, if he loved me and that was the only way we could be together, then, yes, I think I would. Does that mean I love him?"

Vivian shrugged. "I don't know."

"Of course, I am quite accustomed to living that way." Mary grinned. "So it would not be a great sacrifice." She paused. "I don't want to love him."

"It would be difficult to be married to someone you loved and to know he did not love you back."

"Yes. It seems worse to me than going into a marriage knowing neither of you loved the other. If I love Royce and he will never feel the same, I would be condemning myself to a life of unhappiness."

"You say that he 'keeps' asking you to marry him," Lady Vivian said.

Mary nodded. "He has asked me twice, and even though I refused him flatly, he said he would continue. But then he told me he did not wish to bully me into marrying him. I thought he meant he would stop, but he said that he was . . . simply going to try other ways." Mary's blush spoke volumes about what she thought the "other ways" might be.

"I cannot speak for Sir Royce. But in my experience with English gentlemen, if one asks a woman to marry him only out of a sense of duty or honor, a single proposal is considered sufficient. I don't think it is honor that propels a man to subject his pride to refusal after refusal—or to trying 'other ways.'" Vivian's eyes twinkled as she stood up. "I'm not sure if I have relieved your mind . . ."

"No, you have been a great help to me." Impulsively Mary reached out and gave the other woman a quick hug. "Thank you."

She watched Lady Vivian walk down to her carriage, her thoughts humming. Could it really be, as Lady Vivian suggested, that Royce cared more for her than he would admit? That it was not simply out of honor that he asked her to marry him?

With a sigh, she went back in to join her sisters.

Supper was late that evening, as the men had been out scouring the countryside until it grew too dark to see.

"But we will find him," the earl promised grimly. "Tomorrow we will ride out again. In the meantime, you girls must stay close to the house."

"No!" the girls cried, almost in unison.

"We want to help search," Mary told him.

The earl stared at her. "Don't be absurd."

"We're not. Surely it would help to have more people looking?"

"And give this fellow another opportunity to seize you? I think not."

"It's only Rose he wants," Camellia pointed out.

"So you think you'll leave me behind?" Rose asked indignantly. "Just you try!"

"We don't know that it's only Rose he wants," Royce pointed out reasonably. "He could have meant to take all of you. Or perhaps whichever one he could lay his hands on first."

"It doesn't matter because he won't get any of us," Mary told him. "We aren't suggesting that we ride out by ourselves, unarmed. I presume that there are several people searching. We will carry pistols and make part of a party."

"I'm a darn sight better shot than that fellow Geoff," Camellia pointed out.

"And she kept a cooler head," Mary added.

Oliver looked chagrined. "I will admit that my grooms are not accustomed to being fired upon. However, after today, they will be prepared for it."

"Good. Then they will offer even more protection," Mary replied. "And with you three along—I presume you are adequate shots?"

The earl's brows shot up at this provocation, and Royce smothered a chuckle.

"Yes, I believe we are adequate shots," Stewkesbury replied with a visible effort to remain calm. "Fitz, in fact, is considered something of a marksman."

"Good. He and Camellia should go in separate groups, since she is the best shot among us. I presume you are going to split up into more than one party?"

Oliver regarded Mary for a moment, then turned to cast a look at Sir Royce.

"Don't look at me," Royce told him somewhat smugly.

"I have been dealing with this for the past three weeks. It's your problem now."

Oliver swiveled his head back to regard Mary, but before he could say anything, she went on, "Surely you don't think that with you three accompanying us, not to mention the grooms, this man would dare attack us. If he did—do you not think you could prevent him from carrying us off?"

Fitz let out a crack of laughter. "She's got you now, Ol."

The earl sent his brother a fulminating glance, but finally he sighed and said, "Very well. We had planned to ride out in three groups. The gamesmen and gardeners will be on foot and will take the woods to the north. That is the area to which Fitz and Royce tracked the blood drops before they lost him. Fitz, Royce, and I will each take two grooms and one of you girls—Charlotte, I assume you do not plan to insert yourself into these proceedings, do you?"

"Not I," Charlotte answered cheerfully. "Though it's a good thing Vivian isn't here, or I feel sure she would drag me along."

Oliver closed his eyes, looking pained. "Thank heaven I escaped that, at least. I will take two of you—Cousin Lily and Cousin Camellia. Your expertise will make up for my inferior skills, I trust. Rose, go with Fitz, since he is the best shot and you appear to be the prime target. Mary, you will ride with Royce and his men."

"But—" Mary began to protest, but she fell silent at Oliver's flat look. She had won this round with the earl, she told herself; she would not argue at being placed with Royce. Besides, she and Royce had called a truce, had they not?

"Why is someone trying to kidnap Rose, anyway?" Charlotte asked. "I mean, he cannot possibly know her." She looked toward Rose. "Of course, you are exceedingly pretty, my dear, but . . ." She turned to the earl. "Doesn't it seem a bit extreme that he saw Rose and decided to abduct her? And that he is going to so much trouble?"

The earl nodded. "I'm inclined to think it's an attempt to extort money from me. I'm not sure why he has focused on Rose—perhaps that is simply a matter of his liking her looks—but I think that when my new cousins arrived, he must have seen the opportunity to hold one of them for ransom."

His words made sense, Mary thought—and that made it even less likely that Cosmo Glass was involved. She could not help but feel relieved.

The group rode out the next morning at so early a time that Mary suspected the earl hoped the girls would cry off. However, they had long been accustomed to rising early to get the food and cleaning started in the tavern, so they met the gentlemen at the stables in good time.

Royce and Mary rode south from Willowmere, accompanied by two grooms. Royce paused from time to time to pull a small collapsible telescope from his pocket and make a sweep of the area. They found no sign of anyone, confirming Mary's suspicions that whoever had attacked the girls yesterday was probably far away by now. After a time, Royce pulled his horse to a halt. Mary glanced over at him. He was gazing at Beacon Hill, looming in the distance.

"It occurs to me," he said, "that it would be dashed easy to keep a watch on the house and all the land around it from up there."

"You think the attacker watched them ride out from there?" Mary looked speculatively at the hill.

"It seems reasonable to me. With an instrument such as this"—he waggled the small telescope—"he could keep a very good eye on everything going on."

"Then let's go up there."

He hesitated, then said, "All right, but ride behind me.

And if I tell you to get down or to do anything else, promise you will do it."

Mary frowned, and he added, "Otherwise, I will return by myself tomorrow to investigate."

Mary sighed. "Very well, I agree."

She did as he asked, staying behind him as their horses picked their way up the trail to the top of the bluff. As they drew closer, she could see the tumbled stones of the ancient ruin. Royce had taken his reins in his left hand and pulled out his pistol, carrying it at the ready. Mary followed his example. It was almost eerily silent at the top of the hill. Mary turned to look out across the vista. Royce was right. She could see the house and gardens and the lands around them with clarity, even without the aid of an optical instrument. With one, she was sure she could have picked out individuals on the grounds.

Royce dismounted and gave her his hand to help her down. They walked to a low flat rock near the edge of the cliff. Looking down at the ground, Mary could see the imprint of a shoe here and there. But that did not mean their attacker had been here. Surely people came here from time to time to look at the view.

"Look at the scuff marks." Royce pointed to the edge of the rock and the ground beside it. "Someone's been here. Good place to lie down and brace your hands on the rock to steady your telescope."

They continued to walk, moving back from the edge of the hill and weaving their way through the fallen stones and low walls.

"Sir Royce!" one of the grooms called excitedly.

Royce and Mary hurried in his direction. They found him standing in a sheltered corner of the ruin where two of the partial walls came together.

The earth in the area had clearly been disturbed. Holes

had been driven into the ground in a distinct square pattern, and the dirt was scuffed and the grass flattened inside the square.

"A tent has been here. And a fire." Mary pointed to the ring of stones, filled with blackened ashes.

Royce nodded, his mouth pulled into a taut, grim line. "No wonder we heard no gossip of a stranger in the village. He's been camping out up here. Watching our every move."

"And look!" Mary spotted an object lying in the shadow, up against one of the walls. She picked it up and turned to show it to Royce. It was the leather satchel that had held all their papers, now empty and discarded. "My case!"

Chapter 24

The house was abuzz with news of the discovery Mary and Royce had made atop Beacon Hill. Maids whispered about it in the hallways, and Miss Dalrymple described at length the palpitations it gave her. Even the invitation to Lady Sabrina's ball could not overshadow the idea that someone had been spying on Willowmere. Lord Stewkesbury insisted that the girls not ride unless accompanied by himself, Royce, or Fitz as well as a groom, and he increased the number of men patrolling the perimeter of the grounds both night and day.

"I feel as if I am living in an armed camp," Mary grumbled as she left the house a few days later to take a walk in the garden. Royce, hearing her intention, had insisted on accompanying her. "I can't imagine why I need an escort as well."

"Do you really want to entrust your life to a gardener patrolling the grounds?" he asked, raising an eyebrow.

Mary sighed. "Well, come along if you must."

"How could I refuse such a gracious invitation?"

She could not help but smile. "I am sorry. I shall strive to be a more pleasant companion."

"There is no need. I have become quite accustomed to you."

That remark brought forth a full laugh from her.

He smiled. "There. That is better. It has been too long since I have heard you laugh."

She glanced at him, surprised.

"Did you think I hadn't noticed?" he asked softly. "Did you think I did not realize that I have been the cause of your unhappiness?"

"No, I will not lay that upon you," she told him quickly.

"You do not need to. I know what I see. And why." He took her hand, raising it and softly pressing his lips upon the back of it. "I would go back and undo what I have done if I could. I would not have you unhappy."

Mary felt the color rise in her cheeks, and she glanced away, flustered—as much from the feel of his lips upon her skin as from his words.

"I did not act as a gentleman should. I allowed my desire to control me," he went on.

"That is not why I am—why I have been—"

"Unhappy?"

"Yes. No." She pulled her fingers from his grasp. "There is no need for you to blame yourself. I am a grown woman. I knew what I was doing. You did not seduce me."

"Yet you regret it."

"I don't." She looked at him, eyes wide. "I have not regretted it for a moment. How could I? It was—" She broke off, her color deepening, and quickened her pace.

He matched her easily, taking her hand in his once again as they walked.

"What?" he asked. "What was it?" His thumb began a lazy circling over the back of her hand, so light it was barely noticeable, yet it sent shivers running through her.

They were walking toward the arbor, and she could not help but think of the maze that lay beyond it—and what had happened in the maze. She remembered his kiss, his touch, the heady delight that had run through her. Her blood seemed to hum in her veins, stirred by her memories and the soft, insistent pleasure of his thumb stroking her hand.

"Royce, stop." She tugged her hand from his again. "You know what it was like. Why must I say it?"

"Because." He reached out, pulling her to a stop and turning her to face him. "It pleases me to hear you say it."

He raised his hand and stroked his knuckles down her cheek, soft as the touch of a feather. Mary looked up into his eyes, unable to pull her gaze away. It was so easy to get lost in those green depths, to forget everything else in the memory of pleasure.

"It was shattering," she admitted hoarsely.

His eyes warmed, the pupils widening. "Marigold . . . you entrance me. Such honesty. Such lack of guile."

She started to turn away, but he grabbed her arms and held her in place. "No, don't run away. It was shattering for me as well."

Mary's breath hitched in her throat. She was very aware of the heat of his hands on her arms, the sound of her own blood pounding in her ears. She wondered if he had sensed the quiver of desire that his words had sent shooting into her abdomen.

"I don't want to lose that. . . . I don't want to lose you." He bent, brushing his lips against her temple. His lips went lower, grazing the hard line of her jaw, then moving on to her ear.

Mary's insides were suddenly soft and warm, like wax melting over a flame. Her eyes drifted closed, and her hands went to his chest, bracing herself. She shivered as his lips slid along her throat. His hand drifted up her side and curved around her breast. Heat blossomed within her, and her nipples tightened.

His kiss deepened as he pulled her farther into the shade of the arbor, one hand curving down her back and pressing her hips against his. She could feel the hard line of him digging into her soft flesh, and the mere touch brought all the memories of their lovemaking flooding back to her. Mary moved involuntarily, and she was answered by a muffled groan from Royce. He kissed her hungrily, fervently, and his hand delved beneath the neckline of her dress, caressing her naked flesh.

She wanted to yield, to sink into his arms, to fall once more into that swirling maelstrom of emotions and sensation. She struggled to recall why she was resisting him when what he offered was so pleasurable. Would it be so wrong to give in to her desire? To feel the joy and fulfillment when he plunged deep inside her? To belong to him, and he to her, so deeply, so completely, that for the moment nothing else existed?

But she knew what would happen after that moment, the emptiness that would creep in as she realized that all emotion was only on her side. He would press her even more strongly to marry him, and she would have to hold out against him, knowing even as she did so that she wanted desperately to take what he offered. There would be arguments and unhappiness. It would be utterly foolish to open the door to those things.

With a wrenching effort of will, Mary pulled away. "Are you—are you seducing me?" she asked a trifle shakily.

"I am *trying* to court you."

Mary turned a skeptical eye upon Royce, trying to ignore the pleasure thrumming through her body. "Do you honestly believe I will be fooled by this sudden attempt at courtship? That you can make me believe you really want to marry me?'

"But I do want to marry you!" He flung his hands out to the sides in frustration, his voice rising.

"Oh, you know what I mean."

"No, I don't." Royce moved closer, his voice low and intimate. "I want you in my bed. And you want me. You cannot deny it."

"No," she replied honestly. "I cannot. But there has to be more."

"What do you want me to say?"

That you love me. She managed to hold back the words. They had to come from him or it meant nothing.

"I don't want you to say anything." She whirled and strode away.

"Bloody hell! Mary—" He hurried after her.

She stopped at the wall that separated the upper garden from the lower one and stared out over the landscape. She did not turn her head as Royce came up beside her. He positioned himself to face her profile, ignoring the view.

"Has it occurred to you that you might already be carrying my child?" he asked softly. "Would you want your child to be born out of wedlock?"

"No, of course not. If I—if that turned out to be the case, I would marry you."

He moved closer to her, his eyes lighting, and Mary took a quick step backward, placing her hand firmly against his chest.

"No. I won't let you seduce me in the hope I'll get pregnant and marry you."

"Mary . . . you wound me."

Mary rolled her eyes, turning away from him back toward the garden. She stiffened. "Royce . . ." Her voice was unnaturally calm and low.

"What?" He frowned, his eyes searching her face.

"There is a man standing below the gardens. Just outside, beneath that first tree."

He went as still as she. "To my left?"

"Yes." She looked up at him, her eyes wide. "He is just standing there, watching us. He's too far away for me to make out his features."

Royce nodded. He took one of her hands. It was ice cold in his. He raised it to his lips. "Don't worry. Start walking to that bench past the steps."

When he released her hand, Mary turned and began walking as he had instructed. Behind her, she heard a scrape and a thud, and when she whirled around, she saw that Royce had vaulted over the wall and was already running down the path below.

She raced to the steps leading down to the path, then hiked her skirts to her knees and took off at a run after Royce. She could not see the man he chased, but she could hear the intruder's progress as he tore through the garden and into the field beyond.

Royce pulled away from her, gaining on the trespasser, until finally he threw himself at the man, and they crashed to the ground in a heap. Mary slowed as she reached them, struggling to regain her breath as the two men rolled across the ground, grappling and punching. She looked around for a small rock or a branch with which to knock the intruder out, but then Royce flipped the other man onto his stomach, grabbing his arm and twisting it up behind his back.

The man let out a roar of pain and stopped struggling. "All right. All right," a very American voice gasped out. "I yield."

Royce eased up on his pressure, then stood, hauling the other man to his feet. He was a well-formed young man, a trifle lanky, and his open, pleasant face held a scattering of freckles across his cheeks. Gray eyes, crinkling at the corners, looked out candidly from beneath straight brows of the same dark blond as his close-cropped, curling hair.

Mary gasped in surprise. "Sam! It's Sam Treadwell!"

"Hello, Mary," the man responded with a sheepish grin.

"You know him!" Royce stared at her.

"Yes. He—he's from our town." Mary continued to gaze at the man in dismay. "I can't believe that you—Sam, what were you thinking? Why did you shoot at my sisters? Why did you try to take Rose?"

Sam Treadwell's jaw dropped, and he gaped at her with an expression of such astonishment that he scarcely needed to say, "Shoot at—take Rose! What are you talking about?" Worry quickly wiped out the astonishment as her words sank in. "Is Rose all right?"

"Are you telling us you didn't fire a pistol at Mary's sisters?" Royce growled.

"No! Why in the world would I do that?" Treadwell's voice rose in agitation. "Mary, what is going on?"

"If you've done nothing wrong, why the devil did you run from me?"

Sam blinked. "I saw you charging at me. I thought you were going to attack me."

"Bloody hell!" Royce dropped Treadwell's arm in disgust and took a step back, though he kept a wary eye upon the young man.

"Mary, please tell me what you're talking about," Sam said. "Is Rose all right?"

"Yes, she's fine. Someone shot at my sisters yesterday. When we saw you, we thought you were the man who did it."

"But you know I would never hurt Rose!"

"I know. I mean, I *thought* you would not hurt her. What are you doing here?"

"I came to see Rose," he said simply, as if that was obvious. "When I found you had left without a word, I followed you. I've had the devil of a time tracking you down."

"Why were you lurking about in the gardens?" Royce asked suspiciously. "Why didn't you come to the front door if you wanted to see Rose?"

"I'm sorry, sir." The younger man again looked sheepish. "I know I should have, but I wasn't sure how Rose felt about seeing me." He looked toward Mary entreatingly. "I was afraid she was angry at me, the way she left. And, well, the house is so grand. I figured if I went round to the back and waited long enough, Rose would come out, and I could talk to her in private."

Royce heaved a sigh. "I assume that this is one of Rose's suitors?"

"Yes. Not one, I think, who would try to drug us all and carry Rose off."

Again Sam Treadwell's jaw fell open. "Someone did that?" His face firmed, and his hands balled up. "Who? Who's trying to hurt Rose?" He swung toward Royce.

"We don't know," Mary answered.

Treadwell straightened, looking at Royce. "Are you this earl fellow?"

"No, thank God," Royce replied feelingly. "However, I intend to introduce you to the Earl of Stewkesbury right now."

The three of them trooped back to the house, Royce walking behind Mary and Treadwell to make sure that the young man did not take it into his head to bolt.

Mary glanced back at Royce. "I don't think Sam will run away."

"Indeed not!" Sam looked affronted. "As if I would leave with Rose in danger."

"I do not really think so either," Royce answered. "However, for the time being, I'm not putting my entire trust in young Mr. Treadwell."

They must have been spotted trudging toward the house, for by the time they reached the back door, Oliver was standing in the hallway waiting for them. Fitz lounged behind him in the doorway of Oliver's office.

"I see you've caught someone. Good," the earl greeted them.

"But it's not Sam," Mary assured him. "I mean, this is Sam, but Sam isn't the one who tried to shoot my sisters yesterday."

"Indeed?" The earl looked the young man up and down in the cool way that had both infuriated and intimidated others.

Treadwell blushed and straightened even more, his jaw jutting out, as he faced Stewkesbury. "I am Samuel Treadwell, sir, and I'm here to see—"

"Sam! Oh, Sam!" Rose had come down the stairs, followed by her sisters, and now stood at the other end of the hall, staring at Treadwell. Her face was suddenly glowing, her blue eyes sparkling, as a wide grin spread across her face. "You've come!"

She hurried down the hall, almost running, and stopped just short of Sam. Still smiling madly, she dug her fingers into her skirts and gazed at him.

"Rose!" Sam grinned back at her rapturously. He took a half step toward her and stopped, his hands coming up, then falling to his sides. "I thought I had lost you forever! When you left and I didn't know where you were, I nearly went crazy."

"We had to leave quickly," Rose responded. Her smile faltered. "And you—I was not aware you cared."

"I know! I know! I was a fool! I should have asked for your hand. I kept silent, hoping I could change my parents' minds. I thought if only they got to know you better, they would drop their objections to your family. I—"

"Excuse me?" The earl's voice was dangerously silky. "Your family objected to *my* cousin's antecedents?"

Sam and Rose jumped and glanced around, embarrassed, as if suddenly aware that there were other people there. Sam blushed and began to stammer a response.

But it was Mary who jumped in to say, "I believe they objected to the fact that our parents owned a tavern and weren't wealthy. Much the same reasons your family looked down on us, as I remember."

Stewkesbury sent her a long look, then bent his head in acknowledgment, the faintest of smiles tugging at the corners of his mouth. "A direct hit, Cousin."

"It is gracious of you to be so understanding," Sam told Mary gravely. "But it was wrong of my parents to judge Rose. And wrong of me to wait. I should have told them I was going to marry Rose, with or without their approval."

Rose's eyes widened and she clapped her hand to her mouth.

The earl cleared his throat. "I am not sure of the custom in America, but in this country, it is usual to ask the head of the family for permission to marry."

"An antiquated notion," Camellia protested.

Sam, however, nodded, saying, "I intend to, sir, if you will allow me to speak to you in private."

Stewkesbury nodded and swept his hand toward his office. Sam straightened, gave a tug to his coat, and followed Stewkesbury to the door of the earl's office.

"Just a minute, Sam Treadwell!" Rose's voice cracked like a whip down the length of the corridor, and everyone turned to stare at her. Her cheeks were high with color and her eyes blazing. "Now your first concern is whether my cousin will approve of our marriage? I might remind you—*I* am the one you want to marry. So *I* am the one you should be asking."

"But I—I—" The young man gaped at her.

"You assumed I would say yes." Rose crossed her arms. "You figured you had me all wrapped up; nothing to worry about. Well, if I were you, I'd worry less about what the Earl of Stewkesbury thinks and more about what Rose Bascombe intends to do!"

Rose whirled and walked rapidly down the hall and back up the stairs. Sam Treadwell gaped after her. He took a step down the hall, then stopped and turned back toward the earl in confusion.

"I think a drink all around might be in order," Stewkesbury told the young man, and steered him into the office.

Fitz followed them. Royce levered away from the wall where he had been leaning and started toward the office. He paused beside Mary, his eyes twinkling, and leaned in a little closer.

"We could make it a double ceremony. . . ."

Mary's lips tightened. "I'm not certain there's going to be a single ceremony. In any case, I hardly think you and I belong with Rose and Sam."

"If you were to hare off to America, I would follow you."

"Because you are stubborn," Mary retorted. "'Tis hardly the same thing."

Royce grinned and moved on, and Mary joined Lily and Camellia as they followed Rose up the stairs.

*   *   *

"Do you mean to marry Sam Treadwell?" Lily asked breathlessly as soon as they crossed the threshold into Rose's room. "It's terribly romantic."

"At the moment, I have no plans regarding Sam Treadwell." Rose scowled as she paced across her room. "But I fail to see what is so romantic about talking to everyone else about marrying a girl and not saying a word to the girl herself!"

"You have a point." Mary closed the door behind her and watched her sister for a moment. "Still . . . it does show a certain commitment to jump on a ship and follow you across the ocean."

"I know!" Rose cried. "And I was so happy to see him. I wanted to throw my arms around him. You know how I feel about him, Mary, how much I've missed him. He said such wonderful things about how he should have stood up to his parents and asked me to marry him. But then he turns around and speaks to the earl first!"

"Mmm. It is rather annoying. But Sam is a traditional young man, you know. I don't think he meant any disrespect to you."

"Maybe not." Rose turned, her chin set mulishly. "But I am tired of being pushed and pulled about. First Cosmo, always pushing me to marry Egerton Suttersby." Rose gave an expressive shudder, which was echoed by Lily. "Then this person who keeps trying to abduct me, though I haven't the slightest idea why. The earl fancies himself in charge of us all and foists that chaperone on us, who tells me what to say, what to eat, how to act, until I think I shall scream. Now Sam shows up and wants to ask the earl if I can marry him, as if Stewkesbury were the one in charge of my heart!"

"You're right," Camellia agreed. "You ought to tell them all to go jump."

"I have a feeling that Sam will correct his behavior. I think he really loves you," Mary told Rose. "As for the rest of it, I think I have a way of catching this man who keeps bothering us."

"Really? What?" All the sisters turned their attention to Mary.

"All we have to do is convince the men," Mary said, and began to explain.

Chapter 25

They set their plan into motion by first going to ask a favor of Charlotte. She looked somewhat apprehensive when she heard what they intended, but she agreed to carry out her part, which was to inform Miss Dalrymple that tonight was to be a family dinner and Miss Dalrymple's attendance would not be required. Since Charlotte had little more liking for the woman than Lady Vivian did, it was not a difficult task.

When the sisters went down to supper that evening, they were surprised to find that the earl had graciously invited Sam Treadwell to stay for dinner. Before they proceeded to the dining room, Sam went straight to Rose and engaged her in a hushed, earnest conversation. From her sister's heightened color and frequent smiles, Mary assumed that the young man was presenting his case well.

The meal itself passed in the usual way until the time came for the women to retire. Normally Charlotte would have risen to signal their departure, but tonight she remained in her seat, as the Bascombes had asked her to, and it was Mary who spoke.

"We thought we would remain here while you gentlemen have your port."

For a long moment, the three Englishmen simply gazed at her uncomprehendingly. Sam Treadwell, down the table, smothered a grin and began to examine his utensils with the same care Cousin Charlotte was using.

"I beg your pardon," the earl said in a level tone.

"I said—" Mary began, a trifle louder.

"Yes, yes, I realize what you said." The earl started to say more, then turned toward the servants, who were still clearing the table, their movements having slowed down considerably in the past few minutes. "That's all, Bostwick. You can do this later."

"Would you care for your port, sir?"

Stewkesbury shook his head. "I have the feeling I'm going to need a clear head." When the servants had left, he turned back to the Bascombes. "Now, what are you up to?"

"We are not trying to break a sacred tradition," Mary assured him. "We wish to talk in private, and this seemed the best time. You are all three here, and the servants leave you to your port and cigars." She continued in a cajoling manner, "You can still have your port and cigars; we don't mind. We just want to tell you about our plan."

The earl sighed. "All right. Tell me about your 'plan.' "

"We all agree that we're tired of being watched all the time and never being able to go anywhere. So the best thing to do is to capture this man who's after Rose."

"I have made some attempt to do just that," the earl offered mildly.

"I know, and we appreciate it. But the best way to capture him is to set a trap."

"Are you saying what I think you are?" Stewkesbury's brows sailed upward.

"We're saying that we want to lure him out of hiding. We intend to spring a trap on him. And we will be the bait."

"Impossible." The earl shoved back from the table and stood up.

Royce glanced at his stepbrother. "You should have let Bostwick bring the port."

"Do you honestly think I would use my cousins to trap a villain?" Stewkesbury went on, ignoring Royce.

"If you will but think about it, you will see that it is the sensible thing to do," Mary argued. "It isn't as if he's going to shoot us. He wants to kidnap Rose."

"A minor inconvenience," Royce suggested.

"And we aren't suggesting that we face him ourselves," Mary plowed ahead. "Your men can be waiting, ready to pounce on him when he shows his hand."

"It's entirely too dangerous." Oliver shook his head.

"The only alternative is to hang about here for the rest of our lives, waiting for this man to show his face again!" Camellia protested. "What if he's already gone, and we're just sitting here looking like fools?"

"What we're doing now makes no sense," Mary went on. "Your protection is keeping him away, which means he won't be captured. But you can't protect us always. He's bound to pounce at some point—but you won't know when and where, and you won't be able to set everything up so you can capture him."

"We've talked about a trap, of course," Royce told them. "But it was clear it wouldn't work."

"Why is that?"

He looked at her without answering, and Mary could not keep from grinning. "*I'll* tell you why, since I have a pretty good idea. It wouldn't work because you were talking about the three of you pretending to be us or something else that wouldn't fool a three-year-old. The only thing that will deceive him is if *we* are the ones who set the trap."

"Cousins . . ." Fitz took up the argument, smiling in his

most charming way. "You are terribly brave; no one is questioning that. But think how Stewkesbury would feel—how all of us would feel—if something went wrong and you were injured."

The argument continued to go back and forth, with no one making any headway. Royce fell into a silence, watching them, his brows drawn together in thought.

Finally, clearing his throat, Royce said, "Stewkesbury, I have a suggestion."

"Thank God." Oliver turned to him. "I hope it will work."

"I think it will. Why don't you do what the Misses Bascombe want? Set a trap."

Mary turned to Royce in amazement, and he smiled.

"You needn't look so stunned, my dear. I told you I'm a reasonable man."

"You are a madman," Oliver countered. "What the devil are you thinking? Why would I agree to such a scheme?"

"There are several reasons, actually. The first is that the scheme makes sense, and you know it, just as I do. Everything Mary has said is true—you can draw him into a situation where you have the upper hand. The second reason is that these ladies won't stop arguing until you agree. Third—and most important—if you don't agree, they will attempt the plan by themselves."

The earl gaped at his stepbrother.

"Sir Royce is right," Camellia offered. "If you don't want to participate, we will do it on our own."

"It will work much better, of course, if you join us," Mary assured him.

"This is extortion!" Stewkesbury's gray eyes were bright silver with anger, his body rigid, and for a moment Mary feared that he was about to explode in a rage.

He walked away from them, then back to the table. He

stood for a moment, his eyes boring into Mary's, his hands gripping the back of his chair. "All right." His voice was tight. "We will spring a trap, but only if we all agree on the plan first—and if you and your sisters promise you will not attempt anything on your own."

Mary studied him warily. "All right. As long as you promise not to withhold your agreement unreasonably, we promise not to try it alone."

"Agreed." Stewkesbury gave her a short nod and sat down. "How do you propose to set the trap?"

"First, we must have a place to go. Somewhere we can walk to, preferably. It has to be enclosed, so that our rescuers can hide there."

The earl glanced at Fitz and Royce, then said, "The old mill."

The other two men nodded.

"It's picturesque enough that it's reasonable you might want to go there. The walk is long, but not so far that it would seem suspicious," Royce exclaimed. "Best of all, it'll be easy for you to find. You simply follow the river."

"You seem to have thought of everything," Mary commented.

He shrugged, smiling a little sheepishly. "It's where we thought of laying the trap if we could have figured out how one of us could look like Rose."

"There's no need for all of you to go," Oliver said.

"You're right," Mary agreed. "Four of us might frighten him off, after what happened last time. Just Rose and I will go."

Camellia shook her head. "You need me along, too."

"We talked about this, Cam. We'll seem more vulnerable with only two of us. And since you are the one who pulled out a pistol and fired on him, he will be more wary of you. Besides, since you're the best shot, we need you to hide along the way and watch over us."

"What? No." The earl shook his head. "I'll have my gamekeeper and some of his men for that. There is no need for Camellia to risk her safety."

Camellia burst into adamant protest, and Mary shot a dark look at Stewkesbury.

"Would you care to put Cam up against your men in a shooting contest?" Mary asked. "Long gun or pistol, I'll warrant she would beat them all."

"Splendid." Fitz grinned. "I'll participate. We'll set up targets—what you do you say, Cousin—ten paces? Twenty?"

"We are not holding a shooting tournament," the earl told him flatly.

"I know what the villain looks like, too," Camellia pointed out.

"I know you don't know me," Sam spoke up. "But I can tell you that Camellia is as good a shot as any man in Three Corners. I'll volunteer to be a lookout as well."

"And me," Lily added. "I have to do something too. I'm not as good a shot as Camellia, but I *can* shoot, and I'm very good at spotting things."

The earl let out a long-suffering sigh. "Very well, the three of you will hide along the route and keep a lookout for the kidnapper, just in case he tries to seize Rose and Mary before they reach the mill. Royce, Fitz, and I will go to the mill the night before and set ourselves up to capture him if and when he attacks you."

"But we need you here, Cousin Oliver," Mary protested. "I thought we'd stage a scene, something to capture the kidnapper's attention—or that the servants will hear, in case one of them is spying for him."

Oliver stiffened. "You think one of my people is a traitor?"

"No. I mean, I have nothing to show that anyone is. But it seems possible."

"You have to admit, Stewkesbury, that he has seemed quite well informed of the girls' whereabouts," Royce put in. "Perhaps it's just from spying, but . . ."

"Yes, all right. What is it you want to do?"

"We could have an argument on the terrace. Someplace very visible to someone watching the house."

A pained expression crossed Oliver's face. "Loud and histrionic. Lovely." He sighed. "Very well. We will stage an argument on the terrace for all to see."

"Then Rose and I will set out. And . . ." Mary shrugged. "We'll capture him."

Fitz grinned. "Of course we will. You know, Willowmere has been much more entertaining since you girls arrived."

"I could do with a little less entertainment," the earl said dryly.

Oliver brought in a map of the estate from his office, and they used it to finalize their plans, going over exactly where each person would be and what he or she would do. At last the earl rose, shoving back his chair.

"It is set, then. Treadwell, I expect it's easiest if you spend the night here. I'll have a room made up for you. Royce and Fitz, I presume you will leave later tonight and spend the night in the mill. You lookouts will go early tomorrow morning while it's still dark." He glanced around and was met with nods. He turned to Mary and Rose. "And you, cousins, I will see tomorrow morning."

They retired early, none of them having any desire to sit in the drawing room making small talk. However, Mary had few hopes of falling asleep quickly. She changed into her night rail and dressing gown, then sat down to read, but she could not concentrate on the words. Her mind kept skittering around, going first to Royce, then to the day awaiting her, then to the man who had shot at her sisters. Were they wrong not to tell the earl about their stepfather? What if it *was* him? What if they could not control him?

She thought about how Royce had spoken up for her and her sisters, and a smile curved her lips. What if Vivian was right in what she said, if Royce's repeated offers of marriage meant that he was driven by something more than duty or honor? Could there be some knot of feeling for her inside him, perhaps not yet love, but something that, if nurtured, could grow into love? Was that enough to risk the rest of her life on?

Mary glanced up at the clock on the mantel. She wondered when Royce and Fitz were leaving for the mill. She had not said good-bye to Royce, had not even wished him well. Nothing would happen to him tomorrow, of course. Nor to her. But she could not stop the little crawl of anxiety through her stomach. Going to her door, she opened it and peered out into the corridor. There was no sound, no movement. She glanced the other way up the corridor. Light shone beneath Royce's door.

She hesitated for an instant, then flew down the hall on her tiptoes. Stopping to glance around her again, she tapped softly at Royce's door. When he responded with a call to enter, she slipped inside and closed the door behind her.

Royce was standing in front of the walnut dresser, shirtless, looking into a drawer. He turned at the sound and froze when he saw her. "Mary!" His eyes lit and he took a step toward her, then stopped. "Are you mad? What are you doing here?" His voice dropped almost to a whisper, and he crossed the room to her in a few quick strides.

"I-I came to tell you something." Mary's eyes dropped to his chest, taking in the broad expanse of skin, the light brown hairs curling across his chest in an inverted V, dwindling into a line that ran down his stomach and disappeared into the waistband of his trousers. Her breath caught, and she was aware of a strong urge to reach out and tangle her fingers through the curling hairs.

Letting out a curse, Royce turned away, grabbing his shirt and shrugging into it. "You shouldn't be here," he told her gruffly. "If anyone saw you, your reputation would be ruined."

"Then you would win; I'd have to marry you, wouldn't I?"

Royce scowled at her. "I'm not trying to *win*. Blast it, Mary!" He stopped and drew a breath, running his hand back through his hair. Stepping around her, he turned the key in the door and swiveled back to her. "All right. What did you want to tell me? I haven't much time. I have to meet Fitz downstairs in a few minutes. And, for my sake if not your own, pray keep your voice down."

She thought about the foolishly romantic notions that had been running through her head. Clearly, there was no need for any poignant farewell.

"I came to tell you about my stepfather," she said in a cool voice.

"Your what?"

Quickly Mary told him about her mother's second marriage and the unpleasant man she had had the misfortune to choose. Royce listened, frowning, as she went on to describe how he had been pushing Rose to marry one of his friends, Egerton Suttersby, despite the large difference in their ages and Rose's dislike of the man.

"And you think he has something to do with this? Was he the man who tried to kidnap Rose?"

"No. No, that man was far younger and larger than Cosmo. The thing is, I saw—or thought I saw—Cosmo in London. That was where I went that day at the Tower when I left you and the others. I thought I had seen Cosmo and I tried to find him, but then you came along and . . ." She stopped, thinking of what had happened after Royce had found her.

The darkening of his eyes told her that he, too, remembered. Mary glanced away and quickly told him the other things that had made her wonder if her stepfather could be involved—the incident in the maze, and the size and shape of the man who had shot at her sisters recently.

Royce looked at her for a long moment. "Why haven't you told Oliver this?"

"Because I don't know anything for certain! There are many small men. Who's to say that it is he? And . . . I was afraid." Mary looked down.

"Afraid?" He reached out to tilt her chin up, smiling into her face. "You? How can that be?"

"I didn't want Stewkesbury to know we were connected to someone like Cosmo. I didn't want any of you to know."

"You shouldn't worry. Every family has a black sheep or two. And he's not even related to you."

"I know. But everyone already thinks we are unfashionable and improper. Having a stepfather like Cosmo would make us look even worse. We were afraid the earl would regret taking us in. I was afraid you—" She stopped and stepped back, turning her face away.

"You were afraid I would what?" He followed her, reaching out to brush a lock of hair back from her cheek. Her skin flamed to life beneath his fingers.

Mary swallowed. "Turn away from me."

"I would never do that." His voice was low and taut. "Look at me." When she turned her face to him, he went on, "I will never turn away from you."

His words made her tremble, and suddenly Mary's throat was clogged with tears. "Royce . . ."

She could feel the now-familiar warmth spreading through her. It was absurd to react this way, she told herself even as her pulse began to thud in her throat. She swayed toward him slightly, her breath coming faster in her throat.

"Sweet Mary . . ." His fingers continued to caress her cheek. "Do you know what you do to me? How much I want you?"

Mary could not answer. Indeed, the way she felt when he looked into her eyes, she could scarcely breathe.

"You should not come into my room dressed like that," he went on, his lips curving sensually. His hand slid down her throat and edged under the collar of her dressing gown. His fingers moved along the hard line of her collarbone, slipping under her nightgown. "You should run back to your room. Now, while there's still time."

"I don't want to run," Mary answered honestly.

Royce let out a breathy laugh and bent to kiss her. His kiss was slow and leisurely, as if they had all the time in the world, far different from the hard, almost desperate way he had kissed her before. He did not pull her into his arms, only kept tracing his finger along her shoulders and chest and neck as his lips tasted hers again and again.

Mary's body flared to life. Her core was suddenly heated and soft, and a low, slow throb began deep in her center. She dug her hands into the edges of his shirt, pulling him to her, going up on tiptoes to kiss him. She wanted to feel him filling her again, to wrap her legs around him and ride the hard thrust of his masculinity. She anticipated the deep satisfaction, the stretch of her flesh as she drew him into her, the ache eased, the thirst slaked.

"Take me," she murmured against his lips. "Take me."

"Not just yet." She could feel the curve of his lips as he smiled. "This time, I am going to be slow . . . and very, very thorough."

He was true to his word. Untying the sash of her dressing gown, he pushed it back from her shoulders and let it fall to the floor. He paused to kiss her, sinking his hands into her hair, before he resumed the task of undressing her. Sliding the thin cotton gown off over her head, he tossed it aside and picked her up, carrying her over to the bed. His eyes never left her as he shrugged out of his shirt and trousers.

Mary stretched beneath his gaze, a little embarrassed and at the same time aroused. Royce stretched out on the bed beside her, propping himself up on one elbow, and began to kiss her. He kissed first her mouth, then her face, then moved down her neck, tasting, it seemed, every square inch of her body. As he kissed her, his hand explored, lingering, teasing a response from her. Mary quivered beneath his touch, her legs moving in restless desire. Yet still he glided over her with an agonizing slowness.

Gently he opened her legs, his fingers trailing up the inside of her thighs, first one and then the other, skimming close to but never touching the heated center of her desire. He took her breast in his mouth and tended to it with a single-minded devotion, using his lips and teeth and tongue to stoke her pleasure, arousing her to an ever higher peak until she thought she must surely explode.

Then he showed her how far still she was from reaching the heights of her passion. His hand slid in between her legs. She jerked at the intimate touch, gasping. Opening the slick, hot folds, he stroked her, pulling tiny whimpers of need from her, driving her desire ever higher. Mary moved her hips, aching and desperate, and dug her hands into his thick hair, her fingers clenching as desire knotted and coiled inside her.

"Take me, Royce," she said again.

This time he could hold out no longer, and he moved between her legs, thrusting deep within her. Mary choked back a cry of satisfaction as he filled her. She clutched his back as he moved within her. His skin was hot and slick with sweat; his breath rasped in her ear. She was surrounded by the sound and scent and feel of him, melded to him in the ferocious fire of their mutual passion.

He cried out, burying his face in her neck, and Mary wrapped herself around him, clinging to him, as their climax took them both, flinging them into that shattering realm where they existed only in each other.

Royce collapsed upon her. Mary smiled to herself, luxuriating in the weight of him. She wanted to stay in this moment as long as she could, drifting in utter and complete satisfaction, her body and mind drained, connected to .Royce in a deep and primitive way, able to believe that right here, right now, she loved and was loved in return.

There was a light tap at the door, and a voice called softly, "Sir? Sir? Master Fitz sent me up to see if you were ready."

With a muttered curse, Royce rolled from her. "Yes," he called, his voice coming out hoarse and low. He cleared his throat and said again, "Yes. Tell him I'll be right there."

The servant answered and went away. Royce turned to look down at Mary. He started to speak, and she raised her hand, laying it across his mouth.

"No. Please don't. Don't spoil it."

"Bloody hell!" He swung out of bed and came around to pick up his clothes. Shoving them back on, he sat down and put on his stockings and boots, and finally covered his white shirt with a dark jacket.

Royce came back to the side of the bed, looming over her. He bent down, placing his hands on either side of her, and looked into her eyes.

"You will marry me," he said flatly. "I promise you. You will marry me or no one at all."

He bent and kissed her one last time, a hard, possessive kiss, then turned and strode out of the room.

"I know," Mary whispered into the dark. "I know."

*   *   *

Mary dressed and slipped down the hall to her room. Her sleep was troubled, and she sprang awake a few hours later when she heard Lily, Camellia, and Sam leaving their rooms. Mary went to her door and opened it a crack to peer out. Lily and Camellia had already passed by; she could hear their soft footsteps on the stairs. But Sam was still walking along the corridor. A door opened, and Rose stepped out. She was clad in her nightgown, her black hair tumbled around her shoulders, and she reached out to Sam. He took her in his arms and pulled her close, bending his head to hers.

Not wanting to intrude on their tender moment, Mary closed her door. If she had had any doubts that Rose would decide to marry Sam, they were gone now. Smiling, she returned to her bed.

Mary and Rose had breakfast that morning with Oliver, Miss Dalrymple, and Charlotte. Cousin Charlotte was notorious for rising late; indeed, Mary had not eaten breakfast with her since she had arrived at Willowmere. However, this morning she looked as bright-eyed as if it were the middle of the afternoon, and though she managed to keep quiet about the day's events in front of the servants, it was obvious that she was ready to burst with excitement. Mary was not hungry in the slightest, but she forced herself to eat to keep up appearances. Rose, she noted, could only toy with her food.

There were circles beneath Rose's eyes, and though they served only to make her appear even more lovely and fragile, Mary knew it was a sign of great worry. Her sister was an accomplished sleeper, and it took a great deal to disturb her rest. Mary wished she could have taken one of her other sisters with her—Lily, for instance, would have greatly enjoyed the drama of it all—but unfortunately, Rose was the one most essential to the project.

As they left the breakfast table, Mary linked her arm

through Rose's, pulling her close to her side. "It will be fine," she whispered, and smiled. "I'll be right there with you. And Sam will be watching out for us. Not to mention Camellia and Lily and Royce and Fitz."

At the mention of Sam, Rose brightened, even allowing a small smile. Personally, Mary was more reassured by the presence of Camellia and Royce, but clearly it was Sam's protection that meant the most to Rose.

"I know." Rose nodded. "I am determined to be brave."

The hardest part was waiting for another hour, as they had planned. They sat with Charlotte and Miss Dalrymple in the drawing room, but soon Miss Dalrymple began to fuss about the absence of the other girls. Charlotte, for her part, twisted her handkerchief and said little, glancing at Miss Dalrymple as if she wished her far away.

"Where are those two?" Miss Dalrymple asked for the fourth time, turning to look at the clock on the mantel. "It is considered a virtue to be punctual."

"Perhaps they are not feeling well." Mary had not considered dealing with Miss Dalrymple in her plans. "It might be best if we put off our lessons until this afternoon."

Miss Dalrymple began to tsk-tsk, wagging her forefinger at Mary in the way that invariably aroused Mary's resentment. "Now, do not let your sisters' poor behavior influence yours, Miss Bascombe."

"That will be enough, Miss Dalrymple." Charlotte's voice held that indefinable tone of aristocratic authority that Mary was sure she could never achieve no matter how long she studied. "I have plans to spend the day with the Misses Bascombe, so your class will have to be postponed until tomorrow. Perhaps you might spend the day devising something more entertaining for your activities tomorrow. I found their lessons yesterday dry as dust."

Miss Dalrymple looked as if she'd swallowed a spider,

but she only nodded and heaved herself to her feet. "Yes, of course, my lady."

Rose turned to her cousin with awe after Miss Dalrymple had stalked out of the room. "How did you manage that?"

Charlotte shrugged. "One simply pretends to be Aunt Euphronia. However do you girls stand that woman? Viv is right; Oliver should replace her. We shall have to talk to him once all this is over." She turned to look at the clock, just as Miss Dalrymple had earlier. "Is it time yet?"

"It's approaching." Mary stood up. She looked toward Charlotte, who nodded and rose to go out onto the terrace for the first part of their charade.

Mary and Rose went upstairs to get their bonnets and to hide their weapons about their persons. Fitz had lent Mary one of his collection of firearms, a LePage pocket pistol that was surprisingly small and light. Rose chose to carry a small knife with her, feeling that it would be more useful if and when the attacker grabbed her.

Bonnets in hand and weapons safely concealed in their pockets, they went back down the stairs and out to the terrace, where Charlotte and the earl sat looking over the gardens. Charlotte by now had worried her handkerchief into a rumpled ball. The earl looked completely at ease. Pirate, for once, was not at the earl's feet, but stood at the top of the steps, apparently surveying the garden for possible foes.

Stewkesbury stood up at the girls' entrance and bowed. "Are you ready?'

Mary nodded. "Perhaps we should begin by talking a bit."

"Of course." The earl gazed out across the gardens. "Lovely day, is it not? Though I fear it will not be long before autumn is upon us."

"Oh, Oliver, how can you be so—so unruffled?" Charlotte asked.

"Well, I must be, mustn't I?" Oliver smiled faintly. "Otherwise, how can he tell I have become agitated?"

"Do you?" Charlotte asked. "Ever become agitated?"

"One endeavors not to." He shot his cuffs, then pulled out chairs for Mary and Rose. "I think it would be best to urge you to sit down, don't you?"

Mary glanced toward the chairs, but did not sit down. "Yes, and I think we would explain that we should like to go farther afield today." She gestured to the east. "We have heard that there is an old mill, and we would like to explore."

The earl frowned. "I would disagree with that. There is, of course, the danger."

"And I would explain that we would really like to get off the estate for a while. We feel cooped up here." Mary turned toward Rose, who nodded.

"Yes, please." Rose gazed at Oliver in appeal.

Charlotte, playing her part, watched the supposed conversation, turning from the girls to the earl.

Oliver shook his head. "No," he said shortly. "It's out of the question."

"I don't see why." Mary's face turned obstinate, and she set her hands on her hips. Her voice rose as she went on, "We're stuck in here with Miss Dalrymple every day. And we can't even go riding without guards. We're sick and tired of being prisoners in our own home!"

Their volume increased as they found the words falling easily into place. The earl recounted at length each and every scrape the girls had gotten into, and Mary retorted by citing the many restrictions that had been unnecessarily applied to them. Charlotte stood up as the tension built, fluttering back and forth, appealing to them to sit down and talk, not to be angry, not to shout—at least not out here where everyone could hear.

Pirate, disturbed by the disagreeable new atmosphere, began to jump back and forth between the earl and the Bascombes, whirling in circles and adding his sharp high voice to the general clamor.

"Hush, Pirate! Hush!" Rose cried at intervals, but the earl, the only one whose commands he obeyed, made not a gesture toward the dog.

Instead, he and Mary raised their voices to be heard above Pirate's yaps, bringing more than one interested face to a window in the house.

"You cannot stop us from going to the mill!" Mary hurled at the earl.

"The devil I cannot!" Stewkesbury slammed his hand down on the glass-topped table, which sent the dog into a paroxysm of barking. "You will *not* go to the mill! I will not be disobeyed!"

With that, he pivoted on his heel and strode into the house. Charlotte, with an agonized glance at Rose and Mary, hurried after him, calling, "Oliver! Wait!"

Pirate trotted after the earl, then turned and looked at the girls. He ran back a few steps toward them, stopped, whirled, and finally lay down on the terrace between the girls and the door. Mary and Rose faced each other. Their nerves had been strangely calmed by the faux fight.

"How long do you think we should discuss this?" Rose asked, taking her sister's hands and looking into her face earnestly. "I feel a fool."

"Not long. We don't want him to get bored and think we aren't going to do anything if he's watching; but on the other hand, we have to give someone time to get a message to him if there's a traitor among the servants." Shaking off her sister's hands, she turned away, exclaiming, "I will not let that man tell me what to do! He's not my father."

"No, of course not." Rose pursued her, tugging at Mary's arm so she turned to face her. "He hasn't any right!"

"Are the servants watching?" Mary asked in a low voice.

"The windows are full of them."

"There are a number of gardeners peeking out from behind bushes, too. I think we should get going. We can dawdle on the way." She stepped away, saying loudly, "Well, I am going! You can stay here and be Stewkesbury's slave, if you want to."

"No, Mary, wait!" Rose hurried after her sister down the steps.

Pirate ran to the edge of the stairs and barked ferociously. As the girls disappeared into the garden, he tore off down the steps after them.

The first problem, of course, was to elude the gardeners. There was little doubt that several of them had seen the argument; it was unlikely that any of the gardeners would physically try to stop them, but they might very well follow the sisters to make sure they were safe, which would effectively ruin the plan.

However, Fitz had laid out the route himself last night, having used it frequently when he was young, and it was well hidden from the view of most of the garden and quickly led out into the side yard. It was not the most direct route to the river and the mill, but it kept them well away from the gardens. The girls ran as fast as they could, and though they encountered a few amazed stares from some grooms around the stables, they met with no resistance. Soon they were clambering down a small hillside to the river.

"Whew!" Mary plopped down on a rock to recover her breath, and Rose joined her.

They kept watch to see if anyone had followed them from the house or stables, but there was no one. In only a moment, however, a small black-and-white body bounded down the hill. Pirate stopped in front of them, smiling, his stumpy tail wagging.

"Pirate! No. Go home!" Mary tried ineffectually to shoo him back toward the house.

"It's no use. No one can make him mind except the earl."

Mary sighed. "Well, we must hope a dog will not discourage the kidnapper. He looks too small to be trouble."

"To someone who's not acquainted with him."

They set off again, the dog trotting along with them, sometimes bounding forward to inspect the trail ahead, other times chasing off after some elusive scent, but always coming back to rejoin the girls.

"I wish I knew exactly where the others are hiding," Rose said in a low voice as they walked along. "It would make me feel safer."

"We cannot look around for them." Mary kept her eyes on the path ahead, now and then glancing at the river that ran only a few feet away. "Any more than we can look for our assailant."

The girls fell silent. The worst part, Mary thought, was keeping their walk slow. They needed to give the man time to come after them, but with the passage of each second, her anxiety increased. Her ears strained to hear any untoward sound—a twig snapping, the pad of feet on the dirt, birds flying up in fright at the passage of a human. But there was nothing beyond the sigh of the breeze in the trees. The world seemed utterly deserted.

It was almost painful to refrain from looking around for their protectors or their attacker. Mary stuck her hands in her pockets, closing her fingers around the small pistol, reassuring herself that as soon as they heard or saw the kidnapper, it would take only seconds to pull the weapon out.

It was easier when they were walking alongside the river through a meadow. But when the trees and shrubbery pressed in on them, narrowing the path and blocking their vision, Mary's heart sped up and her nerves stretched until she thought they would snap. *What was that noise? The soft plop of a footstep? And the rustle nearby—a person or simply an animal moving quietly through the trees?*

At last the mill came into view ahead of them. Mary relaxed a little, even though she knew that it made no sense. Everyone had agreed that the greatest likelihood of attack would come close to the mill. But at least now they were within sight of Royce and Fitz.

However, the trees began to edge in closer to the river, and shrubs hugged the mill, a dank, dark building of lichened gray stone. They were very close now, and Mary had to fight not to break into a run. Beside her, Rose's steps quickened, and Mary reached out, linking her arm through her sister's.

Rose glanced at her and forced a little smile. "I'm sorry."

"Don't worry; it's almost over." Of course, it wasn't; there was the long walk back if he did not come after them in the next few minutes.

Pirate, trotting along at their heels, suddenly burst forward, barking like a mad thing. An instant later, a man erupted from the bushes in front of them.

Chapter 26

Rose shrieked, and Mary pulled out her gun. She fired, but the shot went wide of the mark, and in the next instant the man was on them. He snatched Rose up, his arm effectively pinning hers to her sides, making it impossible for her to use the small knife she had drawn from her pocket.

He headed back into the trees, and Mary hurled herself after him, crashing into his back. He staggered, and it was enough, combined with Rose's frantic struggles, to knock him off balance. He went to his knees. Mary swung her pistol at his head, and it struck with a satisfying crack. Pirate ceased his jumping and barking long enough to dive in and sink his teeth into the man's ankle.

The attacker let out a roar, lashing out with his leg and sending the dog flying. Twisting, he rose and shoved Mary, but doing so lost his grip on Rose. She flung herself away, scrambling to her feet, and began to run toward the mill. The assailant turned to pursue Rose, but was met by the sight of two men running full-tilt at him, one of them wielding a pistol in each hand.

Letting out a curse, he whirled and ran back in the direction he had come. Mary, struggling to her feet, grabbed at him, but he dodged her. It cost him time, however, and he didn't get far before Royce caught up and launched himself at the man, knocking him down. The two of them rolled across the ground, exchanging punches. Fitz, drawing close, stopped and stood watching them.

Mary ran up beside him. "What are you doing? Knock him in the head!"

"And spoil Royce's fun?"

Pirate seemed to share Fitz's view, for he was dodging around the combatants, yapping happily.

"For heaven's sake!" Mary was about to wade in with the butt of her gun again, but at that point Royce landed a hefty blow, then another, and the man went limp.

Royce raised his fist again, but Fitz gripped his shoulder. "Enough. Enough. I have no desire to carry this chap all the way back to the house."

Royce hesitated, then nodded and stood up. He turned, bleeding from cuts on his cheek and lip, a bruise already forming on his cheekbone, and grinned at Mary. "Not much of a show of fisticuffs, I'm afraid, but it got the job done."

Mary, torn between throwing herself into his arms and breaking into tears, whirled and marched over to Rose. They wrapped their arms around each other and held on tightly for a few moments, letting the tension drain away. Behind them, they could hear Fitz and Royce dragging the attacker to his feet.

The girls turned to see the three men returning to the path, their assailant stumbling along between the other two, and Pirate prancing beside them.

"Is this the same man who attacked you at the summer-house?" Fitz asked as they approached, and Mary and Rose nodded.

"Has a bandage on his arm," Royce commented. "Must be where Camellia winged him."

"Never should've come today," the man mumbled. "Told 'im it'd end badly."

"Did you now?" Fitz asked cheerfully. "Seems you were right. Well, you'll have a chance to tell the earl all about it. You might want to spend the walk back thinking about your best course of action. Is abduction a transportable offense, Royce?"

"I'm sure so—of course, he'll go to the hulks first while he's awaiting transportation. Not many leave there alive."

"Didn't abduct nobody," their prisoner muttered, shuffling along between them.

"Well, it is true you failed each time. You might want to consider changing trades. But I don't think that your failure will weigh much with the judge," Royce remarked.

The man cast a glance at Fitz with the eye that was not swollen shut, then looked around. Fitz shook his head.

"I wouldn't run if I were you. My brother here has already proven he can outrun you, and that was before you were in this condition. Besides, I am carrying a pistol, as you'll note." He gestured. "And, unfortunately for you, I'm an excellent shot. I'll just aim for your leg, of course, since we want answers from you. You might want to start thinking about those answers, by the way."

The man rolled his good eye from Fitz to Royce and over at Mary and Rose, who had picked up an exhausted Pirate and was carrying him in her arms. Pirate was not too tired, however, to curl his lip and growl at the outsider.

"Bloody dog," the man muttered. "Bloody countryside." He favored everyone, as well as the surrounding trees, with a black look, then set his eyes on his feet and trudged along.

Ahead of them, there sounded a long, loud, two-note whistle, and a moment later there was a great rustling in a tree down the path. Limbs shook and a booted figure appeared on the lowest branch, bending down and hanging from it before dropping the last two feet to the ground.

It was Camellia, dressed in boys' clothing, a dark cap covering her bright hair. She wore a rifle slung on a leather strap across her back, and a pistol was stuck through her belt. She grinned broadly at them.

"I see you got him!" she called, and jogged toward them. "I saw you walking over there, Pirate following you. It was all I could do not to laugh." She cast a look at the attacker and noted with some satisfaction the bandage on his arm. "Hah! I *knew* I hit you. I pulled a bit to the right, though."

As they continued along the path, they met Sam trotting toward them. "Heard your whistle," he said a little breathlessly, his eyes going straight to Rose.

At the sight of him, Rose let out a little cry and ran to him. He wrapped his arms around her, and the rest of the party discreetly passed them by. Before long they ran into Lily as well, emerging from a stand of bushes. She, too, was dressed to blend into her surroundings, though her dark green dress was more conventional attire than Camellia's.

Their prisoner seemed to sag a little more at each new addition to the group, and by the time they reached the grounds of Willowmere, he looked thoroughly defeated. His demoralization was completed, apparently, by entering the grand front door and taking the long walk through the marble entryway and down the corridor between large portraits of ancestors staring down their aristocrat noses at all who passed by. Fitz and Royce were as much holding him up as holding him prisoner when they brought him into the earl's office.

Oliver, though he must have heard their arrival, did not even look up when they entered the room. He continued to read his paperwork for a moment before he raised his head, his gaze coolly contemptuous.

"This is the fellow who has been terrorizing my cousins?" he asked finally.

"Yes. We caught him attacking Miss Bascombe and Miss Rose."

"It was 'er as 'it me," the man protested, gesturing toward Mary and reaching up to touch the sore spot on his scalp where she had smashed the gun into him.

"After you grabbed Rose and knocked Mary down." Royce's voice was cold as iron. "I think you should take him down to the cellar, Stewkesbury, out of sight of the ladies. We'll get our answers there."

"No! No!" The man looked around frantically for an ally. "I didn't do nothin'. I don't know nothin'. "

"While I am sure that is in general true," the earl said, rising to his feet, "in this instance, I believe you have information of value to me." He turned toward Royce. "However, I see no need for beating the information out of the man. It looks as though you've done enough of that already."

"That was just to subdue him," Royce explained. "I haven't even started to find out why he wanted to hurt Mary and her sisters."

"I din't!" the attacker cried out. "I din't hurt any of 'em. Least, not till they started 'ittin' me. And it weren't all of 'em."

"No?" Stewkesbury asked silkily. "Which one were you supposed to hurt?"

The man stared at him, making a little choked noise. "None of 'em. None. I wouldn't a ever 'urt any of 'em. Please, just let me go, and I promise I'll not do anythin' else. I'll go back to London, I will, and I'll never set foot out of it again." These last words were uttered with such embittered conviction that Mary felt sure they were true.

"Oh, I don't think there's any possibility of letting you

go," Stewkesbury told him. "You are going to gaol. The question will be, I think, what you are charged with. There is kidnapping, attempted murder—"

"No! No! I never meant to murder anybody!" he wailed.

"Or lesser things such as trespass and assault," Oliver offered. "What I tell the magistrate would depend, of course, on how much you are willing to tell me."

"Tell you? I'll tell you anything you want. Wot do you want to know?"

"Who hired you, for one thing?"

The man stared at him. "'Ow'd you know 'e 'ired me?"

"Yes," Camellia agreed. "How did you know someone hired him?"

"Looking at this chap, do you honestly believe *he* came up with the idea of kidnapping anyone?" Turning back to the assailant, he said, "All right, suppose you tell me your name."

"Jamie, sir, Jamie Randall."

"You were hired in London?"

He nodded. "'E come to me, told me to follow them girls."

"He told you to take one of them?"

"The black-'aired one, 'e said, the beauty."

"Why her?"

Randall shook his head. "'E don't tell me things like that. 'E just says, 'Do it.' "

"So you tried in London?"

"I followed 'em to see wot they looked like. I was goin' to come get 'er later, only there wasn't a chance. So I 'ad to follow when they left."

"And who was it who hired you?"

"I don't know."

"Come, Randall, surely you don't expect me to believe that."

"It's the truth! 'E never told me 'is name. He just tells me wot to do."

"What do you call him?"

"Sir."

The man's response brought a twitch to Stewkesbury's lips, but he quickly controlled it. The earl went at it from several more angles, but the answer always returned the same—Jamie Randall did not know the name of the man who had hired him.

"What did he look like?" Royce asked

Randall gazed at him blankly. "I dunno. Older'n me. Um, not tall." He held up a hand to his arm, indicating someone who came up to his own shoulder.

"His hair?"

"Brownish—and turnin' gray, like. Not white."

Mary's stomach quivered uneasily. Everything Randall had said could describe Cosmo Glass. "What about his speech?" she asked. "How did he talk? Like you or these gentlemen, or more like us?"

The man gaped at her for a moment, then said, "I dunno—sort of like them." He gestured toward Fitz and his brothers.

Mary sagged with relief. Then it wasn't Cosmo, whose speech was more strongly American than that of the Bascombe sisters. She looked across at Royce and saw the question in his eyes, and she shook her head slightly.

Under further questioning, Randall admitted that they had indeed camped out in the ruins on Beacon Hill, though he had found it an eerie place and was certain he had heard ghostly sounds at night.

"'E watched all the time, 'e did, with that little viewing thing. And then 'e would send me out."

"Did he never leave the place himself?" Royce asked.

Randall shrugged. "Sometimes 'e'd go to meet someone. Never told me 'oo," he went on, anticipating Royce's next question.

"Was it someone in the house?" Stewkesbury asked sharply. When the other man only shook his head dumbly, he said, "What about the case? Did you see him bring a leather satchel back to your camp? Or did you steal that?"

"I never stole nothin'. 'E 'ad the thing with 'im one day when 'e come back. Seemed right pleased at first, but then 'e said something 'bout 'ow it wasn't enough or something like that."

"What did he do with the papers inside the case?" Royce asked.

"Folded 'em up and stuck 'em inside 'is jacket."

"He never said why he wanted them?" Mary asked, and the man shook his head.

"'E never told me nothin'."

This statement seemed to be the man's most common refrain. The earl continued to question him, but it soon became clear that they had learned all they could from him. Finally, with a shrug, the earl turned him over to the servants and told them to take him to the magistrate.

After he left, they looked at each other.

"Well," Stewkesbury said at last. "We may not have learned much, but at last we have captured your assailant."

"But what will happen with this man who hired Randall?" Mary asked. "Rose is still in danger, isn't she?"

"I don't think he is likely to try the job himself," Royce said. "He did that once and failed. Everyone agrees that he isn't large, and I think he realizes he's not up to the task."

"The odds are he would try to hire someone else,"

Stewkesbury agreed. "He must be from London; that's where he hired this chap. I would think it would be an entirely different matter to find a ruffian to abduct someone here."

"But he already has another person helping him," Camellia put in. "At least, that's what it sounded like to me. Randall said he didn't break in here to take the case."

Stewkesbury's face darkened. "I cannot imagine any of our people betraying us like that." He glanced toward Fitz and Royce. "Can either of you?"

Royce shrugged. "I wouldn't have thought it, but money is a powerful persuader."

"The footmen have been with me for years. Most of them are from around here."

"Why do you think it's one of the men?" Mary asked. "It seems more likely to me that it's a maid." When the men looked at her in surprise, she went on, "Whoever took my case went unnoticed. The footmen are upstairs occasionally, but it is the women who are in and out of the bedchambers all the time. No one would think anything of seeing a maid carrying something out of my room."

"You think it's Prue?" Rose asked in shocked tones. "Or Junie?"

"No, not really. I would not have thought either of them would do anything to hurt us or the earl. I just think we should not rule them out."

"You're right." Oliver nodded. "We must consider everything. It's possible the man broke in himself. It's not unlikely that thievery is his usual occupation."

"I think we can assume things should be calm now, at least for the next few days," Royce said.

"Agreed," Oliver said. "We cannot, of course, relax our guard. But my guess is he has quit, or else he'll go back to London to hire another ruffian."

"Good." Royce gave a short nod. "Then I shall go to Iverley tomorrow."

"Iverley!" Mary's heart sank, and it was all she could do not to protest.

"You're leaving?" Lily asked in a woebegone voice, expressing what Mary would not allow herself to say. "But what about Lady Sabrina's ball? I was counting on you to ask me to dance so I won't be a wallflower."

Royce laughed. "I sincerely doubt that you will have any lack of partners. However, I promise you that I will be back before the ball. So each of you ladies must save me a waltz."

Mary glanced over at the earl. His face, as always, was inscrutable. But Fitz did not look surprised by Royce's sudden decision. They already knew, Mary thought. Royce had told them he was leaving, but he hadn't bothered to inform her.

Determined not to let him see that she was hurt, Mary said briskly, "I wish you a pleasant journey, Sir Royce. If the rest of you will excuse me, I believe I will go upstairs now. It has been a rather tiring day."

Everyone agreed and began moving toward the door. Mary was careful not to glance at Royce as she made her way out of the room. Positioning herself between Lily and Camellia, she strode along the hall and up the stairs, never looking back.

Though Mary tried her best to pretend that she did not notice it, she found Willowmere quite empty without Royce. She told herself she might as well become accustomed to it. After all, it would be her lot in life once Royce gave up and accepted that she was not going to marry him. Better to get used to it now, when there was something going on—Willowmere was all abuzz with the news that Rose was engaged to Sam Treadwell.

"Sam asked me again last night, ever so sweetly," Rose told her sisters the next day as they clustered about her in her bedroom. "He said I was the only one who mattered, and that he had asked Cousin Oliver for my hand only because he wanted to make sure he did everything absolutely right. I couldn't stay mad at him. I told him yes. Look, he got me a ring. He says he's had it for months."

"What did Stewkesbury say to him? Did he interrogate him about his prospects and whether he could take care of you?" Lily asked.

"Yes! But Sam apparently convinced Stewkesbury that he could support me even if his father cast him off for marrying against his wishes—though he said that he could see that Stewkesbury was excessively annoyed at that thought! Sam has saved his money for years, and he wants to start a drayage company. Coal has been discovered farther west, and he intends to haul it out. The earl seemed quite impressed with his steadiness and business sense. And—you will not believe this—Cousin Oliver is even giving me a dowry!"

"A dowry? How medieval," exclaimed Camellia.

"Apparently not in the circles in which we now live. Cousin Oliver explained it to me himself. He said it was only fair, as our grandfather had cut Mama out of his will. The banns will be read this Sunday and next, and after that we can be married. It's terribly hasty, I know, and I shall have to wear one of the dresses Cousin Charlotte had made for us. But Sam wants to get back to the United States. And I can't wait to marry him!"

"Who can blame you?" Mary asked, going to her sister and putting her arm around her.

"But how can you leave us?" Lily wailed. "We'll miss you so much! Do you really want to go back?"

"Yes. Oh yes, I do. I miss home—the way it looks, the

way it feels. Everything is so formal here; I hate having all the servants hovering around, doing everything for me."

"Oh!" Lily threw up her arms and dropped back onto the bed. "I think it's absolutely wonderful! All the clothes and the parties we're going to have." She looked around at her sisters. "All right, I know. I am the only one."

"No, I like it here, too," Camellia said, surprising all of them. "I mean, the people are awfully odd sometimes, and I hate our lessons with Miss Dalrymple. But those will end eventually. I love riding; I love the horses. Vivian wants me to teach her how to shoot, and Fitz has said we're going to set up targets. I can practice with him. He says he'll teach me archery as well. And croquet." She shrugged. "I like Fitz and Charlotte and Royce and Vivian. I think I even like Cousin Oliver."

Mary nodded. She liked it here too, more than she had ever expected to—if only there weren't that odd, empty feeling when Royce was not around. She smiled and reached out to hug Rose. "We will miss you, but we want you to be happy."

"I will be. I promise you I will be."

"You must write us at least once a week and tell us everything," Lily said, jumping off the bed and going to put her arms around her sisters.

Camellia joined them, and for a long moment they clung together, poignantly aware of the great change that loomed before them. Then, with a little sniffle here and there, they broke apart, and the conversation returned to the question of what they would wear to the wedding.

Only slightly less important than the upcoming nuptials was the prospect of Lady Sabrina's ball three days hence, and the sisters passed many a pleasant hour planning their wardrobes and hairstyles for the first major social event of their lives. The evening gowns Charlotte had brought were far more elegant than any dresses they had ever owned, but Lady Vivian decreed that, while they were perfectly fine for a county assembly or some other such country dance, something more refined was needed for Lady Sabrina's ball.

Therefore, as soon as Vivian had learned of the ball, she had sent a note posthaste to Madame Arceneaux, ordering new ball gowns for the Bascombe sisters. The day before the ball, Vivian arrived at Willowmere followed by two footmen with a trunk.

"I thought it would be a problem coming up with four gowns all white and yet distinctive enough," Vivian told them. "But Madame's taste and ingenuity have won the day."

Prue and Junie took the four ball gowns out of the trunk and laid them across the bed in Mary's room. The gowns themselves were exactly alike—puff-sleeved concoctions of white satin slips over which hung round dresses of Urlings net. Flounces of white Urlings lace festooned the bottoms of the skirts, each point of the festoons anchored by a small cluster of satin roses. The difference among the dresses lay in the color of the satin roses and the ribbons that decorated the short sleeves and ran around the high waists. Blue satin ribbons and roses adorned Rose's dress, while Lily's were pink, Camellia's yellow, and Mary's a delicate lavender. White kid gloves, white satin slippers, and white lace fans decorated with matching ribbons completed the outfits.

"Vivian!" The Bascombe sisters showered their friend with thanks.

Vivian simply smiled and said, "I could not let you make your first public appearance in anything less than an Arceneaux gown."

The following evening, when the girls were dressed, with

their hair done up in curls in the French style, small satin roses of the same color as the trim of their dresses pinned into their hair, the effect of all of them together was both dramatic and sweetly innocent.

As she made her way downstairs with her sisters, Mary knew that she looked her best. She was filled with a jittering anticipation. Royce had been gone for almost four days. He had returned that afternoon, she had heard, but as she had been upstairs in the midst of dressing for the party, she had not seen him. She would never have admitted how badly she wanted to see him, how much she had missed him. How many times a day she had thought about him.

Royce was standing in the entryway chatting with the earl and Fitz when the girls made their way down the stairs. He turned, and his reaction when he spotted Mary was everything she could have hoped for. He took an involuntary step forward, his face suddenly taut, his eyes burning.

"Mary . . ."

She could not hold back a triumphant smile. Perhaps there was hope for them. Maybe if she married Royce, someday his desire for her might turn to love.

Royce bent over her hand, murmuring, "You dazzle the eyes tonight, my Marigold. Every man at the ball will be jealous of me for arriving with you."

"A pretty speech, sir," she retorted. "But we shall see how they feel after they have danced with me."

At the ball, Lady Sabrina greeted them beside her husband. She was coolly beautiful in an ice blue satin gown, pearls looped around her throat and palely glowing in her earlobes. She could have been the goddess of the moon, Mary thought, lovely and unobtainable, the object of any man's desire.

"Darling Mary!" Sabrina greeted her with a smile, but

now Mary could see that it did not reach the woman's eyes. "How lovely you look. I hope you are not too nervous about your first ball. I am sure that you will not stumble or do anything wrong."

"Oh, no, I intend to be too busy having fun to do anything like that," Mary responded easily. "You look very pretty, too. What a lovely dress you're wearing. But where is Lady Vivian? I would have thought she would be here to help greet your guests." Mary had little doubt that Sabrina had purposely excluded Lady Vivian from the receiving line; she would not want the competition of Vivian's dazzling beauty.

"Oh, you know our Vivian." Sabrina smiled noncommittally and passed Mary on to Lord Humphrey. "And Sir Royce," she purred, reaching out to take his hand. "So wonderful to see you again."

"Hello, Lady Sabrina." He gave her a perfunctory bow. "Lovely party." He moved on to shake Lord Humphrey's hand.

Mary danced a cotillion with Royce first, followed by a dance each with the earl and Fitz, so that by the time she was asked out onto the floor by Lady Vivian's stately uncle, her nerves were almost entirely gone, and she was able to get through the steps with only a minor bobble.

She glanced around, happily noting that her sisters all seemed to be dancing and chatting without problem. Even the normally reserved Rose was much more animated tonight, a state due, Mary suspected, to Sam Treadwell's presence by her side. Mary chatted with Charlotte and Lady Vivian, who was absolutely stunning in an emerald silk gown with black lace trim and an elegant little train.

As Mary danced and talked, now and then she glanced around, unable to keep from looking for Royce. Once she saw him dancing with Cousin Charlotte, and another time chatting with an older gentleman she did not know. When next she looked over, she saw him taking the floor with Lady Sabrina.

Mary went still, her insides suddenly chilled. It was a waltz, and she watched, unable to look away, as Royce and Sabrina began to move about the floor. Maddeningly, she could catch only glimpses of their faces. She could not read his expression, but whenever Sabrina's face came into view, she was smiling, her perfect features animated, her blue eyes sparkling. Sabrina was still in love with Royce, Mary realized, and her heart squeezed painfully in her chest.

Mary's fragile hopes earlier this evening seemed quite foolish now. How could she ever hope to compete with this woman? She was Royce's first love, the woman who had turned his heart to stone. All that Mary could ever hope to have was the remainder of the man. Was that enough?

The dance ended, and Mary turned hastily away, not wanting Royce to know that she had been watching him. Fiddling with her fan and straightening her skirt, she did not realize that Royce was walking toward her until he was upon her.

"Oh!" She jumped, startled, when he stopped before her.

"I believe I have this dance." He was not smiling; indeed, his face was sober, almost grim.

"Yes, of course." Mary placed her hand on his arm, wishing she did not have to go out onto the dance floor with him just now. At least it was not a waltz; she would not have to try to keep up a conversation.

To her surprise, however, Royce steered her away from the dance floor. She glanced at him questioningly.

"I have something I want to talk to you about." He guided her through the double doors and into a corridor, then turned and walked to the door at the end of the short hall.

"About what? Have you heard something about the man behind the abduction attempts?"

"What? No. This is something else altogether. It's the reason I went to Iverley."

"Oh?" Mary's curiosity was aroused.

They walked out onto a covered veranda that wrapped around the side and back of Halstead House. He found a dark, secluded corner with a wrought-iron bench and gestured Mary toward the seat.

"Here. Please sit down."

"All right." Mary sat down and looked up at him. He was acting rather peculiarly, stiff and at the same time nervous. She remembered, with a sudden sinking feeling, another time when she had seen him behave this way—the afternoon that he had proposed to her. She started to stand up. "Royce—"

"No." He took her arm and tugged her back down onto the seat. "Please listen to me. I want to do this right this time. The reason I went home was to get something." He went down on one knee on the flagstone before Mary, startling her. "Marigold Bascombe, I am asking you to become my wife."

He reached into his pocket and pulled out a box. Opening it, he held it out to Mary. There, nestled in the satin, lay a deep red ruby ring. Mary took it, holding it up close to look into its red depths.

"It's the Winslow ring, given to all the Winslow brides since 1678. My father gave it to my mother, and now I want to give it to you."

"Why?" Mary asked, watching him.

He sighed. "Mary . . . every time I tell you the reasons,

you get angry. I am trying to do it the right way, to show you—"

"And you think what I want is a ring?" Mary asked, her voice rising.

"No. I mean, well, I don't know whether you want the ring or not." He sounded weary and confused. "But I thought you would understand that I am serious, that I truly want to marry you."

"I understand that. But it is obvious that you don't understand." Mary stood up.

"No." He rose lithely, temper flaring in his eyes. "You're right. I don't understand. When we talk, when we joke, when we do anything, it seems good and right. And when we're in bed together—well, I haven't any words for it. But when I ask you to marry me, you refuse out of hand. I thought it was the way I did it the first time. I was clumsy and stupid and not at all myself. I thought if I went and got the ring, if I gave you the Winslow ring, then I could do it correctly, say the thing that would make you accept."

"I can't!" Tears clogged Mary's voice. "Don't you see? I feel all those things and more. I love you. I can't marry you because I love you, and I can't spend the rest of my life like that, with my heart breaking every day because you don't love me!"

She pushed the ring back into his hand and shoved past him, running back into the house. Royce stood staring after her, the ring cold and glittering in his hand.

Mary darted down the corridor. She had to get out of here. She turned in the direction they'd come, then stopped, unable to enter the ballroom. There was no way she could face everyone now. She wished that she could leave, just run home to Willowmere and cry her heart out. But of course she could not. Her sisters were scattered about, enjoying themselves. It would be wrong to make them leave just because of her own unhappiness.

She would go out into the gardens, she decided. Quickly she walked through the ballroom, looking neither right nor left. She did not want to meet anyone's eye and have to smile or stop to talk. All she wanted was to reach the terrace doors. Once she heard someone call her name, but she did not look around.

The terrace doors were open to admit the cool evening air, and Mary slipped through them. A few couples stood or walked on the terrace, but she ignored them, trotting rapidly to the stairs and down into the garden. She headed toward the fountain—and there, sitting beside the fountain, looking around and impatiently tapping her foot, was Miss Dalrymple.

"Miss Dalrymple." Mary came to a stop, dismayed.

This was the worst possible thing, to have run into her chaperone when all she wanted was to be alone. The woman was staring at her as if she'd seen an apparition, which was most peculiar since they had ridden over in the same carriage. Nor could Mary understand why Miss Dalrymple was sitting out here. She had been so gleeful, even smug, that Lady Sabrina had sent her an invitation of her own—although Mary, with her changed perception of Lady Sabrina, suspected it was done simply to make sure that the Bascombes would have someone to monitor and criticize them throughout the party.

"What are you doing—" Mary began.

"You!" Miss Dalrymple barked, glaring at her. "Why are you here?"

Mary blinked, unsure how to answer.

"That idiot girl! Did she send you? I specifically told her to come herself."

"Who? What are you talking about?"

Miss Dalrymple narrowed her eyes. "Never mind. You will just have to do."

"What?" Mary stumbled as Miss Dalrymple gripped her arm and began to pull her down the path into the garden. "What are you doing? Where are we going?" Mary was beginning to think the woman was losing her mind.

"To find Lily and that boy. I told Rose. I thought she must have told you."

"Told me what?" Mary frowned, her pace picking up as she realized that Lily was in some sort of trouble. "I didn't see any of my sisters."

"Lily went outside with a young man. We can't let her compromise her reputation. It will be a terrible scandal."

"Lily went into the gardens with some man she doesn't know? Really, Miss Dalrymple, are you certain it was Lily you saw?"

"Yes, of course it was. I'm not daft. Nor blind. It's just like her, always full of romantic nonsense."

Mary had to admit that the romantic silliness fit Lily. Still, it seemed peculiar that she would venture into the dark gardens with someone she didn't know. If nothing else, after the scares they'd had the past few weeks—

A chill ran up Mary's spine. She turned and looked at Miss Dalrymple, her steps faltering. Miss Dalrymple gripped her arm so tightly that it hurt as she jerked Mary around the corner of a hedge.

Standing there waiting, holding some sort of cloth in his hands, was Egerton Suttersby.

For an instant, he and Mary stared at each other in amazement. Then his face flushed with fury.

"You! You're the wrong one!" He swung toward Miss Dalrymple. "You fool! You brought me the wrong girl!"

Mary whirled to run, but Miss Dalrymple was still clutching her arm tightly. Miss Dalrymple grabbed Mary with the other hand too and held on.

"What does it matter? She's the one who came out! You said you'd take any of them!"

Miss Dalrymple was stronger than Mary had expected, and that, coupled with sheer surprise, enabled her to hold Mary for a moment. Then Mary let out a loud shriek and kicked her hard in the shins, and Miss Dalrymple let go, crying out in pain. But before Mary could take two steps, Suttersby's arms went tightly around her and his hand clamped over her mouth. Mary kicked backward, twisting and turning frantically. She connected with his leg and heard a sharp oath, but still the man dragged her backward. His hand was tight against her face, but she managed to open her mouth and bite the fleshy pad below his fingers.

Suttersby let out a yelp and jerked his hand away. Mary drew breath and screamed at the top of her lungs. She could feel his grip around her slipping, and she renewed her kicking and struggling.

"Damn it, woman, help me! She's a wildcat!" he roared. He tried to shift his hold on Mary, and his grip loosened slightly.

Mary seized the chance to swing her elbow back as hard as she could, and it connected with the man's midsection. He let out a grunt, followed by a curse as he released her. Mary twisted around to face him.

"It *was* you!" she spat. "All this time, it was you!"

Mary whirled to run, but Miss Dalrymple stood in her way. Mary feinted to one side, then went the other way. Miss Dalrymple followed her feint, but she was able to turn in time to grab Mary's skirt and hang on. Egerton came up behind Mary and dropped the sack he had been holding over her head. He wrapped both his arms around her, pinning her inside the dark sack. Mary could still scream and kick, though, and she did.

"Be quiet!" Egerton roared, knocking her in the head so hard Mary's teeth clacked together and her eyes watered.

Then she heard Royce calling her name. She screamed again, aware now of more sounds—running feet and her name being called. Someone flew by her, knocking into Suttersby and taking him down to the ground.

Released, Mary staggered and fell. Frantically she grasped the edges of the sack and yanked it off over her head. She whirled around to see Royce drag Suttersby to his feet and punch him, sending him reeling back into a hedge. Mary turned and saw Miss Dalrymple going in the opposite direction. Scrambling up, she lifted her skirts and took off after her, but the woman had a large head start and was running with desperation.

Beyond Miss Dalrymple, Mary saw her sisters hurrying toward her, calling her name.

"Get her!" Mary screamed, pointing. "She's part of it! Get her!"

It took her sisters only an instant to understand and respond. They ran straight at Miss Dalrymple. Miss Dalrymple veered onto another path and sped off in a different direction, but Camellia, skirts lifted to her knees, was hot on her trail, with Lily and Rose only a few steps behind.

Gasping for air, Mary stopped and sank to her knees.

"Mary!" Royce ran to her and dropped down beside her, wrapping his arms around her. "Are you all right?" He rained kisses over her head and face.

"Yes. Yes, I'm fine." Mary threw her arms around him and buried her head in his shoulder, breathing in the scent of him, feeling his strength around her, while the shivering inside her subsided. Finally she raised her head. "Suttersby! Where is he?"

"Him? He's not going anywhere." Royce jerked his head toward where the other man lay stretched out inert on the ground.

"Oh. Thank God you came in time. How did you know?"

"I couldn't find you. I wanted to tell you—well, that doesn't matter right now—the point is, your sisters came running up, telling me you had disappeared and they thought you'd been lured into the gardens. So I ran out, looking for you."

"I'm so glad you did." Mary tightened her arms around his neck and stretched up to kiss him.

His mouth fastened on hers, hard and desperate. His arms pressed her so tightly against him she felt she might break. But she wanted him to hold her this way forever.

"Mary! We got her!" Camellia's voice cried. "Oh! Sorry."

Royce let out a curse and raised his head, releasing Mary. With an inward sigh, Mary turned and saw her three sisters standing a few feet away, their faces a blend of curiosity and excitement. Camellia and Rose were on either side of Miss Dalrymple, dragging her with them. Lily brought up the rear, pushing the woman from the back. Miss Dalrymple's hair was askew and falling down on one side, and her cheek was smudged with mud, her skirt torn at the bottom and trailing in the grass.

Royce rose and reached down to help Mary to her feet. At that moment, Fitz and Oliver came striding along the path toward them, followed closely by Sam Treadwell, Charlotte, and Vivian.

"Royce! Mary! What is going on? Sam told me—" The earl stopped and looked beyond them at the form lying on the grass. "Who the devil is that?"

"Your kidnapper," Royce told them tersely. "Along with her." He pointed at Miss Dalrymple.

"I never!" Miss Dalrymple began indignantly. "These

girls are quite mad! Out of control. They don't know what they're talking about."

Royce stilled her with a single murderous glance. "I saw you. That villain was trying to carry Mary off, and *you* were helping him!"

"I knew she was a terrible chaperone," Vivian commented, earning a sharp glance from the earl.

Beyond them, Suttersby groaned and moved his head. Fitz and Oliver crossed the grass and pulled him to his feet. He wobbled unsteadily between them.

"The devil," Oliver said coolly. "He looks worse than the other chap. Really, Royce, you need to control this urge to beat people to a pulp."

"He hurt Mary." Royce's voice was as stony as his face.

"I see. Well, he won't be hurting anyone now." Oliver turned toward the others. "Treadwell, Fitzhugh, let's take this rogue to the magistrate. Go around the side of the house; the last thing we want is everyone seeing this. I'll be right behind you with Miss Dalrymple." He took the woman firmly by the arm and turned toward Vivian, raising a brow. "Lady Vivian? Cousins? If you would be so good as to return to the party . . ."

"Yes, yes, I know. We will go back and act as though nothing exciting has occurred." Vivian linked arms with Charlotte. "Let's see, what excuse shall we give to these gentlemen for leaving the party so abruptly? A digestive problem perhaps?"

Mary's sisters hesitated, looking at Mary uncertainly.

"I'll take care of her," Royce assured them. "Return to the party. I will see Mary home and send the carriage back for you."

"Go ahead." Mary smiled at her sisters. "No need to miss your first ball. Though, Camellia, you might want to pin up that ruffle. It seems to have gotten torn."

Camellia grinned. "I have to say, Miss Dalrymple put up a good fight."

The girls followed the other women back into the house, leaving Mary and Royce alone in the garden. He turned and swept Mary up into his arms and carried her back through the garden, following the path that the men had taken around the side of the house.

Mary giggled. "You don't need to carry me. I can walk. I'm perfectly all right."

"I am carrying you." His voice brooked no opposition, and Mary subsided, happy simply to rest her head on his shoulder.

When he reached their carriage, he placed her inside, telling the driver tersely that Miss Bascombe had twisted her ankle. He climbed inside and took Mary into his arms again, holding her all the way home to Willowmere. Mary did not object.

She did manage a protest when they reached Willowmere and Royce lifted her out of the carriage to carry her into the house. "Really, Royce, this is absurd. I'm not ill."

"Shh. Let me take care of you. I have made a hundred mistakes, and I mean to start making up for them now."

The servants clustered around them with cries of alarm, and Royce sent them scurrying off with a demand for a stiff brandy and Miss Bascombe's maid. He carried her up the stairs and deposited her gently on her bed. Then he stepped out while Prue fussed over Mary, helping her change into her nightgown and brushing out her hair. Mary was relieved when Royce knocked and came back into the room with a glass of brandy and sent the maid off to bed.

"Here, drink this." Royce handed the glass to Mary, who was sitting in bed, pillows stuffed behind her back.

"I'm not in a swoon." Mary raised the snifter anyway and

took a sip. She winced as the fiery liquid ran down her throat and burst in her stomach, then gave a little shiver.

"I am sure you are not, but I hope it will weaken your resistance."

"Are you planning to seduce me?" Mary asked with a sly smile.

"I am planning to propose." He paused, grimacing. "For the fourth time."

Mary giggled and took another sip of the brandy. "I think it's the fifth."

She was already giddy before the liquor hit her. It didn't matter anymore what Royce said; she knew her answer. She had known it when she struggled in Egerton Suttersby's hold, terrified that she might never see Royce again, and had realized how foolish it was to throw away her life with him because she was afraid she might be unhappy. If he did not love her now, she had an entire lifetime to change that. And Mary had never been one who was afraid of a challenge.

Royce smiled. "You are doubtless enjoying my humiliation. You have every right to. I am a fool. I have been a fool for a long time, and the past few weeks, I've been even a greater one than usual. I loved Sabrina years ago—I admit it. It was a young man's passion, and when she threw me over to marry Lord Humphrey, I was furious. I gave up on the idea of love. I tarred all women with the same brush. But I have finally realized how very mistaken I was."

"What do you mean?" Mary set the glass aside on the table and gazed up at him.

"I realized that love is not some idiocy dreamed up by foolishly romantic beings. Or, if it is, then I have succumbed to the idiocy." He brushed his knuckles down Mary's cheek. "I love you. I love you so much more than I ever loved Sabrina that it makes my feelings for her seem laughable. Tonight when I saw her, I felt nothing—not desire, not anger, not even contempt. I felt simply . . . nothing. All I could think about was you and how to ask you to marry me so you would accept. Then, of course, I made an utter mull of that all over again."

"Yes, you did." Mary smiled and took his arm, tugging him down to sit on the bed beside her. Wrapping both her arms around one of his, she leaned her head on his shoulder.

"All of my excuses were drivel," he went on, brushing her hair back behind her ear, "silly attempts to hide the truth from myself. The fact is, I asked you to marry me because I love you. I want to spend the rest of my life with you. When I heard you scream tonight, when I thought I might lose you, I could not bear it."

"Royce." Her eyes filled with tears. "Oh, Royce . . ."

He turned to face her, taking her hand. "Let me do this again, properly. Marigold Bascombe, I love you more than life itself. Will you do me the honor of becoming my wife?"

"Yes." She flung herself into his arms, wrapping her arms around his neck and kissing his face all over. "Oh, yes. I will marry you. A thousand times over, I will marry you."

"I think once will be sufficient." He took her chin between his thumb and forefinger, holding her still as he looked into her eyes. "I intend to take full advantage of the one time."

He leaned forward and kissed her. The familiar heat swept up between them, and he wrapped his arms around her, pulling her to him. He kissed her again and again until finally, with an effort, he pulled away, standing up.

"I should go."

"Why?" Mary smiled at him and lay back on her bed, her arms stretched provocatively over her head, her breasts thrusting up against the thin cloth of her nightgown. "No one else is here. It will be hours before they're back."

He stood looking down at her. Mary's fingers went to the first tie of her nightgown and undid it, her eyes steadily on his. Her fingers slid down to the next tie.

"You vixen." A slow, sensuous smile curved his lips. "I can tell you're going to be a terrible influence." He leaned over her, bracing himself with his hands on either side of her.

"I know." Mary raised her arms, and he sank onto the bed, his lips lowering to hers.

"My beautiful hoyden," he murmured. "My love."

Epilogue

Mary slipped her hand into Royce's beneath the table. He glanced at her, smiling, and laced his fingers through hers. They were at the breakfast table the next morning, and the seating arrangements there were always informal. Oliver, of course, sat at the head, but the rest of them were scattered up and down the table in random order. Even Charlotte had risen early, and Sam Treadwell had walked up from the village inn where he was staying, as he had been doing every day for the past week.

Sam and Rose were seated across from Mary and Royce, and it occurred to Mary that she and Royce must appear a mirror image of the other couple. She had been receiving curious glances from everyone all morning, and she knew that they had seen the difference in her and Royce. Indeed, how could they not?

Until now, everyone had been involved in eating, and any conversation had been restricted to polite small talk. But now, her hunger somewhat sated, Mary was eager to hear everything that had happened.

"I don't understand," Mary began, addressing Rose. "How did you know I was in trouble last night?"

"I couldn't find you. You see, Miss Dalrymple had come

to me and told me she needed my help. She said Lily had gone into the gardens with a young man and her reputation would be ruined."

Lily let out a snort.

"I thought it was most peculiar." Rose smiled at her youngest sister. "It didn't occur to me that Miss Dalrymple was trying to harm me, but I thought someone had tricked her. I wanted to discuss it with you, so I told her that I would meet her outside, but I had to get my shawl because of the chill. I couldn't find you, so I told Sam. We couldn't find you anywhere. Then Lily ran up to us—"

"She had locked me in a room!" Lily jumped in. "Can you imagine? A little tiny thing, hardly bigger than a wardrobe. Miss Dalrymple gave me a note from the earl, or so it said, and he wanted me to meet him in this room. I thought it was terribly peculiar. But I was curious."

"Of course." Mary grinned.

Lily made a face. "So as soon as I stepped into the room, someone shoved me in the back and closed the door and locked it. I got up and started banging on it right away, and finally someone heard me and let me out. Then I saw Rose."

"Obviously something was terribly wrong—though I still assumed someone had tricked Miss Dalrymple," Rose continued. "Sam went to find Cousin Oliver, and I found Royce, and . . . well, you know what happened after that."

"What I don't understand is why she did it," Fitz said. "She must have known that she was risking not only this job but her very future."

"Money." Oliver shrugged. "Besides, she thought she wouldn't get caught. All the things he asked her to do, at least up until this last, were secret—putting laudanum in your soup at the inn, stealing the case, staying in sick one day in the hope that you lot would take advantage of the freedom to go wandering. She believed that if she did them well, she wouldn't get found out. Even last night, she probably hoped to pretend that she had been duped as well."

"She arranged for us to go down to the tarn that day when he tried to take Rose?" Camellia asked.

"She gave you the opportunity. I feel sure Suttersby reasoned that four spirited girls, released from their arduous lessons, would go exploring somewhere. They set up the situation and watched." The earl was silent for a moment, toying with his fork. Then, his eyes on his finger as it traced the whorls on the handle of the fork, he said conversationally, "Mr. Suttersby mentioned another participant. I don't suppose you've heard of him—Cosmo Glass." He raised his head and looked at Mary and Royce.

The Bascombes drew in their breaths sharply. Charlotte and Fitz looked puzzled.

"You might have told me, Royce," Oliver commented.

Royce shrugged. "I would have if it had seemed pertinent. But since Randall said his employer had an English accent, we assumed it was not Cosmo. We didn't realize that Mr. Suttersby, who obviously came from England originally, was involved."

"I'm sorry," Mary told Oliver penitently. "It was my fault. Royce didn't even know until the other day. I-I was afraid of what you would think of us."

"But he is only your stepfather. Why would I think anything bad about you? One can hardly be held responsible for one's relatives—think what trouble we would be in if we had to answer for Aunt Euphronia. One's stepfather is no relation at all."

"No. I can see now that I should have told you. But we thought we could handle Cosmo, if it was him, and we wouldn't have to expose you to more scandal."

"Well, reprehensible as this Cosmo chap seems to be, we

shan't have to worry about him. Mr. Suttersby was quite bitter about his taking off and leaving him in the lurch once things got dangerous."

Camellia laughed. "That sounds like Cosmo."

"I don't understand. Who is Cosmo Glass?" Charlotte asked, and the others laughed.

After Cosmo had been explained to Charlotte, Camellia picked up the questioning. "Here's what I don't understand—why did Suttersby do it? I mean, Rose is beautiful and all that, but doesn't it seem strange to chase her clear across the ocean?" She glanced at Sam, then turned beet red, and everyone broke into laughter again.

"You know what I mean," Camellia protested. "Sam and Rose love each other; he knew that she returned the feeling. But she despised Mr. Suttersby. Rose would hardly talk to him when she lived in the same town. And he was going to kidnap her, not ask for her hand!"

"I don't know that one can really understand an obsession," Oliver commented.

"No, but there was something more," Mary said. "When Miss Dalrymple dragged me down there, he told her she'd gotten the wrong one, and she said that any of us would do, or something like that. And while he was disgruntled about it, he was going to take me instead. Now, would you do that if you were obsessed with Rose?"

Royce shook his head. "There's also the matter of the satchel. According to our friend Randall, he wanted the papers in it. But he also indicated that they weren't enough."

"Enough for what?" Lily asked, and Royce shrugged.

"Excuse me, but what was in the case he stole?" Sam asked.

"Not much," Mary told him. "Some old bill of sale and a deed."

"A deed? To what?" Sam asked. "Perhaps it's valuable

land, and Suttersby wanted it. If he forced Rose to marry him, he could have control of her property."

"It was only a small farm in Schuylkill County," Mary told him. "We lived there for a while, but it wasn't—"

"Schuylkill County!" Sam leaned forward. "That's it! There's coal there."

Mary nodded. "I remember Papa saying that. He wished he could mine it, but it's not feasible. It's too far to haul the coal."

"But not any longer," Sam said excitedly. "They're building a canal." He turned to Rose. "Don't you remember me saying that I want to start a drayage company out west? That's where I plan to go. I'm going to haul coal from the mines to the canal. Then it can be shipped down the canal to Philadelphia."

"Then it makes sense!" Mary turned to Royce. "He could have Rose and money."

Royce nodded. "If he was married to Rose, no one would question his running the thing for all four of you."

"We found the deed on him," Oliver said. "I put it in the safe when I got home last night. Sam, since you are moving there, perhaps you ought to see what you can do with that piece of property. It might provide a nice investment for Rose and her sisters."

"Of course. I don't know much about coal mining, but we could lease it to someone who does. Or maybe I'll have to figure out how to run a coal mine."

Rose grinned. "Or maybe *I* will."

There was the sound of footsteps in the hall, and a moment later, Lady Vivian swept into the room. She was wearing a green velvet riding habit and, if possible, looked even more lovely in it than she had in the elegant gown she had worn last night.

"All I need," the earl muttered.

"I had to come hear exactly what happened last night," Vivian announced, ignoring Stewkesbury. "I didn't even have breakfast." She tossed them all a glittering smile. "Thank heavens you're still eating."

"Please, help yourself," Stewkesbury said as she strode over to the sideboard to pick up a plate.

Lady Vivian tossed a grin over her shoulder. "I had forgotten how foul-tempered you are in the morning, Oliver. Well, I'm glad that Dalrymple woman is gone. She was a dull sort." Vivian made her way down the sideboard, filling her plate. "Though dragging her off bodily did seem a bit extreme, don't you think?"

"Mmm. Perhaps you should remember it next time you set out to annoy me."

Vivian laughed, a hearty, infectious sound that brought a smile to everyone's lips. "Perhaps I will." She brought her plate to the table. "Now . . . tell me the whole of it," she said, sitting down and digging in.

Stewkesbury sighed. "It's not a tale I wish known, my lady."

Vivian rolled her eyes. "As if I would tell anyone."

"'Tis true. At least you're not a chatterbox. All right."

Succinctly Oliver related the tale of Miss Dalrymple's deception and Mr. Suttersby's plan to abduct Rose, his story supplemented by a number of additions from the others. Vivian listened, rapt—though she managed to put away a healthy amount of food as she absorbed the story. When he had finished, she sipped her tea, looking thoughtful.

"I think I can help you," she said at last, setting the cup down in its saucer.

Stewkesbury looked at her warily. "In what way?"

"Oh, don't look at me so. I don't mean with any of this skulduggery. I am sure you will manage to hush it all up excessively well. I'm talking about the girls and their Season." She glanced over at Charlotte. "I am certain you'll agree with me about this, Charlotte." She swiveled back to Oliver. "You don't need a governess as a chaperone. What they need is someone who has been in the beau monde, not just a woman who has worked for those who are. You can hire tutors for dancing or even for music and painting, if you are really desirous of their being well turned-out. But for teaching them how to converse, how to act, how to handle a social situation, you need an actual lady."

"Why do I have the feeling you have just the lady in mind?" Stewkesbury crossed his arms and looked at her.

"Because you are an intelligent man. I do. She is from a very respectable family, the widow of Major Bruce Hawthorne."

"Never heard of him." Oliver shook his head.

"Even so, he existed. He was the grandson of some earl or other, but never flush in the pocket, I'm afraid. He died, leaving Mrs. Hawthorne penniless. She is entirely dependent upon her relatives, and I am sure she would be glad of the opportunity."

The earl's eyes slid over to his cousins. "Do you think she could . . . manage this situation?"

"Of course." Vivan smiled at the Bascombe sisters. "You girls will find her delightful. She will not allow you to stumble into any social pitfalls, but neither will she browbeat you." She turned back to Stewkesbury. "And you will find her demure and practical. Her reputation has always been of the best. She is the perfect chaperone."

Stewkesbury hesitated for a moment, then shrugged. "All right. Write her and see if she would be amenable to taking charge of them. How soon could she come? I can send Fitz to escort her."

Vivian lifted an eyebrow.

The earl sighed. "Very well. Will you write to her, *please*?"

"Of course."

"No 'please' for me?" Fitz asked.

Oliver rolled his eyes. "You must be joking. Now that all the excitement's over, you'll be bored and into some sort of mischief if you don't have something to do. Besides, it's exactly the sort of thing you do well—charm middle-aged ladies." He turned toward Vivian. "She is not very old, is she?"

"Oh, no, not *very* old," Vivian replied. Mary saw a flash of something like amusement in Vivian's eyes before she lowered them to her plate.

"Before we leave," Royce said, standing up, "I have an announcement to make." He turned and looked down at Mary. "Miss Bascombe has done me the honor of agreeing to become my wife."

"About time," Fitz commented, and the girls broke into cries of delight.

After that, there was much hugging and laughing, even a few tears before gradually everyone began to disperse. Royce and Mary drifted out onto the terrace and stood looking out over the gardens.

"Well," he said. "We have the day to ourselves now that you are without anyone to give you lessons all day long."

"And since there is no one hunting us, we can do whatever we want," Mary agreed. "We could go riding or walking."

"Perhaps we might visit the summerhouse."

Mary chuckled at the glint in his eyes. "Maybe we'll do just that."

Royce put his arms around her and bent his head, resting his forehead against hers. "Perhaps we should get a special license and not wait for the banns to be read."

"Hush. We will wait until after Rose is married. She is going to have her special day first. You and I . . . will manage."

"I am sure we will." He kissed her forehead. "God, I love you." He bent and kissed her lips gently. As he shifted his mouth to kiss her again, she heard him murmur, "I cannot live without you."

Mary smiled and gave herself up to his kiss. She had come home at last.

Turn the page
for a special look
at the next sparkling Willowmere romance
from
Candace Camp

A Gentleman Always Remembers

Coming next month from Pocket Books

Chapter 1

In a few days she would be gone. Eve Hawthorne could almost taste freedom.

No more lectures from a stepmother only eight years older than herself. No more tight-lipped frowns at a remark deemed too frivolous. No more having to endure the heavy-handed attempts at matchmaking with whatever widower or bachelor her stepmother hoped might be willing to take Eve off their hands.

When Eve's husband died two years ago, he had left her, at twenty-six years of age, not only alone but nearly penniless. The Hawthornes had never been renowned for their ability to keep money in their pockets, and Bruce, the youngest son of a middle son of an earl, had had no income beyond his military commission, which had made it even more difficult for him to stay within his means. Eve used what little money Major Hawthorne had left her to pay off his debts, and even then she had been forced to sell their furniture and many of their belongings in order to satisfy his creditors. She had had no recourse but to return to her father's home to live.

After almost eight years of marriage and managing her own life and household, it would have been hard in any case to have once more become a dependent child, but since Eve's father had remarried several years earlier, Eve had found herself living not only on the Reverend Childe's charity but on that of her stepmother as well. It had not been a welcome situation for either woman.

Eve faced her stepmother now, determined to keep a pleasant smile on her face. Surely these last few days they could manage to get along without their usual subtle struggle.

"It is a beautiful day, Imogene," Eve observed. "Quite pleasant and warm for September. And Julian has finished all his lessons. Did he tell you how well he did in Latin?"

Eve realized as soon as she said it that her words had been a mistake. Much as Imogene Childe reveled in her son's intelligence and education, it was always a sore spot with her that she herself had not received the sort of classical education that Eve had had at the hands of the Reverend Childe. She did not like to be reminded that Eve helped her father teach Julian, whereas Imogene, his own mother, could not.

"I am aware of Julian's achievement in the subject," Imogene responded, her mouth pruning up. "But he has not made the progress he has by ignoring his studies and running off to play."

Eve knew better than to advance the argument that her half brother needed some time to play just as he did to study. Instead, she said, "But Julian will not be playing; we will be observing nature. The animals . . . the plants . . . the ways in which autumn is making changes in them. Besides, it is important for Julian to observe the beauty and wonder of the world that God has made for us, is it not?"

She smiled at Imogene sweetly, knowing that the pious woman would have more difficulty combating this argument.

But it was Julian himself who clinched it. "Please, Mother?" he asked, looking his most angelic. "Auntie Eve will be here only a few more days, and then she and I can't do this anymore."

The thought of her stepdaughter's imminent departure brightened Imogene's expression, and, with a sigh, she relented. "Very well, you may go with your aunt, Julian." She turned her gaze to Eve. "But pray, do not bring him home muddy again or with grass stains all over his clean shirt."

"We shall do our very best to stay clean," Eve promised her. She no longer tried to make her stepmother understand that one could not expect a young boy to remain perfectly tidy unless he did nothing but sit in a chair all day.

Mrs. Childe nodded, the tight corkscrew curls on either side of her face bouncing. "You had best remember, Eve, that the Earl of Stewkesbury is not looking for someone who will let his cousins run wild. He wants a woman who is a model of decorum. Those girls' reputations will depend on what you do as their chaperone. It is a heavy responsibility, and I hope the earl will not regret entrusting it to someone as young and frivolous in attitude as you."

Eve managed to retain her smile, though it was more a grimace than an expression of humor or goodwill at this point. "I will keep that in mind, ma'am, I promise you."

After picking up her long-brimmed bonnet and tying it on, Eve followed her half brother out of the house and across the yard, cutting through the churchyard and cemetery to the beckoning field beyond. She smiled to herself as she watched Julian race ahead, then squat to observe some insect making its way through the grass.

The thought of saying good-bye to Julian was the only thing that tugged at her heart, marring somewhat the joy of leaving this house. Her half brother had made the past two years bearable, easing her grief over Bruce with his warm affection. Even his mother's rigid rules and sanctimonious airs had seemed less bothersome when Julian slipped his small hand in hers and smiled at her or tilted his head to the side like a curious sparrow as he asked her a question. Eve's marriage had been childless, which had long been a sorrow to her, but Julian's presence in her life had helped fill that hole in her heart.

It would pain her to leave him, but in only a couple of years Julian would be sent off to Eton as his father had been before him, and then Eve would be left in the house with only the company of her studious, abstracted father and her carping stepmother. It was a prospect to make one's blood run cold.

That was why Eve had jumped at the opportunity to chaperone Lord Stewkesbury's American cousins. Lady Vivian Carlyle, Eve's friend since childhood, was also close to the Talbot family, headed by the Earl of Stewkesbury. Lady Vivian had written Eve recently to say that the earl was in desperate need of a chaperone for his young cousins who had arrived in London from the United States. It seemed that the chaperone Stewkesbury had first hired to help the young women enter English society had proved entirely unsuitable. What was needed, Vivian had written, was a woman of good family who could act as an older sister or young aunt to the girls, taking them under her wing and instructing them— as much by example as teaching—in the things they would need to know to make their way successfully through a London Season. Vivian had thought immediately of Eve and wanted to know if she would be interested in traveling to Willowmere, the country seat of the Talbot family, and assume the position of chaperone.

Eve had written back to assure her friend that she would indeed welcome the opportunity to chaperone the American girls. In reply, she had received a letter from the earl himself, offering her a generous stipend for her troubles and stating that he would send a carriage to bring her to

Willowmere—a gesture Eve found most gracious, though it was doubtless inspired more by the fact that she was a friend of Lady Vivian than by any concern for her own person.

The earl had given her two weeks in which to pack and prepare for her journey, which meant that the carriage was scheduled to arrive anytime in the next two or three days. She had only these last few days to enjoy her half brother's company, and she intended to take full advantage of them. So she put all of her stepmother's injunctions out of her mind and followed the boy through the field and down to the brook.

They paused to watch the antics of a red squirrel and later to investigate the remains of a bird's nest that had fallen from a tree. Julian had a healthy curiosity about all things in nature, both flora and fauna, and Eve did her best to read enough to keep up with his questions. She had never thought to learn so much about butterflies, or pheasants and robins, or birches, beeches, and oak trees as she had the last two years, but she had enjoyed exploring such topics—though she could not deny the little ache in her heart when she thought of how it would be if she had children of her own with whom to share these wonders.

Before long they reached the brook that lay east of town and followed it to a large rock perfectly arranged for sitting and watching the shallow stream as it burbled its way over the rocks. Eve took off her bonnet and gloves and set them aside, followed by her walking boots and stockings. She kilted up her skirt and waded into the water after Julian, bending down to look at the little fish arrowing past their feet or chasing after a frog as it bounded from rock to rock.

Imogene's strictures were ignored as they laughed and darted about. Julian had more than one streak of mud upon his shirt, and the bottoms of his trousers had been liberally splashed with water. His hands were grubby and his cheeks red, his eyes sparkling with pleasure. Eve, looking at him, wanted to grab him and squeeze him tight, but she was wise enough not to do so.

She was standing in the brook when she heard the sound of a horse's hooves, and realized that they must have drawn closer to the road than she had thought. She turned to climb up the bank, when a small snake brushed her foot as it slithered by her. Eve let out a shriek, forgetting all about the road and the horse, and Julian fell into a fit of laughter.

"Oh, hush, Jules!" she told him crossly, then had to chuckle herself. She was sure she must have presented quite a sight, jumping straight up into the air as if she had been shot. "'Twasn't funny."

"Yes, it was," the boy protested. "*You're* laughing."

"He has you there," a voice said from behind them.

Eve whirled around. There, on the small wooden bridge that crossed the stream, stood an elegant black stallion, and on its back was a man with hair as black as the steed's. They were both, man and horse, astoundingly handsome.

She felt as if the air had been punched out of her, and she could only stare at the man, bereft of words. The rider swept off his hat and bowed to her, and his hair glimmered as black as a raven's wing in the sunlight. His eyes were a bright, piercing blue and ringed by thick black lashes as straight and dark as the eyebrows that slashed across his face above them. Even on horseback, it was obvious that he was tall, his shoulders wide in his well-cut blue jacket. A dimple popped into his cheek as he grinned down at her, showing even white teeth.

"Hullo," Julian called pleasantly when Eve did not speak, and he splashed out of the water and up the bank toward the man.

The stranger swung off his mount in a smooth motion and led his horse off the bridge and down toward them. "I had not hoped to find a naiad on my travels today," he said to Eve, and his bright eyes swept appreciatively down her form.

Eve was suddenly, blushingly, aware of how she must have looked. Her dress was hiked up, exposing all of her legs below her knees, and her bonnet was off, her hair coming loose from its pins and straggling down in several places, her face flushed with exercise and heat.

"What's a naiad?" Julian asked.

"A water nymph," the man explained.

"And something *I* am not." Blushing furiously, Eve jerked her skirts down and shook them into place. There was little she could do about her bare feet or her hatless state, of course, for her shoes and bonnet lay several yards behind them on the rock. Her hands went to her hair, trying to tuck some of the stray strands into place.

"That is always what demigoddesses claim," the man went on easily, still smiling as he came up to them.

Up close, Eve could see the tiny lines that radiated from the corners of his eyes and the dark shadow of approaching beard along his jaw. If anything, such imperfections only served to make him even more handsome. Looking at him set up a jangling of nerves in Eve's stomach, and the afternoon seemed suddenly warmer and more airless than it had moments before.

"Don't be absurd." Eve tried for a tart tone, but she could not keep from smiling a little. There was simply something engaging about the man's grin, so easy and friendly.

"What else am I to think?" He arched a brow, his blue eyes dancing. "Coming upon such a lovely creature, the water running around her, the sun striking gold from her hair. Even the animals yearn to be close to you."

"Like the snake!" Julian giggled.

"Exactly." The stranger nodded at the boy gravely. He turned back to Eve. "There. Even a child can see it. Though, of course"—he tilted his head considering—"one would think a nymph would be more at ease with the creatures of the fields and brooks than to scream at the sight of a snake."

"I did not scream," Eve protested. "And it wasn't the sight of it, it was the *feel*." She gave an expressive shudder, and both Julian and the stranger chuckled.

Eve was aware she should not be talking with such ease to a complete stranger. Imogene would doubtless have a fit of the vapors if she knew. But Eve was not feeling cautious today. For the past two years she had done her best to live by her stepmother's rules, and soon she would have to be prim and proper, befitting the chaperone of young women. Surely she could steal this day, this moment for herself. She could even, perhaps, flirt a little with an attractive stranger.

"It occurs to me that I should stay and guard you from such dangers." The dimple flashed again as his lips curved into a smile. "Indeed, I should probably escort you home."

"'Tis most kind of you, sir, but I cannot trouble you. You were clearly on your way somewhere."

He shrugged. "That can wait. It isn't every day that a man can rescue a nymph, or even a maiden, from dangerous creatures."

Eve raised a skeptical brow. "I already have a champion." She glanced toward her brother, who had already tired of their conversation and was digging into the ground with a stick.

"I can see that." The stranger's eyes followed hers to Julian. "I can scarcely compete." He turned back to her. "But there may be other times when you are out without your champion. I should be happy to offer you my services as an escort."

"You are most kind," Eve responded demurely, casting a twinkling look up at him through her lashes. It had been a long time since she had flirted with a handsome man. Had she forgotten how pleasurable it was? Or was it this man who made it pleasurable? "Perhaps, if you are in the village for a time, we might chance to meet again."

"I can make sure that I am here for a time." For a moment the laughter was gone from his eyes, replaced by a warmth that Eve felt all the way down to her toes. "If you would but tell me where I might chance upon you taking a stroll?"

Eve let out a little laugh. "Ah, but that would make it far too easy, would it not?"

He moved closer, so that she had to tilt her head back to look up at him. "I do not think that you are making it at all easy for me." His voice lowered. "Surely a naiad should pay a token, should she not, for getting caught by a mortal?"

Her breath caught in her throat. "A token?"

"Yes. A price. A forfeit. They always do so in stories—grant a wish or give a present. . . ."

"I am sure that I have no gift here." Eve knew she should back up, should cease her flirting. But something held her there; she could not look away from his bright eyes, could not suppress the frisson of anticipation running up her spine.

"Ah, that is where you are wrong, my nymph."

He bent and kissed her.

His lips were firm and warm, the kiss brief. And at his touch, everything in Eve seemed to flame into life. She was suddenly, tinglingly, aware of everything—the sun on her back, the breeze that lifted the loose strands of her hair, the scent of the grass from the meadow, all mingling in a heady brew with the sensations, sudden and intense, spreading through her body.

He lifted his head, and for a long moment all she could do was stare up at him, her mouth slightly open in a soft O of astonishment, her eyes wide.

"I . . . I must leave." Eve turned toward her brother. "Come, Jules, we'd best get back."

"Pray, do not leave when I have only just met you," the man protested.

"I fear we must."

"At least tell me your name." He took a step after her.

"No—oh, no. I must not." She stopped and looked at him, still dazed by the swift tumble of emotions inside her.

"Then allow me to introduce myself." He swept her an elegant, formal bow. "I am Fitzhugh Talbot, at your service."

Eve stared at him, chilled. "Talbot?"

"Yes. I have business at the vicarage in the village, so you can see that I am perfectly respectable."

Eve let out a little choked noise, and, grabbing Julian by the hand, she whirled around and fled.

Why oh why did I choose this particular day to indulge in a bit of freedom and flirtation?

Eve repeated this incantation in her head as she ran down the bank of the stream, pulling Julian along after her. When she reached the rock, she picked up her things, not daring to glance back. She could only pray that Talbot would not take it into his head to follow her.

"Auntie Eve!" Julian did not have to be told to pick up his own shoes and stockings; he was clever enough to have caught on to the urgency of the situation. "What are we doing? Why are we running?" He turned his head and glanced back toward the road.

"He isn't following us, is he?" Eve asked.

"No. He's leading his horse back to the road." Julian paused. "Is he a bad man?"

"What? No. Oh, no. Pray, do not think that." Eve paused to put her shoes back on and help Julian into his, then struck out across the field at as fast a pace as her brother could keep up. "I think he is the man who is coming to take me to Willowmere."

Talbot was the family name of the Earl of Stewkesbury. And he had said that he had business at the vicarage, her father's home. It must be that Mr. Talbot had come to fetch her for the earl. She dreaded what he would think when he realized that the "water nymph" he had seen cavorting in the brook, shoes and hat off, hair tumbling down, was the intended chaperone of the earl's cousins. That rather than a straight-laced widow, she was the sort who romped about letting strangers kiss her!

"Then he *is* a bad man." Julian's lower lip thrust out.

Eve glanced down at him and forced a smile. "I am glad that you will miss me, Jules, but you mustn't think that Mr. Talbot is bad. He is simply . . . well, running an errand for the earl."

"But I don't understand." Julian panted as he trotted along beside her. "If he is the man who's come to get you, why didn't you say who you were? Why didn't we walk back to the house with him?"

"If we hurry and take the back way, we can get to the vicarage before he does. I must change clothes before I see him."

"Oh."

"You know how your mother feels when you are messy and dirty? That's why we always tuck in your shirt and try to clean up before we return to the house. Well, I think that Mr. Talbot may feel as your mother does."

"But he was quite nice. He seemed to like you."

"That was when he didn't know who I was. You see, it's

all very well to like someone when you think she is just a . . . an ordinary person, but it changes when that person is supposed to be in charge of a group of young girls."

"I don't understand." He looked up at her, frowning.

"I know. It's something that makes more sense as you get older. I just need to make sure that when he sees me again, I look much more like a mature, responsible woman."

"And not a naiad?"

"Definitely not a naiad." Taking Julian's hand, she broke into a run.

Fitz stood still for a long moment after the woman ran away, staring after her in amazement. Sudden flight was not typically the feminine reaction to his name. At thirty-two years of age, Fitzhugh Talbot was one of the most eligible bachelors in England. He was the younger half brother of the Earl of Stewkesbury, and though his mother's family was not nearly as aristocratic as his father's, the money that she and her father had left Fitz more than made up for that minor flaw. These factors alone would have made him well liked by maidens and marriage-minded mothers alike, but he had also been blessed with an engaging personality, a wicked smile, and a face to make angels swoon.

Many regarded him as the perfect picture of a gentleman, and indeed it would take a determined soul to find anyone who disliked Fitz. Though he was clearly not a dandy, his dress was impeccable, and whatever he wore was improved by hanging on his slender, broad-shouldered body. He was known to be one of the best shots in the country, and though he was not the horseman his brother the earl was, he had excellent form. While he was not a bruiser, no one would refuse his help in a mill. Such qualities made him popular with the males of the *ton*, but his skill on the dance floor and in conversation made him equally well liked by London hostesses.

There was, in short, only one thing that kept Fitz from being the perfect match: his complete and utter disinterest in marriage. However, that was not considered a serious impediment by most of the mothers in search of a husband for their daughters, all of whom were sure that their child would be the one girl who could make Fitzhugh Talbot drop his skittish attitude toward getting married. As a consequence, Fitz's name was usually greeted with smiles ranging from coy to calculating.

It was not with a noise somewhere between a gasp and a shriek and taking to one's heels. Still, Fitz thought, he did like a challenge, especially one with a cloud of pale golden hair and eyes the gray-blue of a stormy sea.

When he reached the road, he swung up into the saddle and turned his stallion once again in the direction of the village. He did not urge the animal to hurry; Fitz was content to move at a slow place, lost in his thoughts. He had been willing enough when his brother Oliver asked him to fetch the new chaperone for their cousins. Fitz was often bored sitting about in the country, and though the Bascombe sisters had certainly kept things lively since they arrived at Willowmere, the week or two until Mary Bascombe's wedding had stretched out before him, filled with the sort of plans that provided infinite entertainment for women and left him looking for the nearest door. So he had not mind the trip, especially since he had decided to ride Baxley's Heart, his newest acquisition from Tattersall's, in addition to taking the carriage. That way, he could escort the doubtlessly dull middle-aged widow back to Willowmere without having to actually ride in the coach with her.

But suddenly the trip had acquired far more interest for him. His plan to return to Willowmere the following day now seemed like a poor choice. Surely there must be an inn in the village where he could be put up for a few nights.

There was not, after all, any need for the girls' chaperone to be at Willowmere immediately. What with Cousin Charlotte as well as Lady Vivian overseeing the wedding preparations, not to mention Aunt Cynthia, Charlotte's mother, who had shown up as well, there was more than adequate oversight of the Bascombe sisters.

Fitz could take the time to look around the village and find his "water nymph." First, though, he would pay a call at the vicarage to meet the widow and tell her that they would be leaving in a few days. He might have to pay another courtesy visit to the vicarage in a day or two, but other than that, he would be free to find his naiad and spend his time in a light flirtation—perhaps, even more.

He thought of the girl's slender white legs, exposed by the dress she had hiked up and tied out of the way . . . the pale pink of her lips and the answering flare of color in her cheeks . . . the soft mounds of her breasts swaying beneath her dress as she hopped from rock to rock . . . the glorious tumble of pale curls, glinting in the sun, that had pulled free from her upswept hair.

Yes, definitely, more than flirtation.

He considered how to go about finding her. He could, of course, describe her to someone like the local tavern keeper and come up with a name, but that would scarcely be discreet. And Fitz was always discreet.

He supposed that she could be a servant sent to tend the boy. However, her dress, speech, and manner were all those of a lady. On the other hand, one hardly expected to find a lady splashing about like that in a stream. And who was the child with her? Could the boy have been hers? There was, he thought, a certain resemblance. But surely she was far too young to have a child of seven or eight, which was what he had judged the lad to be. Fitz would have thought that she was no more than in her early twenties. But perhaps she was older than she appeared. There were mothers who romped with their children; he had seen Charlotte doing so with her brood of rapscallions.

Perhaps she was the lad's governess—though in his experience governesses were rarely either so lovely or so lighthearted. Or maybe she was the personal maid of the boy's mother. Personal maids were more likely to have acquired the speech patterns of their mistresses than lower servants, and they also frequently wore their mistresses' hand-me-downs.

None of these speculations, however, put him any closer to discovering the girl again. She had hinted that he might come across her walking through town, so perhaps she regularly took a stroll. Still, he could scarcely spend his entire day stalking up and down the streets of the village.

Lost in these musings, Fitz was on the edge of the village almost before he knew it. Indeed, he had almost ridden past the church before he realized where he was. Reining in his horse, he looked at the squat old square-towered church. A cemetery lay to one side of it; Fitz had gone past it without a glance. On the other side of the church was a two-story home, obviously much newer than the church but built of the same gray stone. This, he felt sure, would be the vicarage.

It was a rather grim-looking place, and he could not help but hope, for his cousins' sake, that the widow who resided there was not of the same nature as the house. He thought for a moment of riding past it, but a second thought put that idea to rest. In a village this size, it would be bound to get back to the residents of the vicarage that a stranger was in town, and they would feel slighted that he had not come first to meet them. Fitz knew that many deemed him an irresponsible sort, more interested in pursuing his own pleasure than others' ideas of his duty, but it was never said that he ignored the social niceties.

Besides, he thought, with a little lift of his spirits, as he swung down off his horse and tied him to the lowest branch of a large tree, he would have an excellent reason to keep his visit short, since he needed to get his animal stabled and find himself a room. Brushing off the dust of the road, he strode up to the front door and knocked. A parlor maid, who goggled at him as though she'd never seen a gentleman before, quickly answered the summons, but when he told her that he wished to speak to Mrs. Hawthorne and handed her his card, the girl whisked him efficiently down the hall into the parlor.

A moment later a woman of narrow face and form entered the room. Her dark brown hair fell in tight curls on either side of her face, with the rest drawn back under a white cap. Her face was etched with the sort of severe lines of disapproval that made it difficult to guess her age, but the paucity of gray streaks in her hair made him put her on the younger edge of middle age. She had on a gown of dark blue jaconet with a white muslin fichu worn over her shoulders and crossed to a knot at her breasts.

Fitz's heart fell as he watched her walk toward him. Poor cousins! He had the feeling that the girls had merely traded one martinet for another, and it surprised him that the lively Lady Vivian would have recommended such a woman. However, he kept his face schooled to a pleasant expression and executed a bow.

"Mr. Fitzhugh Talbot, ma'am, at your service. Do I have the honor of addressing Mrs. Bruce Hawthorne?"

"I am Mrs. Childe," she told him. "Mrs. Hawthorne is my husband's daughter."

"A pleasure to meet you, madam. I am the Earl of Stewkesbury's brother, and I am here to escort Mrs. Hawthorne to Willowmere. I believe he wrote to her regarding the matter."

"Yes, of course. I have sent a servant to tell Mrs. Hawthorne that you have arrived."

She gestured toward the sofa, and Fitz sat down, relieved to learn that at least his American cousins had escaped living with this woman—and that he would not have to endure two days of traveling with her.

Mrs. Childe took a seat across from Fitz, her spine as straight as the chair back, which she did not touch, and inquired formally after his trip. They made polite small talk for a few moments before there was the sound of hurrying footsteps in the hallway. A moment later a tall, slender woman dressed in a gown as severe and dark as Mrs. Childe's, her blond hair pulled back and twisted into a tight knot at the crown of her head, stepped into the room.

Fitz shot to his feet, his customary aplomb for once deserting him. There was no mistaking the woman despite the complete change in her attire. The tightly restrained hair was the same pale ash-blond, the eyes the color of a stormy sea.

The middle-aged widow he had expected was, in fact, his water nymph.